WE ARE FAMILY

Fabio Bartolomei

WE ARE FAMILY

*Translated from the Italian
by Antony Shugaar*

Europa
editions

Europa Editions
214 West 29th Street
New York, N.Y. 10001
www.europaeditions.com
info@europaeditions.com

Copyright © 2013 by Edizioni E/O
First Publication 2018 by Europa Editions UK
This edition, 2019 by Europa Editions US

Translation by Antony Shugaar
Original title: *We Are Family*
Translation copyright © 2018 by Europa Editions

Library of Congress Cataloging in Publication Data is available
ISBN 978-1-60945-503-3

Bartolomei, Fabio
We Are Family

Book design and cover illustration by Emanuele Ragnisco
www.mekkanografici.com

Prepress by Grafica Punto Print – Rome

Printed in the USA

CONTENTS

For Monica, who invented all the games I know

Children know something that most people have forgotten.
—KEITH HARING

WE ARE FAMILY

PART ONE

1.

This year here is 1971, and it's called that because every-thing in the world has a name, except for the years, which have numbers instead. In the year called 1971 a whole bunch of things are breaking. A piece of Pakistan called Bangladesh broke off, a friend of Papà called Jim Morrison got broken, and also I hear that a valve broke on the spaceship Soyuz 11. Mamma always says that when one thing breaks, then other things break in a chain reaction, that's what she said just last week when the blender, the washing machine, and the record player broke. So now that the flames are breaking this plastic wastebasket, I blame the washing machine. Or maybe Jim Morrison. My mother's exact words were these: "Try to be good for ten minutes. I have to go talk to your teacher and will be right back, is that clear?" My mother is an old lady, age thirty-five, with dark brown hair, and when she talks to me with her eyes glued to me that way it means I'm supposed to answer her: "That's clear, Mamma," but not just any old way, I'm supposed to say it really carefully, staring her in the eyes. Her name is Agnese because she's very pretty, otherwise her name would be Carla or Gertrude, which seems obvious, right? My father says that she looks like Princess Grace, and that the big difference between them is that the other one has the finest makeup artists and hairdressers constantly on call, while Mamma uses practically no makeup and she cuts her own hair. Anyway, the old lady told me to be good and I said to her: "Got it, Mamma," or actually: "G-g-g-got it, Mamma," because I'm four years old, I have black hair, and I have a stuttering problem. According to my father, it's an ignition problem, our Fiat 600 has the same problem and the mechanic said it isn't serious. Sometimes we both get our motors flooded, me and the 600. Mamma asked me if I understood and I answered yes, properly, with the gaze that always works and that made me an angel in the Christmas pageant. I'm not a disobedient little boy, it's just that I constantly have to fight some idea that's just popped into my head. I'm going to climb on top of the table now, no I have to be good, I'm going to go in the bathroom and play with water now, no I have to be good, I'm going to throw something out the window now, no I have to be good, I'm going to climb up the bookshelf now, no I have to be good, I'm going to take a roll of toilet paper and throw it down the hallway now, no I have to be good. But you can't win them all, so the wastebasket burns. When something catches on fire, Mamma asks me: "Why did you do it?" That's a tough question. I took a box of matches because on August 12, 1969, Papà said: "In this house, there's no such thing as mine and yours, there's only ours"; I hid the matches in my pocket because at my house they hide everything, the jelly, the cookies, the toys, and all I've done is to watch and learn; and I set fire to the edge of the wastebasket because I felt like it, and that's that. A few days ago Papà had a long talk with me about the value of objects and respecting things that belong to others. That was a strange subject for a conversation, but talking to Papà is a happy thing and so I told him that I understood, even if I wasn't that sure I had. Stealing, breaking, and burning are only wrong if you get caught, is that right? In fact, I try to be very careful, I only want to melt a little bit of the edge of this wastebasket, let a few flaming drops fall onto the floor, and call the firemen. And do it fast, because the bellman is arriving. From what I've been able to figure out, he's in charge of the hallways and the bathrooms. The classrooms, on the other hand, belong to the Mother Superior, and the bellman is only allowed to come in every now and then to yell at us and say that us boys need to pee sitting down too, otherwise we make a tremendous mess.

"What's that terrible smell? . . . Have you been burning something?" he asks me with a mean look on his face.

Papà says that I'm a great actor, that with this little angel face of mine I can con anyone. "To con" means to open my eyes really wide and make people believe that I really don't understand what they want from me.

"Me? No, no," I reply.

We stare each other in the eye, but since I practice every day with Mamma, I win the contest.

"It must be that damned electric plug again! If they don't fix it, this whole school is going to go up in flames!"

While the janitor goes into the classroom and gets down on his knees to sniff at the dangerous holes where you put electric plugs, I get tired of being a good boy and decide to go down to the end of the hallway, behind the door to my teacher's office. In there, people are talking about me, about Al Santamaria. Credit for the fact that my name is Al is due to my grandfather. Papà told us that Grandpa never asked for a thing in his whole life. He didn't talk much, if he wanted water he'd flick a fingernail against the edge of the glass, if he wanted silence he'd just say: "Oh!" The longest conversation in his life was with my father a minute before passing away. No, but the thing I have to remember to ask Papà is where he passed away to, exactly, and when he will be coming back. Anyway, a minute before passing away he said: "I was thinking that I'd like to be remembered, I'd like to ask you to give my name to your firstborn son. Oh, and one more thing, get that hair of yours cut." My father did as he'd been asked: he cut his hair very very short, after all, in a year it would grow back, and he named me Almerico, after all, everybody would just call me Al.

"Al is a very bright little boy, intelligent, surprisingly intelligent, believe me," says the teacher, "but I just can't get him to participate in classroom activities."

"Does he get distracted?" my mother asks.

"It's not that he gets distracted, it's that he just gets bored. He puts his fingers in his ears when the other children try to count to ten. He bangs his head on his desk when I try to teach them the sounds that the animals make . . . but believe me, this is good news. Your son's intelligence is far above average, it's a natural gift."

"Ah."

A few seconds of silence.

"What's wrong? You seem upset by the news," says the teacher.

"No, it's just that I thought I'd been a really good mother, and instead it's just . . . a natural gift."

That's simply the way Agnese is, sometimes she says funny things, but there's no two ways about it: on the hit list of Mammas, she's number one with a bullet. The teacher recommended that she have me do some things that are called "tests" and to send me straight to first grade. My mother said that she'd talk to her husband about it, and then something else about being normal and being happy that I didn't have a chance to hear very clearly because the man with the bell must have found the melted wastebasket, and started yelling.

I know I'm special. I write, read, and speak better than my sister, and she's four years older than me. I'm better at everything than her, though that's not saying much because Vittoria is a klutz. She's good at school too, sure, but she's been trying to tie her own shoes for two months and she still hasn't been able to do it once without knotting her finger into the bargain. I get bored at school because we always do the same things: we sing, we learn the colors, the names of things, and then we draw and draw and draw. All my classmates draw the same thing, their family standing next to a little house with a pointy red roof, two square windows, and a door in the middle, clearly they must live in the country. I live in a tall, light-brown apartment house, so I draw my family standing next to an apartment house that's tall and light brown. The only thing that's fun at school is when Sister Taddea tells us stories about the saints, who are the religious superheroes, but always sad. No one listens to her though, because while she talks she projects a series of badly drawn pictures on the classroom wall and everyone tells themselves their own personal stories with happy endings, without burnings at the stake or crucifixions. When Vittoria and I come home, Papà always greets us with the same wisecrack: "Did you get a nice thorough brainwashing today?" And we always say: "Yes, Papà, washed and pre-washed." The only reason we say it is so that Mamma will come out of the kitchen and glare at us. She says that it's one of the best schools in the city, that it costs an arm and a leg, and that knowing the story of God and the Ten Commandments never did anyone any harm. I have to agree. And I'd also add that it never did anyone any good, either.

2.

The headquarters of the Santamaria family is in Rome, in a neighborhood known as the Quartiere Ostiense. You enter a light-brown apartment house, you take the elevator, you push the button with the number four, then you ring the doorbell to apartment twelve and if Grandma doesn't have the volume turned on too high on the radio, you come right in. Inside there's a long hallway, on the right is the room Vittoria and I share, Grandma's room, then the bathroom and the kitchen; on the left is the living room with the sofa bed where Mamma and Papà sleep. It's our apartment, in exchange Papà only has to give the man who lives on the top floor a white envelope every month. The Santamaria family is "handy and conveniently compact," as my father likes to say. A grandmother, an uncle, and that's all, because what counts isn't quantity, it's something else that now I can't remember.

I'm very sorry for all the other children but in this family we've had shameless good luck, because not only do we have the number one mother, but we also happen to have the world's best Papà. His name is Mario but everyone calls him Elvis—everyone, except for my mother, who's too embarrassed. Elvis is his favorite singer, and he's so crazy about him that he not only listens to his songs, he even imitates the way he dresses and combs his hair. Papà is an astronaut first class; just for now he drives buses but in a few years he's going to get a license to become an Apollo commander. My mother, on the other hand, is a housewife, because when Mario Elvis is up in space, she'll have to become the chief officer of the earth base at Via del Gazometro 25, and that means she can't have a job, she has to be ready to take command whenever the need arises.

"Al, please, can you just sit up straight," Papà says to me.

"Stop being a dope and sit the way you're supposed to," Vittoria adds.

The first message comes in from outer space so my sister, who's in charge of radio communications, relays it to the control room. Just the way you see it in the movies. Vittoria has big front teeth like a rabbit, which is a word that we aren't allowed to use in our house. She has one jug ear, the right one, but then "jug" is another forbidden word. Her nose turns down at the end, and in fact, "aquilon," meaning north wind, or the place name "Aquitaine," or the saint "Thomas Aquinas," and especially the adjective "aquiline" are all words that we cannot utter. The strange thing is that all these mismatched pieces of her face, when put together, fit quite well and form a lovely sister. The real problem is her temper.

"Are you going to sit up straight?" she shouts.

My head, arms, and chest all point toward my plate, my legs gaze out at the toys scattered across the carpet, under the TV. It makes them mad.

"You see, Papà? He won't listen to me!" my sister complains.

By the time Mario Elvis turns around to look at me, my legs have rejoined the rest of my body. I manage to get a: "Good boy!" Let's see how the radio communications officer likes that. Mamma shows up with a panful of spaghetti, and as usual she serves my father first, because he's the man of the house, the head of the family, and that's just how it's done. The spaghetti lifts out of the pan in a single clump, like a flying saucer. Her work as a cook is clearly deep cover, Mamma is clearly meant for other duties. Grandma Concetta, who as a young woman, before becoming my grandma, was Agnese's mamma, must not have been briefed on the Santamaria family space program, because she shakes her head at the sight of the flying saucer made of pasta. At school they told us that old people are very wise, and in fact the president of the Italian republic and the pope are always very old, whenever they speak we must pay attention because we can learn a lot of things from them. That's why everytime Grandma Concetta speaks Vittoria and I turn to look at her and listen very closely. We've been doing it for years.

"You should have used a little more olive oil," says the old sage.

Mamma looks at her with a twisted, angry face. She ravages the flying saucer with savage blows of the fork.

"You do that, you'll scratch the pan," grumbles the old woman, wise and courageous to boot.

The future commander of the Apollo mission comes to the aid of the future commander of the earth base.

"It smells wonderful," he says.

From the mother ship, five drooping little shuttles break off and land on our plates.

"What do we have for the main course?" asks the radio communications officer.

"Meatballs."

Now the time comes to lay a booby trap for Mamma.

"What k-k-kind of meatballs? The ones all covered in sauce or the ones with nothing on them?" I ask.

"The kind you like, with nothing on them."

"*No-o-o*, I wanted them with sauce!"

3.

Sunday is my favorite day. Right after Mass, at 10:30, the Santamaria family climbs into the car and sets out in search of the promised home. Mamma and Papà say that it's out there somewhere, but they don't know where. All they know is that it's beautiful, roomy, and full of light.

This is how the game works: we pick a neighborhood and we drive around in it—actually, we jet around in it in our space vehicle—singing at the top of our lungs, while Vittoria and I keep our eyes peeled for signs reading "For Sale."

"C-c-commander Santamaria, for sale sign sighted on the right, street number 36," I announce.

"That's on the left, Al," the radio communications officer points out.

"For sale sign sighted . . . decipher secret code," Papà says.

Mamma jots down the secret code on a sheet of paper and the space vehicle zooms off in search of the nearest phone booth. "Only Mamma and Papà are going," she says when we spot one.

The old woman is joking. The sardine game is a happy thing and no parent can expect we're not going to play it every blessed time, even if it's 105 degrees in the shade, for the rest of our lives.

But it turns out I'm wrong, the old woman isn't joking: she puts on a serious face, levels her finger in our direction, and heads off, convinced she's settled the question.

"I HAVE A LACK OF AFFECTION-N-N-N-N!" I shout out the car window.

In one of Grandma's newspapers I read that "the violence spreading throughout the world of the young can be attributed to a lack of affection suffered during childhood." I didn't really understand it all, but it clearly means that if your parents fail to do what you tell them, then when you grow up, you're likely to wind up joining some motorcycle gang, robbing banks, or even shooting someone. Agnese knows this and in fact she comes galloping back to the car, claps her hand over my mouth, and drags me out. A second later all of us are in the phone booth, packed in nice and tight, because everybody knows: if canned sardines aren't snug up against each other, they're likely to rot and then they'll stink.

"Mamma, Al must have started to rot."

"That's not true!"

"Your feet are rotten!"

"Quiet now, Papà has to make a phone call," Mamma says.

"Hello, I'm calling about the apartment for sale."

Everyone holds their breath, the Agnese sardine clinging to the Mario Elvis sardine.

"Ah . . . I was hoping for something a little larger. What about the price? Well, the price is certainly reasonable . . . All right, let me do some thinking about the square footage, in any case, I'll call back. Thank you . . . have a nice day."

"Is this it, Papà?" Vittoria asks.

"I'm afraid it's not. The Santamaria family home must be in some other part of town."

Then he transmits a secret message to Mamma: "Thirteen

hundred square feet plus three hundred square feet of ter-
race."

"What about the price?" she asks.

"Don't ask . . . "

Mario Elvis is very tall, I can't touch his chin even if I stand
on tiptoes and I stretch my arm as far as I can reach. He says
that when I'm tall enough to do that, then we'll start to have
some serious conversations, and then, when my head is tall
enough to touch his chin, we'll have some very serious conversations, and when the tips of our noses are at the same height,
we'll even have some secret conversations. Last of all, when the
tip of my nose touches his forehead, we can start to just talk
nonsense, because spending a whole lifetime talking about
serious matters isn't good for you.

The other thing I like about Sunday is going to visit Uncle
Armando, who was Mamma's brother when he was young,
because it means we can have lunch with the whole Santamaria
family, all in one place. Papà and Uncle Armando compete to
see who can eat the most, because Mamma makes special
meatballs with lots of bread crumbs so that there's more of
them and we don't have to spend a lot of money on meat.
Because for some reason, spending a lot of money on meat is
wrong. Uncle Armando says that Vittoria and I are both going
to become scientists, that he's never seen two children as sharp
as us, and that Agnese and Mario Elvis ought to find a way to
make use of our talent.

"Al, concentrate . . . this one's hard. Understood? You need
to gather all your intelligence and concentrate on this answer,"
Uncle Armando says to me.

"Understood. Go ahead."

"Milan-Juventus?"

"Two," I reply.

"No overtime?"

"If Bettega and Anastasi are playing . . . "

After lunch, we all pile onto the couch. While Mamma and Grandma finish clearing the table, me, Vittoria, Mario Elvis, and Uncle Armando play with the tape recorder. The tape recorder was a gift from Mamma for Papà, it's the size of a brick, it has a nice black leather case and a microphone with a long cord. On it is written "Grundig," which looks like the snarl of a ferocious animal but actually means that it's German and therefore that it's good. Mamma bought it because Mario Elvis is studying to get his accounting degree, which is necessary if he wants to get his space pilot's license. Having the tape recorder means he can listen to the lessons again while he drives the bus. It's a very important exam, and Mamma really cares about it. Right now, though, Mario Elvis is using it to sing songs into it. Me, Vittoria, and Uncle Armando go: "Dum dum dum dum dum dum dum," while he sings: "*This crazy heart that chases after you, and day and night thinks of nothing but youuuu!*" But this is only the beginning of the game, because then he rewinds the tape and the tape recorder, which must have learned it all by heart, repeats it word for word. Hearing Papà's voice come out of the Grundig drives us crazy, we laugh and laugh until our tummies hurt.

"Now c-c-can I sing?"

"No, me first!" Vittoria shouts.

"It's not a toy! Papà needs it to study!" Mamma says. But she's not being serious, it's obvious that it's really a toy. And in fact when Mario Elvis pushes down the button with the little black triangle and turns the volume all the way up, she breaks out laughing too.

"What could be better than this?" Mario Elvis asks me and Vittoria.

"Nothing!" we reply.

Papà always says: when you have a family like the Santamaria family, you have everything. He also says that nothing is impossible for the Santamaria family. And that as long as we remain united, we're as strong as Spartan warriors. My father says lots and lots of happy things.

Outside the sun shines, Vittoria strokes my hair, Mario Elvis and Uncle Armando sing "La spada nel cuore," and from the kitchen comes the aroma of a chocolate *ciambellone*, an Italian variant on the bundt cake. I'm the luckiest little boy in the world.

4.

They swore to me that this doctor lady doesn't give shots. "Cross my heart and hope to die: she doesn't even have syringes." But I only feel calm now that I've entered her office and I immediately saw that there's neither the glass cabinet with the needles in it nor the horrible little bed, the one that looks like a padded stretcher. The doctor is a very calm lady, she smiles a lot and talks as if her batteries had run down. Very, very slowly she tells me that I'm certainly a nice-looking little boy. Since Mamma told me that I'm not allowed to answer: "I know," all I do is smile and she asks me whether the cat's got my tongue which is a dumb joke that they always ask us kids but that only makes old people laugh. Mamma smiles, I reply: "No." The calm doctor lady is trying to make friends, she keeps talking, she tells me that she has a grandson my age, that she likes my T-shirt, and that I'm certainly tall. Of course, I'd have to be, the world is full of tall things, first of all, doorknobs and the handles on wardrobes and refrigerators, and then there are tables, bicycle seats, cookie cabinets, the shelf where they keep matches, this chair I'm sitting in . . . It's all about stretching. The day they decide to keep putting the handles higher and higher, people will keep growing until they're ninety. But I don't want to make friends with her so all I say is: "Yes."

"Do you want to play a nice game?" the doctor lady asks me.

When an old person says something like that, it's usually because they want to trap you into some kind of ambush game like statues or the silence game. I reply that "I can hardly wait," that "I'd be delighted to play," that she's "making my dream come true."

"Don't pay any attention to him . . . " Mamma says. "He's such a joker . . . " and she jerks my arm.

The lady doctor smiles and with her batteries increasingly drained, she lays three squares of cardboard with strange markings on them in front of me. Then she puts three more into my hands and asks me to lay the right square on the table, the one that I think completes the family. I complete the family of squares, the family of triangles, and then the family of circles. After every game, she tells me: "Good job, Al," and looks down at her watch, so I understand that this must be a timed test and I make a special effort to work faster and faster. I construct figures, I guess which alarm clock is half an hour slow compared to alarm clock A and how many triangles make up the pyramid drawn on the sheet of paper. I try to make families of objects work by inserting the missing piece, which is an easy game because all I need to do is think about the Santamaria family which has all the right pieces, and so I fill in the empty spaces with an airplane, a dog, a screwdriver, and a lightbulb, and every time: "Good job, Al."

"This is the last game," the lady doctor tells me.

"Twenty-one cats," I reply.

"Are you just trying to guess? You barely looked at it . . . "

"Come on, Al, it's the last one, try to do a good job," Mamma tells me.

"I did a very good job, the number of cats increases by two, four, six, eight cats in each square. So the number th-th-that's lacking to make the family of cats grow is twenty-one, and the lady doctor can stop the timer."

"My, we did that one quickly . . . " she says.

"Can we do some more?" I ask.

"Now your Mamma and I need to talk alone for a little bit. Can you wait for us outside, Al?"

I knew it. All grown-up games are the same, they never last long enough.

"Can I have the lollipop, now?" I ask.

"Certainly. What color do you want?"

"Yellow. And can I have an orange one for my sister? Do you want one too, Mamma?"

"No, thanks, Al."

Too bad, if I could only have had three, Vittoria might even have had a chance of getting one for herself.

I'm standing in the metal bucket that Grandma uses to wash clothing. I wound up there because I hate taking my afternoon nap. Agnese said: "There's just nothing I can do today, he's too agitated," and Grandma replied: "Give him to me and I'll take care of it." It seems to me that I've been there other times before, but I don't really know, my memories are all mixed up. There's red wine on the bottom of the bucket, Grandma is dipping the sponge into it and massaging my legs. Then my belly and my arms. There's that good smell that comes from Papà's glass when we're eating dinner. The old woman really focuses on the arms, the chest, and the neck. I like it, the smell gets strong. Who knows why they feel so certain that after this little bath I'm going to take a nap, massage me all you want, I'm not sleepy in the slightest, Huey, Dewey, and Louie have come to see me, we're going to play with the Play-Doh that smells just like wine, what did Grandma just say? No, I'm not starting to feel sleepy one bit, I want to play with my fast cars, put my toy soldiers on top of them, have some crazy crashes, and then I want to try that wine . . . I mean try flying . . . off the table . . . down . . . black cape . . . like the Bat Man . . .

"Mamma-a-a . . . "

"It's the middle of the night, Al! Go back to sleep!"

Still? They already got me to take a nap in the afternoon, who knows how they did it. How much sleep do these people think I need? I have a lot of things to do.

"It's turned sour!"

I'm talking about my thumb. I personally don't agree, but Mamma says I'm too big now to use a pacifier so she makes me suck my thumb with sugar on it. But the sugar is gone almost immediately.

"Would you just go to sleep!" the radio communications officer repeats.

"Did you say your prayers?" Mamma asks.

"I did, Al didn't."

"Oh yes I did! I said them with C-c-casimiro!"

For some reason I don't understand, when I say: "Casimiro," everyone pretends they didn't hear. Even the radio communications officer. Casimiro is my imaginary friend, in the sense that I play with him and I talk to him while the others, unable to see him, can only imagine him.

My bed is a secret bed. By day the whole world thinks that there's only one bed in the room, Vittoria's bed, but then, when it gets dark, Mario Elvis comes in, lowers the blinds so no one can see in, and pulls it out from under my sister's bed, nice and ready. As soon as the lights go out I slip a foot under Vittoria's covers and push it against her butt because, for a few seconds, the darkness is really black, there's nothing left, and I feel all alone. She must feel the same way because, though she isn't one of those cuddly sisters, when it comes to keeping company with my foot, she doesn't have anything negative to say.

My bed is surrounded by an enchanted forest. I can only manage to glimpse it when the darkness turns less black and they leave the lights on in the other room. The path from my bed to the enemy encampment is the most dangerous route on the planet, riddled with ambushes and sentinels with very itchy trigger fingers. But we knights are fearless and so, the minute Vittoria starts to snore, I set out with my trusty page Casimiro, and we slither down off the mattress to begin our nighttime attack. We advance silently through the stand of carnivorous plants, we bravely make our way down the quicksand hallway. The encampment is illuminated by a large bonfire upon which appears the image of Dracula, who in reality is actually called Christopher Lee and is an actor with pointy teeth so whenever they need someone to play Dracula, they call him. These are the most daunting last few yards. We need to hold our breath and wait for the moment when the sentinels are distracted. They're talking in low voices.

"He's an extraordinary child, the lady doctor said that she's never seen anything like it," says the female sentinel in a happy voice.

"If we don't treat him like a normal child, we could do him some real harm," replies the sentinel with the Elvis quiff.

"Gifted as he is, he's destined to achieve great things."

The sentinel with the quiff turns around to look at the female sentinel.

"He might discover the cure for cancer or became a great statesman, what do you know . . . " she says.

Cancer? *Statesman*? I'd need the book of words to understand the language of the sentinels, but knights are men of action and they can only move forward. Now! Under the sofa bed!

"We'll see, he can decide for himself when he grows up."

"Of course, we just need to help him find his way."

On top of the mattress something's happening. The metal

springs start to move, and I hear some strange noises, it might have been a kiss. A whole family of kisses.

"Someone like him could save the world," whispers the female sentinel.

"Really?" asks Casimiro.

"Al!"

5.

Since last night I haven't done a thing to save the world. While Sister Taddea tells us one of her stories with an unhappy ending, I think back to my expedition into the enemy encampment and to one phrase in particular that I overheard: "He needs to find his own way." The meaning is clear, I have to figure out what particular route will allow me to save the world, but the word "way" for some reason makes my thoughts turn strange and I imagine the way as a street, paved with asphalt, with white lines painted on it. Perhaps my way is just like the promised home of the Santamaria family, maybe it's hidden somewhere and I ought to go out every Sunday to look for it. Mario Elvis said that we'll recognize the promised home the minute we see it, as soon as we set foot in it, we'll know if it's the right place or not. It probably works more or less the same when it comes to my way. Then there's another thing I don't understand: Why does the world need to be saved? What is it that isn't working? Evidently things aren't working out there the way they are at my house, maybe not all the Papàs start the day by singing Elvis songs, not all the Mammas make chocolate *ciambelloni*, not all the families play with a fine German tape recorder. I need to learn more, I need to study.

"She looks like Snow White," Roberta whispers behind me.

Sister Taddea has projected onto the wall the picture of a woman dressed in white and light blue.

"It's Saint Lucy," I reply.

The saint has a handful of greenery and a little plate in the other hand. She must have been a cooking saint. Like all the religious superheroes she is looking upward, because she knows that all trouble will come to her from that direction.

"Why are they dressed the same?"

"Bec-c-cause Saint Lucy wants to get engaged to the prince but Snow White finds out and scratches her eyes out."

"That's not true."

"Wait and see."

"Almerico and Roberta! Aren't you interested in the story of Saint Lucy?" Sister Taddea asks us.

"Yes, we are," we reply.

"Knowing about the lives of the saints will be a big help when you grow up. You, Roberta, what do want to be when you grow up?"

"A saint."

Sister Taddea smiles and nods. Here's the first lesson that will come in handy when we grow up: it's not important to tell the truth, what counts is to always say what will make other people happy.

"What about you, Almerico?"

"I'm a genius, I'll probably save the world, but I still need to find my way."

From the look on Sister Taddea's face it occurs to me that I haven't been as good at answering as Roberta was. The nuns aren't bad people, they're just obsessed with this matter of good and bad. Goodish and baddish don't exist, on any given question there's always the risk of getting it wrong and winding up in hell. To say you want to have the same job as your Papà or be a soccer player or a doctor is good, to say that you're a genius and you want to save the world is bad. Normal is good, genius is bad.

"Oh no, sorry, I want to be a fireman," I correct myself.

Right answer, the nun smiles.

"Good boy, firemen do a very useful job, they save people."

I didn't tell a lie, being a fireman really is the job that I wanted to do before finding out I'm a genius. So it's not really a lie, it's more like a postdated truth. I can't disappoint Agnese and Mario Elvis, I can't disappoint the world. I'll become a genius and a savior, and a fireman if I have any spare time.

I'm not happy with my body. The brain transmits commands and my body never seems capable of responding properly. The order is: "Run!" and the legs start spinning out of control, skidding, reaching a decent speed only once they start following the head as it falls forward. Stopping is always a problem. Asphalt, cobblestones, and marble are all hard materials that I learned to recognize early, the ones I scrape my elbows and knees on every day on account of Ezio, a mean kid that even the fifth graders steer clear of. The fifth graders, though, have no reason to run when they see him, because his favorite target is me. Ezio has lazy, troublesome speech, when he talks you can't understand a thing, so he's gotten used to saying the things he thinks with gestures. But since his thoughts are always nasty, the way he gestures is to slap, shove, and trip you. Outdoor recess is never a happy thing. We leave the classroom in double file, we walk down the stairs, we join the other classes, we cross the courtyard stamping our feet hard on the ground the way the nun tells us to, and if you ask me she's an outstanding general. As soon as the nun tells us to go play, my brain orders my body to vanish as fast as a missile. After losing my balance on the wet grass, after running straight into a tree that jumped out in front of me, and after falling to my knees in an effort to catch up with my head—and at least my head has the right idea and moves fast—I take refuge in the furthest corner of the garden, next to a high metal gate that leads out onto the street. I've inhaled so much cold air all at once that now I feel as if I have a saliva-flavored popsicle stuck in my throat. Luckily, Ezio is nowhere in sight. Right now there must be another little boy in the courtyard trying to understand the meaning of: "Your sandwich mine now I'll smack your face." But I make the grave error of failing to vanish behind the bush, Roberta spots me and comes running in my direction. She has very long black hair, green eyes, and a very obedient body. She doesn't slip on the grass, she avoids trees, she stops in front of the gate with a nice graceful leap. Her cheeks seem to be colored with that stuff they put in candy to make it clear that it's strawberry flavored, a lock of hair is stuck to her lips. She smiles at me, I don't respond otherwise she might get the idea that she can stay here with me. She taps my shoulder with a finger, I don't turn around otherwise she might get the idea that she can talk to me.

"My mother says that your father is a clown."

"No, he's a top-ranking astronaut," I tell her.

"Ah, too bad."

"Hey, look, being a top-ranking astronaut is a very g-g-good job. He'll go to the moon and to Mars, too!"

Every time I happen to be close to Roberta at the front door, some parent will ask if we're going steady. I don't think I'm ready for that, even though I know everything there is to know about girls: when you choose up teams you always pick them last; better leave them alone because they'll start crying at the drop of a hat and the nuns have giant hands; when they play with dolls they always make little voices, unpleasant ones for her and idiotic ones for him; they're always looking for some excuse to kiss you and leave a wet patch on your cheeks.

"What are you doing here?" she asks me.

I'd almost forgotten: they always ask you: "What are you doing? Where are you going? What are you thinking about?"

"I'm t-t-trying to find my way."

She puts her head between the bars of the gate. She looks outside.

"Is that it?"

"I d-d-don't think so. My way must be really wide and lined with trees."

"Downstairs from where I live, there's a way like that."

"Well, then, starting today, you and me are engaged. It must be destiny."

"What does that mean?"

Destiny is the person who makes things happen, but how can you explain that to a girl?

"It means that you have to g-g-give me your hand."

She looks at me.

"And what are you going to give me in exchange?"

6.

If you want to go look at certain homes, you have to dress up. Why? Because they're pretty and they'll only sell them to well-dressed people. Why? Because if you're dressed up nice everyone will think that you're also important, reliable, and serious. Why? Just because. So Papà put on his Black Herringbone suit, the same suit that Elvis wore in 1969 to sing in the city they call Las Vegas, and Mamma put on her checkered overcoat with the fuzzy sleeves. Then she borrowed a couple of rings from Grandma, but Grandma has big hands so Mamma has to keep her fingers pressed together, otherwise the rings will fly off. Vittoria and I, on the other hand, put on our school uniforms, which are the fanciest things we own.

The apartment that we're seeing has soft floors. In every room there's a big carpet that they can only have installed with a helicopter, after taking the roof off. We walk from room to room without making the slightest noise, something that makes me think of increasingly daring nighttime missions. On the furniture, which is all white and shiny, there are lots of colorful objects, a long-necked yellow telephone, smooth pink and sky-blue stone eggs, a sort of luminous torpedo in which large bubbles rise and fall. Mamma reads my mind.

"Don't touch a thing."

It's not my fault that when I was little I must have swallowed a magnet. Papà says there's no other explanation, if my fingers seem to stick to anything colorful I see, it must be because when I was little I swallowed a magnet which wound up in my stomach and then from there it went back and forth through my body until it got stuck in my fingertips. I feel a mysterious force emanate from that strange torpedo and reach my hand.

"What did I just tell you, Al?"

"This apartment is perfect for a family like yours," the house man says, "it even has a nice big office . . . What kind of work do you do, sir?"

"I'm in the transportation sector," Papà replies.

Mamma looks at me with a tight-lipped smile. The message in code is: you're in trouble if you open your mouth. I'm not stupid enough to go around spilling the beans to some total stranger that Papà is an astronaut first class. First they tell you you're a genius and then they treat you like a cretin.

"Papà!" Vittoria shouts in delight. "The stop for the 170 bus is right downstairs . . . so we can wave at you when you go by!"

I smile at Mamma Agnese and the coded message is this: sure, you do have an idiot child, but it's not me.

I tried to play with Vittoria and her girlfriend but we fought right away over a stupid matter of apparel. There was a dance and Ken showed up bare-chested, in bermuda shorts and with a rifle in one hand. The Barbies didn't appreciate it.

Mamma says that soon I'll have lots of friends and I'll be able to invite them home every day. Friends must be like the promised home and my way, they must be out there somewhere, we just don't know where. The one thing I know for sure is that they aren't here in our apartment house, since the youngest child who lives here is eleven and is some kind of technological pirate: he uses the phone in his house to play pranks on people he doesn't even know and he goes from one apartment house to another, ringing doorbells. At school maybe, but not in my class: I don't know how to play with people who mix up snipers, cowboys, and ancient Romans.

Ken was taken from me and, while the Barbies' big evening begins, I start leafing through Grandma's magazines, which are full of photographs, have big headlines and lots and lots of exclamation points.

"So delightful, this party, don't you think, darling? Certainly, darling. Shall we dance some more? Certainly, darling," says Vittoria.

"Doesn't Ken know how to say anything else? Only 'C-c-certainly, darling'?" I ask.

"Mind your own business!"

"C-c-certainly, darling," I say.

"Mamma! Al's being a pain in the neck!"

"That's not true!"

You can tell an angry mother by her footsteps. When the floor shakes, trouble is coming.

"Grandma isn't feeling well! You'd both better be good!" she shouts at us.

"It's his fault!"

"It's her fault!"

"It's his fault," says Vittoria's friend.

Two against one. Mamma's next word is going to be: "Al."

"Al, cut it out! How many times do I have to tell you . . . but what are you doing?"

"Nothing, I'm just reading the papers. A d-d-dog that got lost on holiday found his family after two years."

Actually, I was reading: "Witnesses in the Manson trial speak out: HOW I BECAME A SEX SLAVE OF SATAN!" and "Charming indiscretions from the housekeeper in the Onassis home: JACQUELINE'S SECRET LIFE!" but I can't tell her that, because I only have permission to read the pages with pictures of animals. Mamma believes me and makes the face I like so much. That face of someone who's in love with me that so irritates Vittoria.

I spoke my first word at five months, I started reading at age two, and when I was three I was already writing. I can do mathematical calculations in my mind that are challenging for a fourteen-year-old, I have a gigantic memory, and I read publications for grown-ups with names like *Cronaca Vera*, *Stop*, and *Novella 2000*. Also, I very much enjoy reading the dictionary, which is a book where all the words in the world are collected. I learned that collections are made in order to save things from universal deluges, people build arks of wood or paper so that the survivors will be able to go on enjoying animals and words forever, because these are happy things. To me, what I do seems perfectly normal, but I understand that this isn't the case when I find myself with other children my own age. If someone asks us how old we are, the best they can do, after a good half hour of sitting there with their mouths hanging open, is to hold up their hands and waggle their fingers. In contrast, I immediately reply that I'm four years and seven months old. And then, if I want to make a good impression, I tell them my age in the total number of days. As far as I can tell, that means I'm a genius, so I'm all right and my life is going to be very easy. Agnese and Mario Elvis have decided to put me right into first grade. They say that I'll get along with older children much better and I'll be able to make lots of friends. I can't wait I want to have someone I can invite home too, so I don't have to listen anymore to all the nonsense the Barbies spout.

"Now, that's enough dancing. I'd like some champagne . . . "

"C-c-certainly, darling."

7.

The days go by and I still haven't saved a single thing, I can't even seem to save Vittoria from the suppositories that prickle. I go and poop without complications: hot milk with a triple helping of cocoa, cookies, and then I'm off to the bathroom. Not my sister, though, she's lazy inside and out, nothing will convince her to go, not even the fear of the homemade suppository constructed out of scraps of bar soap. I tried it once, I was just too curious, I figured that after I put it in, I'd just extrude lots of soap bubbles. Instead, the skin in there started burning really badly and there wasn't so much as a single bubble. Grandma Concetta is a peasant, but that doesn't mean that she tills the soil, it just means that she's stubborn and she's obsessed with poop. You have to poop every day. Right after breakfast, while I'm thinking about ways to find and worlds to save, she asks us: "Have you gone to the bathroom?"

"Yes, yes," I reply. I always say yes twice, because Grandma is a little hard of hearing.

"Well, sort of . . . " Vittoria replies.

"Then she does it on purpose," I think to myself. All she needed to say was, "Yes, yes," to save her ass, and instead the big whiner said, "Well, sort of," and Grandma Concetta starts moving like my little toy robot after it's just been wound up. She turns around, goes over to the cabinet, takes a small pan, turns around, goes over to the sink, pulls open a drawer, and gets out some scrap chunks of bar soap, she turns around, she turns around, she turns around, she finds the matches and goes over to the stove top. Nothing's going to be able to stop her until her granddaughter's taken the suppository.

"Errrrgh," my sister sighs as the kitchen begins to smell of Camay bar soap.

The mush is ready, and Grandma starts shaping it into a bullet shape. Vittoria watches every movement of her fingers, I'm happy because in the pan there's also a piece of yellow soap, the kind they use to wash laundry, and that really burns. Then the phone rings and Grandma leaves the suppository in Vittoria's hands.

"You can put it in yourself. And push down good and hard," she tells her.

My sister is a very obedient little girl, anything they tell her to do, she does. So I set aside my bowl of milk, I turn my chair around and, with both elbows on the table, I get ready to enjoy the scene. She pulls down her pajama pants and her underpants, then she starts touching herself here and there between her butt cheeks. Her gaze focused up on the ceiling lamp resembles that of a couple of the protagonists of Sister Taddea's stories.

"D-d-does it have to take you so long?" I ask after a while.

"Listen, it's not as easy for me as it is for you, you know?" she tells me. "At least there's no risk of you putting it in the wrong hole!"

That's exactly what she said: "At least there's no risk of you putting it in the wrong hole." That's right, I heard her loud and clear. There's no doubt about the meaning, she has more than one. Now I understand those strange words: "We're different, you and me," "You have a peepee, I don't." I can't seem to think about anything else, this story about how girls have two butts is driving me crazy.

"And just who would this little angel be?"
The picture of Vittoria naked with a couple of butt cheeks

in front and another pair in back makes way for a face full of wrinkles, with two lines drawn by a felt-tip pen in place of the eyebrows and a cigarette that's been stuck to the lips for centuries.

"Al, answer the lady," Mamma tells me.

"The little angel is shy! How old is he?"

After which she does the three things I hate most: she gives me a pinch on the cheek, uses the idiot voice people use with puppies, and says the words slowly because she's afraid I won't understand her. Okay, she asked for it.

"I'm f-f-four ears old," I say, holding up all five fingers.

"'Four ears'?" she repeats, amused.

With a glance, my mother begs me to stop.

"Yeth, four ears and . . . and . . . a widdow bit moah!"

"Why, what a little love . . . what a sweetheart," and at last we can start looking around the apartment. The lady tells us not to pay the condition the place is in any mind, it's been unoccupied for two years, and that before deciding whether or not we like it, we should try to imagine it repainted and furnished the way we'd like it. I look down the hallway and I imagine it furnished with a really long electric racetrack and little Formula 1 model race cars that zip back and forth; I imagine the children's room with just a single bed, my own, and on the floor a huge army of toy soldiers, so densely ranked that I can walk on top of them; I imagine the master bedroom with the trundle bed for Vittoria in a corner; I imagine the bathroom with a giant bathtub always full of water so I can get a running start from the hallway and do cannonballs right into it; the kitchen should be Mamma's pride and joy and I imagine it with a nice little fireplace where I can do my experiments with matches. Yes, I like this place just fine, and Mario Elvis and Agnese must like it too, because they wander from room to room with dreamy looks on their faces.

In the elevator Mamma and Papà let go of our hands, which means that now Vittoria and I have permission to speak.

"Is that the place?" we ask immediately.

"I'm afraid not," says Papà.

"It seemed like a happy house to me!" I say.

"No, Al. It seemed like it, but that's not the place."

Mamma leans her head on Papà's shoulder.

"But it really was beautiful."

8.

This is the year they call 1972 and things are happening that I can't understand: a woman from Messina woke up one morning with holes in her hands and instead of taking her to the hospital, everyone started to pray; an old actress in her seventies married an old man in his thirties and the whole thing made Grandma grumble for two days; Nicola di Bari won the Festival of Sanremo even if he's not friends with Papà; the ocean liner Queen Elizabeth was destroyed by flames, in a harbor, with all the water they have in harbors.

The experiment I was doing in the sink to prove that you'd have to be a fool not to be able to put out a fire in the middle of the water cost me a week's punishment, luckily interrupted after four days thanks to Vittoria's birthday and a word you can find on page 109 of the dictionary, "amnesty." Seeing that my sister also has good grades on her report card, Mamma and Papà have decided to give her a puppy, a little mutt, which was the item that led the wish list for Father Christmas for the last three years, something that however he never brought her because he's allergic to dog hair. Vittoria and I are both thrilled, the puppy sleeps on a pillow under the radiator but we're not allowed to start playing with him until we've listened patiently to all of Mamma's advice and shown how mature we are and, more in general, that we're not actually two children aged five and nine.

"Having a dog is an important test," Mamma tells us, "a dog is a very sensitive animal, you need to take good care of it, just as if it was a person, otherwise it suffers. Is that clear?"

"Certainly," Vittoria replies.

"C-c-certainly," I say as I think of the best way to harness a cart to the dog and get him to haul me at top speed back and forth in the park.

"You're going to have to take care of him, it won't be easy but I trust you, I'm sure that you'll show me what big kids you are, and that this experience will help you to grow up even more."

"Yes, Mamma," says Vittoria.

"Yes, Mamma," I say, having in the meantime solved the problem: I'll use Papà's suspenders and one of Grandma's girdles.

"You'll feed him in the morning and you'll feed him at night. You'll always take him out for a walk together as soon as you get home from school, and you'll never cross the street, is that clear?"

"Certainly, that's clear."

"Perfectly c-c-clear," I say as I think about where to find a riding crop.

"Very good, good children, now you can go and play with Ciccio."

About the name, it's the puppy's own fault, he screwed himself with his own paws. Papà says that dogs choose their own names, all we can do is suggest options. And so while he was sitting there we started taking turns calling him. Grandma: "Lampo," Mamma: "Rex," Papà: "Aaron," me: "Onassis," Vittoria: "Ciccio!" and the idiot turned around.

Grown-ups write fairy tales. That much I understand. They write them to help children get to sleep, and also to earn a little money. Okay, that's clear. They invent fantastic worlds where a skinny kid can easily pull out a sword stuck in a stone and a white knight can kill a dragon as tall as an apartment house, and you'd better believe them or the grown-ups will get their feelings hurt. But that's only at night. Because during the day, if you try to pull out the knife stuck in the watermelon or shoot at the neighbor lady's vicious dog with your sling-shot, then they'll tell you not to, that it's dangerous, that it's not right, that it's against the law, and that you shouldn't believe in fairy tales. This game of making you dream and then yanking you back to reality makes all my thoughts turn strange, it makes me angry, and that's why the parents of the Santamaria family no longer tell fairy tales. Now they just tell us that if we want to know what witches and various monsters are like, we only need to take a stroll around the apartment building. There's the old man who rides the elevator up and down all night long, the lady who never comes out of her apartment—no one knows how she can survive without buy-ing groceries—and a gentleman who always reeks of wine, and another one you should never say "Buongiorno" to, otherwise he'll reply, "Buongiorno my . . . " followed by a word you're not supposed to say. And then there's Signor Tuzzi, the man on the top floor. He's tall, super-skinny, and capable of staring at you for twenty minutes at a time without uttering a word, the same way I do. But the reason he doesn't talk is that his throat is dead and he can't get the words out without the assis-tance of an electric device. He presses it against his neck, his neck vibrates, and the words come out in little fragments, with a strange sound that gives you goose bumps. Signor Tuzzi comes to our front door at the end of every month, always at night, because Papà has the white envelopes. His arrival in the afternoon is an odd occurrence, so I go to the door and hide behind Mamma's legs.

"What? . . . I'm sorry, I didn't understand . . . Would you

mind saying it again, it's my fault, I'm a little hard of hearing . . . Would you rather write it down? Do you want a sheet of paper?"

The man pulls out a very short pencil and a notepad from his jacket pocket, writes something, then turns the sheet so Mamma can read it.

"You bought a nice dog."

"It's only a puppy," says Mamma.

"He must eat a lot."

"Not at all, seriously, and just imagine, he loves stale bread."

"This year I'm going to have to raise the rent."

"But why? We pay our rent on time, the apartment is in perfect shape, where else are you going to find such wonderful tenants as us?"

Signor Tuzzi puts his notepad away in his pocket and turns on his electric device.

"Ddddoooonnnn'ttt wwwwooorrryyyy . . . I-I-I-I-I cccaannn fffiiinnnddd ttthhheeemmm . . . bbbyyy tthhee ddooozzzzeeennn."

I put my hands over my ears and when Signor Tuzzi went away I started laughing. But Mamma had the wrong expression on her face, the one that's neither angry nor cheerful and only makes me feel strange. I follow her around for a while, she does various things, she washes a clean glass, dusts a dresser that doesn't need dusting, opens and closes a drawer without getting anything out of it, behaves as if I wasn't there, keeps her back turned to me the whole time, and then shuts herself up in the bathroom without playing the game of the smile that vanishes behind the door. I wonder what's going on. I go to see Vittoria. She's sitting on the bed and brushing Ciccio with Grandma's hairbrush.

"Vittoria? Is this our home?"

"Certainly it's ours."

"So that means no one c-c-can kick us out?"

"Why should they kick us out? As long as we pay, we can stay here forever."

"Wh-wh-what's a rent? Signor Tuzzi says he wants to raise ours."

"Oh, really? What do you care? We have Papà's salary and Grandma's pension . . . "

"Are we rich?"

"Rich people have Ferraris, television sets with lots of buttons, and wardrobes full of fur coats."

"Then are we poor?"

"Poor people live under bridges and have yellow teeth."

"Then wh-wh-what are we?"

"Al, give me a break, we're just a so-so family."

9.

The search for the promised home has become a lot less fun. Mamma and Papà are always in bad moods, we no longer sing in the car, the sardine game has been forbidden, and then nobody will explain to me why we keep looking at smaller and smaller apartments.

"It's a nice place," Papà says.

"The apartment house isn't bad either," says Mamma.

We ring the buzzer, we tell them that we're the Santamaria family, we cross the courtyard, we say how nice it is, we step into the elevator but since it takes a ten-lire coin to make it work and none of us has one, we get back out. As we get out, we say how nice the elevator is, too. We climb the stairs to the fourth floor, and no one manages to like the rotten door and the piece of broken wall the doorbell hangs off of. The interior of the apartment unfortunately doesn't resemble the neighborhood or the apartment house or even the elevator, it's just as nasty and broken as the door. The owner of the apartment is a gentlemen you'd want to take a good long look at. He's wearing a plum-colored suit, a sky-blue scarf around his neck, and he wears a pair of perforated fingerless leather gloves. He doesn't touch anything, he opens the doors by pushing them with his elbow, and he ends every sentence with the recurrent phrase: "but after all . . . "

"The facilities are all fine, there might be some minor work to do, but after all . . . " he says, looking at Mamma and Papà.

He accompanies us into the living room, opens the door with his elbow, and stands in the middle of the room.

"There's plenty of space, it's not a palace, but after all . . . "

The kitchen might need a little touching up, the bathroom is normal, the two bedrooms are the way they are, but after all . . . for a family like ours it's fine, he makes up his mind to say at the end of the tour. While Mamma and Papà go back to look at the living room, the man goes out to dust off his elbows with a handkerchief made of sky-blue cloth.

"This can't be it, c-c-can it?" I ask Vittoria.

"I certainly hope not. There's no room here for a little room all my own."

I could gladly give up Vittoria's bedroom, but not Mamma and Papà's happiness. Where are the nice faces they had when we were looking at the apartment with soft floors? Mamma isn't talking about walls to knock down and big mirrors to put up here and there, Papà isn't talking about his little nook where he can play the guitar, he isn't wandering from room to room trying to decide where to install his private bar. This place isn't right.

"So you're the little genius . . . "

Everyone wants a genius for a son, but since I'm already Mamma and Papà's son, Dottor Bernabei is acting all obnoxious.

The son he got is Gianmaria, second-best student in the class and former teacher's pet.

"How old are you?" he asks me.

"F-f-five years, two months, and a week. Eighteen hundred and ninety-five days."

"Oh, really? When were you born?"

"March 14th."

His staring eye and quivering lip tell me that he's multiplying three hundred and sixty-five by five. He was pretty quick, I have to admit. Now he squints and waves the fingers of his hand because he's adding the two months, then the week. And he smiles.

"The little genius is going to have to study his mathematics a little harder," says Bernabei. "Five years, two months, and a week makes eighteen hundred and ninety-three days, not eighteen hundred and ninety-five."

Following the advice of the editor in chief of *Cronaca Vera*, in reply to the letter from Piero A. in Foggia who asked how he should behave when dealing with rude and arrogant people, I act as if he didn't exist.

"Papà, both 1968 and 1972 are leap years, so the exact number of days is eighteen hundred and ninety-five," I say.

"Two days more, two days less . . . what difference does it make," Mario Elvis says to me.

"And then we'd have to check to see if those are leap years, I don't remember offhand . . . " Bernabei replies, somehow convinced he still exists.

"There's nothing t-t-to remember, Papà, if the last two numbers of the year are divisible by four, then . . . "

"That's enough, Al, we'll check later," Papà says.

"Yeah, yeah, kid, I'd really be interested in knowing if it's true . . . " Bernabei snickers, doing his best to end with a tie.

Unfortunately for me, the Santamarias are very sociable people. Living in a family of sociable people means that your parents try never to fight with anyone and especially that they always take you to parties, even if you don't want to go. I hate birthday parties because I always wind up in a corner watching the others play and waiting for my turn, which never comes. The most odious things are parties at a park, because Papà stays there the whole time telling me over and over again: "Come on, go play with them," "Come on, go tell them it's your turn now," and I run back and forth after that band of kids who are too fast and never pass me the ball. Agnese and Mario Elvis were so hoping that I'd get along with the older kids, and to keep from upsetting them, I try to get involved. I do pretty well at hide-and-seek. I've been behind a bush for ten minutes. I have branches and twigs sticking out of the neck of my T-shirt and the waist of my pants, I've blackened my face with mud, and all around me, hidden behind benches, water fountains, trees, and, I swear it, pages of newspapers, the others are dropping like flies. From my hiding place I see Mario Elvis off on his own. He's wearing leather pants, pointy boots, and a black shirt with the long collar, the Black Suit, the special outfit that Elvis wore in 1968 for his concerts on TV. The other parents are all looking at him, a few of them tilt their head in his direction and laugh, one of the mothers brings him something to drink and then immediately turns to go. Maybe they're just shy because he's too good looking. I like it when Papà worries about me: until just a moment ago, he seemed distracted, but now he's pacing back and forth, looking around, trying to find me. If an astronaut first class can't see me, it means that I'm really hidden well.

"I found you all!" Michele shouts.

Loser, you haven't found me.

"No . . . " I say, with my mouth all twisted so it sends the voice far from my hiding place.

"Now let's play dodgeball!" says Michele, and I try speaking a little louder: "You still haven't . . . found Al!"

All the children run to the middle of the lawn. Michele, who already has the ball under his arm, starts dividing up the teams. Inside me I feel something bad that I haven't encountered before, it grows in my stomach, it reaches my throat, and it heats up my cheeks. There must be a name for this feeling, like there is for everything else in the world, what do you call it when you don't want to come out of your hiding place because if you do everyone is going to look at you and realize that you'd been forgotten? Maybe this thing that's freezing me in place is so bad that it doesn't even have a name, or else maybe it doesn't have one because it's never happened to anyone else before. Luckily it doesn't last long. Papà saw me, he's not mad at me. He walks over to the bush, takes me by the hand, smiles at me, and picks the twigs and branches off of my T-shirt.

"You even blackened your face . . . " he says to me, "you're just too good, Al." I know, Casimiro always tells me the same thing.

10.

I read that a famous gentleman named Isaac Newton made a very major discovery while lying under an apple tree. That's because brilliant ideas don't just happen anywhere, you have to make an appointment to meet in a specific place. I don't have a lot of choices, here on the balcony there's just a vase of geraniums that are decidedly much less powerful than apple trees because after half an hour the only idea that's showed up for the appointment is this: I need to help my parents. Vittoria says that it's normal, you can't be happy every single day, no one is. To me it seems crazy not to at least try, maybe the problem with the world is that everyone else thinks the way she does. But I'm different. What good is it to possess an extraordinary brain if you don't use it to make yourself happy, along with your family and therefore, by extension, yourself?

Vittoria can leave the courtyard and walk all the way around the apartment house, Mamma said so, and I can too but since no one has said so, I'll have to sneak out to do it. For today I'll settle for looking at the other buildings here along the street, if I'm fast enough and my mother doesn't start leaning out the window and calling me, I can make it all the way to the intersection. I'll have to spend a couple of days exploring this area, because maybe the promised home has always been here, just a stone's throw away, and we just never noticed. Crossing the courtyard and getting out the front door onto the street won't be a problem. I just have to make up my mind whether to use my superspeed or one of my supercamouflages instead. If I come home covered with mud again, though, Mamma will kill me, so I opt for the superspeed. To the naked eye, there's nothing the red blur of my T-shirt, and maybe you'll hear a boom when I break the sound barrier. Ready, set, go!

"Hi, Al!"

"Where are you running to, Al?"

"Careful not to fall and hurt yourself, Al."

"Have a good day, Al."

It went well. Aside from the usual old pains in the neck, everyone else must be asking themselves whether what they saw go racing past was a missile or a lightning bolt.

This is the first time that Casimiro and I have gone out alone, we're very excited. Walking without holding hands with Mamma or Papà is so special, it makes everything seem brand new. Just a few short steps and already we're looking at a very nice building. When I walk this way with Mario Elvis, I always just watch our shadows, I run ahead to make them the same height or else, if I understand that he's in a hurry, I make him drag me, I tell him that I'm tired and ask him if he'll pick me up and carry me. That's why I'd never noticed this building before. It has a lovely yard, there's a lemon tree and lots of dirt to dig holes in. Maybe this is it, maybe we wandered around in vain for months while the whole time the promised home was waiting for us just a slingshot's throw away from our front door. I try to see what's behind the windows but they're all dark. The iron bars on the low garden wall are so widely spaced I should have no problem getting through them.

"Let's go into action," I say to Casimiro.

I insert a leg, it gets through right away, then the belly, the chest too, now the other leg . . . and the head. Sideways, maybe, because it's not getting through like this. Ouch, it hurts. My head is bigger than my chest, how can that be? My ears are ripping off. My brain is so big it won't pass through the bars!

"Holy Christ! Who on earth are you?" a lady asks me from the window.

"Al Santamaria . . . I come in peace . . . "

The lady did just like Tarzan that time he freed Jane from the carnivorous plant. With the strength of her hands alone, she managed to widen the bars just enough to set me free. She told me never to try that again, that it's dangerous and lots of those kind of things, where once you've listened to the first two all you need to do is keeping saying: "Yes," with a sorrowful look. The apartment was nice enough, but it certainly wasn't the promised home. When I went inside, I didn't feel that certain I-don't-know-what that Mamma and Papà always talk about, just a bad smell of soup made with stinky vegetables. I could have taken a look at the apartment next door, but Vittoria tells me that I always overdo it, and so I decided to just go back home at a velocity that leaves nothing but a red blur. This mission is too important for me to let myself be found out on my first excursion.

It's nice to get home after being out in the world. Everything says hello to me. The steps on my staircase. My window on my landing. My carpet in front of my door. My doorbell.

"At last!"

My mother.

"When I call you, you have to come straight home, understood? . . . What's that smile, Al?"

"Nothing."

"What have you gotten up to?"

"*Noth*-ing."

"I'm going out for five minutes," Mamma says, "don't make Grandma mad."

When would I ever do such a thing? In fact, I steer well clear of her, because I have no desire to spend the afternoon rolling balls of woolen yarn and answering: "Yes yes, I went to the bathroom already." The minute the apartment door closes, I go into the kitchen, I get the matches out, and I start scorching the edges of the trash bag. It's too bad I'm destined to do great things because it really would have been nice to become a fireman. I like to set fire to things. I look at the flames, the way things crumple up and change color, then I say that the blaze is out of control, I call the firemen, and I put out the fire. Little yellow flames start growing on the trash bag. Nothing much. I keep it up. Plastic burns nicely, I think to myself, it's not like carpet fringes. Wow, it's really burning now. Niiiice, the plastic sack has burst into a fireball.

"Hurry, c-c-call the firemen!"

I'm not allowed to go get the water unless first I make the sound of the siren.

"Weee-woooo-weee-woooo!"

I pour a glass of water on the flames, but they've already consumed the handles. The bag collapses on the kitchen mat.

"Weee-woooo-weee-woooo! Hurry, more water!"

The second glass hits the target too, but by now the flames are raging high and are consuming the carpet.

"Weee-woooo-weee-woooo! Hurry, c-c-call the reinforcements! . . . Grandmaaaa!"

"Al, it won't do you any good to put on a captivating smile!" Mamma shouts.

"Captivating" is a very nice word, what it means is that I shrug my shoulders, I tilt my head to one side, I show all my little teeth, I make my eyes look sweet, and I get out of trouble. Usually. "Do you know that you're a very smart little dead kid? You could have burnt our house to the ground stuck living out on the street because you're little in America!" Being shouted at by two grown-ups at the same time is no fun at all. At first you can't understand a thing. But then, thanks to my superintelligence and the fact that they've started taking turns talking, I understand that I'm too smart of a little kid to do such dumb things, that a kid my age is dead now because of this kind of foolishness, that another kid set his apartment on fire and now his family is stuck living out on the street, to say nothing of the shoe repair man's son who got bad burns and is now having an operation in America.

"I must have told you a thousand times but you don't listen!" Grandma shouts at me.

"Just why is it that you don't listen?" Mamma asks me.

It's not hard to understand, the whole world talks to me, everyone calls me at the same time, everyone has something important to tell me, and they all demand my attention. Right this very second, my mother is calling me, and so are the colorful lighter on the table, the new toy soldiers still attached to the plastic strips, the tube of Crystal Ball magic bubbles, and a spider walking on the bottom of the shelf. I don't know how old people can handle it. Doesn't anyone call them anymore?

11.

I'm lucky, I was born in the years when anything is possible. Science and technology are so good now that with just a few bucks you can solve any problem, it says so in the papers. "Brand-new mathematical method to win twice a month at Lotto and the Totocalcio soccer pool, 2,500 lire," "TALLER WOMEN TALLER MEN with a world-renowned system. Rapid, guaranteed success, 2,400 lire," "Giulio Capece SPECIALIST IN LOVE POTIONS makes them in 99 different ways, 3,000 lire." Once I've figured out what's going wrong in the world, I'll be able to solve those problems by means of spectacular, inexpensive inventions. In the meantime, I go on studying. Car trips are very useful when it comes to understanding the world. Observing it from the car window, I've noticed that very few people smile. They don't smile in their cars, they don't smile at the bus stops, and they don't smile on the sidewalks. Seeing that, as far as I can tell, people aren't happy when they're on asphalt and cement, it seems to me that getting rid of them might make everyone happier. Still, there's something about this thought that doesn't work. A few days ago, while Mamma was listening to the radio, I heard that a young man, a left-winger, which must mean that he used his left hand to write just like I do, was stabbed to death in a park and that a man shot his wife to death in their home. And in both cases, asphalt and cement had nothing to do with it. So maybe I should take a different approach to the problem. Killing someone else is the worst thing that an old person can do, it's like how stealing someone else's snack is the worst thing that a kid can do. So are these men capable of killing a left-handed young man and a wife nothing more than snack-thieving children who've gotten older and therefore meaner? If that's the way it is, why bother to wait, why not just catch them in kindergarten and throw them in prison? It seems easy, but in Papà's newspaper, the one with floppy pages and tiny words, I read that they're still looking for the people who years ago put a bomb in a bank and killed seventeen people. They must have been some very very old people. Like, in their eighties, because if even at age twenty you're capable of stabbing to death a left-hander you don't much like, it must take some time before you can get so mean that you'd kill seventeen strangers you've never even met. One solution might be to keep an eye on all the old people, from seventy-five years and up. I'd already figured out that Grandma's magazines didn't tell the whole truth about the world, that the famous actor who left his wife for a ballerina couldn't be the planet's principal problem, but the floppy newspapers, the radio, and the TV news aren't doing anything to help me see things clearly. But for now, I'm going to have to set aside the issue of saving the world, because we're on the last verse of "Surrender," Mario Elvis is singing, "*Be mine forrreeveeer . . .* " and now it's Vittoria's and my turn.

"*Be mine to-niiight!*"

Papà slowly slips the key into the lock. He turns it very very slowly because otherwise you can hear the click. He was really good, we put our hands over our mouths because even our laughter is supposed to be silent. Now Papà blows on his fingertips, warms up his hands, and starts opening the door, one millimeter at a time. One millimeter. Two millimeters.

"Use the felt pads, I just waxed the floor!" Mamma shouts from the kitchen.

Once again, Agnese wins. Mario Elvis shakes his head and smiles, he can't believe that he has such an excellent wife that, after waxing the floors, she develops the superpower of ultra-hearing. He steps onto the felt pads and slides off, with both hands behind his back. When he reaches the end of the hall, he turns a graceful pirouette. Vittoria and I put on our little felt skates and set off down the hall, hand in hand, just like on the cover of *Hans Brinker, or the Silver Skates*.

"Agnese, come on! The ice is stupendous tonight," says Papà.

"No."

"Oh, come on!"

From the kitchen comes the sound of a pan dropping and Mamma snorting.

"Anyway, I don't know how to ice-skate . . . I don't know how to do anything at all!" she says.

We exchange a glance.

"Princess of Monaco treatment?" Vittoria asks.

"Hmmm, I think that's exactly what's called for," Papà replies.

The Princess of Monaco treatment is something that Papà invented as a way of telling Mamma that she's the finest woman on earth without resorting to words. This is how it works: you kidnap the princess from the kitchen, you ignore when she protests: "No, no, everything'll get burnt," and you make her sit on the throne, which is of course just the armchair in the living room. Papà stands behind her and massages her temples, Vittoria and I sit in front of her, we each take one foot, and we start caressing it. If Princess Grace of Monaco is pretty, it's because she lets people massage her for two hours a day. But since Mamma is prettier, ten minutes every so often is enough for her.

12.

While the other children chase after Roberta, who runs back and forth in the backyard for no good reason, the explorer Al Santamaria takes advantage of a momentary distraction on the part of the mothers and vanishes into the hedge. Did anyone see me? No, to the other children I'm invisible and to the mothers, for the past twenty minutes all that exists are those little plastic vases which must be much more than just food containers, otherwise there would be no explanation for all of those "oooohs" and "aaaahs." All the better, that way the search for the promised home won't have to stop for a stupid party. On this side there's nothing interesting, only a row of identical houses that seem to be made of sand, with the same rectangular pail. On this side, on the other hand, things look better. The apartment house with the big marble lions near the front door might be the right one. From the apartment on the second floor comes the smell of homemade cake. That's a sign.

"Who is it?" asks an old voice from the intercom.

"Hello, my n-n-name is Al, can I have a glass of water?"

It's not really all that hard to get into the homes of old people. Two of them live in this place, they have the agreeable manners and quick way of speaking of people who have a lot to do. The man is painting the stable of the manger scene, because "if you don't get these things done in the summer, you never do them at all"; the lady is ironing sheets with an iron that you don't plug into the dangerous holes, but that you put on the stove like a frying pan. The apartment is so silent that it seems like no one has ever uttered a word in there. The silver objects on the dressers and credenzas are covered with large sheets of plastic. There are lots of carpets but the two of them play a strange game, they go from one room to another without ever walking on them. They step around them, they jump over them, it must be some kind of game: whoever touches the carpet dies. The apartment is big, if you walled off part of the living room there would be a bedroom for each of us.

"Does your mother know that you're out and about on your own?" the woman asks as she fills the glass with water.

By now, I've figured it out: all old people belong to a secret organization established to keep an eye on us kids.

"Yes, she gave me permission. As long as I d-d-don't go far or cross the street," I tell her.

"Do you want another?"

"No, thanks . . . Is the electric wiring new?"

The woman puts a hand on her hip and looks at me.

"Giulio, this little boy wants to know if our electric wiring is new!"

The woman's voice runs down the hallway, across the living room, and reaches the man's ear. Since it's an old lady's voice, it runs very slowly and the answer takes a while to come back.

"It was put in in '39 . . . they did things right in '39 . . . We astonished the world in . . . "

The last "thirty-nine" never gets there. It must have gotten lost somewhere in the hallway.

"Can I see the balcony?" I ask.

We walk along next to a very long carpet, we edge around a wide carpet, though in the end I step on it with one foot, just to see if anything will happen. Nothing does. There's one last carpet, a little one. I jump on it behind the woman's back and then I walk out onto the balcony.

"It's nice!" I say.

"In the evening, we sit out here and enjoy the cool air."

"Are you s-s-selling this apartment?"

"Why, do you want to buy it? No, dear, we're going to live in this apartment until we die."

"So h-h-how is your h-h-health?"

I didn't ask to go to Roberta's party. No. This idea of moving me up a year really screwed me, now I have to go to the parties of my new classmates and also to the ones of my old classmates, a double ration. I'm in trouble because when I get back from my expedition, instead of running after the other children, I choose to sit by myself reading magazines near the women who were playing with the plastic containers. When Papà came to get me, Roberta's mom immediately ratted me out, saying: "I'm afraid that Al didn't have much fun. What a strange child, I wonder who he takes after."

The trip home isn't a particularly nice one. Papà doesn't sing the way he usually does.

"Listen carefully to me, Al," he says.

After all, I know what you want to tell me, but I listen to you all the same. I stop thinking about that strange piece of news about something called the "vote of confidence" that's constantly in the press, and I listen to you.

"Knowing how to keep company with other people is important. You need to learn how to play with other kids, even if you don't like their games . . . just for the fun of being together."

The fin that's at the end of the fish is called the caudal fin.

"That's part of the process of growing up, your intelligence is nurtured through regular contact with other people."

I want to become one of those magicians who saw women in half. Who knows if they just let you start sawing them, or if you have to take a class first.

"Believe me, Al, being intelligent won't do you a bit of good if you don't know how to get along with other people . . . you son of a bitch!"

What is it Papà called that driver? "Son of a bitch"? Did I hear him right?

"In other words, you're a smart kid, try to make friends with all your classmates."

I know "bench," "batch," and "blanch."

"Is that clear, Al?"

"It's very c-c-clear, Papà."

When we get home, Papà is happier. Talking is a very important thing to him, and in fact I always let him talk.

Mamma is outside the street door with a number of other ladies from our apartment house.

"Agnese, where are you going?" Papà asks as he greets the other ladies with a deep bow.

"Back to the fruit vendor, look at the disgusting tomatoes he palmed off on me."

Yes, no, should I try, I shouldn't try, good bad right wrong, what should I do, should I try?

Sure, I'll try.

"Fruit vendors really are a bunch of sons of bitches!"

At the base of those sons of bitches of the KGB in Berlin, Generaless Agnesova and General Elvisovic are exchanging secret messages. Hiding like a genuine son of a bitch, secret agent Al is eavesdropping.

"They say she's not long for this world . . . " Agnesova whispers.

"If you want, we can bring her home," Elvisovic reassures her.

They're talking about Grandma Concetta. She's been in the hospital for days but, according to what those sons of bitches the doctors say, the disease must be terminal and she can't come home.

"I don't know, she doesn't recognize anyone anymore . . . why inflict that on the children?"

That last phrase is mysterious. Even Casimiro isn't understanding a thing by now.

"Mario, how long can we survive without her?"

"Don't think about that now, we'll be fine for a while."

"We already pay too much rent."

This must be a secret code of some kind. We can't have suddenly become poor. Could that be? Is all you need a Grandma in the hospital and a so-so family becomes poor?

"Oh my God, that smell, I can't take it anymore . . . pass me the pomade," says Elvisovic.

The whole Santamaria family has been walking around with smears of mentholatum under their noses on account of that little son of a bitch Ciccio. He stinks to high heaven because he has a skin disease that can only be cured by a special soap that costs too much. Since the little mutt has hairy armpits just like Mamma and Papà—I know because I picked up his paws and saw it—I thought I would solve the problem by putting deodorant on him. It didn't go well, now Agnese is angry because she found tufts of dog fur under her armpits, Ciccio stinks twice as bad as before, and no one, except for me, finds the idea of the menthol-mustachioed family funny.

13.

For a week Mamma and Papà have sent us to the secondary headquarters of the Santamaria family, the one where Uncle Armando lives. It's much smaller and there aren't any forbidden games because after all everything's already broken. The television set is held together with duct tape, the sofa is stained and has a tear on the right armrest, the only vase still even resembles a vase because of a spiderweb of glue that holds the pieces together. It's heaven on earth. At my house, there are objects everywhere, all of them are fragile, and Mamma has scattered them here and there to make sure that every corner of the apartment is the wrong corner to play in. I have to take care not to scratch the table, not to knock over the bric-a-brac and conversation pieces, not to break the windows, not to destroy another lamp. I've only broken one of them, the one in the living room, with a soccer ball I kicked. Mamma got really mad, according to her it was impossible not to know that if I kicked a soccer ball indoors I was bound to break something. I even considered offering her an explanation: "You know, Mamma, this is how it works, first of all, you need to forget all those old-people ideas like 'the principle of cause-and-effect' and 'the analysis of consequences,' you always talk to me about these things but the only things I know the meaning of are 'now,' 'right now,' 'immediately,' and what I wanted, now, right now, immediately, was to kick that soccer ball." In the end, though, all I said was the usual: "I'm sorry, I didn't do it on purpose." With Uncle Armando we did whatever we wanted, when I started making waves in the bathtub and when Vittoria set a hot frying pan down right on the table, all he said was: "The water on the floor will dry eventually," and: "These days polka dots are in fashion, all you need to do is make a few more burned spots like that one and it will look like a super-modern table." At night we always had a very important job to do: Uncle Armando has lots of girlfriends but he has trouble making up his mind which one to pick, he says that his tastes are just too finicky. After dinner he'd put us to bed and then he'd get out a magazine full of pictures of women because there's even a mail-order catalogue for girlfriends, which clearly cost less, just like the shoes that Mamma orders. Uncle Armando told us that we needed to choose one by looking at the face, because the important thing is the eyes which are the mirror of something or other, while the other parts of the body can trick you. He would leaf through a few pages and then ask us: "What do you think of this one?" and he'd fold the page so we could only see the face. Uncle Armando's girlfriends were beautiful even though they always had too much makeup on and their mouths puckered up as if they were blowing out candles on a birthday cake. The final runners-up were Ramona, who was Uncle Armando's choice, Chéri, picked by Vittoria, and Cindy, who wore a cowboy hat and was my favorite. Unfortunately, Mamma and Papà came to pick us up before we could crown a winner.

When we get back to the Santamaria family central headquarters, Grandma isn't there. Mamma tells us that she's gone.

I ask where she went, Mamma picks up a vase with a little green plant in it and tells me that this is how life works: first we're little tiny sprouts, then we grow and get tall and strong, then we start to yellow and wither. The question is: why did they forget to water Grandma? Then Mamma gets out the book on birds, points to the drawing of a seagull skeleton, and tells me that this is all that's left of us when we pass away, but that we shouldn't be sad because the most important thing is our soul, and our souls are eternal. From Mamma's smile I gather that being eternal is a fine thing.

I'm not sad, it's just that my thoughts are all mixed up. I can't sleep, I'm feeling too many things all at the same time: Grandma Concetta is gone, she passed away, an angel carried her off, now she's in heaven, she's a seagull skeleton, her soul is floating around someplace, in other words, she's dead, and no, Vittoria can't move straight into her room.

"C-c-casimiro, did you hear what Mamma said?"

"Grandma is dead."

"No, the l-l-last thing that she said."

"That Grandma is in h-h-heaven, and that an angel took her there, that is: she's dead."

"No, she said that Grandma is l-l-looking down on us from up there!"

"Yes, and then she said that she's d-d-dead."

"H-h-how can she look down on us from up there when it's cloudy?"

"Will the two of you just cut it out? Al, Grandma's dead, period!" the radio communications officer breaks in.

"I g-g-got it, she's dead! But will she come back now and then, or is she dead forever?"

Mamma gave Vittoria a diary. I personally have never much cared for diaries but the minute I saw it in my sister's hands, it became the thing I wished for most in all my life. On the cover there's a nice little padlock because it's a secret diary, Vittoria can write whatever she wants in it and no one will ever be able to read it. When she misses her, she can even write to Grandma Concetta, who when she lived here at home couldn't see a foot past the tip of her nose but, now that she's in heaven, can apparently read words from miles and miles away, even with clouds in the way. The padlock has a key, in the store all the diaries had two but when I mentioned that to Mamma, she replied: "No, no . . . really? . . . It must have gotten lost."

In bed, Vittoria has permission to keep the light on for ten minutes so she can write in her diary. I start coloring in the book full of drawings with numbers in them. According to the coloring book factory I ought to use blue where it says 1, yellow where there's a 2, and green where it says 3. But I don't take orders from someone I've never met, not me.

"Wh-wh-what are you writing?" I ask Vittoria.

"None of your business."

"Can I read it when you're done?"

"No, Al, ask them to give you one of your own."

"If you let me read it, I'll let you c-c-color in my coloring book."

"Look what you've done with those felt-tip markers . . . your hands are all dirty!"

"I'll wash them later."

"Wash your hands right away, the ink is bad for you."

"Why?"

"Your skin has pores, your pores absorb the ink, the ink winds up in your blood . . . and from there it goes into your heart and brain!"

"Really?"

Please say yes, please say it's not a fairy tale.

"Certainly, Al, everyone knows that. Where do you think sweat comes from? From the pores, so if your skin is perforated then it means that things can come out and go in, too."

It's not a fairy tale, pores exist, I know that, I'm on page 579 of the dictionary. That means that you can write things on your heart and your brain. My right hand is the most secret diary in the world, and the only one in human flesh!

14.

"Santamaria residence? Signora Agnese? . . . Just a moment, let me pass you your son."

"Mamma! C-c-come quick, I've found the promised home!"

"Al, where on earth are you?"

"I'm right here, c-c-come quick!"

"Where? Give me the address! Put the lady back on the line!"

"The address is on Via delle C-c-conce . . . number eleven . . . apartment two. I've found it, Mamma, there's an old lady in it, but this is it!"

"Al! Stay there, I'll be right over . . . " Mamma tells me. "Stay there with the lady, understood?"

"I'll stay here with the old l-l-lady, over and out!"

Adults are designed to ruin your happiness. There are always rules to be respected. But why don't they say something beforehand! Instead, no, they wait for the last minute to tell you that this is how the game works: 1) the promised home can't already be inhabited; 2) the promised home can't have five rooms and a yard as big as a soccer field; 3) the promised home can only and exclusively be found among those that have a sign out front reading "For Sale." I had decided to keep a long face all evening long but when the curfew game started, I just couldn't resist. The curfew is something that they had during the war to make cities invisible so the enemy bombers would get lost and bomb their own homes. The rules of this game are that as soon as your homework is finished, you have to turn out the lights and do everything with just two candles lit. At dinner, Papà and Mamma, who are living on a diet of tea and melba toast, tell us all about the war and how they used to race for the bomb shelters, they're stories that strike fear into your heart, much more than the fear you feel when you watch the movies I secretly watch from under the sofa bed. Agnese gets scared too sometimes, like the time that an ambulance went by and Papà shouted that it was the air raid siren.

When it's time to go to sleep I'm so agitated that they have to say goodnight three times, bring me a glass of water, give me a little back massage and two kisses with loud smacks to get me under the covers. How does Vittoria manage to lie there, so still and good?

"H-h-how much fun it is to play blackout, right?" I ask her.

"You really are a cretin."

"N-n-no, you are."

"This isn't a game, we've become poor!"

I mean, is this really the life that awaits me? Games, surprises, inventions, and candlelit evenings? I'm so happy I could set my mattress on fire. In the other room, Mamma and Papà are whispering, I've run out of excuses, I ought to go to sleep but I'm just too curious. If I want to go into their room to see what's so much fun in there, all I need to do is show up with my hand on my forehead. Or would it maybe be better to show up with a frightened face and tell them I had a bad dream about bombardments? No, hand on the forehead, I'll tell them I don't feel good and then I'll get coddled. I start acting about halfway down the hallway, and when I open the door I seem like a genuine invalid. In the darkness I see one black figure sitting on the bed, Papà, and another black figure down on her knees in front of him, Mamma.

"I don't feel good," I say in the voice of someone with their hand on their forehead.

"Al!" Papà shouts.

There's something odd. Maybe they didn't see the hand on my forehead, because what they usually do is turn on the light and get out of bed, instead they just stayed perfectly still, my mother didn't even turn around.

"Go to bed, Al!" Papà shouts again.

Maybe they didn't hear me.

"I don't feel good," I say again.

"Go straight to bed or Papà will come in there and tell you why!" he says.

What about Mamma? Doesn't she have anything to say?

"Get going!"

I'm going, I'm going. I go back to bed, but now I'm upset. I hate it when things don't go the way they usually do. Now I'm going to have to think over and over again about what I've seen, about why they didn't worry about my health one bit and why Mamma didn't even open her mouth. With all the worries I have! With the promised home, my way, saving the world, and all the rest! Ah, at last he's here. Papà comes into the room, sits on my bed, and puts a hand on my forehead.

"Your forehead isn't hot, how do you feel?" he whispers.

"Wh-wh-what were you doing?"

"Nothing, Al, just tell me how you feel."

"I just didn't feel very good . . . why was Mamma on her knees?"

"Mamma on her knees?" asks Vittoria.

"Why doesn't anybody get any sleep in this house?"

15.

Sometimes Mamma kneels down for no good reason, other times she says that she has a headache, she lies down on the sofa, and she puts a cotton ball under her nose, a cotton-ball that's soaked in that liquid they use to remove fingernail polish. She's been doing it every now and then, since Grandma passed away. The cotton ball treatment works, she falls asleep for a few minutes, then she gets up and comes over to see us, walking all off-kilter, to tell us that we're the lights of her life. The way she talks, it's impossible not to believe her, as if she were one of those wooden Russian dolls and the words were coming straight out of the very littlest doll, the one that's solid wood, with nothing hidden inside of it. Today, she used the cotton ball, so it's easy to tell her that Ciccio is lying in the middle of the street with his tongue sticking out.

Vittoria wanted to take him for a walk in the park without the leash, because on Sunday there are practically no cars around. Ciccio is very lazy, he never wants to get out of our shadow, and in fact we had a colored tennis ball that seems to be the only thing that he cares about in life. Just a short distance from the park, as we were crossing the street and I was thinking about all the things that a mother can do on her knees, my sister took the ball, waved it in front of Ciccio's snout, and got ready to throw it onto the grass. Vittoria is pretty but she's no athlete. In her case, the athletic action is merely a facial grimace accompanied by pointless, ill-timed movements of the rest of the body. In other words, she stuck her tongue between her teeth, she furrowed her brow, she stretched out her left leg and wound back her right arm. Out of all this preparation there emerged a very slow toss, a throw straight out of a cartoon that, instead of winding up on the grass, ran smack into the rearview mirror of a parked car not even a yard away from her. The tennis ball bounced into the street, Ciccio went streaking after it, and so did a fast-moving Alfa Romeo Alfasud.

Seeing that it was Vittoria's fault but the woman with

the knees wants to pretend it's not, she has decided to buy her another animal right away. She picked one that you can't find on the page of animal noises, one of those animals that since they don't lick your hand, you're allowed to think that they're stupid, and they don't suffer even if they get hit straight on by an Alfasud. As soon as Papà gets off his Sunday shift, he takes Vittoria to play in the courtyard, so Mamma and I can sneak out to the amusement park. There's a stand there with lots of glass bowls, with a goldfish in each one. For a hundred lire, they give you ten white ping-pong balls and a goldfish for everytime you get a ball in the target.

"Pick the one you want and throw a ping-pong ball into its bowl," Mamma tells me. She sure has some nice knees.

"What are you looking at, Al? Look at the goldfish and pick one!"

"That one, Mamma! It's the goldest one of them all!"

"Go on, throw a ball."

"Just one? Look at how big the ball is and how little the opening of the bowl is in comparison . . . " I say.

I throw all the balls at the same time, and in the swarm of bouncing balls one of them winds up in the bowl.

"I won!"

"Aaah, you're a clever little boy, aren't you?" says the gold-fish lady.

"I'm a genius," I say before Mamma has a chance to clap her hand over my mouth.

"A genius! So what do you want to be when you grow up? A scientist?"

"I don't know, I'm still trying to f-f-find my way."

On the way home, I pester her until she lets me carry the plastic bag with the goldfish inside. My mother is happy, the lady at the amusement park laughed and laughed and said lots of nice things to her. I like seeing my mother on her feet and happy, I like the idea that I'm what's making her so happy. I've got her in the palm of my hand, the old woman.

While Vittoria does everything she can to forget that she killed Ciccio, Mamma and I put the goldfish in a glass salad bowl. Since there's no way to suggest a name to a goldfish because goldfish don't have ears, without even asking him what he thinks of it we decide to name him Clay, like the Ferrari race driver. This is because he's certainly going to be a fast goldfish, who'll race through the water and leap in the air on my command. And after all, he's gold. While Mamma tells Papà the story about the big balls and the little fishbowl mouths, I have permission to give the fish a little bread. But my plan fails to meet with their approval.

"No, Al, we have to give the fish a little bit every day . . . A whole bread roll all at once and then another a year from now won't work, understood?"

"Now we'll hide it and at dinner we'll spring the nice surprise on Vittoria," says Papà.

"Can I give her the goldfish?" I ask.

"Certainly, but it has to be a surprise, you can't tell her anything about it until the last minute, understood?" Mamma warns me.

The plan seemed perfect to me but when my sister came back from the courtyard, I started to feel all agitated. The present is a wonderful thing, you can smell it in the air, it's here, right now. Why can't everything just happen all at once? Why is there always something that has to be done later, and why is that something always something nice?

"Th-th-there's a surprise for you!" I tell Vittoria the minute I see her.

"Al!" my mother shouts from the kitchen.

"What is it? What's wrong, Mamma?" she asks.

"Al . . . " says the woman with nice knees, appearing in the hallway.

"Not now, Vittoria. Later," I tell her.

"What surprise?"

"Mamma, can I just t-t-tell her that it's a gift?"

"Al, preparing a surprise mean surprising people, not keeping them in the dark until the last second."

Of course, it's just like my album of stickers about the planet Earth: "When a volcano's magma chamber is full of lava, it seeks a natural outlet toward the exterior." And by now my head is a magma chamber full of the words "gold" and "fish." No living creature will be able to stop them.

"Vittoria, it's a surprise, so it's not a goldfish."

16.

To find out why mothers get down on their knees and all the other things that the old folks don't want to tell me, there's one infallible method. At school they assigned us to write a little essay: "My Favorite Animal." I handed my essay in to the teacher, she read it, she thought it over a little, then she reread it and called me to her desk. Under the essay, on which as usual she'd only been able to add a comma and take off an extra swirly loop from the capital T, she wrote: "Good job but you strayed off topic." Then she told me to get Mamma and Papà to sign it. Which is why I'm now here walking with Mario Elvis.

"It's nothing, Al, I was just tired, I was on edge about work, you know how it is . . . "

"No, h-h-how is it?"

"It's like when Mamma is tired and we give her the Princess of Monaco Treatment."

"A-a-ah, g-g-got it."

"Grown-up things . . . nothing in particular."

"And wh-wh-what does the treatment involve?"

"Nothing in particular, Al! I told you, like for Mamma . . . massages . . . things . . . "

"What things?"

"It's just a manner of speech . . . 'massages,' 'things,' meaning massages and that's it!"

Well, you tell me, what kind of an explanation is that? It's useless, worse than useless: until I'm tall enough to touch his chin with my finger, I'll never be able to have a serious discussion with him. It's all just a succession of "you'll understand later"s, "when you're a grown-up the same thing will happen to you"s, and "tomorrow it'll make perfect sense"s. Nothing ever happens *today* in the world of kids.

"Would you at least mind telling me what this treatment is called?"

"I wouldn't mind at all. It's not like it's a secret. Why would I mind? It's called . . . the . . . Prince of Wales Treatment."

O-o-oh, well, that was a lot of work! So now I know. Mothers on their knees are giving the Prince of Wales Treatment! Nice, good to know, now I'll write it down in my human flesh diary.

Mamma and Papà have been in the kitchen talking for hours. They left the television set on and when the evening news broadcast starts I take advantage. I lie down on the carpet with my felt-tip markers and pretend to draw. The news is being read by a sad man that maybe they put on TV when the news isn't good. The news must always be a complete disaster because I haven't seen the happy man, the one who reads the good news, even once. He always has the same look on his face, he sits as stiff as if the Mother Superior were there to keep an eye on him, and his voice always sounds bored. Half of the things he says are incomprehensible. He talks about disorder in the streets and the need for law and order. I think that must mean that the police came out to tidy up and sweep the streets nice and clean, but the pictures I see on the screen show lots of smoke and policemen clubbing other people who seem angry. I don't get it.

"What are you doing, Al?" asks Mamma from the kitchen.

Five minutes of silence and sure enough she starts to get worried.

"I'm drawing."

Before two minutes are up, she'll stick her head in to see if it's true, so I start drawing the sky. The blue marker is always the first one to run out because I used to draw the sky by just coloring the strip on top, but then Vittoria told me that the whole background of the drawing has to be blue because the sky is everywhere, it reaches all the way down to the ground, just stick your head out the window and you'll see it's true. After that, blue everywhere, even it that means it's harder to figure out where Grandma and Ciccio wound up. The sad man on TV uses lots of words I don't know: inflation, devaluation, corruption, Cee Dee, Eye Cee Pee. I need to read even more, I need to do a better job of studying the ark of words otherwise I'll never be able to figure out what's needed to save the world.

"Everyone at the table, because Papà needs to talk to us!" says Mamma.

"Co-o-o-oming," I say.

"Right away, Al."

"Just a minu-u-u-te."

"Now!"

I turn off the television set. A click and the sad man becomes a small luminous ball at the center of the screen that fades until everything turns black. Is that what death is like?

"Al!"

I go into the bathroom, I turn on the faucet, because after all I know perfectly well that unless I let a little water run, there's no chance of sitting down to eat. When Mamma sets the table in the kitchen there's always some important piece of news, and we have to talk it over far from the television set, so the sad man and the young lady with the puffy hair can't hear it.

"Papà wants to tell us some news," says Mamma.

Mario Elvis pours himself a glass of wine, drinks it, and looks at us.

"We've decided that starting next month we're going to go live in another apartment," he says.

"The promised home? Have you found it?" I ask.

"No, we're going to live in another place precisely so we can save up the money to buy the promised home, the minute we find it."

"The new place is smaller but it's very nice," says Mamma. "It won't be for long, a year at the most, just long enough to save up some money."

"Will there be a little room just for me?" asks Vittoria.

"No. When we find the home that we're looking for, then maybe you can have your own little room."

"Maybe . . . " repeats the complainer.

"No one knows that the promised home is like. When we find it, we find it, and we'll have to take it the way it is," says Papà.

17.

It's 1974, the year of messages. The Red Brigades send a message that they kidnapped a man named Mario but it's not Papà because his last name is Sossi; the Turks try to communicate something by occupying part of the island of Cyprus without paying rent; the courts inform women that since they wanted the right to wear trousers, now if they go out after nine at night they should expect to be assaulted; the Pioneer probe is traveling into deep space with an aluminum plaque depicting the human race, which we want to describe as follows: men, who stand one step forward, waving in a friendly fashion; women without genitalia, who stand one step back and have a grumpy attitude.

We, after celebrating, with fruit juice and chocolate *ciambellone*, the first anniversary of my liberation from the persistent stutter, are on our way to Torvaianica in our Fiat 600 loaded with an unbelievable amount of luggage, launching a controversial message to anyone who sees us: we are the average Italian family on our way to the beach, in February. The plan to save up money so we can buy our promised home is starting to drag out. In the time since we left our official residence on Via del Gazometro, we've rotated through a cellar apartment, abandoned after a few weeks because it was infested with mice; a tiny apartment across the way from Cinecittà, where we held out for a year even though Mamma and Papà slept in the kitchen; and six months in a garret apartment in the San Giovanni neighborhood with ceilings so low you could just reach up and touch them and where, in the summer, you could hard-boil eggs without need of boiling water. The promised home continues to elude us but Mario Elvis says that we've done it, this is the last move before finally moving into our final destination.

In my human flesh diary I've written lots of things, including these: "Deposit monthly allowance in a numbered Swiss bank account. Ask for more information," "Girls' second butts have a scientific name: vagina," "Giving the wrong answers to your classmates on quizzes only makes you happy for the moment," "If you're on the left or the right, there's a good chance you won't live to see age twenty-five, that's why there are so many Christian Democrats," "The most important thing in the world is a full-time job," "Consider the hypothesis that the United States and the Soviet Union are just spoofing the rest of the world," "There's been an economic boom and the

Santamaria family never even noticed. Look into this." A separate section of the diary is dedicated to notes that may prove useful to my plan to save the world: "The theory about asphalt should not be dismissed out of hand," "Parliamentary democracy is very nice but it doesn't work," "Is it enough to just go to America to become rich, or once you're there do you actually have to do something? If it turns out that just going is enough, then let's go."

The apartment in Torvaianica is in a building far from the center of town. In February the atmosphere is spectral. Deserted streets, roller shutters lowered in front of shops, only a few scattered signs of life. It seems like one of those cities devastated by a virus that's plummeted out of the sky on a meteorite or else hit by one of those bombs that disintegrate human beings but leave buildings intact. Intact, so to speak. Seen from up close our apartment house appears to be in a state of abandonment, the rust has vigorously begun that slow process of erosion that, over the coming centuries—though it actually may only take a few decades—will pulverize the structure, leaving in its place a canyon of reinforced concrete. The paint on the handle of the front gate crumbles onto my hand, the hinges creak and rattle, begging for a squirt of oil, while the stairs are covered with a veil of sand. We climb up to the second floor, never daring to take the elevator. The apartment itself isn't bad, all the windows and the long balcony have views of the sea, which as the crow flies can't be any further that two hundred yards. There's a big room where Vittoria and I will sleep, a living room where Mamma and Papà will sleep, a spacious kitchen, and a tiny bathroom. The heat is electric, in each room there's a metal panel with a grate and two buttons, each with a little red light next to it. They seem like the electronic calculators in a poorly made science fiction film. When we turn them on, a tepid waft of air comes out of the grates, smelling of dust and chestnuts. The furnishings, as Mamma says, are what someone somewhere ordered to put into all the beach apartments in the whole world: wooden furniture painted sky blue and scattered seemingly at random, each item with its own little defect that they meant to fix right away, but instead just accumulated with all the others, summer after summer. Democratically, there's one defect for every piece of furniture. One lacks a leg, another lacks a knob, one cabinet door won't shut properly, another has the key broken off in the keyhole. We put our own furniture in the cellar of one of Papà's friends. A week ago, someone tried to force the door, and Mario Elvis decided to sleep there until they fix it, because he says we can't afford to have all our possessions stolen.

As usual, we spend the first few minutes telling ourselves that it's not a bad place to live, that we'll be alright there, that after all, we're only going to live here for a few months. Vittoria doesn't take part in this phase of bolstering morale because now she's become a "young lady," and eleven-year-old young ladies are always in a bad mood when they have to say goodbye to their friends. In contrast, I'm only seven, so I'm fine wherever I am, as long as I have my big box full of toys. The first thing Mamma does is turn on the refrigerator to keep the meat safe. The preservation of the meat has been her sole concern throughout the journey. No heating in the car, and windows rolled down the whole way. Once we have successfully completed the rescue operation for the few slices of beef, she extracts from the cooler a package wrapped in aluminum foil, containing the cadaver of Clay, which is actually Clay VI though Sister doesn't know it. We take the little coffin and head down to the beach to give it a fitting burial. Aside from Clay IV and Clay V, who died of natural causes, the others fell victim to Vittoria's loving distraction. Until Clay VI, we were able to conceal the deaths and replace the fish without Vittoria noticing a thing. Each time, Mamma limited herself to generic advice such as: "Even if it's hot out, you probably shouldn't put the fishbowl in the refrigerator." The farce ended with this last imitator of Clay I who died right before her eyes. "Well, this time it was just bad luck," we told ourselves, because it's hard to accept the idea that a member of your family is an exterminator of pets. We put the blame on the new faucet in the kitchen of the last apartment, the one in the San Giovanni neighborhood, and the fact that no one had bothered to explain to my sister just how to use that mysterious lever, so different from the two faucets, one for hot and one for cold, that we were used to. It all unfolded under the eagle eyes of Mamma, who was pretending to stack dishes while Vittoria changed Clay's water. She carefully caught the fish with the little net, she quickly popped into a basin, cleaned the fishbowl, and then picked Clay up again with sufficient care to persuade my mother that her fake dish-stacking could come to an end. And so my sister was all alone when she pulled that handle. It was just bad luck, she only realized that the water that was filling the bowl was hot when steam began to rise from the surface. Mamma was frantic, she tried everything to save Clay. The goldfish flapped his tail for the last time, his body completely covered with Prep medicated cream.

18.

The evenings with all of us together at the dinner table seem like a distant memory now, something to talk about with a sigh, like the races to reach Mamma and Papà's big bed when there was a bad thunderstorm, or else the poop that you could carry around proudly in the little potty so everyone could tell you how proud they were of you. By now we only see Papà on Sunday, on account of the blockade of the Suez Canal and the austerity policies, he has to walk the whole way from the train station. When he gets home, we throw a huge party for him, but by then he's so exhausted that all he wants is to go to bed. Every time we hear a noise from outside we rush to where he's sleeping, in the hopes he might have woken up and could be in the mood to play. We tiptoe to the door of his room, but he's asleep, he's always asleep, until Agnese goes to wake him up and tell him: "It's time to go." The days have grown shorter. There's not much time for breakfast because it takes Mamma an hour to get us to school, then she spends the rest of the morning looking for work, until it's two in the afternoon, time to come pick us up. We sit down to lunch around three, we eat quickly and without appetite, we tell her what we did at school today, even though it's obvious that she's left her thoughts in some office, in a shop, in the waiting room of the employment office. There was a time when it seemed as if she couldn't live without news of our school days, now there's always something, far away, outside the window, that interests her more. When Papà is away, Agnese is terribly afraid. One night she called the Carabinieri and said that someone had tried to break into the apartment. They squad car showed up twenty minutes later, my mother showed them scratch marks on the door, and the officers reassured her, it must have been an amateur because he had used a screwdriver and hadn't done any real damage. The "amateur" had been my mother. She told us so herself: "That way, the next time I call them they'll know the way and get here quicker," she told us. That's why today I'm angry and I have no intention of running away from Ezio.

Papà says that people who are intelligent like me don't need to resort to violence, they can defeat their enemies by the sheer force of thought. That's why, Ezio, I am going to vanquish you! The sheer force of that miracle of nature that is my mind is focusing itself into a single overwhelmingly powerful ray that will defeat you. Stop, Ezio!

"That's enough, Al. Keep it up and you could disintegrate him!"

"We need to stop him right away, Casimiro. A guy like him would be capable of stabbing somebody when he grows up, or planting a bomb, or bringing down the government over a disagreement on ministerial positions!"

I'm focusing the sheer force of my thoughts upon you, stop in your tra-a-a-acks!

"Your snack mine now," Ezio says.

Wandering through the deserted streets gives me a sense of omnipotence. I can throw rocks at the shutters, chase cats, and shout that I'm the king of the neighborhood without getting so much as a raspberry in response. I have permission to stay out until four in the afternoon, then as soon as the sun touches the sea, I have to come home. Since all the apartments and houses are empty, I can go without interference into the backyards, the gardens, and even the buildings, just to come up with a first, summary selection of possible promised homes. I'll have to complete this exploration before the end of March, when the killer virus will attenuate its effects and the apartments will fill up again on the weekends.

This place, for instance, isn't bad. You can't see the water from here, but the view over the countryside must be nice, there in the distance is the military airport of Pratica di Mare, and I can already picture myself looking out the window with Papà to see the Fiat G-91 fighter jets taking off. In order to inspect the place, I have to climb over a gate. The toes of my shoes are empty so I can't get a foothold, the hems of my trousers get caught on a jagged edge, and my wool sweater snags relentlessly on all the patches of rust. This is no way to work. Everything I wear is two sizes too big for me because Mamma says I grow like a weed. Actually, I'm growing at a perfectly average pace, and the result is that by the time sweaters, trousers, and shoes all start to fit me perfectly, they're so ragged they're not worth keeping anymore. The family specialty is sweaters. Mamma started making them at home after the fraud of the "woolf" label. She thought it was an indication of pure wool, but instead it was a trick and they got all matted after being washed just once. I don't understand why she took it so hard, it wasn't her fault that no one had thought to require factories to declare the actual materials and ingredients in their products. One day or another she'll realize that the cans of creamed salmon that she buys every Christmas are nothing but a concoction of second-rate fish, full of artificial color and fake aromas. The real problem with homemade sweaters, though, aside from the inevitable embroidered reindeer, is that Mamma gets the wool from old clothing, which she unstitches, obtaining nice big balls of yarn that she skillfully knits into sweaters that are matted from the get-go.

Once I get over the gate, I have no difficulty getting into the building because the front door is broken. On the second-story landing, I identify the apartment door. It hangs ajar. I go over to it and I realize that it's been forced open, either kicked open or crowbarred. Better run away. Or maybe I can run up to the door, take a quick look, and then take to my heels. I choose the option that entails more fear. I take a nice deep breath and go for it.

"A-a-ah!" I shout in front of the door, and then I turn and run down the stairs.

I hide behind a low wall. No noise except for my shout, which echoes down the stairs

"If you're brave, you'll do it again," Casimiro tells me.

"It's not so hard to do. . . . "

"Then this time if you're not afraid, you'll even put a foot inside the door."

I take a nice deep breath, run up, open the door, and jump inside.

"A-a-ah!"

"Fu-u-u-uck!" shouts a figure in front of me.

I just jumped in front of an old man, not as old as my parents, but he must certainly be at least twenty-five if he's a day. He is carrying a black bag in one hand, and he's wearing a sweater that looks like it was made by my mother and a wool hat on his head. I say the first thing that pops into my head: "Is this apartment for sale?"

The man is having a hard time breathing and he's all red. The first thing he manages to do is lean out onto the landing. The hand holding the bag is trembling.

"Are you alone?" he asks me.

"Yes."

"So what do you think, is that the way to enter someone else's home? Get out of here, I've got work to do, go on!"

"I didn't think it was occupied. Are you the owner, sir?"

"Sure . . . I mean, no . . . I'm the guy in charge of doors."

"Can I see how you fix a door?"

"No, you can't see how I fix a door, I'm not here for my amusement! I've got a lot of work to do, around here there's lots of two-bit doors . . . and lots of thieves."

"Yes, there are lots and lots of doors like this one. In the apartment house at number 54 on Via Albania they're all like this, except for apartment 7 which has a door that's all metal. And there's a very similar model in the apartment houses at 71 and 73. On Via Romania they're the same as this one, but they have two locks instead of one, with the exception of the little house at number . . . "

"What do you know about them?"

"I've seen them. I know all the apartments around here."

"Oh, really? Hold on a sec." He pulls a sheet of paper and a pen out of his trousers pocket. "So, now, you were saying . . . "

19.

We find ourselves in the teacher's lounge in the following formation: the teacher in the center, me and Ezio standing facing her, the respective Papàs sitting next to us. For the minor problems, they call the Mammas, but when they want the spankings and face slaps to come with some force behind them, they call the Papàs.

"Your son headbutted Ezio!" the father of the future criminal begins.

We each tell our version of what happened. Due to a set of factors, my version proves more convincing. Ezio's limited vocabulary and wobbly grammar make his account as difficult to tolerate as a set of fingernails scraping along a chalkboard. His rehearsal of the mysterious phrases that I was muttering as he drew closer proves absolutely incomprehensible. The teacher half-shuts her eyes and compresses her lips as if each solecism were a knife being plunged into her back. Her hand quivers, she'd like to scrawl a nice fat red F, but she doesn't know where. When it's my turn, in practically perfect Italian I tell the story of how Ezio came nearly every day to steal my snack. "Your snack mine," I quote him, obtaining the disconsolate confirmation of the teacher when she is summoned to identify the corpse of Italian grammar. I then declare that it was Ezio who gave me the head butt, only he aimed poorly and his nose smashed into my frontal bone causing me abrasions with subcutaneous bleeding, healable in four days. I conclude my account with a reference to Article 51 of the Charter of the United Nations concerning the inherent right of collective self-defense. As we leave the teacher's lounge, I write in my human flesh diary: "A well-told lie works better than the truth poorly told." In addition to the head butt, Ezio also received a sharp smack from his father, accompanied by a liberatory movement of the teacher's hand. Papà kept a stern expression on his face until he reached the front gate, then he told me that he already knew everything, that his duty as a father would be to tell me that "I shouldn't do this, it's not right, it's not proper, the value of dialogue here, the pointlessness of violence there," but seeing that we're talking about Ezio, he doesn't want to ruin what ought to be a day of celebration for the Santamaria family.

Papà snaps his fingers and I start off from memory.

"NSU Prinz 4L! Five standard seats, price 750,000 lire plus 20,000 lire for the front disc brakes!"

"And what did the Santamaria family say about the front disc brakes?" Papà asks.

"Plththththth!" Vittoria and I reply.

"Go on, Al!"

"This is the price of the NSU's comfort and safety. Just think: to travel from Milan to Rome in the Prinz 4L costs only 810 lire per passenger in fuel!"

Today the Santamaria family is celebrating the purchase of the new car. The Fiat 600 is broken and Papà decided to get a new car. That's not all: as long as we're spending money, he also decided to repair at his own expense the cellar door: from now on he'll sleep at home like all the other Papàs on earth. Now he'll be taking us to school, which means the car will run in third gear, and even in fourth, and it will last forever. Mario Elvis pretends to turn on the car radio he didn't buy, Vittoria switches on the portable tape recorder, and he sings a song by his friend Donatello: "*Like a rock tha-a-a-at, plunges into the de-e-epths, I get lost in the blu-u-ue, of your beau-u-u-tiful eyes!*"

We've already started the second verse when Papà yanks the tape recorder out of Vittoria's hand and turns it off.

"Hush, children, hush!"

He immediately pulls over and stops the car. Mamma is just

getting into a taxi parked in front of the gate. As soon as she sees us she runs over to the window of our Prinz 4L.

"Armando is dead," she says.

Then she strokes my hair and Vittoria's with a sad expression on her face, as if telling us: yes, he's dead, but it's not serious, don't worry about it. Mamma goes back to the taxi. I look at Papà, instinctively I try to figure out the scope of what's happening. He heaves a sigh, he seems upset, he's pale, he says nothing. It confuses me. I look through what I've written over the years in my human flesh diary, but I find out I've been very generic: "Separation between body and soul," "Heaven," "White clouds for good men and black clouds for bad men." Where is heaven? What cloud? What's a soul? Why is it separated from the body? Does it separate so it can go somewhere? Is Uncle Armando's body going to become a seagull skeleton? Or a faded ball of light?

"Where's Uncle Armando?"

"What do you mean where, didn't you hear? He's dead," Vittoria tells me, her eyes glistening.

"I understand that he's dead. What I meant to say is: Now that he's dead, where has he gone?"

"To heaven."

"Where's heaven?"

"This isn't the time, Al," says Papà.

"It's in the sky," says Vittoria.

"Where, exactly?"

"This isn't the time."

"So you don't know."

"Yes, I know, it's everywhere, the whole sky is heaven!"

In my human flesh diary I write that the whole sky is heaven, that heaven reaches all the way down to the earth, and so everything is heaven except for the earth, which is where we are.

20.

After the funeral, my thoughts become clearer. Not so much about what is gone, but about what has remained. To see Mamma with her eyes all red and wet is the clearest explanation about death that I could have hoped for. I like growing up, but sometimes I wish that Mamma and Papà would grow with me, because there's nothing more reassuring than discovering the world from safe behind their legs.

They expect me to understand everything that they tell me, though I swear I've done my best. Grandma, Ciccio, the various Clays, and Uncle Armando are in heaven, which means that they're dead, which means that we'll never see them again. It also means that in some way the event must be connected to that disgusting dog carcass that I saw on the side of the road, with maggots crawling out of it, and therefore Uncle Armando must have maggots in his eyes and fragments of fur with bones jutting through it. That means that Uncle Armando and the dog carcass can be connected to those bodies I saw on the evening news, they said they were dead, but one was writhing on the ground and was clearly suffering. Therefore there's some sort of transitional phase between life and death in which you writhe in pain and that's very simply unacceptable. It's already pretty ridiculous to take people and put them on clouds, I don't see what good it does to make them suffer this way. How old is Donald Duck? Could he die of a heart attack like Uncle Armando did? And if he can die, who's going to take his place in the next issue? So this means that Wile E. Coyote suffers too, suffers like a dog as he falls into the canyon and we laugh, that his bones are shattered as he hits the ground and we roll in our seats as we see the little cloud of dust rise. Does that mean someone rolled in their seats laughing at Uncle Armando's death? And what about the Italian aviators hacked to death in the Congo, how badly must they have suffered? If a machete is twenty times bigger than the kitchen knife I cut my finger with, then I can establish the scale of the pain by multiplying that sharp hurt by twenty and then multiplying the product of that hurt by the number of machete blows received.

"Mamma?"

A heart attack is like a machete blow to the heart? So Uncle Armando suffered just like the Italian aviators and like me, only twenty times worse?

"Mamma! Look what Al's doing!"

Sooner or later, we all have to die, Papà said so, but that's not enough for me, I also want to know how. I want to know if my heart is going to be cut in half, if I'll wind up crushed in an out-of-control elevator, or if I'll die the same tragic death as the little girl in Carpi crushed by her grandfather's tractor!

"Mario, hurry. Al isn't well!"

Apparently when you speak deliriously and fall to the ground clenching your teeth, then you have to go see the calm lady doctor. We talk for an hour, just the two of us. I feel like those days when as soon as you're done with your homework you go out to play and it's pouring rain. I have a nice fat soccer ball under my arm and I don't know what to do with it, that's what I feel like. As if I knew that now it's going to rain for the rest of my life.

"What do you like to watch on TV? Do you like Laurel and Hardy?" the lady doctor asks me.

"No."

"Don't they make you laugh?"

"They're dead. They shouldn't broadcast the movies of dead actors, otherwise you'll think they're still alive. Then when you find out they're dead, you'll think that all dead people wind up on TV and then you'll spend hours and hours in front of the screen, waiting to see Grandma Concetta again."

The calm lady doctor listens to me, then she asks me to

draw something. I know what it means but I don't have any fake messages to send her. I draw Papà and Uncle Armando having a contest to see who can eat more meatballs. Then I think that maybe it was all those meatballs that killed him, so I take my eraser and erase my picture. I draw Mamma kneeling in front of Papà while Vittoria and I play with a kite. Then I think of Benjamin Franklin's kite and since I don't want a thunderbolt to strike Mamma while she gives Papà the Prince of Wales Treatment, I take my eraser and erase the picture. I draw a mushroom cloud sweeping away houses, then an African dictator eating a child, an airplane falling apart, and every time, I erase the picture. I give the lady doctor the sheet of paper, and all it has is a big hole in the middle of it.

When Mamma and Papà come in, the lady doctor gives me two lollipops and tells me to wait outside. I thank her, I shut the door, and with Vittoria I press my ear against the door and start listening.

"Just listen to that . . . the young master is stressed out . . . " the radio communications officer informs me.

"What's that mean?"

"That you're crazy."

"That's not true!"

"It is so!"

"Shut up, let me listen . . . There, I knew it, if you do something once, then they say you 'always' do it!"

"You always do it."

"No, just once I got up at five in the morning to go steal the newspapers from the newsdealer, just once!"

"What about that time that you started reading them in the trash can?"

"The newspapers were in the trash can, I got them out, and I read them outside of the trash can. Not in the trash can!"

"Mmm-hmmm, when she starts behaving like a fanatic, I just can't stand it!" says Vittoria.

She goes back and sits down with a pout. In there, Mamma is talking about how I read the encyclopedia and that I secretly bought a transistor radio so I could listen to the news broadcasts.

My chat with the calm lady doctor did Mamma and Papà a lot of good. At dinner, they were very cheerful, and instead of the TV, Mario Elvis turned on the Super 8 projector that we haven't used in such a long time, and we watched a short documentary about the animals of the savanna. The goodnight was fantastic, instead of a kiss on the forehead, Mamma gave me the lioness's lick on the cheek. There was one all ready for Vittoria but she didn't want it because young ladies are fussy that way.

The darkness in the bedroom has brightened, all around me I start to be able to make out the houses on the outskirts of Saigon. But tonight there's not going to be any raid on the enemy base.

"So all of a sudden, Uncle Armando up and died. Apparently it was a heart attack."

"What's a heart attack?"

"It's when your heart breaks. You know, like a sudden fright, a piece of bad news, and it can break."

"And why did his heart break? Was he sad?"

"No, quite the contrary, before dying he thanked us all, because he was very happy as long as it lasted."

"How old was Uncle Armando?"

"Forty-four."

"And how old is Mamma?"

"Thirty-eight."

"So in a few years . . . "

"Will you just cut it out?" Vittoria tells us.

"Casimiro can't sleep," I explain to her.

"Casimiro, go to sleep, everything's all right," she says.

She turns over on her side, her back to me. Then she takes
my foot and braces it against her butt.

"You go to sleep too," she tells me.

She mutters something, then she does that wonderful thing,
she strokes my foot, up and down, from the big toe to the heel.

21.

In my human flesh diary I jotted down Mamma's expression and I wrote that looking for work is bad for you, it ought
to be work that looks for you, otherwise your face goes all
wrong. These days she needs the cotton ball every day. Vittoria
and I spy on her while she's sleeping on the sofa and the
minute we see that she's about to wake up, we run into our
room and pretend to study. Mamma comes right in to see us.
We can hear her slippers dragging on the floor. She sticks her
head in the door, she smiles at us, she goes over to Vittoria.

"Look at my Vittoria's hair, so nice and thin and fine . . . "

Vittoria smiles, Mamma strokes her head. She sinks her fingers into Vittoria's hair, runs them the length of that hair. She
does it once. Twice. A third time. A fourth time. A fifth time.
Vittoria smiles at her again. A sixth time. A seventh time. An
eighth time. Signorina Vittoria starts to get irritated. A ninth
time. A tenth time. An eleventh time. I slam a book shut loudly,
Mamma stops, startled, turns to look at me, and I savor my
ration in advance.

"Look at your poor knees, my darling," she tells me, "all
filthy black and covered with scabs . . . "

A minute later I'm sitting on the kitchen table while she,
sitting on the chair in front of me, tries to make them glisten
with the rough rag that she uses to wash dishes. They certainly
are black and scabby. There's not a single game that doesn't
leave its marks on the knees. I recognize all my scabs: the two

big ones in the middle are from when I fell off my bicycle
while riding with no hands, the long and narrow one on my
left knee is from when I made a spectacular dive to block a
penalty kick by Rocca, the other two that look more like
scratches are the work of a tuff-stone wall that I climbed in a
hurry because I had thrown a rock at a stray dog who took it
the wrong way. I don't have any real alternatives to these
games, because of the calm lady doctor I'm not allowed to
watch TV, listen to the radio, or read newspapers, magazines,
or even the encyclopedia. The only positive aspect is that now
I have a ton of free time that I can spend lying under the vase
of geraniums and devoting myself to the purpose for which I
was put here on earth. Today, for instance, I leafed back
through the notes I jotted down in my human flesh diary and
I started off from the observation that gathering around the
dinner table with the television turned off at least once a day
is the best way to iron out any international controversy. At
the UN, there are plenty of tables but not a sign of food, and
that's almost certainly why it doesn't work very well. There's
no two ways about it, in front of a plate of french fries or a
slice of chocolate cake, you can think more clearly. Therefore,
this could be a preliminary solution: the delegate who has a
proposal has to make something for everyone to eat before he
can set it forth. A second solution to improve the quality of
life on the planet could be the application of the Criterion of
Direct Assumption of Responsibility: every delegate who
announces an initiative to the council must specify in whose
name he is speaking. In the name of the president of the
republic? The king? The minister of defense? And what is the
matter at hand? An armed intervention? An embargo? An air
raid? Whatever it is, the UN Security Council will ensure that
behind the wheel of the first jeep to enter enemy territory, on
the bridge of the first cruiser to intercept the supply ships, or
in the cockpit of the first fighter plane to drop a missile, will

be the president, the king, or the minister who first introduced the idea. No more cowards like Mauro, who encourages us to steal colored chalk from the janitor's closet and then
sits safe and sound in class while we do it! It will be hard to
talk them into doing it because there's a basic problem
upstream: the old men in suits and ties who make those decisions. Maybe it would be a good idea to force these gentlemen
to do a year of voluntary service before taking office. Six
months at a hospital and six months at an insane asylum. The
first six months so that they'll always remember what it means
to be hurt or sick and in the future will always only make decisions that make people well and happy; the second six months
so that they can immediately recognize madness, and then
when one of their bosses wakes up one morning talking about
a thermonuclear attack or "making war for peace," they'll
know how to intervene.

Excellent, there's more than enough here to win not one
but two Nobel Prizes. Have they ever given two to the same
person before me? As I observe the contrast between my right
knee, by now gleaming white and redolent of Comet cleansing
powder, and the left knee, ruggedly handsome and looking
lived in, I decide that the real problem is persuading the world
to put these ideas into practice. I am reminded of a note I jotted down years ago, one of Papà's sayings: "Revolutions
always begin from below." He said it the time that we convinced Grandma to move the scheduled Sunday breakfast
from 8 A.M. to 9:30. An invaluable note, nice work, Papà. The
changes have to come from below, it needs to start from one
cell and then contaminate the others with an effect that might
be slow but remains continuous and unstoppable. Everything
needs to come at the initiative of a superior creature, capable
of becoming a guide to mankind at large. Now it's all much
clearer, my way is no longer an unknown place, it starts here
and runs straight down there, toward the horizon. The dawn

of a new day for the human race will spring from the hand of the chosen one!

"Al, sweetheart, get down off the table . . . " my unsuspecting mother tells me.

22.

This is the time for action. My plan for the salvation of the world certainly needs a major planning phase but also a solid base of departure that must be constructed by resolving various practical problems. I can't limit myself to the secret search for our promised home, and unless I want to go down in history as nothing more than a brilliant theoretician, I'm going to have to get busy.

"Well, what did your customers tell you?" I ask.

"That it's better than the one I usually sell . . . you can tell that it's homemade. How much should I charge?"

"My mother says twenty percent less for the first six months, then the same price as the one you sell now. Plus free breakfast for me and my sister every Monday morning. Minimum order of three a week."

I secretly took one of Mamma's chocolate *ciambelloni* to the owner of the café outside the school because, if you ask me, the prepackaged ones that he sells can't even begin to compare. I even gave him the whole morning to test the product and gather impressions from his clientele. The result was a foregone conclusion. My mother's chocolate *ciambellone* is not only better, it's from another planet, and that fact makes me reflect. She buys the cheapest flour, butter, eggs, and chocolate she can find, she'd walk two or three miles just to save fifty lire, so I ask myself, what the hell kind of ingredients are the major pastry and baked goods manufacturers using? Of course, before shaking hands the old man tried to bargain with me:

"Twenty-five percent discount for the first year," and I promptly put him in his place, telling him that: "My mother already has other offers and isn't interested in dropping her price." And now I can't wait for Mamma and Papà to come and get me.

Waiting with Vittoria was pure torture, my head felt like it was about to explode. "I have a surprise," "a nice surprise for Mamma," "a surprise that has to do with her chocolate *ciambelloni*," "that conerns her chocolate *ciambelloni* and the café right outside the school." Having spoiled the surprise for my sister in five minutes flat, I made up my mind to take a more grown-up approach with Mamma. In the car, the topic comes up immediately.

"Al, the *ciambellone*'s gone, you wouldn't know anything about that, would you?"

"What *ciambellone*?"

"You know perfectly well! It was supposed to last all week."

"Huh, who knows."

"What did you do with it? Did you eat the whole thing? Did you sell it? Did you set it on fire?"

"Just guess . . . "

"Al, tell me right away what you did with it!"

If you spill the beans straightaway then you spoil the surprise, if you create a little suspense then they get mad, it's no good, whatever you do is wrong.

"It was supposed to be a surprise, Mamma . . . I sold it to the café at school, with a special promotional price for the first sales period, a little under market price, and then rising to standard market price. The supply contract calls for three *ciambelloni* a week, for a full year. We're rich."

A certain Daniela from Bologna has been elected the perfect Italian wife. She passed her tests with flying colors in the fields of general knowledge, child rearing, floral arrangements, cocktail preparation, and, also according to the newspaper article, she enchanted the judges with her baked lasagna. Signora Daniela is proud to wear her pageant sash but she only enjoys that privilege because none of us thought of trying to run Mamma in the competition. She may not be much at floral arrangements and she doesn't have the foggiest idea of how to make a cocktail, but she'd be able to enchant the judges with her dazzling smile alone, the wonderful smile that has started to appear on her face regularly since she's been able to tell everyone that she's a pastry chef. I went back to see the man who fixes doors because Agnese and Mario Elvis went to vote and I thought he might enjoy my company. I found him inside a detached home. We chatted for a while, his name is Raul, he told me that he's a highly respected professional, he used to work in Rome, but now he's commuting between Ostia and Torvaianica to attract new customers. He says that every now and then it's good to move on to greener pastures. Then all of a sudden he pulled a Monopoly box out of his bag and told me to get out of there because he had no more time to waste with me. At that point it dawned on me that there is no single recipe for making people happy, saving the world is going to be a titanic undertaking.

When Mamma and Papà get back I'm waiting for them in the living room, bent over my schoolbooks just as I'd promised.

"Well, have you exercised your rights as citizens?" I ask.

"Yes, Al . . . " Mamma replies.

"Have you voted according to conscience?"

"No matter what you ask, it's useless, we're not going to tell you how we voted."

"I understand . . . which means that you implicitly authorize the keeping of secrets within the nuclear family."

"Al, cut it out, we voted 'no.'"

"Oh great. I have parents who are opposed to the abolition of divorce . . . who call into question the survival of the family, this basic cell, this instrument of progress, this guarantee of continuity, fertilizer of the earth, great mother, hearth and home capable of warming and fostering ideas and affections, cradle of the most fervent sanctity!"

"It's the nuns, I told you . . . " Papà gets argumentative with Mamma.

"So you want to keep divorce? Then you'd better be well aware that next comes abortion. And after that, homosexuals getting married. And after that, your wife might very well leave you to run away with the maid!"

"No, I know who it is . . . " Mamma replies, "this is Fanfani at the rally of the Christian Democrats . . . Al, you've been listening to the radio again!"

23.

When Torvaianica finally started to seem like a normal city, with lots of shops open for business, lines of cars, and loads of people on the beach, we were forced to take shelter back in Rome, in a one-bedroom apartment on the Via Casilina. The landlord had told Mamma and Papà that for the month of August they could either give him triple the rent or else they were free to get the hell out. We went back to the beach in September, yearning to enjoy the last few days of summer, and we found the door broken in and the whole place upside down. It took me a whole day to track down Raul, but in the end I found him and I convinced him to change our lock. It wasn't easy, I had to beg him and play the captivating smile card. I discovered that he's actually a very shy person: when I introduced him to Mamma he bowed his head and stayed that way until he was done with the job. He didn't want to accept payment, he only took an espresso and a slice of cake.

Vittoria has gone back to hanging out with the same group of friends she managed to assemble before our first exodus from Rome. I don't understand why Mamma and Papà don't say something to her, and yet I know they've seen these kids. They're between eleven and fourteen years of age, nearly all of them have flunked a year, and the ones that aren't repeating a year over have quit school entirely. They walk along dragging their feet like the living dead and all they talk about is soccer and pussy, subjects they're especially expert on because those are the same subjects their fathers and older brothers mastered. I've made friends with a kid myself, a boy my age. His name is Raimondo, and he really had no say in the matter. He works behind the counter at the local café so if you order something and talk to him, he's forced to listen, I knew that because I saw it in a movie once. His parents are always cheerful and laughing, but they're not really happy, they have coin-operated smiles. They work like pay phones, pinball machines, and jukeboxes. They turn on the cheer when a customer walks through the door and they turn it off again the minute he leaves, to save on power. I like Raimondo because he seems shy but the minute his parents leave him alone, he livens up, and sometimes veers into the diabolic. He's a very talented musician, the only one I know who is able to play the cardboard box that contains liquorice strings. He made a big circular hole in it, and attached rubber bands from one side to the other, varying the tension in order to obtain high and low notes. Of course, he can only play his cardboard box when he's alone, when his parents are out running errands. They're worried at the thought that their son might have a different talent than what is needed to manage a bar.

I leave Mamma whistling in the kitchen as she listens to

one of Papà's tapes, actually a mix tape, with a lesson on esti-
mating land revenues for fiscal purposes and a couple of Elvis
songs, a double-entry accounting lesson with a song by
Bobby Solo following it. She kneads and bakes chocolate
ciambelloni all day long. On her ID card, she has drawn a line
through "Housewife" and written in "Pastry Chef," with a
pen. According to Papà, sooner or later they'll arrest her. I go
straight to the café. All the kids drop by to put a few coins
into the pinball machine on their way back from the beach.
They come in dripping wet, barefoot, and the minute they
start to put their coins into the metal slot an array of spectacular white and blue sparks appears. Two of them have gotten stuck to the pinball machine, and one—this I witnessed
personally—to the jukebox. In the end Raimondo's father
decided to insulate them by putting wooden boards under
the legs, and since then it's been necessary to come up with
new ideas to have fun.

I walk into the bar and I go over to the counter. Raimondo
doesn't even say hello, he just tips his head toward a little kid
drenched from head to heels, furiously playing the pinball
machine. Water sprays from his hair.

"This damned pinball machine doesn't work right, the spe-
cials don't light up!" says the kid.

Raimondo puts on that smile I like so well.

"It's probably because of the plug, it might not be snug in
the outlet . . . " he tells him with disarming promptness.

A second later, the kid, still dripping seawater, is behind the
pinball machine, fooling around with the plug.

When I get home I see Vittoria walk into the courtyard
where the bicycles are stored and I hide behind the street
door. She immediately notices the flowers on the bike seat. She
looks around. She seems to be stunned. This morning I left a
big paper heart for her, but she must have thought it was for

somebody else, that whoever it was had just left it there. Now she has no doubts and she smiles, the idiot. Yesterday she came back from the beach with her face all gloomy. "What's wrong?" I asked her and she said: "My ankles are fat." "Who says so?" "Everyone." And I realized that our last few days of vacation were about to turn into pure hell. A practically adolescent girl who's depressed because she thinks that her ankles aren't skinny enough is a ticking time bomb and I don't particularly feel like having my vacation days ruined because Cristiano, or Cris as he likes to be called, or "everyone," as my sister chooses to call him, has just found out that Vittoria wasn't constructed in the Mattel laboratories. "Your ankles are fine just the way they are," I told her, and she said: "What do you know about it." Nothing, never mind, what do I know about it. I have my dreams too, you know, I'd like to be able to bend a lamppost with a single punch like Spiderman, but still I'm not willing to ruin my summer because the most I'm able to do is bend a fork or because Mamma isn't thrilled with my displays of strength. I come in and she immediately hides the flowers in the bike basket.

"What are you doing?" I ask her.

"Nothing, just going out for a spin. Leave the door open for me, the electricity has gone out in the whole building."

"Oh right, at the café too."

There's something powerful about what I've done. This morning Vittoria leapt out of bed and ran down into the courtyard to pump up the tires of her bicycle, or at least so she claimed. She couldn't wait to see whether her secret admirer had left her another present. When she came back upstairs she seemed to be in a trance, even more than usual, I mean. The anonymous message composed of letters cut out of the newspaper must have worked.

"Vittoria, what are you planning?" my mother shouts.

"I'm co-o-oming," she replies from the bathroom.

"What the hell has she been doing in there for the past hour . . . "

"She's brushing her hair," I say.

"Does it have to take so long?"

"If you brush your hair like Rita Hayworth, yes . . . "

"Al, you shouldn't peep through the keyhole."

"I just wanted to make sure she was still alive."

"If she's putting on this whole production because she thinks she won't have to go to the beach, I'll fix her little red wagon. I don't want to hear another word about her ankles," Mamma mutters.

Vittoria walks out of the bathroom in her swimsuit, with a sarong wrapped around her waist, and a mouthful of lipstick. Her hair, electrified by the excessive brushing, whips the air wildly.

"Oooh, how pretty we are," says Mamma.

Vittoria replies in a bored tone of voice, she's felt pretty since yesterday afternoon, and she already seems to be tired of the idea. She leans against the doorjamb and crosses her legs. Her hair levitates and sticks to the wooden doorjamb, in search of a ground.

"I'm guessing that you're going to the beach," Mamma says to her.

"Of course I am, we're at the beach, where else would I go."

"Fine, but take off the lipstick."

"Oh, come on."

"No argument out of you!"

"She put on perfume, too . . . " I say.

My mother investigates, sniffing the air.

"It's so I don't reek of the stench of Al's feet," says the lovely Vittoria.

"Take off that lipstick and come eat your breakfast."

The diva sashays lazily to the bathroom. On my heart and on my brain I jot down this note: "Making a woman happy is easy, remember to do it every day. For your own good."

24.

"Al, not today, I'm begging you! We have to go to the lady doctor and today I don't want you to play the fool! Understood?"

"Ah'm vara sarra, Mamma, bat tadaa Ah'm anla asang tha vawal 'a.'"

"Why on earth would you do such a thing? Get going, it's late, too! You will be in big trouble, Al Santamaria, if you make me look like a fool today in front of the lady doctor, I swear you will catch it tonight . . . first from me and then from your father!"

We get to the office of the calm lady doctor after a car trip that lasts an hour and twenty minutes plus a short walk that consisted of much jerking along by the hand and a string of threats. How can I make them understand that I don't want to go to this lady doctor anymore? Once we've determined that I'm a genius, enough is enough, right? Why keep hammering at it?

"Hello, Al, how are you today?" the lady doctor asks me.

My mother glares at me. She clenches my hand tightly.

"Well, ve-e-e-ery well," I say, and my mother heaves a sigh of relief. "Bet Decter? De yee mend mech ef tedey Eh enly ese the vewel 'e'?"

I don't have anything against this lady. In her way, she's even likable. If you ask me, she uses the cotton ball the way Mamma did before becoming a pastry chef. She's never in a hurry, she's loving, she doesn't seem to have anything else to do but tend to me. But the point is that I don't really like seeing

Mamma and Papà wasting money on these visits, if then when we finally find the promised home, we won't have enough left over to buy it. The sleepy lady doctor is very good at drawing words out of me but I know that I need to be careful and the whole time I make a special effort to talk about harmless topics, like school, my friends, my sister, my dreams of becoming a superhero. It wasn't easy, but it seems to me that it went quite well.

"Al, do you mind waiting outside while I talk to your Mamma?"

"Certeenly, Decter."

The absurdity of grown-ups. They still believe that if they tell me to leave the room just when they're getting to the interesting part, I'm going to just sit down and be a good boy, instead of gluing my ear to the door.

"Believe me, Signora, I've never had a thing like this happen before. We spoke for a solid half hour and I kept forgetting I was sitting across from a seven-year-old child," says the lady doctor.

"What did he talk about?"

"About the new law on public financing of political parties, about the inflation, about al-Fatah, about the commercials with Pippopotamus . . . "

"Oh yes, he loves him."

"No, Signora, he hates him. He sees him as a crowbar to force open the consciousness of the public and induce them to purchase needlessly costly consumer goods."

"Pippopotamus?"

"And he believes that financial restitution to the former colonies is only just and fair. Your son is a happy boy, he adores his family, but there's something oppressing him, he seems anguished . . . "

"We do everything we can to keep him from reading the papers and watching TV . . . I don't know how he finds out about certain things, my husband and I never talk about politics."

"He's surprisingly precocious but don't be fooled, he's still a child and there are certain things that are too grown-up for him, he's not capable of processing them . . . "

"I can process them perfectly well, actually!"

"Al, stop eavesdropping!" shouts Mamma.

There, now they're whispering and I can't understand a darned thing they're saying. Too bad for them, now I'll get bored and there's nothing in the world more dangerous than a bored little boy, right, Casimiro? Anyway, I know exactly what they must be saying to each other. So long newspapers, so long TV, hello parties with my friends and soccer cards. Oh God.

"What's that smell?" the lady doctor asks from inside the room.

"Al!"

"What smell?" I ask.

"You're burning something!"

"Me? No, no."

Wake u-u-up . . . wake u-u-up . . . my amazing brain is sending you impulses ordering you to wake u-u-up . . . don't try putting up any resistance, it's futi-i-i-ile . . . I'm looking at you intensely and my massive brain which is already so active at four in the morning is establishing contact with your sleeping pastry chef brain . . . let yourself be guided by my superior impulses . . . when I count to three you will awaken . . . one . . . two . . . three-e-e-e . . .

"A-a-al . . . " Agnese mutters from between the sheets.

It works!

"What are you doing up? . . . What time is it? . . . "

"I've had a great idea, Mamma."

"You can tell me tomorrow, now scoot back to bed . . . "

"It'll only take a minute! You need to put a chocolate

meteorite in the *ciambellone*. In the *ciambellone-e-e-e* . . . you understand, Mamma?"

"What? . . . "

"A chocolate meteorite, a bigger chunk of chocolate than the others, much bigger, and whoever finds it gets the slice for free. You understand, Mamma? It'll make sales sky-y-yrocket! Listen to me-e-e-e . . . "

"Yes, yes, I understand . . . but now, I'm begging you, go back to bed . . . "

Do you hear me? This is Al's extraordinary brain talking to you . . . the supremacy of my brain cells orders you to put a chocolate meteorite in the *ciambellone-e-e-e* . . . and while you're at it: it's time to cut it out with these visits to the way too calm lady do-o-oct-o-or. Now go to sleep . . . slee-ee-eep . . . slee-ee-ee-eep . . . and when I count to three you'll sleep and you'll give rest and recuperation to your exhausted body . . . one . . . two . . .

"Three!"

"A-a-al!"

25.

The cold has driven the vacationers extinct. From one week to the next, the children with their life preservers and swim masks have vanished, as have the mothers with their straw hats and transistor radios, the fathers with their binoculars and sports dailies, the grandmothers with their pans full of rigatoni with meat sauce and breaded cutlets. Filling my leisure time without annoying anyone is a challenge. Raimondo swung by to play Papà's guitar, I was hoping to have a little time to play with him but he could only stay for ten minutes. His parents had to go to Rome and to make sure he stays at the bar they call every half hour, he has five minutes to call them back.

Vittoria's friends have left and there's no chance that any class-mates come out here before next summer. What we need is a stroke of luck, what we need is for the promised home to pop up unexpectedly.

Given the general state of desolation, Mamma gave me per-mission to watch TV, but only in the afternoon and only with Vittoria next to me. After turning the two antennas in all pos-sible directions we can only manage to see the first RAI chan-nel. And then the picture will only stay clear if you plant a foot on the round antenna and remain motionless for the entire duration of the program. We laugh with Loretta Goggi, Alighiero Noschese, and Enrico Montesano, we wait in vain for the Kessler Twins to make a mistake, we imitate the gri-maces and smirks of Mina and Aldo Fabrizi, and sometimes, when Papà is home, we put on a chorus of Ricchi e Poveri, just to annoy him. Today, after rejoicing at the announcement by the young lady with the puffy hair: "And now, in an unsched-uled surprise, a cartoon of *Popeye*," we watch Raffaella Carrà dance with a blonde male *ballerino*. After their performance, my sister has an idea.

"Should we do it ourselves?"

"Do what?" I ask.

"The dance. I just lift you onto my shoulders, I let you slide down my back, then I grab you by the neck and between my legs," she says.

In other words, Carrà's part is for me. Concerning this point there's not a lot of argument because my sister is taller and heavier. Acrobatic dancing might not be my favorite pastime but, seeing that Vittoria already feels like a grown-up and the opportunities to play together are drastically waning, I reply in the affirmative. As the tape recorder plays "Jailhouse Rock," my sister and I go for it, trotting and pirouetting and all the rest.

"Okay, now take a running start . . . " says the *ballerino*.

It all happens very quickly. The *ballerino* takes the young

Raffaella Carrà by the waist, she leaps into the air and remains suspended over his head, arms spread wide, then she slides trustingly in an angel's pose down his back and, smiling, hits her head right on the floor.

I'm brought back to consciousness by Raul. He was installing burglar-proof security hooks on the roller blinds and when he heard the thump, he was the first to come running. Stretched out on the bed with a wet rag on my forehead, I try to reestablish contact with the blurry reality around me.

"Signora, he's regained consciousness," Raul tells my mother.

At the recommendation of the door repairman, Mamma, who places a lot of trust in the advice of specialists, goes to the kitchen to get a steak from the fridge. She comes back with a mustard-colored package in one hand.

"Darn it, we're all out of steak, would these be all right?"

I wake up with a handful of beef strips on my forehead. The cold bovine blood streaks down my temple and fogs my vision even more. The picture of Mamma, Vittoria, and Raul looking down at me in silence flickers up and down like on the television set when Papà tells me to stabilize the resolution and I go over and give it a good hard smack. Raul slaps my face gently, human heads and television sets aren't really all that different after all, and the picture grows clearer. Vittoria is smiling, but Mamma's not.

"Can you tell me exactly what happened?" she asks me.

"I fell down."

"And how did that happen?"

"I was being Raffaella Carrà."

26.

Mamma dressed Vittoria down good and proper, and that evening Papà performed an encore every bit as intense. Not since the days of breeding lizards in Agnese's jewel box had anyone gotten such a scolding around here. I'm so used to being the guilty party that with every new incrimination I felt like saying: "I swear I didn't do it on purpose!" Vittoria took it badly, because her status as a grown-up young lady had been repeatedly called into question. On the other hand, I wasn't mad at her, because I'm the genius of the family, and a genius should never entrust his own invaluable gifts to Vittoria "Ricotta-Fingers" Santamaria. In any case, I wrote in the human flesh diary: "The murderer of household pets has taken her crimes to a new level. Beware!" Because of this accident I was forced to postpone a highly sensitive mission for forty-eight hours; until yesterday my head hurt so much I couldn't even comb my hair. Nothing could be worse than to have a brilliant plan and be forced to postpone it. The only positive aspect is that I thus had more time to work out the details and foolproof the plan even more securely. I'm about to do something that's against the rules, but then again the factory workers at Fiat Rivalta have organized against the increase in ticket prices announced by the private transportation company, and six hundred Turin families have occupied the apartment houses in the Falchera quarter, so one thing is clear: you're allowed to break the rules if it's for a good cause. I glance at my watch, in mere minutes Mickey Mouse's arms are going to reach my second-favorite position, after the one that means 9:15: the one with both arms straight up. In the darkened room, I've put on six T-shirts and two woolen sweaters. Now my new jacket, which according to Mamma's plans ought to have fit me perfectly by the time I got to high school, is fittingly filled out. A fake Zorro mustache, a bag with everything I'll need, a chocolate *ciambellone*, plenty of money. I've got everything. No! I almost forgot the hairy hand! Don't worry, Al, it's still five minute to midnight. I tiptoe across the room, I take the jar of glue from my table, I slap a healthy helping onto the back of my hand, I count to ten, and then I sprinkle it with a shower of Vittoria's hair that I cut when she wasn't looking. A masterpiece.

I take forever to make my way through the apartment because everything squeaks or creaks, except for the front door which I took great care to oil in advance. I time my moves to Papà's rhythmic snoring and then I go, I pull the door open, and . . . I'm out, and I close it behind me. I head downstairs, out the street door, and from there I run to the car, taking advantage of a cloud that covers the moon.

"If the Prinz starts up on the first try, the mission will have been a success."

"If it starts up on the first try, it'll be a miracle, more than anything else," says Casimiro.

The gods are favorable, and the car starts right up. The theory that children learn quickly is accurate, and if the children in question are geniuses then all it takes is a couple of drives with Papà behind the wheel to figure out the use of the instrumentation and such basic rudiments as balancing the gas pedal and the clutch. We get started a little jerkily, but we do get started. I wait until we round the curve before switching on the headlights and I follow the directions on the road map that I memorized before setting out. Take the first right, straight for two-thirds of a mile, take the second left, the first right, straight until you reach the stoplight, turn right there, and keep going until the roundabout. Driving isn't hard, you just need to be cautious and straddle the double white line on the asphalt, the same as the little racing cars on the electric track. I'm sitting on the very edge of the seat and pushing the pedals takes so much effort that my legs are already numb. Am I going to be able to keep this up for six hours? Go through the intersection, continue until you see the sign that says "Highway," and then turn right. There's not another car in sight, and if I'd known that in advance I could have spared myself the camouflage until I reached the tollbooth. Staying on the white lines isn't easy, especially on curves, but after a couple of miles I already feel much more confident.

At the end of a straighaway, the Prinz's timid headlights illuminate a row of flickering smudge pots and a line of wooden barricades.

"Don't worry, Casimiro, there's not a single successful mission that didn't start out with a snag or two."

"The Battle of Taejon in the Korean War . . . " he reminds me.

"The storm over the English Channel on June 5, 1944 . . . "

Here, on the other hand, it's a detour due to construction underway that plays hob with my mental road map. I start wandering around the outskirts of Rome, down dark streets and past rows of gray apartment houses that strike fear into my heart. I drive down long boulevards, hoping the whole time that I'll fetch up against the tollbooth in the end. Then I decide that the tollbooth must be outside of town and the minute I spot a little greenery, I head straight for it. I wind up on a road that seems to be leading right out into the countryside. I'm a good hour late on my original schedule, I can't waste any more time, I'm just going to have to ask someone for directions. I drive slowly along the sidewalk hoping for help from some late-night stroller, and after I round a curve, the car's headlights illuminate a house. And a large wooden sign. On it is written, "For Sale."

"Casimiro, technical intermission for home inspection."

We get out of the car, leaving the engine running. We cautiously approach.

"Spacious, understated, surrounded by greenery," says Casimiro.

"Sign reading, 'For Sale.'"

"Do you feel what I feel?"

"Yes, Casimiro, this is the place . . . "

Now I understand just what that certain something is that

allows me to recognize the promised home: It's the activation of dreams. I don't have to make the slightest effort, I don't need a real estate agent to tell me to imagine the place personalized to suit my preferences. It's the house itself that suggests it to me. Here Agnese and Mario Elvis can lie in the sun, here I can splash with Vittoria in a nice inflatable pool, I measure the length by my strides. One . . . two . . . three . . . four: Mamma and Papà's bedroom. Five . . . six . . . seven . . . eight: my room. Nine, ten, eleven, twelve, thirteen, fourteen, fifteen: the living room. Sixteen, seventeen, eighteen, nineteen: the kitchen. Twenty and . . . almost twenty-one: Vittoria's little bedroom. This is the place!

I'm strongly tempted to head straight home to tell everyone else, but there's another mission to be accomplished. And so I go in search of landmarks, after which I retrace my route to get the name of the street, and on my way I also find a sign pointing me to the highway. This will be remembered as the magic night of the Santamaria family. I need to make up for lost time, but I don't want to overdo it, I'll floor the accelerator only once I'm on the highway. Within sight of the tollbooth I pull over to touch up my disguise. Even though there should be no need to say a word, I try out my voice, I trained for the whole week, if I pull my head down between my shoulders and stiffen my neck, I can talk like an old man of at least twenty. I get a little overwhelmed, and when I start up again, the engine cuts out. Come on, just this one last little obstacle and then it will all be highway. The tollbooth is scary, it's shrouded in a light mist that creates strange haloes around the lights. I proceed slowly out of fear that the engine might die again, and I keep one foot on the gas pedal while I use my other foot to offset it with the clutch. My leg muscles are exploding. When I pull up to the booth, I adjust my fake whiskers one last time, and roll down the window with my eyes straight ahead. Out of the corner of my eye I observe the tollbooth attendant as he hands me a ticket without so much as a glance, I reach out my hairy hand, I take the ticket. He ignores me, doesn't even look my way. I put the ticket on the dashboard, pretend to adjust my jacket, and he doesn't even turn a distracted eye in my direction. All this work for nothing? I wave my hairy hand to attract his attention, and then in a nice deep voice I ask: "Is this the right way to Milan?"

"Signor Mario Elvis Santamaria? . . . My name is Mancuso, I work at the North Rome tollbooth and I have your son Almerico here with me . . . Listen, don't ask me."

Casimiro, my friend, we're in trouble deep. Now how are we going to explain this to Papà? It was all supposed to be a nice surprise. This time we're getting the belt, I think.

"You're in for it now, kid," Signor Mancuso tells me.

"I am, aren't I?"

"There was a tone in his voice . . . just look: I got goose bumps, and I don't have anything to do with it!"

"I don't have an-n-n-nything to do with it either! All I wanted was to export Mamma's *ciambellone*!"

"What did you want to do?"

"Mamma's *c-c-ciambellone* with the chocolate meteorite inside! . . . Would you care for a slice?"

"So that's what that smell was. But wait, where did you want to take it? To Milan?"

"I read that th-th-they have the biggest pastry company in Italy there . . . How is it?"

"Excellent, absolutely outstanding."

"Too bad, though, if you'd found the c-c-chocolate meteorite you could have taken another slice."

This is one of those moments between father and son. One of those moments that occur when the son gets up to something serious and bad and the father, instead of pounding him within an inch of his life, decides to have a man-to-man talk with him, just eleven years early. Even though the decision is absurd, it strikes me as intelligent to reward it, and so I go along with it. We stroll in the park, in silence, every so often we talk, but about other things. A nice tree, a nice butterfly, a nice bright sun that, oddly enough, is warm. This interlocutory phase is starting to get on my nerves.

"You see, Al . . . "

Here we go, this is it.

" . . . sometimes we make mistakes, even with the best intentions."

He looks at me, I look at him.

"It's the hardest thing to understand, I know, but you're a big boy now."

He smiles at me, I smile at him.

"Don't think for a second that I haven't figured out the reason why you stole the car . . . "

He laughs at his own joke, I laugh along with him.

"It's admirable that you wanted to do something good for your mother, but you were really too reckless . . . "

He nods at me, I nod back.

" . . . you could have hurt yourself or someone else, lots of people are killed in car crashes."

He looks at me, I smile at him. Holy cow, I just made a mistake!

"What do you have to laugh about?"

"Nothing, nothing, sorry!"

"What did I just say, Al?"

"Eh-eh-eh . . . car crashes! You were talking about 'car crashes'!"

"Right, and before that?"

"Eh-eh-eh . . . "

"Al, you haven't been listening to a word I've said! What the devil have you been thinking about?" he shouts at me.

I try my famous captivating smile but it doesn't work. I turn to run.

"Al! Come here, right now!"

I'm sorry, I was thinking about the promised home.

"Al, don't do this, it'll only make it worse!"

I've found the promised home but I can't tell you now, when you're angry.

"Al, the minute I get my hands on you . . . "

When he doesn't specify, it's really going to hurt! I try again with the smile.

"This time you asked for it!"

Okay, I confess, I was actually thinking that in the promised home there's going to be a long hallway to do cannonballs into the bathtub! Bewildered gaze! Captivating smile! Beginning of tears! Stop, Mario Elvis, this is the power of my mind commanding you, sto-o-o-op no-o-ow!

27.

I don't know, I can't really imagine that such radically different things can happen on the same plane. The world that plans the first trip to Mars can't possibly be the same world that devises the destruction of the Earth, the world that works to save poor children can't be the same world that kills them by dropping bombs pretty much at random. Maybe there's a parallel world, subterranean, gray, and wrong, like in the comics, if that were the case, then all we'd have to do is put big blocks of cement over all the manholes. My moments of meditation under the vase of geraniums always seem to abound with answers and solutions. Even though I'm preoccupied today because Papà went to take a look at the promised home. He'll come back overjoyed, he'll throw his arms around me, he'll tell me that I was a genius to find it, because the darned thing really was well hidden. But enough of that, the chosen one has other things to think about. It's not like the only problems the world has involve unhappiness and cruelty, there's also the problem of generalized idiocy. The Americans and the Russians claim that they possess a nuclear arsenal powerful enough to destroy the planet four times over. I don't get it, after the first time, what's the point? Could it just be a manner of speech? "I hate you so much that I'd kill you four times!" Or maybe it's like when Walter brags, thinking he can buffalo us when he says that he knows a way to kill us just using his pinky finger. Men are just bigger, hairier kids, they talk about the Cold War and the strategy of tension, and with these big important-sounding words they can fool anyone, but not a kid. You're not strategizing tension, you're just boasting, the way Walter does. But this isn't the only absurd aspect of it. In my secret diary in human flesh I jotted down certain phrases that old people really seem to like: "Live every day as if it were your last," "Carpe diem," "The grave's a fine and private place, but none I think do there embrace," "Live as if there's no tomorrow." The old people know perfectly well that to be happy they ought to think the way we children do, but then they keep forgetting that fact and scold us continuously because we children don't think the way they do. Why do they do it? Are they confused? But if they're so confused, then how do they manage to rule the world? The unmistakable tractor-like sound of the Prinz's two-cylinder engine distracts me. I can't wait to lock eyes with Papà and drink in his astonished and grateful gaze. I run out onto the road, I pull open the door even before the car brakes to a stop.

"Well, Papà? What do you say?"

"Al, I'm dead on my feet, it took me an hour to find it . . . "

He gets out of the car and slams the door.

"It's no good, it's not even a house," he tells me.

"Why not? It's got everything, four walls, windows, doors . . . "

"Yes, it's even got too many doors . . . Al, I thank you for what you tried to do, but now let us handle the search for a new home, that's the right way to do it."

"What did I do wrong?"

"These are things for grown-ups, Al. The structure itself is very spacious, the place is out of the way but quite charming, the price would be perfect, but to choose a house you have to take too many things into consideration, you can't know them all."

"Can't we talk about it?"

"No, Al, we can't."

I take note of the fact that helping grown-ups really isn't easy.

"Why can't we?"

"Because we can't."

And that saving the world is going to be a long and arduous undertaking.

"Papà?"

"Yes, A-a-al?"

"Just don't complain about the fact that I have an imaginary friend."

28.

Given her natural talent with household pets, Vittoria decided to show up at home one day with a stray kitten. The kitten, which must have sensed the danger in the air, decided to skip the suffering entirely.

"It was meowing when I picked it up!"

"Vittoria, it must have been very sick, maybe its mother abandoned it and it froze to death. You see that it's not breathing?" Mamma says to her.

"But what if it recovers?"

"Put it out on this woolen rag, that'll keep it warm. If it doesn't recover in an hour, that means it's dead and we'll take it out into the field and bury it. All right?"

We put the cat in a sheltered corner of the balcony, nicely wrapped up in the woolen rag.

"I swear that it was meowing when I picked it up," Vittoria says again.

"Do you think it'll recover? It looks pretty beat up to me. Just look how skinny it is, all those scabs on its eyes . . . "

I read in a magazine that a dead kitten was brought back to life by keeping it in a lit oven, like an incubator. Vittoria wants to give it a try. I raise the objection that it strikes me as dangerous. She says that there's no danger because we'll keep the oven at a low heat, very very low, barely warm. I'm so curious to try that I drop my objections, but I make a resolution to watch her step by step to make sure she doesn't pull one of her boneheaded moves. We wait for Mamma to lie down for a nap and when the coast is clear we shut ourselves up in the kitchen.

"How high should I set the temperature?" Vittoria asks me.

"I'd say between 85 degrees and 105 . . . closer to 85."

She opens the oven door to slide the kitten in. I stop her.

"Hold on, first let's check to make sure the temperature is right."

We stick a hand into the oven, the heat is faint and pleasant. The thermostat in Mamma's new electric oven works very well. We wait a little long to make sure that the temperature has stabilized, then we slip the cat into the oven. We shut the door.

"Just to be safe, let's leave it open a crack to let in air," Vittoria suggests.

"Good idea."

"Now let's go into our room to pray to the Madonna, and we'll come back in ten minutes."

I check the time on my watch, I stick my hand in to feel the temperature one last time, and then I leave the kitchen.

"What do you say, should I turn on the light in the oven? If it wakes up and sees everything's all dark, it might get scared . . . " Vittoria says.

"Go on, turn on the light and let's go to our room before Mamma wakes up."

Vittoria goes back, pushes the button that turns on the light, and together we go to pray in front of the little painting of the Madonna.

"Hail Mary, full of grace. The Lord is with thee . . . Do you think that the Madonna will have time to look after kittens?" she asks me.

" . . . blessed art thou amongst women . . . If Superman can find the time, then the Madonna can find it, too, no?"

" . . . and blessed is the fruit of thy womb, Jesus . . . Superman doesn't exist."

" . . . Holy Mary, Mother of God, pray for us sinners . . . Then I'd say it looks bad."

"Now and at the hour of our death" is a premonition that remains graven in our hearts, petrified by Mamma's scream. I've never heard one like it. Not even that time that I set Grandma's fox fur stole on fire.

At dinner, Mamma remains shut up in her room. Every now and then we hear the frightful sound of retching. Papà would like to encourage Vittoria but he can't find the words. He keeps slapping his thighs and biting off his sentences: "Sure, but . . . ," "Well, if you ask me . . . ," "Still, what I can't understand is how . . . " Vittoria sits there pouting. She's a faint shadow of her former self, I can pilfer her fried potatoes without having to resort to the stratagem of the dropped napkin or the cockroach on the carpet. But it's no fun this way, so I try to explain to Papà that I was an eyewitness and can testify to the fact that Vittoria did everything by the book, scrupulously and with great care.

"I blame the engineer who designed that oven, only an idiot could have put the button for the light right next to the button for the broiler!" I say.

In the other room, Mamma vomits.

29.

"Did you see what happened to Mario Elvis?"

"No, Casimiro, what?"

"How can you ask, he was right there on the floor, I didn't think he was capable of falling. He was passed out, his eyes were all white . . . "

"That's not true."

"Of course it is, he was there right in front of us, you can't have missed it."

"Never seen Mario Elvis fall down in my life. As far as I can remember, he's always been up on his feet, good and sound, solid as a rock."

"But I tell you he was flat on his back."

"That would be completely inexplicable, like some bad dream."

"I didn't dream it."

"Then how do you explain?"

"I have no explanation."

"It was just a bad dream, Casimiro . . . don't give it another thought."

For no good reason that I can see, Papà has spent four days in bed. The doctor said that it's just exhaustion, his body must have rebelled against too heavy a schedule and maybe one worry too many. I know that because I eavesdropped on the conversation through the kitchen wall. I pressed my ear against the bottom of a glass, the way Grandma Concetta used to do when the neighbors were fighting. These are things we do in pursuit of the truth, she would say, because afterwards everyone in the apartment house gossips and there's no telling who's wrong and who's right. Mamma's version of the doctor's diagnosis is interesting. She told us that Papà's only problem is that he's behind on sleep, which means that if you don't sleep eight hours every night, your body keeps track of the shortfall and sooner or later presents you with the bill. It might say nothing for a whole year and then, without warning, demand all its back pay, and you can't ask it for more time, you're obliged to stay in bed until you've paid back every last second of sleep. In other words, Papà has been burning the candle at both ends, his body noticed, and he was forced to sleep for ninety-six hours in a row. This morning he got up early and drove away in the car. Mamma started ironing, when we asked her where Papà was, she said that she didn't know, maybe he'd just gone out for a drive. As she irons the towels, which she usually just folds and puts away nice and stiff the minute she takes them off the drying rack, and also the shirts that she's already ironed once, she hums under her breath the tune of "Sugar Baby Love," the beginning of the song, which you don't need to know English to sing, because all it says is wat-choowarree. After twenty minutes of it, Mamma's humming isn't funny anymore, and after two hours it's like being in a horror movie, the kind with the possessed girl and the evil spirit that sort of sings something to lure her into its trap. Vittoria is exhausted and tries to interrupt the hellish refrain.

"Sugar baaaby lo-o-ove! . . . " she suggests loudly.

"Wat-choowarree, wat-choowarree-warree!" the possessed woman continues.

I gather my courage and I take her Big Jim's luau shirt. When I get there she's ironing the hem of her skirt and she doesn't even give me a chance to speak. She just takes the micro-shirt and starts removing the creases with tiny little delicate taps with the tip of the iron. Then the phone rings and she goes running into the living room, leaving the hot iron on the shirt, which slowly melts and adheres to the face of the iron.

"Mario, well? . . . Really? . . . Oh my God, that big? Are you sure we can afford it?"

Once we figure out the subject of the phone call, Vittoria and I press in close around Mamma. After all these years, we play the sardine game again.

"And where is it? . . . Where? . . . Certainly, it's a little out of the way, but a thousand square feet . . . How on earth did you manage to find it? . . . Al? He found it?"

So I was right after all, that really was the promised home, and I'm the one who found it! Mamma gives me a wink, I shut both my eyes because I don't know how to do just one.

"What's Papà saying? Huh, Mamma, what's he saying?" I ask.

"He's saying that when you're not attempting suicide by fire or stealing cars, you really can make yourself quite useful."

I get the impression that Mamma feels like running, maybe even shouting. We go into the kitchen to make a pizza and throw a nice celebratory dinner. We stick our hands into the flour, we start kneading the dough while Mamma slowly adds the water. No one has anything to say about my black fingernails, we forget the salt, we're out of olive oil, but none of it matters because the fingernails, the salt, and the olive oil are all things that are here, and in our minds we're already in the promised home, intently gazing at that thousand square feet and imagining the same things, the round table here, the corner sofa there, the tub for cannonball dives over there.

30.

Al, the chosen one, has succeeded in turning time back to when the Santamaria family used to pack into the car together and sing happily at the top of their lungs.

"You see these apartment houses? Noisy neighbors, endless condo meetings, forget about all that!" Papà declares.

"Shall we forget about all that?" Mamma asks, seeking confirmation.

"Music playing full blast? We're free to do as we please. Dancing at three in the morning? Yes we can."

"Playing soccer indoors?" I ask.

"No, no we can't. Everything else, though, yes."

"So it's not this fine apartment building here, either . . . " Mamma asks.

"A rat warren, an architectural monstrosity from the 1960s. We're almost there, now shut your eyes, shut them!" Papà shouts.

"Eyes shut!"

"Okay, now. Before you open them again, try to imagine what it will be like once we've done all the work. Understood? Don't let yourself be influenced by what's in there now, just evaluate the structure and the thousands of opportunities that it offers us . . . There, open your eyes!"

"Where's the house?" asks Vittoria.

Soon we'll have our promised home. Right now it's occupied by a tire repair shop, but Mario Elvis has already drawn up plans. Mamma and Vittoria have the wrong looks on their faces because they can't imagine it finished, without the stacks of tires and all the rest.

"It's not even a house," Vittoria tells me, "I won't be able to invite anyone over . . . Oh God, I'm so ashamed."

"There's even a view of the countryside," I tell her.

"What countryside are you talking about, it looks like a dump."

Mamma and Papà hold each other close and stroll toward the house. It's a very simple structure, long and low, a cement parallelepiped with two large metal roller shutters in the front and long, narrow windows in the back. It's going to be the largest home we've ever owned.

"Just try to imagine, Agnese . . . Instead of that roller shutter, we'll put in a great big window. It'll be enormous and it'll fill the place with light."

From inside the house comes the hiss of an air compressor and a belch. Mamma pays no attention, she looks at Papà's hand that trembles as he points to the roller shutter, it trembles in a frightening way. His voice trembles too as he says that we'll have to keep the other one, that for a while we'll just have to get used to having it as the front door of our home. I've never seen him tremble like that, he must be incredibly cold.

"There's no shame in having a roller shutter for a front door. We'll paint it white and it will be lovely," says Mamma.

"Over there will be Vittoria's room," says Papà.

"Where, Papà? Where?" she asks, all excited.

It didn't take much to purchase Vittoria's consent. But Mamma's isn't going to come so easy. Right now she's not saying a thing, she clutches Papà close and nods at everything he says, including the plan to build a second floor in the future. I think that when Mamma was small, she too spent years at a time drawing cozy little houses. That's why she's having such a hard time now recognizing this as our promised home. It doesn't have the red pitched roof, it's not square, it doesn't even have the two little windows and the door at the center; still, though, this is it. The Santamaria family's promised home.

Are you able to hear me-e-e? This is the prodigious brain of Al Santamaria establishing direct contact with yours, the brain of an elderly and baffled pastry chef. Do not put up resista-a-ance . . . the cells of which I am composed are unrivaled in

nature . . . surrende-e-er . . . the place you saw today is the pro-
o-omised ho-o-ome . . . register this information: it–is–the–pro-
o-omised–ho-o-ome! Do not put up resistance, all your negative sensations will vanish when I count three-ee-ee: one . . .
two . . . oh wait, one last thing: the next time you go out to buy
chocolate wafers, buy the big pa-a-a-ckage. Now register the
information and re-e-est . . . one . . . two . . . three-ee-ee.

PART TWO

31

The year 1981 began as a year of records. Ronald Reagan is the first actor to become president of the United States, Tiina Lehtola the first woman ski jumper to surpass 100 meters, and in Italy it was finally possible to overturn a royal decree allowing citizens to go around armed with sabers. I'm fourteen years old, I'm taller than Mamma now, and most important of all, I'm in time to become the all-time youngest savior of the world, even though the preparatory phase of my project is taking its time, as does everything in the Santamaria family. Obtaining the promised home that, in Papà's intentions, was going to be taken care of in just one year, actually took an extra six. After the pinwheel of Roman apartments and the eight months, tops, of exile in Torvaianica, which turned into twenty-six months, if not more, we went back to the Italian capital, and there we touched bottom: a cellar apartment, 320 square feet, so damp you could easily identify north by the moss on the walls. Aside from Raul, who came to see us in each of our new apartments, and Raimondo, who is willing to put up with as much as two hours on the bus for a guitar lesson, we're always alone. Mamma and Papà have lost touch with even their last few friends and Vittoria, who's by now legally an adult, only comes home to sleep. It's the last effort, as Mario Elvis told us every day, and in the end he was right. With the money we've set aside by living in those hovels, we've got enough money for a down payment, and we've bought the promised home with a twenty-year mortgage.

Elvis Presley died on August 16th, four years ago. Papà dreamed that sooner or later he'd come to Italy to give a concert. Instead, the only live performance we'll ever listen to will be by Papà, on the annual Elvis Day celebration held by the Santamaria family. Very likely there will be an Al Day too, eventually, as a worldwide secular festivity, but in the meantime I'm sowing my crop of relics: just last week I donated a photograph of my skull to science. Mamma and Papà were worried about something, I heard them whispering with the lady doctor about some strange things I'd supposedly said and some others that I'd supposedly done, and so I was forced to get another X-ray plus a triple ration of tests, the results of which they're now anxiously awaiting. In my human flesh diary, I wrote, "If worrying is the work that parents do, when they retire, do they stop worrying?"

For the first time, the Santamaria family is all together in the promised home. We can't believe it's true. We're all sitting on the couch, exhausted from the move, truly dismayed at the sight of the mountain of cardboard boxes that we're going to have to unpack sooner or later. We're tired but soon we'll celebrate the historic event with a big party. For the moment, the most we can manage to do is hold hands. Mamma holds mine, I hold Papà's, and he holds nobody's because for the past few years Vittoria has been sitting as if she were immune to the force of gravity. She's lying on the floor with her feet propped up on the armrest and her ears anaesthetized by an Italian imitation of a Sony Walkman. Mario Elvis is the tiredest one of all, but he can't seem to stop talking. He praises the fine workmanship of the floors, the excellent job that the mason did in transforming one of the doorways into a giant window, the remarkable skill of the cabinetmaker who put in the handsome walnut doorway, a door that, after we lower the metal shutter, we can consider burglarproof.

"With the first money we get, we'll build the inside walls!" Papà shouts in a vain attempt to involve Vittoria in the conversation.

One of the curtains we've used to partition the rooms only now realizes just how provisional it really is and slams to the floor. We don't even have the strength to jump at the noise.

"First the kitchen, Mario, otherwise the odors . . . " says Mamma.

"But that's the fashion nowadays, open kitchens!"

"First the bathtub, Papà," I suggest.

"Al, you're obsessed with this bathtub . . . first we enclose the kitchen and then the bedrooms!" On "bedrooms," he tries to drag Vittoria into the conversation by lightly elbowing her foot.

"Oooouch!" she complains, as if he'd clubbed her over the head.

"Do we know anything about getting the electricity hooked up?" asks Mamma.

We know nothing about getting the electricity hooked up, or for that matter the natural gas, or the phone service. No one can give us any answers. Maybe they just haven't figured out that the Santamaria family is here. Luckily, we get a little light from the streetlamp outside, weak but more than sufficient for a family well trained in the rules of the curfew game. As for phone calls, there's a booth right next to the house, if we built a little window into the wall next to the front door, we'd be able to stick our hands out and pick up the receiver. Mamma doesn't like the phone booth, she says that people will stop to make a call and we'll always have someone in our house, or maybe she just hopes so, because in the time we've been here, not a single car has gone by. I saw one the day I came here with Papà to deliver the first load of furniture. It came racing up at top speed, then we heard the screech of brakes, and a few seconds later, we heard it drive away. A half mile or so further along, the road comes to an abrupt end. From what we've been able to learn, the original intention was to build a large supermarket here, but then they must have run into trouble with their permits, because the plan was abandoned. Beyond the Santamaria home, no more light poles, no more road—after us, nothing. But what matters is that we've put an end to our long wandering in the wilderness and we've become members of the Italian elite of homeowners. For a few more days we'll go on cooking with the propane tank, dining by candlelight, fantasizing about what the house will look like when it's done. This is a new beginning, I'm so excited. "Al! Did you burn something?" asks Mamma, venomously.

"Me? No, no. I just lit the candles."

"I smell the stink of burnt varnish!"

Does a person think they can go ahead and use a spray can as a flamethrower just because now they live in a thousand-square-foot house? Well, they're wrong, even if it was ten thousand square feet, she'd still be able to smell the odor instantly.

"It must be coming from outside," I say.

32.

"Stop staring at that lady," Papà whispers to me.

"But did you see her? She has the longest earlobes in the world . . . "

"Sssh!"

Doctor Livingstone used to do the same thing. The first time that he found himself face-to-face with the pygmies he stared at them one by one. There's nothing strange about it. I stare at people because there's always something to discover: the tribe of women with withered earlobes, the tribe of dyed hair and the acne tribe, the tribe of geometric moles, of little handbags, the tribe of eyeglasses with tinted lenses, the tribe of the mohawks and the tribe of white cotton socks. Papà tells me that at my age it's not right, I ask him why, and he replies, just because. Therefore, I consider myself free to ignore his request.

"That structure doesn't belong to this district," the clerk tells my father, "you're going to have to ask the people over in the nineteenth."

"But it was the people in the nineteenth who told us to come here."

"Well, they were wrong . . . that section of road doesn't come under our jurisdiction."

"They said that Via del Fossone comes under your jurisdiction, it's in your district."

"Listen, the districts have very precise boundaries, and Via del Fossone comes under our jurisdiction right up to number 123, but we don't even show the existence of a number 125."

"But the house is registered with the city real estate registry!"

"Then the people at the real estate registry made the mistake! We don't see any sign of it, after street number 123 there's nothing but countryside."

"There's some countryside and then right after a curve in the road, there's my house, with a paved street and a light pole. Who's in charge of the maintenance of that light pole, which district?"

"How should I know, it's not like we take care of those things! You'd have to ask the road maintenance office."

This clerk, like so many others that we've met, must have other plans in life. It's clear from the bored expression he puts on when we come in, and he reiterates the point with his increasingly abrupt irritated replies. He didn't graduate from high school, just scraping by with the lowest possible grades, and he didn't procure a highly placed recommendation just so he could be a paper pusher, shut up in a hermetically sealed compartment walled off from the rest of the world. No, he has grandiose plans, and a desperate need for a tidy little pile of cash to achieve those dreams. His is the face of someone hoping for a punch in the nose as the great opportunity of a lifetime. A month convalescing, a lawsuit won from the outset with a million dollars in damages for a fracture of the mandibular condyle and an acute atlantoaxial subluxation. I know that, my father knows it, and so we walk out of the office leaving him unhurt.

As far as I can tell, the odds were a billion to one against me and Vittoria ever being born. When Agnese and Mario Elvis were young, they must have been so good-looking that it's a miracle they weren't just cut down by fulminating heart attacks the minute they laid eyes on each other.

Lying in the shade of the vase of geraniums, I look over at Papà, and I have to admit there are few men on earth who can be so striking as they dry their hair in the sunshine, wearing a sleeveless undershirt and a hairnet.

"It's not as if I were asking to get them for free, electric power, gas, and a phone line!" he suddenly blurts out. "I'm just asking them to hook me up to the network, so I can enjoy the privilege of being plundered by the monopolistic regime, but there's just no way!"

By now, I'm almost big enough to bump the top of my head against the bottom of his chin, which is why Papà starts talking to me about serious matters.

"If there were free market competition, everything would work perfectly, they'd be stepping all over each other!" he goes on.

"It's not a question of monopoly, it's a question of mentality," I reply, "what the people who run this country lack is a long-term strategic vision. Even if there were no longer a monopoly, the result would be a series of companies competing to see who can rip off their customers in the cleverest fashion. The average Italian executive reasons like a shopkeeper."

Vittoria says that I seem like a well-trained dog, I say and do intelligent things just I can hear the usual "good job" and get the occasional pat on the head.

"Good job, Al."

It's so irritating to realize that she's right.

"It's a good thing I have a beautiful family, I don't give a damn about the gas," says Mario Elvis, and he goes back to enjoying the sunshine.

That's right, ignore all the rest, only think about us.

Behind the promised home there must be fifteen acres or so of untilled land enclosed by the road, which runs around it in a large horseshoe arc, picked out by plane trees. On the left is a very dense growth of underbrush, thornbushes, and low trees, and from there runs a row of holm oaks about a hundred yards into the field. This, along with the plane trees, creates a second barrier separating us from the first apartment buildings; on the left is a small tuff-stone hill covered with brushwood and blackberry and laurel bushes; stretching out before us, on the other side of the road, is open countryside until you reach the first monstrosities of the outskirts of the city. In other words, there's plenty of greenery around the promised home, but I insisted on the geraniums, I knew that in the long run they'd work. I looked at Papà, I thought about the words of the clerk in the city administration, and the idea just popped into my head, unannounced. Like Newton, I managed to transform an accidental event into a great intuition, the key that I was seeking to give meaning to all the random details that had emerged so far. In my biography, it will be written: "This is the story of Al Santamaria, the greatest genius of the twentieth century who, in 1981, his *annus mirabilis*, transformed the potentially disastrous neglect of the administrative bureaucracy into the beginning of a memorable enterprise for his family and for the world at large!"

But now I don't want to spoil everything, I have to manage to keep the secret and spring a nice surprise. I'll work in the shadows, no one will have the slightest idea of my mission, to all appearances I'll be the same old Al, the good, altruistic son, the model student, mild-mannered and affable, but with every passing day I'll spin the web of my project, I'll honor the mission that History has assigned me. I scan the horizon, the line upon which my exploits will be indelibly impressed.

"Al, get down off the table," orders the clueless father.

What you are experiencing is a stream of thought. Mario-o-o . . . don't try to put up any resistance, the supremacy of my brain cells is establishing direct contact with you-ou-ou . . . Did you hear the message of the thought stream? Everything . . . is . . . under . . . contro-o-ol, I repeat: Everything . . . is . . . under . . . contro-o-ol. This is the promised ho-o-ome. Even if it doesn't belong in any particular district, even if we don't have electric power, gas, or telepho-o-one. When I count to three, you'll no longer have any doubts . . . one . . . two . . .

"A-a-al . . . "

"I didn't say 'three' yet."

"Huh?"

Sleep . . . put up no resistance . . . sle-e-e-ep. It's Al ordering you to sleep, it's History-y-y-y itse-e-elf. One . . . two . . . three-ee-ee-ee.

33.

The imposing body mass of American Marines makes their incursions into enemy territory much more complicated. It's easy to slip past enemy sentinels when you're a slight Viet Minh, but if you're forced to scamper on all fours between curtains and packing boxes with all those muscles on your frame, then you must really be good at it. The extremely muscular Sergeant Al creeps furtively through the forest right up under the enemy HQ, bound and determined to find out what has been upsetting the opposing generals since this morning. Private Casimiro holds his breath, for now all we can hear are sighs and the rustling of sheets.

"Poor little thing . . . that kind of permanent damage from a dumb stunt," says the Generaless.

"Sssh! Don't talk so loud!" orders the General.

Too late. The commando raider Al is already poised in ambush under their bed, and thanks to a secret technological device, he's able to pick up even a whisper from half a mile away.

"Agnese, no one could have known, kids hit their heads all the time and are none the worse for it . . . "

"And instead he hits his head once and . . . what did the lady doctor say?"

"Arrested development of his personality at the age of the trauma. But, you know, that lady doctor always exaggerates."

"No, she doesn't exaggerate. She said that he's still the seven-year-old kid that she saw last time! I know there was something wrong, poor Al . . ."

Poor Al? Casimiro! They're talking about me, about the knock on the head I got when I was dancing with Vittoria! Well, aren't they happy now? I don't understand them, they've just had full confirmation that nothing's changed, that I'm a genius just the same as when I was seven, and these two are practically in tears?

"He should have been taken to the emergency room."

"Agnese, it's no one's fault, and after all, she was only talking about his personality, nothing about his intelligence or his ability to learn. Don't be like this, come on."

More rustling in the sheets. Lots of rustling. Let's head back to the base, Casimiro. It's all just a false alarm, the enemy generals were just looking for an excuse to kiss and hug.

Every day I go with Papà to the grocery store. Since for the moment, the promised home doesn't even exist as far as the postman is concerned, the grocer has let us put a label with our name on his mailbox. Unbeknownst to him, Mario Elvis acts under the guidance of my cerebral force: the other day, after noticing that, for what must have been the tenth day in a row, no one had replied to any of his certified letters, he believes that he had the idea of purchasing a diesel-powered electric generator. Thanks to Raul, who obtained it for us second hand, we now have sufficient power for lighting and for the refrigerator. At night, we have to turn it off because it's a little noisy, but all in all, we can consider the problem solved. Now that the promised home is starting to take shape, the family seems to have benefited from the change. For the past few days, we've spent much more time together, everyone's more affectionate, and they all make a great show of curiosity about my intelligence.

"Say, tell me something, Al . . . " Papà asks me, "if a man has a car that gets 47 miles to the gallon and he decides to drive around the world along the equator, how much would he spend if the price of gasoline is 3,400 lire a gallon?"

All right, let's say the man starts in Ecuador. He drives across South America. Then, Africa, from Libreville to the mouth of the Jubba River. Then Indonesia. I'll rule out Micronesia, but toss in 60 miles just to be sure.

"Approximately 337,000 lire, give or take 5,000 lire."

He takes a sheet of paper out of his pocket. He reads it. He seems worried.

"No, Al, he'd spend more than 1.8 million . . . "

"One point eight million? A-a-ah, I see what you did. You meant the whole distance around the equator, including the ocean. You should have told me that this was an amphibious vehicle because in my calculations I took into account that you'd ship the car, and therefore spend nothing on gas, so that on dry land it would barely cover 4,700 miles, starting out from Quito, Ecuador, by way of Macapá, Brazil . . . "

"Okay, okay, that's perfect, good job."

As we're heading home, Papà seems overjoyed. The table is set and, as usual over the past few days, I catch a whiff of one of my favorite foods. Today it's tortellini. Vittoria pours me some water, Mamma fills my plate and then turns to look at Papà who gives her a wink.

"Listen, Al . . . " he says to me, "I just can't seem to finish the crossword puzzle because I can't remember the name of the pope of the Great Refus . . . "

"Celestine V. Dante mentions him in the third canto of the *Inferno*," I reply.

Vittoria, Mamma, and Papà all exchange a glance, forget to say: "Good job, Al," and start eating with expressions of relief.

"Papà, the TV news," I say.

"No news broadcasts during dinner, we won't digest our food."

"But we never watch it."

"Just eat, Al."

"The truth is that you're all worried about me!"

Goodness, I managed to attract a lot of attention with that sentence. So I say it again.

"You're all worried . . . but I'm a big boy now, I know the way the world works! And I can process information just fine! That will be clear, as long as we interpret the results of the exams correctly! When they get here . . ." I add, vaguely.

Mamma and Papà exchange a quick glance.

"And after all, what kind of atrocities can you imagine me finding out about that I haven't already encountered while studying the World Wars, eh?"

"You're already studying the World Wars?" Mamma asks me.

"No, I just went ahead on my own . . . I mean it's not like I can spend a whole month on the Eastern Roman Empire!"

"Al, we're not worried about you," says Mamma. "How can you worry about a son who's getting straight As?"

"In fact! I don't know what else I can do to keep you from worrying . . . Hey! Hey! Mamma!"

"What is it?"

"Gre-e-e-en beans, you know that Casimiro never eats them . . . "

34.

Out here everyone's crazy, it took me a while to figure it out because the Santamaria family is a wonderful place to grow up in, but for that very reason it fails to educate you in the slightest about the dangers of the outside world. After years of study and collecting data, I've come to the conclusion that it is possible to summarize the world as follows: it works just like a high school class year. There are the leaders, groups form, the groups compete, the competition is almost always unfair. In each group there are spies, traitors, double agents, diplomats, and the loyalists willing to subscribe to even the worst causes. Then there are the neutrals, like me, who are held in the lowest esteem but, since they're useful, they're able to prosper in blessed peace. It's a cold war climate, full of false smiles and angry glares by turns, creating an atmosphere of instability that systematically degenerates into periods of crisis marked by small-scale acts of intimidation and the occasional test of strength for trivial reasons. The fact that the maneuverings of a community of adolescents in the throes of hormone storms should so closely resemble the maneuverings of international politics and the ploys of the most refined minds on the planet is dismaying, to say the least. Day by day, I'm increasingly convinced that my undertaking is not only memorable, it's above all necessary, because the discovery that things don't work as well out there as they do in the Santamaria household would even be acceptable if it weren't for the fact that the outside world just won't stop undermining our happiness. We're running headfirst up against a coalition of powers that seem to have it in for us even though we haven't done anything wrong, aside from failing to be rich. We have blindingly obvious evidence, in the fact that after years of searching for a home, we are being told that responsibility for its proper functioning falls under no one's jurisdiction, and the fact that a candy company copied the idea of the chocolate meteorite and now Mamma's chocolate *ciambellone* is stocked in only two cafés, to say nothing of the fact that Papà's office manager has it in for his hair, as if the image of the bus company depended on that, rather than the buses which are at least twenty years old. There's no more time to waste, the plan is ready. I just need to put aside a little money to finance the undertaking and then hope for a miracle: Mamma and Papà going away for a few days.

So, lost in my thoughts, I got out at the wrong stop, now I'm also going to have to take quite a hike to go see Raimondo. Yesterday I remembered that he lives in an apartment building that has the longest, steepest garage ramp in the world, a good hundred feet of cement with a super-rough surface that ends in a sharp elbow turn sprinkled with fine gravel. Many years ago, after trying unsuccessfully all afternoon to break our necks, we found ourselves at the top of the ramp on our high-handlebar banana seat Graziella bikes, and he told me: "We need to take the descent pedaling as hard as we can go, then hit the curve without once touching our brakes." A minute later—just long enough for me to convince him that he'd had an excellent idea and that therefore, according to my theory concerning the direct assumption of responsibility, he ought to be the first one to go down the ramp—he wound up running full speed against the wall. The marks are still there. On Raimondo, not on the wall.

If he only had different parents, Raimondo and I would be great friends. We'd spend all our Saturday afternoons together, we'd have our own gang and pretty girls to go around with us. Instead, in the winter he never goes out because he has to work at the family bar over the Termini train station, and the same thing in the summer because his folks keeping taking over the operation of the bar in Torvaianica. Managing to play together is quite an undertaking, one that always requires a gigantic subterranean organizational machine. As soon as his parents loosen their grip just a bit he hurries over to my house, and I think that means that I'm his best friend, even if then he spends most of his time playing Papà's guitars. He adores the Martin D-28, which, according to my old man, is a guitar that was made to play Elvis songs even though, for the past few years, it's been doing a first-class job of playing Italian artists like Baglioni, Battisti, and Celentano, too. It must be horrible to be born to parents who only think about working. Raimondo isn't even allowed to decide what to wear and, in fact, just like me, he's the favorite butt of his classmates' jokes. Leather loafers, wide-wale corduroy pants, white shirt, and sleeveless wool sweater, that's how you ruin a son. I suggested he talk to them, but he told me it's pointless. His mother has a perennially intimidatory attitude, every word that spills out of her mouth comes with an exclamation mark attached. From "*buongiorno*" to "*buonanotte*," every word seems like either an order or a threat. She's fixated on discipline and the impor-tance of focusing on priorities. One time, Papà asked her if she could drop Raimondo off at our house on a Sunday. The woman said no, Raimondo had to attend mass and then head straight over to the bar to help his father. Papà insisted, it struck him as absurd that the boy couldn't come over at least once to play. She replied that "Playing! isn't! a! priority!"

Luckily Raimondo is in the yard, so I don't have to ring the buzzer and risk having to speak to the old woman on the intercom. Hidden behind the wall, I try to catch his attention.

"Raimondo . . . Raimondo-o-o."

"Hey, Al! What are you doing here?"

He's inspecting the windows of the house and he comes over with a broad smile on his face.

"What are you doing?" I ask him.

"At New Year's I'm going to set off a bang that everyone else can only dream about . . . "

He points toward the section of the garden where he had been sitting. Concealed under a bush are a dozen or so boxes of firecrackers and a shoe box half full of black powder.

"All I have to do is make a hole in the box, insert a fuse . . . and they'll hear it go off all the way to Milan!"

No mentally sound person would do anything of the sort, I have to make him understand what a terrible mistake he's making.

"Raimondo, trust me, you're doing something stupid . . . "

"Why?"

"What do you mean why? If you pack it like that, your super-firecracker will just emit a burst of flame and a cloud of white smoke. If you want black powder to explode, you need to compress it and seal it!"

35.

At the Santamaria home, we've gone back to candlelight dinners. I blame the increase in the price of diesel fuel for the generator. The shadows trembling on the walls like in a horror movie, the liquid wax that sculpts stalactites down the shaft of the candle, the flame over which you can heat up the handle of Vittoria's fork, just for a laugh. I'm the only one who finds it exciting. I ask Papà to tell me a story about the air-raid shelters, Mamma asks me to leave him alone because he's tired, I suggest to Vittoria that she hurry up and eat her meal because otherwise it'll get cold, Papà tells me that if I've heated the handle of her fork again I'll catch it this time. A grim evening. That's another mysterious aspect of the world of adults: they lose their enthusiasm. If I like something, I like it every time. Not them, the magic of dining by candlelight has already begun to pall. And then Mamma is more irritable than anyone else.

"Mario, please, can you keep this table from rocking?"

"Al, stop jiggling your leg."

The furniture in our house seems like so many veterans of the Napoleonic army who are accompanying their general on a last mission. A handful of broken-down old men, sorely tried by the succession of moves, but still staunchly performing their duty. Instead of a medal as their reward, they're given a saint card of the Virgin Mary folded in four under their wounded leg. Then that odious thing happens, and it always confuses me because it reminds me that my happiness isn't enough to make everyone else happy. There's something else in the world, aside from me, and it gets the better of me in the most unpredictable ways.

"There, you see, now it's all ruined!"

While she was reaching for the bread, Mamma burned the sleeve of her sweater on the candle.

"Let me see," Papà says to her.

"What do you want to see . . . I'll just have to throw it away . . . like everything else in this house!"

"Agnese, it's just a sweater, we'll buy you another one."

"Certainly, and now we'll go shopping for sweaters when I don't even have enough money to buy groceries! Do you know that three ounces of salami costs eighteen hundred lire now?"

Vittoria huffs and gets up from the table. Because of the burnt sweater sleeve, I learn that fifteen thousand lire a week isn't enough to do decent grocery shopping, that there was a job as an office worker but my father turned it down, no he didn't turn it down, yes he certainly did turn it down, and that now Papà is running the risk of being fired, it's all on account of his hair, the hair has nothing to do with it, it has everything to do with it, actually, because when you're twenty it's all fun and games, at thirty it's eccentric, but at more than forty it's just pathetic and sad. Then I learn a bunch of other things that tell me a great deal about the exact location of the human soul. I've always wondered about this, the important organs are always well protected, the brain in the skull, the heart in the chest cavity, behind the ribs, but what about the soul? Where is that hidden? I wrote in my human flesh diary that the soul is in the stomach. Because when Mamma said that we'll all wind up out on the street, Papà replied that she could have just married someone else and she retorted that that probably would have been a better idea, and that's when I felt the broken fragments dropping.

I go to see Vittoria who's lying in bed on her back with her legs propped at a ninety-degree angle straight up the wall. I wish I had a counterfeit Walkman to plug up my ears with. As soon as I get there, she heaves an exasperated sigh and turns her head in the opposite direction. Even if it's hard to interpret the gesture as an invitation, I go ahead and sit down beside her. From her headphones blasts protest music at top volume, the piece is "Hula Hoop" by Plastic Bertrand, the protest is obviously against my father. In the other room the argument is spreading like wildfire until it reaches a not-otherwise specified offense dating back to the summer of 1965, I cover my ears with both hands, I sing the theme song to *Judo Boy*, Vittoria puts her hand on my knee. That works even better than a saint card of the Virgin Mary folded in four.

I won't get much sleep tonight, either. I thought I'd solved the economic question by launching Mamma's chocolate *ciambelloni*, but it seems that was not enough. Inflation has hit seventeen percent and the only improvement brought about by the extra earnings is that Agnese and Mario Elvis's periodic diet based on tea and zwieback toast has been upgraded to tea and regular toast. And then, if Papà actually lost his job, disaster would ensue: so long, toast of any kind, so long, sweet home. I'll find a solution, though. I'm a big boy now, and I'm certainly not frightened by the idea of carrying my family on my shoulders.

"Al . . . "

Vittoria is still awake, I'll have to be quieter. Maybe I should start studying economics. If I really worked hard, in just a couple of years I could become an expert and launch the family into daring financial maneuvers.

"A-a-al . . . "

She has superhearing, just like Mamma. The problem is that we need an immediate solution, in another couple of years we could already be living on the street. It's a good thing I have broad shoulders, these problems would be enough to crush another young man with less personality.

"Al . . . don't move the bed!"

"Just for tonight."

"No, you need to get used to sleeping alone."

"I *am* alone! There's a curtain between us!"

"Only for tonight, then starting tomorrow you'll put your bed back on the opposite side of the room!"

In my biography, they'll write: "Because of his family's

economic problems, Al was forced to grow up in a hurry. A carefree youth was a luxury he was never able to afford."

36.

"Well, how is Raimondo?" Papà asks me.

"He doesn't have anything serious wrong with him, but he's grounded. He's not allowed to receive visitors."

"Grounded even in the hospital? They could have at least waited for him to get home!"

"Did he say anything to you? When are they going to release him?" Mamma asks.

"I don't know, I waved to him from the hallway and all he said to me was 'All good!'"

Truth be told, Raimondo gave me a thumbs-up and told me: "Super-firecracker test went okay!" but I don't really want my folks to know he's even more of a moron than they already think.

"Even psychological torture . . . they only let him see his friends from the hallway."

"Mario, he could have been killed. What kind of games are these, I swear I don't understand kids these days . . . "

This is one of the last generations of adults who don't understand the games kids play, perhaps the last one who can bust our chops with the usual refrain about how we don't know how to have fun, all they needed was a kite and a little wind. Soon my generation will take the helm, the generation of teenagers who fried their neurons in front of a television set with endless matches of Pong, who spent hours on the beach in the hot sun playing with a Zoom sliding ball on strings, holding our arms out wide to make that oval plastic rugby ball slide from one end of the strings to the other for no good reason, who experimented with the hallucinatory effect of the colored keys and electronic sounds of the Simon game. A kid from the early eighties will look at the absurd games of the children of the new millennium and if he even knows the meaning of shame, he'll say nothing.

With the long walk to and from the hospital, my tongue is as dry as a piece of cardboard. Now I go over and lie down on the sink, with my mouth open under the water faucet like Sylvester the Cat when he bites into a chili pepper instead of Tweety Bird.

"Al, Vittoria's inside with a friend . . . leave them alone, they'll be going away soon."

"I'll just go in for a second to get a glass of water and then I'll come right back out."

I go in and take a seat in the living room.

"Ciao," I say to Vittoria and her friend.

"Al, this is Giancarlo."

His hair is long, he has a messianic beard, his jeans are torn, he wears a long white smock of a shirt that hangs down to his knees, and a colorful headband across his forehead. When I say hello to him, he replies by holding his fingers up in a V sign. Unfortunately for him, it does him no good to smile at me because I already dislike him intensely, and I'm not about to change my mind just because I happen to find out that he's intelligent, likable, a blood donor and a war hero. I'm not jealous of my sister, at all, she'd be welcome to date Pol Pot as long as she refrained from bringing him home. The point is that I know how it's going to turn out with these boyfriends she chooses without consulting me, they are just playing, and she's not, and then I'm the one who's going to have to put up with months and months of depression and hysteria. I jam two fingers down my throat to make it clear to Vittoria just how disappointed I am and go off into the kitchen. She pretends to ignore me.

"Do you want something to eat?" she asks Giancarlo.

"Yes, Duck," he replies.

I retrace my steps. I stick my head in and silently pray I misheard.

"He calls me Bucking Duck . . . it's my Indian name."

What could be more obvious? The most normal thing in the world is a girl from the outskirts of Rome with an Indian name.

"Are you one of those people who were rooting for the cowboys to win? If you knew the story of the Indians, you wouldn't turn up your nose like that . . . " Giancarlo butts in.

Here's another reader of *Tex Willer* who thinks he's an authoritative expert on the subject. Vittoria realizes that this is going to end badly, but still she has no way to stop me.

"I've studied it, as a matter of fact, and I call them Native Americans, not Indians, a term that actually applies to the inhabitants of India, obviously."

"Which means, for instance, that you know all about Sitting Bull and the Apaches?"

"A little something. For instance, I know that Sitting Bull wasn't an Apache at all, but a Hunkpapa Sioux, that the correct translation of his name would be Sitting Bison, since bulls and cows weren't found in America prior to the arrival of the Europeans. Oh, and actually the name Apache itself is a misnomer because the tribe's real name was . . . "

"All right, all right, I give up. You know the history," he interrupts me, clearly annoyed.

"Al, stop acting like a smarty-pants with Solitary Puma."

Here's a nice way of clarifying matters: he is the super-cool Solitary Puma and she is the silly Bucking Duck. Puma tries to change the subject.

"The renovation is inching along here, isn't it?"

Vittoria hastens to justify the situation.

"We're getting close, the bricklayers should be here any day now."

"Wait, for real?" I ask her.

"Al, don't be a pain in the ass . . . I'm sick of being made to look like a fool in front of my friends!" she whispers to me.

Even considering the issue of what that native of the Garbatella thinks of us strikes me as absurd, but there is no doubt that the situation needs to be resolved. Already, Papà has contacted the bricklayers and masons three times, only to cancel the work at the last second. First it was because he had to get the car fixed after Vittoria crashed it during her first driving lesson, then to pay the dentist who was about to take us to court, and then finally because we had to buy a new refrigerator and washing machine after they refused to accept the last jury-rigged repair and simply gave up the ghost after being starved for too long of spare parts.

The two of them are going out to a party. Vittoria has put on an oversized white T-shirt with shoulder pads, red high heels, and leg warmers like the ones Olivia Newton John popularized. The puma isn't about to let that pass, he criticizes her apparel as "a modern young person's uniform." Instead it was perfect. While she was getting ready, I couldn't resist, and I slipped a note into her jacket pocket: "You are the prettiest Santamaria there ever was. (So try not to pollute your genetic patrimony, thanks.)"

My classmates went to a party, too, but they only invited me at the last minute, hoping I wouldn't go. I decided to make them happy. In order to keep from needlessly worrying Agnese and Mario Elvis I put on my wide-wale corduroy pants, my wannabe Clarks desert boots, and the sweater without reindeer, and I went to the bus stop. As usual, I'll ride from one end of the route to the other a few times, I'll jot down brilliant ideas in my human flesh diary, and then I'll go home and tell a bunch of amusing episodes that took place in my imagination. Turns out my mother's prediction that I'd have lots of friends in high school was wrong, as was my father's prediction, though he'd moved up the happy event to middle school. My classmates are all fifteen or sixteen years old, they think about nothing but motor scooters and girls, and if you don't have one or the other, you're cut out. Raul said that the motor scooter is not a problem, he can get me one cheap, then it's just a matter of reissuing the registration and paying for insurance. Maybe I'll be able to afford it in a couple of months, we'll see, in any case chasing after my classmates would be a pointless, endless pursuit. Even if I had a motor scooter, they'd treat me like a penniless wretch because I don't own a jacket with goose down filling, and once I'd bought that they'd keep it up because I can't show off a portable stereo in my room with two turntables and at least four stacks of cassettes. Every so often I got the impression that there were also normal people in their ranks, like Federico and Luca, who had started to devise a plan to attempt an expedition from Rome to Stockholm by motor scooter. But their enthusiasm waned day after day, and in the end it became clear that the purpose of the trip was to pick up chicks and in fact, they turned to the simpler solution of making a short film so they could stage auditions with all the girls in the school. I'm interested in girls myself, but they seem to be suffering from some kind of illness, the dating disease. I've got a date with this one, I've got a date with that one, oh how I wish I could get a date with this other one. I've had a date, I was excited, I was expecting who knows what, but after a couple of hours at the park I was bored out of my skull. I wanted to play, but that girl must have had low blood pressure or something because every five minutes she was lying down on the grass.

37.

No one can stop the Santamaria family. Mamma's baking *ciambelloni*, Papà has started getting overtime again, and I've started selling classwork. Latin, Greek, and Italian at five thousand lire apiece, math at seventy-five hundred because the math teacher likes to use guerrilla techniques and the margin of risk is greater. The damned old woman paces continuously up and down the aisles between desks, whips around without warning, then sometimes she pretends that she's reading her gradebook with her head bowed, but actually she's got her eyes focused on the class the whole time. There are even times, and in those cases there really is nothing you can do, when she sits behind her desk on the raised dais, motionless, wearing sunglasses. There are other strong students you could ask for help, but I'm the only one who's never been caught. Their stratagems are limited to pens stuffed with notes and the dangling cableway with invisible nylon fishing line. I have one and one alone, and it's infallible: finish the quiz in the first twenty minutes, when most of the kids are still struggling with the translation of the first sentence in the text or the first basic steps of the equation, at a point when no teacher would ever suspect you might have finished and therefore the monitoring is far looser. It was important never to give in to the temptation to hand in my paper before the time was up, that way my teachers might have an idea that I'm a good student but they'd never dream just how fast I actually am. With this approach I've saved up 250,000 lire in the first quarter alone. Last year I'd doubled my capital by investing the whole sum in phone tokens just a few months before their value rose from fifty to a hundred lire; unfortunately, though, given the initial investment, I only made 20,000 lire. Until just a few weeks ago, I was hoping to take advantage of the tensions between the United States and Iran by investing all my money in gold, but now a much tastier opportunity has presented itself. Since we're in Italy, the sex education of unprepared female students was entrusted to two sophomore girls who offered special accelerated courses. The advice offered by the two tutors fell along these lines: five days before and ten days after your period, you can have sex without contraceptives and not worry about it, always keep your panties on when you're jerking off a boy because sperm can cover distance, if by mischance someone happens to come inside you, climb up on a chair and jump off with your legs spread, repeat at least fifteen times. Then a senior girl got knocked up by a recidivist in her class, so-called because he had already gotten a girl pregnant two years earlier, the general level of trust in the two experts collapsed, and I decided to sink my funds into condoms. Ninety-five percent of the daring fornicators in this school would be willing to pay three times their market price just to avoid the embarrassment of having to buy them at the pharmacy.

I have some excellent prospects of making money, but first I need to stop wasting money on Roberta, my ex from elementary school. One day she said: "Help me with this quiz, I haven't studied at all," and I replied: "Five thousand lire," and she replied: "I don't have enough money, I'll give you two packs of cigarettes," "I don't smoke," "I'll let you see my tits. With my bra on, though." Every time I tell myself this is the last time, that I'm a dodo, that I should think about my family's welfare, that I don't need to pay to see her tits because I can see Vittoria's whenever I want, but the minute Roberta takes me by the hand and takes me into the bathroom, I lose all self-control. What I need is a girlfriend, someone whose tits I can look at for free, but after the misguided episode of the reenactment of the partisan bomb against the Nazi troops on Via Rasella, I sort of became the laughingstock of the school. At recess everyone locks themselves in the bathroom to do forbidden things, and so do I. They smoke and neck, I get out my toy soldiers and organize blitzkrieg battles on the toilet lid. Since there's never much time, I have to opt for something quick, the failed American raid on the embassy in Tehran, for instance, or the partisan attack on Via Rasella, as I mentioned, the kind of thing you can pull off in a few minutes, just enough time to line up two columns of German soldiers and then blow them away with an explosion. There were those that decided however that I'd been spending too much time locked in that stall and so they climbed up to look over, thinking they'd catch me doing who knows what. I doubt that there's even one of the three hundred students in my high school who hasn't been informed of my embarrassing little foible. If I haven't been completely marginalized and if anyone still speaks to me at all, it's only because of how useful I am for class assignments and quizzes. I don't really mind it, I have little enough in common with my immature fellow students.

"Okay, that's enough, you win . . . " I say.

"Al, we don't stop playing the game just because you're losing!" Vittoria objects.

"But after all, you've already won!"

"You drove me crazy for an hour so I'd play with you, and then you just quit the game like that . . . You're a poor loser!"

"Don't use that word!" I say and run out of the living room.

"Los-er!"

"Don't say it!" I shout and lock myself in the bathroom.

"Almerico is a poor loser!" she says to me through the keyhole.

"That's enou-ou-ough!"

God I hate her when she's like this. So, I'm a poor loser, what about it? What do you do, shatter the need for family harmony of a fourteen-year-old? Since when does growing up mean learning how to lose? Have we lost our minds?

No one will leave me alone! I live to hear people tell me: "Good job, Al." So? What's wrong with that? "Nice dive, good job, Al," "Nice drawing, good job, Al." Now, that's the life!

"Mamma, Al's crying because he lost at Monopoly!" says the spy.

I blame Papà and that nonsense about how you're never supposed to cheat. Certainly, if you cheat and then you have scruples about it, Papà's right, it's best to lose, but I enjoy the victory all the same, and anyway I sleep like a rock every night! No one understands me. They turn it into a question of right/wrong while here it's a matter of beautiful/ugly. Cheating a little helps us to make our days, our lives, the world more beautiful.

"Aesthetics is the basis of morality!" I shout.

"Mamma, Al has lost his mind . . . "

38.

After a couple of weeks of blessed peace the powers that be started attacking us again. Some kingpin somewhere decided that soon the 170 line, the bus route that Papà drives, will be eliminated because it has too few passengers. After such a long time, Mamma had another of her collapses of self-esteem, she's afraid that along with the bus route they might eliminate the jobs, and I understand her fear, Mario Elvis is getting old and if they fire him he can forget about his space program.

"Get that nasty thing off your face," Vittoria tells me as I gaze into the mirror, admiring the development of my secondary sexual characteristics.

"Quite a mustache, eh? It covers the whole lip, at this point," I reply.

"It looks like a hamster's belly."

"Nice mustache, right Mamma?"

"Nice nice nice, soft soft soft . . . " says Agnese teetering in my direction.

Now we'll give her a half hour of the Princess of Monaco Treatment to remind her that she's a wonderful pastry chef and a woman of great taste.

How do you increase the volume of passengers on a bus route? How do you persuade people that are used to driving or taking the metro to hop onto an old-fashioned, uncomfortable, and noisy means of conveyance? To find out more I decided to stake out a strategic location. The end of the line is ideally placed, right across from the post office. But it's just that not even fifty yards away, there's also a metro station. This is the real problem: the competition. I take note of the fact that the workers at the ministry all leave the office at 5:30 P.M. sharp. There are hundreds of office workers, but they all head straight for their parked cars and for the metro, there are only six of them who board the 170 bus. Unfortunately, if I want to convince adults to change their habits, I almost always have to rely on a falsehood. As it happens, I just happen to have one in mind. I walk out of the metro station and stride up the line of employees running late, the diehards who leave the office at 5:40 P.M.

"The metro's not running," I say.

"What? The metro's not running?" a guy asks me, clearly exasperated.

I throw my arms wide in helpless resignation.

"Yeah, and it looks like it's going to take a while, I waited half an hour and I'm still here."

In an instant, the rumor spreads. "Not running?" "Again?" they ask.

"And now what are we supposed to do?"

That was the question I was waiting for.

"Well, anyone who needs to go downtown can take the 170."

"Oh great . . . and how long is that going to take?"

"No, it's actually fast, the end of the line is right here and the bus is usually empty. Whereas the metro always pulls in packed with passengers."

"But does it go by Via Cavallari?"

"Certainly, you just get out at Via Ignazi and from there it's a short walk."

So I head off toward the bus stop with fifteen or so people trailing along behind me while the rumor spreads and the bad news causes a domino effect, spreading dismay among dozens of office workers.

"What a pleasant surprise. Are you going to take a ride with me?" Papà asks me.

"Yes, Papà. But you need to go right away," I whisper to him.

"I'm supposed to leave in five minutes."

"No, Papà, right away . . . trust me."

"Why?"

There, that's the look I hate. He thinks that I must necessarily have done something wrong.

"All right, I convinced them to take the bus by resorting to a ploy. But now you'd better not disappoint them. So leave right away."

Mario Elvis starts the engine. The passengers' sigh of relief convinces him that he's made the right choice. He takes on a couple more late arrivals, pulls the lever that works the hydraulic pistons to shut the doors, and with a whoosh of air and three metallic clangs he seals the still doubtful office workers into the vehicle. We pull out.

"If I ask you to do something, will you promise to do it without a lot of objections?" I ask him.

"That depends."

"Yes or no."

"No, Al."

"Instead, say yes . . . and sing."

"Sing? Why should I sing?"

"It's a long story, but you just sing."

"I can't sing while I'm driving my bus."

"Papà, these are laws of the market. The 170 route can't

compete with the metro. You need to offer an extra service. Just like with laundry soaps. When you don't have anything better than the competition, then you need to stuff a baseball card or a soccer card inside the box or you add a lemon scent, and watch your sales skyrocket. It's the mechanism of perceived differentiation. What's more, you need to consider the importance of consumer loyalty. If you sing well, they'll come back."

"I don't understand a thing . . . "

"What the devil good is it to have a genius son if you never listen to a thing he says?"

I go and take a stance in the middle of the bus, ready to launch a series of messages. I cross my arms over my chest, meaning: I'm all alone in the world, no one understands me, and all I have on earth is what I'm hugging at this very moment. I clamp my mouth shut, letting my lower lip protrude, which means: I'm not going to cry because I'm a big boy now. I look at Mario Elvis and then I turn away the minute he returns my glance, which means: I'm mad at you and I don't want to meet your gaze because that would suggest we're on the same wavelength, decidedly out of the question as has already been made clear by the arms crossed over my chest. Papà gives me another glance in his rearview mirror, again I pretend not to notice, and so he starts singing. He sings and looks into the rearview mirror. He starts singing a little louder and when he sees that people are starting to look at him, he gets shy and begins whistling instead.

"What's he doing? Is he singing?" asks a little old lady.

"Yes, they call him Elvis . . . he's an outstanding singer, I take the 170 just to listen to him," I tell her.

A few passengers smile, others exchange puzzled glances. A few gentlemen comment on his appearance but about his voice there are no complaints.

"Well, as far as his talent, he's talented," says an office worker in his early fifties.

"I've heard that there are people who take this bus just to listen to him," a lady replies to him.

Three stops short of the end of the line, Mario Elvis has broken the ice.

"And this one's for you, my dear lady with the grocery bags! *Are you lonesome toni-i-ight!*"

Being the genius of the family is a big responsibility. You need to keep an eye on everything, show that you're always a strong and authoritative leader. It also takes real sensitivity to skillfully pilot the inevitable handover of power between parents and prodigy son, leaving them with the sensation that they're still in command. My memorable project is finally getting in gear, I read as much in Papà's eyes at the dinner table. He told Mamma everything and we had a cheerful meal. "Let's just hope it lasts," she said, immediately finding the reassurance that she had been looking for. Yes, it'll last, because I'm going to lurk outside the metro station three times a day for a week, I'll bring new customers for the 170 bus, and in the course of a month, in part thanks to word of mouth, I hope to have a reassuring number of loyal customers. I stretch out a foot and slip it under the sheets, against Vittoria's butt cheeks. She doesn't say anything because she's too busy, she's been fooling around all day with her transistor radio in search of her favorite songs. As soon as she finds one, she pushes the "Rec" button on Papà's tape recorder and captures it on tape. After a day's searching she has "Tunnel of Love" by Dire Straits, without the beginning and with Mamma coughing toward the end, and "Enola Gay" by OMD, with me coughing on the first chorus, plus me coughing again and her yelling at me over the second chorus. Now she's looking for "Johnny and Mary" by Robert Palmer, and I can already feel an irritating scratching in my throat.

39.

I just adore the day they give out report cards, I have top grades in everything except for history, a subject in which I got a B+ because of an argument with the teacher. She didn't consider pertinent my analysis of the Italian Middle Ages that established a link of continuity between the establishment of fiefs and the ultimate influence of the Christian Democrats in southern Italy and the Lockheed scandal. Actually, doing well in school is easy, all you have to do is memorize and regurgitate, remember all the dates—which always makes a strong impression on your teachers—and refrain from any personal comment or analysis. I dedicate less than a minute to reading the report card and then I go back to reading the janitor's newspaper. As a reflection of the basic anomaly of the system, the janitor buys a different newspaper every day, to keep an open mind, he says, while in the principal's office all you can find is the *Corriere dello Sport* and the *Guerin Sportivo*. The Italian stock market has risen 2 percent, a miserable increase compared to the double-digit growth in my condom sales. Still, I'm not satisfied, it's time to start diversifying my investments. I could establish an agreement with all the students in all five homerooms of the sophomore year for an exclusive purchase of their Ancient Greek dictionaries. That would allow me to corner the market and impose a much higher price on resale of those used textbooks. Only then I'd have to wait until September to earn back my money, and I can't afford that. Maybe I'm taking the wrong approach. Civil and well-mannered systems aren't going to lead to anything good. Every time I read an article about Renato Vallanzasca, I'm astonished at the vein of benevolent approval of certain journalists. They refer to him as "*il bel René*," news reporting slides into the realm of hagiography. I can certainly understand that in a country largely populated by squalid bribers and tax evaders, even a common bandit like him can start to look like a romantic personage, and the moral of the story is that due to an excess of good manners, I've chosen an excessively tortuous path. A brief criminal career might help to give my undertaking a jump start, as well as adding a picturesque note to my life story. I try to imagine. "*Il bell'Al . . .* " and things have already taken a bad turn. Compared with "*il bel René,*" it really sounds pathetic. "Handsome Al," it just doesn't cut it. How about "Brilliant Al . . . " Even worse. "Amiable Al . . . " Much better. "Amiable Al, the most extraordinary genius of the twentieth century, had a troubled childhood. Forced by events beyond his control, he devoted himself to a life of crime, pulling off a number of daring capers that are still studied today by detectives and police around the world."

"How did it go?" Roberta asks me, with no idea of who she's talking to.

"Excellent, top grades in all subjects. How about you?"

"Fine, except for philosophy. I'm going to have to do a makeup class in the second quarter."

"How hard could it be . . . "

"It could be plenty hard, seeing that I haven't even cracked the book yet."

"Wait, you have Balestra, too, right? Don't worry, he always asks the same things, at the very most you'll only have to study twenty pages or so."

"Sure, but which pages? Will you help me? Can we make the usual trade?"

"E-e-eh, I don't think that'll be enough . . . I have to reread the whole book, type up the important passages, make a well-thought-out summary."

"I'll let you lift my skirt."

"If this were the first quarter, that would be a reasonable exchange, but since this is the second quarter, at least two oral exams, both of them crucial . . . "

The amiable Al was cold, pitiless, calculating.

*

Now what should I write in my human flesh diary? "Never pull surprises on adults"? What's the lesson? If the Santamaria family really lacks nothing, then why did Papà feel the need to kiss that woman? There shouldn't be people in the world with tits bigger than Mamma's.

"Mario Elvis is tired."

"I know that he's tired! But what's that supposed to mean? Mamma and I are tired too, but we don't go around kissing women with mega-tits!"

"Mario Elvis isn't to blame, it's that woman's fault. She wants to break up our family."

"You're right, Casimiro, it's her fault. But now what do we do?"

"You could try explaining it to Agnese. Not directly . . . the way you know how to do, in other words."

"Maybe I could try telling Vittoria first."

"Vittoria is going through one of her bad moments."

"Right, so as usual I'm going to have to take care of it myself."

"It's the curse of all geniuses."

I need to act with great cunning. What I need is a sophisticated plan, something subtle and psychological that can make that woman cease and desist immediately. The tip of my nose is starting to itch, mucus is collecting in my throat, my eyesight is turning watery, I put a hand on Casimiro's shoulder because this was the last thing he expected, he'd gone to the garage to show his report card to Mario Elvis and talk over a few changes in the schedule of the 170. Witnessing a scene like that was too hard a blow, but crying won't do any good.

"Hey, youngster . . . everything all right?" asks a gentleman.

Wait, now what's going on? Is there a youngster in trouble? But where? Ah, he was talking to me.

40.

Casimiro is right. He does his best when he's around us, he acts more and more confident, with a beaming smile, but Papà is exhausted. The idea that his son is a genius must be very comforting, but then you need to take into consideration Vittoria's idiotic escapades, and the effect is neutralized. A tired man can make a mistake, he might feel the need for a distraction, I get that, it's just that everything always happens at the same time, the coup d'état of Antonio Tejero, the P2 Masonic lodge, the decision to find everyone innocent of the Piazza Fontana bombing, the attempted assassination of the pope, Rino Gaetano's poor driving, the Israelis' Operation Babylon, and the collapse of the stock market. And then this overwhelming impulse to tell Mamma that I'd seen Papà kiss the woman with the huge tits, but the point is, I really wouldn't know exactly how to do it. "You know, she had a really prominent bosom, she was quite pneumatic around the chest area, there was quite an imposing accumulation of fatty tissue, you know the solar X-ray photon fluxes around Venus?"

"Mamma! Al isn't feeling good!"

"Bobby Sands and Bob Marley are dead . . . The Grey Wolves on the other hand are alive and well and so is General Jaruzelski and the women with all those . . . "

"Al, what's happening to you? Speak to me!" Agnese shouts at me.

"We're in danger. The world is full of bad people, Gelli, Moretti, Ali Ağca, the women who have . . . "

"Have what, Al?"

"The hidden powers that lurk in the Italian parliament, in the senate, under the scanty blouses . . . "

"Tell Mamma, what is it?"

"THERE'S A GLOBAL THREAT OF LESS THAN AGILE WOMEN!"

*

Papà says that choruses are killing good music. The same thing goes for people's lives. The endless refrain of crisis/calm lady doctor is killing me. I'd hoped that as I grew up, I'd get rid of her, but here I am, back again. The hallway with the hardwood floor, the darker parquet that always creaks, the painting with the basket full of grapes and the dead fish, the little black leather armchairs, the lady doctor with the cigarette in one hand smiling at us from the door. An elbow pokes me in the ribs.

"Al, get your hand out of your pants," Mamma whispers to me.

Al, don't do this, Al, don't do that. Now what is it!

"Stop touching your peepee . . . "

Oh, is that what I was doing? I hadn't even noticed. So I can't even give myself a little squeeze in front of other people, heaven forbid. My nose, fine, my ears, sure, but not that, it's not a good thing to remind other people that you've got exactly the same equipment as every other male on the planet. God, I'm so out of sorts today.

"Well, Al, how are you doing? Is it going better with your classmates?" the lady doctor asks me the minute I sit down.

"Na."

"Why not?"

"Whan Ah'm wath tham I faal laka Ah'm all alana."

"And when you're alone, on the other hand, how do you feel?"

"A hava lats af naca thangs ta thank abaat. Tama flaas."

"And exactly what nice things do you think about?"

"How much will you pay me if I tell you?" I ask.

"You want to be paid? Wouldn't you rather just tell me because we're friends?"

"Wha af caarsa . . . "

41.

"Al, how are you?" I'm not like Vittoria myself, if every-one expresses interest in me, I enjoy it immensely. But I keep from saying it, instead I say: "A little better," "oh all right I guess," because the family has adhered again around my minor malaise. Mario Elvis and Agnese smile constantly, we play together, at the dinner table we talk about the world, about life, and about how magnificently harmonious and astonishing everything is. I'll be "all right I guess" for at least the next ten years. I'm really just fine, the role of shadow paterfamilias is a burden but I can't complain. I think about what my life would be like if I were the shadow paterfamilias of Raimondo's family. A brother who doesn't know how to put together firecrackers, a pair of parents who care only about how to increase sales of sandwiches. Or of Flaminia's family, which we call the "Oh, Well, We" family, people who gauge the quality of life according to engine displacement or linear inches. Mario Elvis and Agnese take it as a game, they talk with the parents and they say: "We bought a Prinz," and the parents say: "Oh, well, we bought a Simca 1100"; "We had mussels for dinner," "Oh, well, we had mussels, and they were THIS big!" Things wouldn't be much better for me with Roberta's family, all her parents talk about are the Lions Club dinners, the Lions Club meetings, and the people they've met at the Lions Club dinners and Lions Club meet-ings. If I think about it, I realize how miserable the founda-tion is that we're starting off from, and just how long my plan might take.

Even if I've taken great care not to talk about matters of politics, domestic and international, with the calm lady doc-tor, Agnese and Mario Elvis have once again banished televi-sion, magazines, and newspapers from my diet. In order to satisfy my thirst for knowledge and prevent nocturnal raids on the newsstand or the local dumpsters, we watch the evening news together. A speech by Reagan offers a demonstration of the greatness of a nation where any citizen, I mean literally *any* citizen, can reach the highest office in the land; the recovery of John Paul II is a startling demonstration of the triumph of good over evil. Even Vittoria, who is forming her own political ideas on the general principle of I Hate Everyone, goes along with the game, nods, reassures me, tells me about how kind an old gentleman was, how he followed her for half a mile to give her back the wallet that she dropped on the metro. I pretend to believe the stories they tell me and to accept the lady doctor's recommendations. I feel almost sorry for them because of how antiquated they are, they prevent me from reading the newspapers when we're in the 1980s and all I need is a couple of phone tokens to make use of modern technology and listen to the news report over the telephone.

Now I have to operate on two separate fronts. First: get the woman with the overabundance of tits out of the way; second: distract Mamma and Papà from my passing malaises by introducing them to a girlfriend. I had no difficulty solving point one. I wrote the homewrecker a nice love letter, all in block capital letters to make it look more grown-up, and in it I deployed my cunning by praising the beauty of her eyes. That ought to work on someone like her, who must have a hard time even getting her oculist to look her in the face. I signed the letter "A bachelor admirer" and, just to convey the point that I'm not a bachelor because of any lack of expertise, I scented the paper with two strokes of my stick deodorant as a crowning touch. If I mail one of these letters every week, her relationship with Papà ought to break down in the course of a couple of months, tops, and then we'll be united just like before. For the second point I've enlisted Roberta, with whom

I already have a well established commercial relationship. In exchange for a weekly house call from her, I've indebted myself until graduation.

We stroll hand in hand in the backyard, talking about this and that as we proceed toward the living room window. I don't need to look inside. I can just imagine my folks, they must be peeking out from behind the curtains, in the shadows, modestly proud of their son's success. Roberta smiles and waves with one hand toward the slightly overestimulated parents: they're in front of the curtains, in full daylight, giggling and gesticulating without so much as a crumb of style.

"Don't you think we ought to kiss?" she whispers to me.

"You think?"

"If you ask me, if we don't, your folks won't fall for it."

"All right then."

"But keep your hands to yourself or your mother will think I'm a slut."

She takes me under the tree. She waits. I wait.

"Wait, what is this, your first kiss?" she asks me.

"What do you think?"

What does this girl think, to talk like that? I must have kissed at least a dozen girls. Nicoletta, Claudia, Giovanna, Paola, Serena, Isabella, who can even remember the names? I have problems with the subsequent steps, all right, but where the courtship and kissing are concerned, I'm unbeatable. We sit down on the grass because Roberta thinks that's more romantic, I pop a mint into my mouth because she says that's what you're supposed to do, I put my hands around her back but I don't squeeze her too close on account of that whole slut thing.

"You're supposed to say something nice to me first," she adds, as a last observation.

"You're my favorite business partner."

She seems resigned, and I make a mental note of this

aspect, which must be the distinctive expression of female mammals about to agree to intercourse. She shuts her eyes, I keep mine just slightly open because I don't want to miss so much as a single instant of everything that's happening. Our lips touch, everything is going fine until I feel something pressing against my teeth. Roberta is pushing with the tip of her tongue, trying to pry my mouth open. Instinctively, it strikes me that the right thing to do is fight back, so I clamp my lips shut and push her tongue away, but then I have a flash of intuition: this is a kiss like in the movies! I decide to open my mouth, but I'm just a second too late, and her voice echoes through my cheeks: "Hey, idiot, are you going to open your mouth or not?"

42.

There has to be a good reason that Galileo Galilei took forty years to perfect his telescope, and in fact he was no doubt distracted continuously by his family problems. I was feeling fine out in the backyard, stretched out in the shade of the geraniums, when Vittoria showed up and told me to go to my room because she had to have a talk with Giancarlo. To get ready for her little chat she spent an hour and a half in the bathroom, because when she wants to fight with a boyfriend she needs to feel pretty, it gives her an added layer of confidence. Unfortunately the Eighties have gotten off on the wrong foot, to see that we only need listen to the words of the designers. An actual quote: "Clothing is a symbol of daring and revolt with which women give themselves the gift of a break in which to amuse and enjoy themselves, to don the costume of the character they like best. Clothing is the joy of inventing oneself." And so, with red ballet flats on her feet, pastel pink trousers, and a blouse that matches the shoes, Vittoria has just stepped into the costume of a character afflicted with red-green color blindness whom I've never met, and has invented herself with glitter on her cheeks and curly hair. The very minimum required for an argument that's *with it*.

I wanted to eavesdrop on the conversation but the voices are so loud that I can perfectly overhear everything they're talking about from the desk in my bedroom, while with the left lobe of my brain I study, with the right lobe I think about my memorable exploit, and with the frontal lobe I plan a launching ramp for my toy cars. Vittoria has a decisive attitude, a firm and authoritarian tone that, since it's completely alien to her, requires an excessively elevated outlay of energy. I'm willing to bet money, in two minutes she's going to burst into tears.

"You told me this would be forever!" she says.

"I never said any such thing, I told you over and over again that I don't want anything serious!" Giancarlo answers her.

Did he say that over and over again? No.

"Wrong, handsome!" I shout from my room. "What you said is: 'I've never wanted to be tied down before but now I sense that something has changed, when I'm with you it's as if I *was* . . . '—using the wrong form of the verb, your trademark—'on another planet.' That's what you said, handsome!"

"Mind your own business, retard!" he shouts at me.

I run to the window because that sound of a wet rag slammed onto the floor can only be a slap in the face. Hidden behind the curtain, I peek out to see Giancarlo walking briskly away, hand on his cheek, Vittoria standing with her right arm still extended. The super-cool puma just took a smack in the face from a duck. My sister came to my defense! Well, after that, what do you want, regrets are just part of her nature, and after begging him to come back, she returns home in a fury.

"You need to mind your own business!"

"This *is* my business."

"No, Al. Things between me and Giancarlo don't concern you!"

"Yes, they do, they concern me, because the two of you fight every day, you're always on edge, you're rude to me, and we haven't played in months!"

"I'm sick and tired, you're all on me constantly! I can't stand you anymore, I can't stand this house without walls . . . I'm going to get a job and go and live in a real house!"

"This is the real house, the promised home . . . "

"There is no promised home! That was just a game! This is the only house we could afford, it's certainly not our dream house! Why don't you get it?"

Actually, though, I understand perfectly. Exactly as I was just trying to explain to her, Giancarlo isn't the right guy for her, he makes her too intractable. Vittoria is still too young to find a boyfriend all on her own, she likes extravagant, unpredictable types, and then she complains that they behave extravagantly and unpredictably. On the other hand, I can understand that taking my advice makes her dismiss lots of young men who, no matter how dumb they might be, are still perfectly nice people. Here's what she needs, a calm, mature young man who knows how to restore her love of play. In the meantime, I'm going to have to bring back her secret admirer because I can't stand looking at her by the window waiting for the return of the antisocial feline.

43.

Vittoria spends hours on end in the phone booth. A pile of phone tokens on top of the phone, her finger twisting the wire. Papà says that he can't understand how she can stay in there for so long, it isn't good for her, the telephone shouldn't take the place of social relationships. In his day, they only used the phone for important calls.

"But why don't they just see each other and explain everything face-to-face?" he asks Agnese.

"You'll see, she'll get over it . . . "

"This is what I don't like about technology, it makes relationships so much colder . . . all these young people locked up in their rooms or in phone booths whispering—some progress."

"We would have done the same thing when we were young."

"Are you kidding, we saw each other, we'd walk hours just to meet. This generation, on the other hand, always attached to the telephone . . . if you ask me, they're going to turn into morons. A young person should be out in the open air."

"That girl might even go out too much . . . Vittoria, that's enough!" Mamma tells her.

"Just another minu-u-ute."

This morning is one worth framing. Luckily, our moods aren't timed to match the hours of the stores, so we aren't the kind of people who find Sundays boring. Agnese is sunbathing, Mario Elvis mows the lawn, I work on processing toxic waste and the welfare of the planet.

"Al, look what you're doing to that hand . . . " Papà says to me.

"I'll wash it later."

I'd be crazy to, this is precious stuff that needs to go straight to my brain. When the time is right, all these notes will prove fundamental. Addendum to the Plan for Salvation drawn up by Almerico Santamaria, age 14. Draft VIII. In order to guide the planet toward a more ethical and enlightened form of development, we must call for the adoption of the Regulatory Criterion by the legislative body of every government. The Regulatory Criterion is designed to determine the quality of all laws, proposals, initiatives, and projects, in the fields of finance, energy, society, and diplomacy, and it consists of three simple questions: 1) Does it contribute to the physical development of children? 2) Does it contribute to the mental development of children? 3) Does it contribute to the happiness of children? Any law, proposal, initiative, or project that fails to respond affirmatively to these questions will be considered contrary to the interests of mankind. I feel ready, the outlines of the undertaking are increasingly clearly defined, the money I have set aside is more than sufficient, now all I need is for Mamma and Papà to clear out and let me work uninterrupted for at least a day. In twenty-four hours I can get this done, it won't be easy but there's no point in hoping that the most homebody parents on earth will give me a broader margin to work with.

Vittoria goes over to Mamma. They sit down face-to-face to paint each other's toenails, near them is a table with four bottles of citron juice and a transistor radio that changes stations according to the whims of the wind, with me and Papà in the foreground: he's amusing himself by whipping the electric lawnmower as if it were an ox harnessed to a plow, while I'm creatively incinerating the brushwood. If I wanted to send one of those postcards reading "Hello from . . . " that are so fashionable these days, that's the picture it would have.

"Can we burn the brushwood without having to call the firemen?"

"It's all perfectly under control, Papà." And I toss a balloon full of alcohol onto the burning grass. "Napalm effect!"

Papà walks toward me, gives me a kiss on the forehead.

"What would I do without you?" he says, while he pulls the old gag of the out-of-control lawnmower that drags him away.

This is a hostile act. An unmistakable aggression. I had to call Casimiro because I couldn't even believe it was really happening.

"Casimiro, we need to react with resolve."

"Yes, Al, there's a limit to everything!"

It's absurd, she had the nerve to go right past our house. She felt confident that no one would recognize her but she was wrong, I know who you are, you damned homewrecker. The worst thing was seeing Papà, who stopped mowing the lawn, got in the car, and told us he'd be right back.

"You understand, Casimiro? Not half an hour after saying to me, 'What would I do without you'!"

"They're a couple of filthy pigs . . . "

"Now I'm going to talk to Mamma and ask her to come take a walk with me!"

"No, Al, you'd better not."

"Yes, instead, I better had. Enough is enough!"

"Al . . . what are you muttering about?" Mamma asks me.

Mamma, stop lying in the sun and come with me, we need to go get Mario Elvis back. It's a miserable story, you're going to be upset because you're going to feel betrayed, and I don't blame you because that's how I feel myself, but it's not his fault, the one who's at fault is that woman who isn't satisfied with having a marvelous secret bachelor lover, she wants a married one too, with children, now let's go and fetch him back, then we'll deal with the situation like grown-ups, calmly and rationally, we'll brood and sulk for a few days, we'll get him to swear that he'll never do it again, and then, don't worry, I'll take care of making sure that chesty glutton ceases and desists once and for all.

"Nothing, Mamma, everything's fine."

44.

Next to the table we've set up the folding ladder, its top covered with a sheet. It looks like a monument to the bricklayers, awaiting its inauguration. Papà know that he's not supposed to ask us any more questions because a surprise is a surprise, we won't tell him anything until Mamma brings the food to the table. While we're waiting, he tries to take his mind off it.

"Let me tell you, you can't guess what happened yesterday . . . " he tells us. "Agnese, do you remember Sandra, the one from the personnel office? The one who's a little zaftig?"

"Maybe so . . . Sandra? I don't think we ever met though."

"Well, last night she came home and the street was full of people, police, firemen . . . a fire had destroyed her house."

"Oh my God, that poor thing, what happened?"

"Well, this is the interesting part. The firemen said that it wasn't an accident, that this was a case of professional arson . . . Al, there's nothing to laugh about! . . . That poor thing doesn't have a place to live, and she was so scared that she went home to her mother in Campobasso."

"But wasn't she supposed to be a terrible loan shark?" Mamma asks.

"I don't know, there were rumors. Anyway, if it's true then that means she went up against the wrong person . . . Al, what's gotten into you tonight?"

Mamma goes into the kitchen to sample the chicken, she's not entirely satisfied so she asks my advice. I taste it, I taste it again, and I'm not entirely satisfied either. I ask Vittoria what she thinks of it, and she nibbles at the bite of chicken and stalls before finally giving her approval. Since Papà makes us suffer every time he has a surprise, we've decided to make him pay. These five minutes of supplementary waiting have the desired effect: as soon as Mamma sets the pan down on the table, he snaps.

"All right, will you explain to me just what that catafalque is?!"

"It's an idea of mine, Papà," I say, "mine and Vittoria's some, too . . . We decided that, along with Elvis Day, we're going to celebrate," and here I whip the sheet off the ladder, "Santamaria Day!"

There was a very good reason that King Arthur and his knights gathered around a table. Sitting side by side they'd tell each other: "Do you remember how much we laughed in that one battle?" and memory after memory gave them the feeling that they belonged to a single family. That is how they became invincible. On the top of the ladder we fastened the Super 8 projector with the lens pointing downward. When I turn it on, the beam of white light hits the table at an almost perpendicular angle. I move the bottle of mineral water so that Mario Elvis can have a perfect view of Agnese's face. Look at how beautiful she is as she poses on the beach, pretending not to know that you were filming her. Unless this really is a world of lunatics, VHS cassettes will soon be forgotten, their inexplicable popularity at an end, and we'll all go back to using film projectors. The sound of the film as it runs, pulled headlong by the toothed sprocket, the heat of the lamp, the image that every so often bounces and blurs: nothing that so closely resembles memory can ever be forgotten. Vittoria runs over the cups and plates wearing the crocheted swimsuit that Mamma made her, she comes over to me as if to play with sand on the bread basket. She talks to me, I talk to Casimiro. Then Papà arrives, glances toward the lovely director, takes us both by the hand, and does the routine of the circus strongman. An instant later we're both in the air, we kick our feet, holding tight to his hands. Now we push aside the roasting pan with the chicken to get a better view of Papà playing his guitar, little Vittoria holds out her hands, she wants the movie camera, Mamma lets her have it, the picture jerks and swerves, then it spins dizzyingly and stops on a blurry extreme close-up of the sand. End of the reel. The sprockets continue to spin, the tail of the film slaps at the projector as it whirrs. Mario Elvis wants more.

"You were great . . . what a great job . . . "

Agnese sighs, Vittoria asks me to run the other film, the one of her gymnastic tryouts, Papà stares at his plate as he toys with his fork. He seems to have lost something among the pieces of chicken with red peppers. I climb the stepladder, make sure that the projector is still solidly battened down, and rewind the film.

"What else could the Santamaria family ask for?" I say.

"Nothing!"

45.

The Santamaria family is once again discussing Vittoria's bad luck. Mario Elvis laughs and shakes his head, Agnese says that bad luck has nothing to do with it, that girl just doesn't have an ounce of gracefulness. I limit myself to commenting that with the money we spent on six years of gymnastics, we could have put in a jacuzzi. In other words, she's pulled another one of her classic stunts, this time on the road. Vittoria is really good at English, and in order to take her mastery of the language to another level, since they couldn't afford to send her to boarding school, Mamma and Papà sent her to work as an au pair with a family in Manchester. The evening she got there she called us, she told us the house was beautiful, extremely nice and well cared for. The mother had done it all with her own hands, she spent hours stitching curtains, decorating the walls with stencils, and caring for the plants. In this home-sweet-home, my sister, having noticed the absence of a bidet, decided the right thing to do was climb up onto the sink. It was obvious it wasn't going to support her weight but I know my sister well, and even if I wasn't there, I know exactly what happened next. She decided: "If I'm very careful I can do this. Here, I'll climb up on this stool and then

I'll just lightly rest my weight . . . gently, ever so gently." The way I imagine the scene, a second later my sister lost her grip, fell full-force onto the sink, and knocked it to the floor where it shattered into a thousand pieces. And this was only the appetizer. The mother, who of course loved that sink as if it were one of her children, went into a full-blown hysterical fit. After a day of chilly distance during which she stayed in the garden, pruning the hedges, and my sister stayed in her room, burning with shame, the woman took a step toward détente and invited the toilet acrobat down for a cup of tea. According to Vittoria's account, there are two armchairs in the living room upholstered in hand-sewn fabrics, carefully pleated, covered with exceedingly intricate floral patterns with colors ranging from gray to dark brown. Hues that are damned close to the colors of the woman's Yorkshire terrier. My sister went down to the living room, apologized for the hundredth time, and in her portrayal of the role of the young woman at her wits' end, she let herself flop backwards into one of the armchairs. The Yorkie's favorite armchair. The Yorkie the woman loved as if it were another one of her children, a brother to the sink.

Papà went to get her at the airport, my sister landed at 6:50, about an hour late, but twenty-six days earlier than the day she was expected back.

After dinner, while Agnese and Mario Elvis try to resolve a difference of nine hundred twenty lire between the total predicted by Mamma's pocket calculator and the numbers printed out by the cash register at the supermarket, I try to distract Vittoria with a game of Scrabble. Vittoria writes "dance," "university," "boyfriend," "travel," and "television." I write "trauma," "thoracic," "neck," "broken," "quadruped," and "English."

"Al, in your opinion, am I a beautiful woman?"

"You're not a woman, you're my sister . . . anyway, yes, you just become prettier all the time."

"Really?"

"Casimiro says so, too."

"Do you think I'll ever be famous?"

"Famous how?"

"Well, famous like I take my degree, I publish a bunch of papers, and maybe I even make an important discovery, and so they interview me and invite me to appear on TV."

It's not my sister's fault that she asks so many stupid questions. It's a result of the proliferation of television networks, of cameras, and of the exponential increase in the number of people who, almost invariably unjustifiably, are allowed to enjoy a few minutes of fame. Even scientists no longer dream of being published in specialized journals and the recognition of the scientific community, they prefer to appear on the small screen and to receive the canned applause of the television audience. They'll get over it, in no more than a decade everyone will get over it.

"We're all going to be famous," I reply.

"Why?"

"When Papà becomes an astronaut . . . "

Vittoria toys for a few seconds with the plastic letters.

"I'm perfectly happy with Papà as a bus driver," she says.

"So am I, but he shouldn't give up his dreams."

"I don't think he really ever dreamed those dreams. I think it was only a joke he played on us when we were little."

I have better plans for him, better than he can even imagine. But I'm certainly not going to stand in his way if he wants to take part in the space program.

"I thought it was true myself until just a few years ago, but then I understood," Vittoria continues.

Mamma will take a chocolate *ciambellone* to the technicians at the NASA control room. It will turn into a regular thing.

Everyone waits eagerly for the arrival of Signora Agnese and her good-luck cake.

"You can only write one word at a time!" Vittoria complains.

All right, all right, I'll take away "Yorkshire," and I'll leave "dead."

46.

Good News, I adore you. I cut a meatball in two and there's almost no bread inside, so this must be really big news. What can it be? Are we about to start construction on the interior walls? Or maybe the bathtub? Of course, they must have decided to give precedence to the tub!

"Mario, let's tell them right away, otherwise these two are going to choke on their food."

"We said after dinner. After the espresso, and after the grappa . . . "

"No-o-o!"

"Okay, okay. Well then . . . Mamma and Papà have made a decision. We've spent a few challenging years, we've waited so long for everything to be settled once and for all, but seeing that there are always going to be problems, we just told ourselves: enough is enough. It's now or never."

"What's now or never?" Vittoria asks.

"Mamma and Papà are leaving, we're going to have our honeymoon, in Venice."

"Bravo!" Vittoria shouts.

"Yes-s-s-s!" I yell.

"When are you leaving?" Vittoria asks.

"In a few days, we've found a little pensione in Mestre and we want to take advantage of the opportunity."

"And how long will you stay away?" I inquire.

"We're leaving on an open-ended basis, as long as our money holds out."

"Ten days at the very most, then . . ." Mamma jokes.

Perfect. I was ready to put the plan into effect in twenty-four hours, but instead now I'll have plenty of time and I'll even be able to devote myself to refining the details.

"Maybe we'll win something at the Venice casino and we'll be able to stay longer," says Papà.

"If you set foot anywhere near that casino, I'll head straight home, this is a honeymoon!"

"Right, it's a honeymoon, having fun is out of the question."

"Mamma, remember to take a *ciambellone* with you, the northeastern Italian market is an important one," I say.

"Certainly, Al . . . But here's an important point, I'm going to need a phone number to reach you. Tiziana's number?" Agnese asks Vittoria.

"Yes, that's good."

"Wouldn't Lorenzo's be better?" I ask my sister.

"What does Lorenzo have to do with anything?"

"No, I was just saying. On account of you always go over to his house. Even when you say you're going over to Tiziana's."

The gazes of Mario Elvis and Agnese, perfectly synchronized, swivel to focus on Vittoria's bright blush.

"That's not true! I sometimes go over to Lorenzo's just because we're studying together for an exam!"

"Come on, you two, don't fight. Let us go on our honeymoon without worries," says Agnese. "You're big kids now, Vittoria is legally an adult . . . Understood, Al? While we're gone, you're going to have to do as your sister tells you."

She's gone mad. The head of the family is going to be Vittoria. How long do I have left to live? Twenty-four hours, forty-eight at the very most. She'll blow up the house with natural gas or jump on the bed and break my neck. They must have told her that just to prop up her morale after what happened with the Yorkshire terrier, there can't be any other explanation. Anyway, it's a secondary matter, the important thing is that this the opportunity I've been waiting for. A sign of fate. As long as I've been in this world, my folks might have gone out for the evening maybe a dozen times, the farthest they've gone is say from Rome to Torvaianica. It's unmistakable, then, I have a divine investiture. I need to call Raul.

47.

We have the whole house to ourselves. Actually, I have the whole house to myself because, two hours after the old folks leave, Vittoria has cut and run. She told me that she was going to go to the university, then to Lorenzo's to study, then over to Tiziana's. Her role as the adult head of household with responsibity for my care is evidenced by the following fine list of admonishments left on the table: go to school, lunch is in the fridge, so is dinner, do your homework, turn off the generator before going to bed, don't set the house on fire. I file the note away in a plastic bag with a label reading "Exhibit A." Right now I won't say a word because the situation happens to be to my advantage, but when the old folks come home we'll have a laugh. Raul will be here any minute, I have a million things to do and I need to get them done fast, if Vittoria goes over to Lorenzo's, she's quite likely to come home ahead of schedule. He's dating Caterina but they're having troubles, technically it's as if they had split up, and Vittoria is an ideal specimen to keep falling for such ridiculous stuff. If she shows up again with puffy eyes and starts whining about it, I'll just ignore her this time. Among the many tasks assigned to me by History, taking care of that train wreck certainly isn't one of them.

For certain undertakings, Raul is the ideal partner. Most people might have told me: "You can't do that," "It's not legal," or "You're crazy," while instead he said: "Just think, I always wanted to tell you that you were being idiots about this." It was easy, after telling him the lie that Agnese and Mario Elvis were in agreement, all it took was six hours of work and seventy thousand lire's worth of materials. We dug a ditch a foot and a half deep, installed cement conduits, laid the cables, and covered everything up carefully to make sure there were no traces of our intervention. I was a mess afterward, my clothing is drenched in sweat, I have cement in my hair, my fingernails are filthy, and I have a second skin of dirt all over my body. What would a real man do now? Certainly, a nice restorative nap on Vittoria's bed.

I cross the living room at a dead run, Papà is right behind me, he tries to pass me, the living room never seems to end, in the middle there's also the kitchen with Grandma melting soap bars, I'm the first to get to the bathroom door, I yell, I leap in the air till I graze the ceiling lamp, I fly over the tub.

A thunderous roar. The panes of glass shake. Sitting up on the bed I try to splice together the echoing thunder and the shaking house with the reality I prefer, the one from before, suspended in midair. I run to Mamma and Papà's king-size bed, I look out at the rain slapping the window, I try to recover from my fright. I've never seen a downpour like this one, and look at the rain, it's not drops but ribbons of water.

"Vittoria?"

Wait, how long did I sleep? It's pitch black outside.

"Vittoria?" I shout.

I switch on the light on the side table. It's two in the morning. Can Vittoria really not have come yet?

"Vittoria, are you in the bathroom?"

I need to bolster my courage. I get out of bed, I turn on another light. The noise of the rain on the roof sends shivers down my back. I go back into Vittoria's room. She's not there. On the bed I see the outline of my second skin that has disintegrated into the sheet. My fear made me spontaneously shed my skin. But who would leave a brother at home all alone in the middle of such a rainstorm?

"I'm here, Al. Don't be afraid."

"Casimiro, what should we do?"

"Let's get in the big bed with all the lights turned on, and we'll stand guard until tomorrow morning. We'll take turns sleeping. Shifts of three hours each."

Excellent idea. That way, if Vittoria returns home, we'll hear her immediately, and if she doesn't, we'll be well rested so we can pitch an unforgettable scene tomorrow morning.

Eight A.M.?

"It's eight in the morning, Casimiro!"

I get out of bed and first thing I do is run to the window. The blue sky, without so much as a trace of clouds, seems to be claiming that it had nothing to do with the tremendous mess of the night before.

"We can't be late!"

I can't possibly miss school today. We have a class exercise in math today and if the bus comes right away, best case scenario, I'll get there in time for second period. Right now, there must be a dozen classmates who need my help.

"I'm losing money by the handful!"

I ought to get washed up and change my clothes, but I don't have time to waste on such frivolous concerns. I tear outside, my feet sink into the mud up to my ankles. On the bus everyone looks at me as if any moment I might start singing and begging for spare change. The only two passengers who want to chat are a couple of old people, they talk about the cloudburst, they say that on the seven o'clock news it said that this was the worst storm in the last seventy years. They put on an expression as if to say they were there in 1911 and they can remember the cloudburst in question perfectly. I go into the school, the janitor doesn't know where to begin and he turns and leaves, throwing an "I didn't see a thing" over his shoulder, I knock at the classroom door and open it without waiting for the teacher to say "Come in!" and I tell them that I fell over on my bike and landed in a mud puddle, I sit down at my desk, ignoring the gazes of my classmates. I start copying down the equation written on the blackboard which, open square brackets, is a trifle multiplied by, and here open round brackets, the number of my classmates multiplied by their IQ divided by the number of hours they spent getting ready for this written exam, which is to say zero, close brackets both round and square. I turn in the exam without having a chance to pass it around, I return the payments that I had demanded in advance, I get shoved around a little, along with a referral from the gym teacher because I forgot my workout uniform, I trot out the same story about falling off my bicycle to my Italian teacher who sends me to the bathroom to "freshen up a little," and there I meet Roberta who gives me a discount and, for 4,000 lire, reminds me that maps printed on oilcloth and slate blackboards aren't the only happy memories I'll have of high school.

I devote the trip home to a dress rehearsal of the scolding I'm going to give Vittoria: I'll make my entrance with a loud door-slam, there'll be a substantial central section with plenty of shouting and insults, and a grand finale with my disappearance and late-night return after worrying her to death. All pointless, because at home all I find is a short note: "Ciao Al, call me at Tiziana's as soon as you get home," which I file away with a label reading "Exhibit B." Now she's going to hear from me. Disappearing for two days when she only had permission to stay out until nine at night. What kind of manners are these? Is that how you're supposed to take care of your brother? Here I am, knocking myself out for the good of mankind, and she doesn't give a damn. It's all crystal clear, she had a fight with

Lorenzo and now she's at her girlfriend's house, licking her wounds. I take five tokens and go outside to let off some steam.

"Vittoria!"

"Ciao, Al . . ."

"Oh, that's great, at least you remember your brother's name!"

"Sorry, I had to study, things have just been so crazy . . ."

"There was a thunderstorm and you left me all alone!"

"You're right, I'm sorry, but they moved up an exam . . ."

"I don't care what happened, I have my own problems and, believe me, they're much bigger than yours! Do as you like, all I want is for you to come home when it's your turn to cook and to let me know immediately whenever Mamma and Papà call. I'm still waiting to find out whether they reached Venice!"

"You're right, Al, excuse me . . ."

"Would you just quit apologizing? So did Mamma and Papà call?"

"Did they call? Oh, yes . . . they got there, everything's fine. And how are you?"

"I'm fine, I'm fine . . . for all that it matters to you! When are you coming home?"

I take care not to ask her how she's doing because her voice is a mess, she's got a gallon of snot in her nose, and she sounds like she's choking.

"Listen, I don't think I'll be home today, maybe later but I really don't know. Don't wait up for me, I might stay at Tiziana's again . . . after all, the fridge is full."

"Living your life at Tiziana's, eh?" I say ironically.

"Yes, we're having fun. Ciao, Al."

Exactly. It's mathematical. She and that boy spend more than half an hour together, and they have a fight. I know how it went. She couldn't help but ask him whether he had any plans for the future involving her, he must have retorted that he's a free spirit, and here's the result. Now, I'm done worrying about Vittoria, here in my human flesh diary I have a long list of things to do.

48.

Here she is, here she is! I'm so happy to see her arrive that my whole plan of scolding, tantrums, and sulking vanishes in a puff of air. Maybe later I'll take the opportunity to launch a few darts of reproof, but right now I'm beside myself, I want to show her the fruits of the past few days of hard work, open her eyes to my great project. Now what I need to put on is a nonchalant attitude. I go out to water the plants. She looks at me, I pretend not to see her. She crosses the street, she stops, she must have seen my latest masterpiece, I hear her footsteps on the grass.

"Al . . . "

"Hi, Vittoria."

Oh lord, look at that face. How does she work herself into these states every single time? The circles under her eyes have to be some kind of record, this dark and sallow I'd never seen them, not even when Giancarlo was around. And what's this? Am I getting a hug from my sister? She's afraid of my temper, isn't she? I can feel the tip of her nose on my neck, it's cold and damp.

"You're going to strangle me."

"Sorry."

"It was just a joke . . . "

Whatever, the hug is over. By now her attention has been captured by my creation.

"What's that?" she asks me.

"What's what?"

"What do you mean, what's what, that flag."

"Oh, the flag . . . It's the coat of arms of the principality. Just keep in mind that for now it's only basted together," I say nonchalantly.

"What principality?"

"The principality of Santamaria."

It's so nice to see Vittoria smile.

"No, wait, you can't hug me. This is serious business, not just some game!"

The positive aspect of her state of emotional fragility is that, in contrast with what I expected, she doesn't tell me that it's foolish nonsense, quite the opposite: she unfurls the banner, she admires the lion rampant and the stylized Elvis standing back-to-back, surmounted by a crown and the slogan *In Elvis We Trust*.

"I had a seamstress make it . . . with my own money."

"And what's it for?"

"We'll fly it by the front door. It's our banner, the Santamaria banner! Do you like it?"

"The principality of Santamaria?"

"Did you see that the lion has fringe on his paws just like Elvis's jacket? Anyway, it's just a first rough draft, if you want to add anything . . . "

"No, it seems perfect just as it is."

"Whoa, contain your enthusiasm."

"Would you explain to me what it means?"

This is the ideal moment. The pangs of love make her as biddable as a kitten. She looks at me with glistening eyes, playing tug-of-war with a drop of mucus that appears and disappears at the tip of her nose. I explain to her that, after having sent the last few certified letters to the utilities company to obtain the hookup of electricity, gas, and phone service, and after obtaining the usual silence in reply, our promised home is finally ready to take its first steps toward full independence.

"Independence from what?"

"From the Italian republic, from the rest of the world!"

"But what does it mean?"

"Look here."

I turn on the outside light and I point to the lamp over the door like a magician gesturing toward the rabbit he pulls out of the top hat.

"I don't understand. The light's turned on, so what?"

It's not her fault. Two geniuses in the same family would be too many.

"Don't you hear anything?"

"No, Al, I don't hear a thing. Just a few birds twittering, nothing else."

"Exactly, Vittoria. You can hear the birds because the diesel generator isn't working."

"Then where is the electric power coming from?"

I point to the light pole on the street.

"Oh lord, Al . . . you can't do that."

"Not according to the Italian republic, true, but we are the principality of Santamaria, so we don't care what they say."

I tell her that with Raul's help, I've made an underground hookup to the light post outside and that now we have unlimited quantities of electric power for lighting, to keep the refrigerator turned on day and night, and also for the heating system which, once we've bought it, will run on efficient electric heaters. Thanks to this spectacular move, and thanks to her idea of getting her scooter stolen last week, we have freed ourselves at one fell swoop from the bonds of the oil companies, electric companies, and insurance companies. Now we can say farewell to the natural gas as well because with all the electric power that we'll have, we can reinstall the electric stovetops. For the water, we'll go on using the cistern on the roof which is supplied by an undeclared pipe, but since that questionable setup was the work of the tire repair guy, the principality declines all responsibility in that connection.

Still she seems absent, she looks around and grows distracted. She still doesn't realize the scale of this new development.

"Did you make any other changes while I was away?" she asks me.

"Why? You don't think this was enough?"

"No, what I meant was . . . I don't know, there's something strange. Doesn't it strike you that there's more space between the house and the street than there used to be?"

I've disoriented her. Perhaps I was too precipitous.

"Vittoria, I very much doubt that the street can have moved, there's just a lot more mud on account of the downpour . . . but is that all you have to say?"

"Al, it's really a beautiful idea, I mean it . . . " It looks as if she's about to burst into tears, but then she smiles. "It's just that I don't think it's strictly legal . . . forget about the unauthorized electric hookup, I'm talking about the principality itself, I don't think that you can just take a house and say that it's no longer part of the Italian republic."

"Actually, it was the Italian republic that made the decision in the first place. We don't exist on the maps, we don't belong to any district, we don't have rights to any of the services provided to all the other houses. We're simply acknowledging the state of affairs."

She'll need a little more time to get used to it, but in the end she won't be able to keep from recognizing the magnificence of the concept. The principality of Santamaria. Mario Elvis and Agnese Santamaria: reigning prince and princess. Almerico and Vittoria Santamaria: heirs apparent to the throne!

"Al . . . what's that look you've got on your face now?"

"I'm just thinking about Mamma and Papà when they find the coat of arms over the door and discover that they've become prince and princess."

49.

"A letter from Mamma and Papà has arrived!" Vittoria tells me when she gets back from the grocery store.

"What do they say, when are they coming back?"

"I don't know, Al, I still haven't read it."

"It was a trap, good for you, you didn't fall for it . . . "

"Do you really think that I'd read it without you?"

They were as good as their word, in the last phone call to Tiziana's place, they had told Vittoria that in order to save money, they'd start writing letters. We look for the right place because this is the first letter we've ever received from Mamma and Papà, the very first one in our whole lives, and we can't just read it like this, unceremoniously, standing here. We sit down on the sofa, we try various positions but none of them feel right. We lie down on Vittoria's bed, first on our tummies, and then with our legs up on the wall, but it's a nice day and in the end we just go outside, on the lawn behind the house.

"'Dear Vittoria and Al . . . '"

"Wait, who's doing the writing?" I ask.

"It's Mamma's handwriting. 'Dear Vittoria and Al, Venice is beautiful and our feet hurt from all the walking we've done in the past few days. We miss you oodles . . . '"

"Mamma wrote 'We miss you oodles'?"

"Why?"

"Let me see . . . "

Vittoria hands me the sheets of paper. Second line, we miss you oodles.

"That must have been a suggestion from Papà," I say, "those two are having the time of their lives, forget about them actually missing us!"

"I think you're probably right." Vittoria picks up the sheets of paper and starts reading again: "'We miss you oodles but, if you don't mind too much, we'd like to stay here a while longer.

There are so many things to see, and who knows when we'll ever have a chance to come back.' What do you say?"

"Certainly they can stay, I don't have any problem with that. Why, what about you?"

"As long as they have the money, they should stay. So we'll write back and tell them that we're fine with it."

A few extra days is exactly what we need to give them a fitting welcome when they return. I want to do a plaster cast of the principality's coat of arms to put over the door. Plus I need to think about the letterhead stationery for official communications, send out my request for UN recognition, and get down to work on drafting the constitution. So go on and enjoy Venice, the islands, the photographs with pigeons in St. Mark's Square, high water and seafood feasts, and when you get back you'll discover what a memorable exploit Al has undertaken!

"A-a-al, it's six o'clock!" Vittoria shouts from the kitchen.

A new day shines its rays on the principality of Santamaria. I need to gather the courage to get out of bed, elbow my way onto the bus, and smile for the two hundred forty-fourth time at the wisecrack: "Look, it's Al Santamaria, the human case of diarrhea!"

"Come on, there's a surprise!" she tells me.

"What surprise?" I ask, jumping out of bed.

"Look here . . . "

"A frittata?"

"It's not a frittata, it's Mamma's chocolate *ciambellone*! It just turned out like this because I was in a hurry . . . "

I immediately sample a slice. I can taste the butter, the eggs, the flour, and the sugar. It's just that I taste each one separately.

"Not bad . . . " I say, to keep from hurting her feelings, "but maybe you should have kneaded it a little more thoroughly, and given it more time for the yeast to rise."

"The yeast! I'm such a mess."

Behold Vittoria Santamaria, who got Papà's eyes, nose, and hair, and Mamma's sense of self-respect. Her eyes, which until just a moment ago were smiling, dim and turn opaque.

"Shoulders back, chest out, and pride up! You're the future princess of Santamaria!"

Vittoria straightens her shoulders, takes a deep breath and puffs out her chest, and lifts her chin.

"Future Prince Al, the future princess is going to be running a little late today," she says.

Well, that's hardly a surprise. Princess Vittoria has had bags under her eyes like a scrubwoman for the past two weeks. When is she going to stop letting herself be tortured by that commoner Lorenzo?

50.

Dear UN, . . .

Friends at the UN, . . .

Esteemed Envoys, . . .

How the hell do you start a letter to the UN? If I were sending the application for recognition of the principality to an Italian state agency, I'd have no doubts, I'd begin with Most Illustrious Excellencies, but there in the Glass Palace on the East River, I'm assuming they are actually people with a certain degree of class, indifferent to the standard servile approach.

"A-a-al?"

Looking out the window, I see Vittoria standing motionless in the street. She came home on time today, just when what I need more than anything else is another hour of blessed peace. I don't want to interrupt my work, I'd better just not answer.

"A-a-al!"

It's no good, a future reigning prince can't even have five minutes' time to focus on a fundamental passage in the life of the principality. What the devil is she doing out there, why doesn't she come in? Another lizard taken for a poisonous snake?

"What is it? I'm busy!" I shout.

"Come see!"

I'm coming! I'm coming! If this is about another baby bird we need to let die inside one of my socks rolled up for a nest, I swear that . . .

"You see?" she asks.

"What?"

She takes long strides toward me.

"One . . . two . . . three . . . almost four. Don't you remember that when we first got here, you used to play at jumping from the door directly into the street to scare Mamma?"

"This thing with the street again? Anyway, yes, I remember, and I also remember that Mamma never got scared precisely because the street was so far away."

It's no good, she's not convinced. I've already figured out that this is going to be her new fixation. For that matter, she's the one who after the Seveso incident turned intermittently purple because she had decided only to breathe every once in a while, in order to avoid contamination. I'm tempted to laugh.

"Al, I'm serious!"

Unless I pretend to take some interest, this is going to be a long and drawn-out thing. I offer her a long glance to the right and another to the left, I scratch my chin, and I make an insignificant evaluation of the stretch of ground between street and door.

"No, Vittoria, I really don't think that the road has moved."

Since I'm eager to get back to the more urgent matter of foreign policy, I take the shopping bags out of her hand and take them to the kitchen table. I start rummaging through them.

"But you didn't buy any of the things I wrote on the list!"

"'Chocolate, popcorn, chocolate cookies, chocolate wafers, powdered cocoa, red pizza, whipped cream in a can, assorted chocolates . . . ' Do you think that's a shopping list? I'll be in charge of these things, all right?"

I'll have to give some ground to her, constitutional monarchies are in general opposed to the centralization of power and the ministry of shopping strikes me as an acceptable sacrifice.

"What are Mamma and Papà's covers doing on your bed?" she asks me.

"Nothing."

"Nothing" is the most slothful word in the whole dictionary. At least until you get old. It comes out of your mouth with a meaning of approximately "no big thing," "zero activity," "absence of problems," and it reaches the ear of your listener transformed into "reason to worry," "shady business," and "problems." And in fact there she is, pulling the curtain aside and checking. Now she's going to bust my chops, tell me that I shouldn't be playing around with Mamma and Papà's bedcover, that it cost a lot of money, that I've ruined it, and so on and so forth. She says nothing because she wants me to turn around and see how wide-eyed she is. I don't fall for it, I keep rummaging through the grocery bags, myself.

"It looks like a nice thing, but what is it?" she asks in a faint, uncertain voice.

Here we go. She's started using drugs.

"It's a surprise for Mamma and Papà . . . " I say.

I go over to her, her pupils look normal.

"They're album covers, now . . . let me show you how it works."

I carefully arrange the cover on the bed, I get under it in the proper position to read. Vittoria gets comfortable next to me.

"You wrote with a magic marker on the covers . . . " she says.

There, now I recognize her.

"If you want, I can sew on some little labels," she adds.

No, no, she's definitely on drugs.

"You see?" I tell her. "For now there are only two strings. One of them ends where I wrote 1967 and one where I wrote 1968. Pull the string for 1967."

Vittoria pulls the string and a line of silhouetted cardboard tabs pops up, just like in my favorite old book of fairy tales.

"Look, there's Mamma all pregnant, Papà looking at the moon, the car rushing to the hospital, and then there's me," I explain to her.

"How nice . . . you're in the bright sunlight, everyone's laughing, and then what are those two? A couple of big birds?"

"No, two angels . . . is it too much?"

"It's perfect."

Vittoria pulls the string for 1968. There's the scene of her putting me in the trash can. She laughs, she sniffles, a tear rolls down her cheek, what kind of a fool sister do I even have?

"Shall we do 1969 together?" she asks me.

51.

I didn't like this latest letter, not one bit. I'm miffed, terribly miffed. I don't give a damn if someone my age isn't supposed to do such a thing. I go over and stand in the corner and scratch the paint on the wall with one finger.

"Now they're overdoing it," I say.

"Why, Al?"

"Does this strike you as normal? What kind of honeymoon is this?"

"Al, it's a honeymoon they've put off for years and years."

"Sure, but do you think it's right that they don't miss us even a little bit?"

"What are you talking about?! They spent eighteen whole years with me and then with the two of us, day and night! So, even if they decided to spend the next eighteen years all by themselves, I wouldn't see anything odd about it. And anyway, they only mentioned a couple of months."

"But everything's ready here! The flag, the coat of arms over the door, the drafting of the constitution is well under way, we have letterhead stationery, and our answer from the UN is bound to arrive any day now!"

"Al, try to understand, they're not having fun. Papà found out that he's been fired! Forget about a honeymoon trip, they're really worried about paying the mortgage."

"If they find jobs they'll never come back."

"Al, they're looking for odd jobs until Papà can find another job back here. You know what they're like, they can't wait to get back here. And then we can make use of this extra time to do something exceptional for the principality. Just think of when Mamma and Papà come back and see the flag flying outside and all the rooms separated by wonderful walls!"

Sure, that's right, I pay her my compliments, I'm no longer so terribly out of sorts. I'm sick of doing everything on my own and the fact that Vittoria too has entered into the spirit of the thing comes as a relief. She's right, Mamma and Papà ought to find the principality completely finished. The next expenses we'll have to undertake will be, in order of importance, the bathtub, the hot water heater, the electric stove, at least three heaters for the winter, walls and doors for the individual rooms.

"The bathtub isn't urgent," says Vittoria.

"It's a gift for Mamma and Papà, they deserve it, think what a nice surprise if they can have a nice hot bath when they get back."

"It costs too much, Al. We need to buy another scooter first thing."

I can't expect too much from her.

"You need to make an effort, Vittoria . . . we-are-an-inde-pendent-principality. No motor scooter, no car, nothing that can obligate us to sign contracts and get ripped off by the companies of the Italian republic!"

I cut off the conversation because it's been an hour since Raimondo started playing the guitar and now, as per terms stipulated last week, an hour of playing together awaits us.

"Raimondo, it's time!" I say.

"Just another five minutes! The last song!" he shouts from outside.

"No, right away! I've already got the plastic army men set up!"

Raimondo comes back inside, kisses the body of the Martin, and carefully sets it back in its case. As he walks toward me, his fingers are still playing arpeggios.

"Are your folks still away?" he asks me.

"Yes, for a while."

"What incredible luck . . . your parents are legendary."

Soon the sun will break over the horizon and bless the principality of Santamaria with its early beams. It's time.

"A-a-al . . . please turn it down . . . turn it do-o-own," Vittoria mutters from her room.

"What do you think of thi-i-is o-o-o-one?" I ask her.

"Don't you ever sleep?" she shouts at me.

"How on earth am I supposed to sleep! History is made by the waking! And after all, it's five thirty, you would have been awake in half an hour anyway."

She must have inherited her personality from Grandma Concetta. Mamma and Papà don't jump in the air for every little thing, but she has that foul peasant personality. She stumbles over to the table, smells the coffee and then, when I turn down the volume, looks at me with a wrinkled grimace in the shape of a smile.

"Well, what do you think of it?" I ask her.

"Of what?"

"Of the song, as the anthem of the principality!"

"No, Al. Not 'Galactica' by the Rockets, please, no."

I put another cassette in the tape recorder.

"Well, it was a tribute to Papà. How about this instead? It's a little softer, right? *Meteor, meteor, meteor ma-a-an . . .* "

"I think that the anthem ought to be an Elvis song, like say 'Mystery Train' or 'Suspicious Minds.'"

"Of course, we'll choose the final anthem with Mamma and Papà when they come back, but for now we need a temporary one, something to play while we raise the flag at daybreak."

"Come here . . . "

"No, stop laughing . . . and don't hug me! You aren't taking this seriously! That's enough, you're suffocating me! Seriously? Never an intermediate attitude, either irritable or all sugary!"

There's no middle ground with Vittoria, but the ground that's covered with hugs, kisses on both cheeks, and raspberries on the back of my neck is by far the one I prefer. We listen to other songs as we have breakfast. We choose them at random, we pull out Mamma and Papà's old cassettes, we take turns sticking them into the tape recorder, and we rewind the tape a little to hear the last song they listened to. We skip over "Parole" by Nico e i Gabbiani, "Resterai" by the Corvi, and "Only the Lonely" by Roy Orbison. During "Forever and Ever" by Demis Roussos it gets late, we need to make a decision. We solemnly unfurl the flag at dawn and, as the sun blesses the principality with its first rays, we put on the last song we can remember dancing to with the old folks. Hands on our hearts, we sing "We Are Family" by Sister Sledge.

52.

We read the long letter from Agnese and Mario Elvis like good siblings, grabbing the sheets of paper out of each other's hands and fighting over whose turn it was. They write us every day but they only mail the letters every so often to save on stamps, and maybe to keep from boring us, I'd guess. They were angry that I forced open the token box of the phone booth. It seemed to me like a good idea, by getting all those tokens we'd be able to call them free of charge whenever we wanted. Vittoria was happy about it, too, and in fact she told me to write our folks about it immediately. It didn't turn out well, they wrote back that the Santamaria family has always played by the rules and that the fact that the law isn't protecting our rights isn't enough of a reason to just break it. Obviously, living outside the country, they aren't getting a clear idea of how things are going in Italy, they don't realize that we'd be freeloading on the phone company of the only country on earth where the oil companies have taken to peddling contraband and have defrauded the state of 2 trillion lire, no less. Since I'm going to have to mention the electric hookup on the light pole sooner or later, I decided not to press my point too heavily, for the moment, it's probably best to let it slide. We concentrate on the good news: Mario Elvis has found a position as a singer, Agnese is still looking for new pastry shops, they've rented a small but cozy room near the club where Papà is performing. Then there are a bunch of questions, and we're answering them now.

"'Did you set fire to anything, Al?'"

"Say no," I tell her.

"You set fire to the curtains."

"That was a controlled fire, it doesn't count. And after all, I only burned a little bit of the fringe. I don't like curtains with fringes."

"What about the fire in the garden?"

"That's what you're supposed to do, Vittoria: you pile up the brushwood and then you burn it."

"But you're not supposed to throw balloons of alcohol without Papà's supervision. All right, let's do this, I won't say anything, but you cut it out with the fires, I don't like lying."

"Right, good idea, so let's write them that four evenings out of seven you don't come home to sleep!"

"I'm all grown up, I can come home when I want."

We avoid discussing fires and late-night escapades, and we shift over to more innocent subjects: my grades at school are excellent, Vittoria already has lots of friends at the university, the house is in fine shape.

"Speaking of the house, we ought to deal with this matter of the . . . " says Vittoria.

"I'm not talking about it."

"Mamma and Papà wrote that they thought it would be the best solution."

"It's out of the question, this is our promised home! Are you kidding? They leave for a couple of months and we sell the house . . . "

"We could take away all the furniture, all our memorabilia, it's just four walls."

"We had an understanding, Vittoria. Mamma and Papà are going to come home and they'll find their house transformed into a principality."

"I don't know how much longer we're going to be able to pay the mortgage, and I'm positive we can't go on living hooked up to a light pole."

"My how bourgeois you've become . . . "

"Al, try to be reasonable, it's not our fault, there's the economic crisis, inflation, there are no jobs . . . Mamma and Papà know it perfectly well."

"It's the system that's in crisis, not us! If the system is in crisis, then all we need to do is live outside of the system. And after all, who is the firstborn here?" I ask.

"I am."

"In the dynastic line of the principality, only the male offspring count . . . anyway, we'll stay here, we'll proclaim ourselves an independent principality, and we'll cut all ties with society and with the economic downturn."

We don't have a single day to waste. We can't remain linked to a country governed by people who see nothing scandalous about the fact that forty-four members of the Italian parliament went around wearing the aprons of the P2 Masonic Lodge, black hoods over their heads, candles in hand, and then censor a television news investigation of prostitution. You can't halt History in its tracks. My plan to save the world needs to pivot to the live, operative phase, the time is ripe. Vittoria has become sufficiently grown-up and weak that I can bend her to my will, Mamma and Papà will find themselves face-to-face with a *fait accompli*. I can just see them returning home, their eyes filled with pride, Papà putting a hand on my shoulder and telling me: "You're a genius, Al," or perhaps: "You're a real man, Al," or even: "You're the pride of the human race, Al."

Young normally endowed woman, stop grinding your teeth and rela-a-a-ax . . . accept into the folds of your brain this stream of superior thou-ou-ou-ght . . . it's your brother who's spea-ea-eaking to you . . . the principality of Santamaria is a reality . . . put up no resista-a-ance . . . we are the chosen family . . . we are the healthy cell that will bring welfare and prosperity to the rest of the pla-a-a-anet . . . the history has been written: joy and abundance will reign from today for a thousand millennia . . . on the count of three let my will be done . . . one . . . two . . . thre-e-e-e.

53.

If we're not careful, the ants are going to ruin everything. The deal was total anarchy until twenty-four hours before our folks get back, then we'll scrub the place till it's spic and span. But that was when we thought Mamma and Papà were going to be away for ten days or so. Without really discussing it, we tacitly decided to stick to the same understanding all the same. The result is that my clothes have moved house and now live outside of the wardrobe, in a heap next to the bed, while Vittoria's clothes have moved to the chair and are now slowly taking possession of the living room couch, a little at a time, starting with the armrests. The bathroom is a spectacular array of underpants, bras, various spray cans, and toy soldiers. The dust has glazed over floors and furniture. The kitchen is our masterpiece, nothing remains clean, the cabinets are all empty, we only wash what we need from day to day, wafting out of the garbage can are mists and vapors of alimentary bog and methane. The one thing missing was ants. They walk, undisturbed, unhurried, in a long procession that underscores the burgeoning chaos. Because of them we find ourselves at the point of no return, with no alternative but to do major household spring cleaning. Vittoria is going to see them and declare, enough is enough, we can't go on living like this! So the thing to do is get rid of them. Grandma used to take a newspaper, crumple it up, set fire to one end of it and pass the flame over the whole line of ants. She'd use it as a flaming whisk broom, and with slow movements of the wrists she'd sweep the insects away, incinerating them, disinfecting, freeing burnt confetti into the air that descended to earth as if in slow motion. If a person wanted to be less bloodthirsty, they could just work upstream along the procession of ants, identify the entrance to the anthill, and set out a nice morsel of food nearby. It is intelligence that ennobles mankind, not brute force, even if the latter is always much more fun, and now that I think about it, there's also a nice newspaper winking at me from the table.

When Vittoria comes home from her meeting with my teachers, the kitchen is spic and span, that is, still a mess but without ants. Now that Agnese and Mario Elvis are away, she is the one who receives my teachers' compliments for my academic performance. We've decided to say nothing to anyone about our parents' extra-large honeymoon, and only in the case they should ask, to say only that they're on a business trip. If you ask me, there's no real need to lie, but I love the idea of sharing a lie with Vittoria, it reminds me of when we played Secret Society and when we spoke in pig latin at the dinner table.

"What did they tell you?" I ask her.

"The usual, you're a great student . . . but you need to tell me when you're not going to school. Your teacher Professoressa Sardi told me that you skipped your Ancient Greek test and I had to make up a story."

I was wrong, Vittoria hates telling lies without adequate prior preparation. When she tries to improvise, it's immediately obvious that she's lying. First of all, she repeats the question that she was asked, and she must have said something along the lines of: "Why didn't Al come to class for the test? Ah of course, he didn't come in for the test because he was very sick. What was he sick with? Scuvry or a carbuncle, the doctors still aren't sure."

"I went on strike," I explain to her. "Those sneaky classmates of mine have started buying just one essay and passing it around . . . stingy jerks!"

"You're never going to make friends like that."

"I wouldn't make friends anyway. I don't say 'fuck' and 'I mean' every three words."

"Al, come here."

"Why?"

"I'm just happy today, come here . . . "

"Hmmm, you're really happy . . . super-happy . . . over-joyed . . . "

There was a time when an indicator Vittoria was super-happy was any hug lasting longer than five seconds. But ever since Mamma and Papà left on their honeymoon, she seems like a different person. She's full of thoughtful gestures, she cuddles with me, she almost never gets mad. I think she must be growing up, having passed the age of competitiveness, I guess she's resigned herself to my superiority and realized that a brother who's a genius isn't a threat, he's a resource to be treasured dearly.

"I found a job," she says.

"A job? Mamma doesn't want you to."

"Let's just say it's a secret . . . "

"What are you going to do about the university?"

"It's a part-time job, I'll go the university in the morning and work in the afternoons."

"And what kind of job would it be?"

"Secretary."

"But you don't know how to type."

"They were looking for a person who knows how to speak English well and is available to travel."

"What are you talking about? You're not available to travel!"

"I inquired into it, Al. The destination is Milan and most of the time I'll go up and come back on the same day."

"Then I want a job, too."

"You're still in high school."

"So what, I have my afternoons free, too, I can study at night and on weekends!"

"Al, you can work when you start attending the university, like me. For now, be a good boy and keep the secret."

Of course, I'll keep the secret. With the money I'm setting aside plus Vittoria's salary, we won't have any problems paying the mortgage, and what's more, we'll be able to start construction soon. The principality will be finished in a blink of the eye, when Mamma and Papà come back, and we'll welcome them with a nice hot bath in a tub the size of a swimming pool.

54.

The Italian Defense Minister has minimized reports that Sicily was about to become an American atomic arsenal. He said: obviously, the very idea, but who did they take him for? The missiles will be deployed in a "deserted wasteland." Today three hundred thousand people took to the streets, declaring loudly exactly what they think of a cabinet minister, paid a lavish salary, who looks at an old military map of the Royal Army, sees that the location selected for stockpiling the missiles is called "Contrada Deserto," and accepts the proposed deployment without trying to find out whether, by any chance, over the past century, a thriving agricultural economy hasn't sprung up in that supposed wasteland. The idea of installing a hundred and ten cruise missiles among the greenhouses and wheat fields earned that cabinet minister a generous ration of specially dedicated choruses, rich with specific suggestions. My research was encouraging: in order to prevent that miscarriage of justice young people and old, priests and Leninists, from the south and the north of the country, all mobilized. There is fertile soil in which good ideas can take root, a foundation upon which to establish the new world order. I swore it before each of those faces, smooth-shaven or mustachioed, wearing Ray-Bans or eyeglasses repaired with scotch tape, in hoodies or Sicilian flat caps: the principality is going to put an end to these follies.

The fact that our house attracts so many people flatters me, I realize that a happy island, independent and free of prying parents, is an irresistible attraction. Still, a few nights every so often, I wish I could come home and find only Vittoria. But instead, this time, it's out of the question, there's a scooter parked near the phone booth.

"Vittoria, I'm home!"

"S-s-sh! Be quiet, Al, we have a guest," she whispers to me.

"I saw. Who is it?"

"It's Adele, a friend of Tiziana, she's going to be staying with us for a few days."

"Free of charge?"

"Certainly, Al! Try not to make any noise and one more thing . . . she has a black eye. Don't ask questions."

"How did she get it?"

"It was her boyfriend."

"Were they playing?"

"No, Al, her boyfriend is an asshole, he beat her. Now you have to swear on the constitution of our principality that you won't stare at her and you won't ask her any questions."

"Yes, yes, I swear."

"Al . . . "

"I said that I swear!"

When Adele woke up, it was super-easy to keep from looking at her face. She walked into the living room wearing a skimpy T-shirt and translucent white panties deserving of the utmost attention. When she saw me, before vanishing behind the curtain, she yanked her T-shirt down to cover her thighs, and in so doing uncovering her breasts. Even my sister couldn't have done any better. Once you know what all that stuff is good for, it's hard to think of anything else and to accept the idea that you can't put your hands on it, even if you ask pretty please.

"What are you doing, you don't stare at people like that!" Vittoria scolds me.

"She came out in just her panties!"

"S-s-sh!"

Adele reemerges from behind the curtain a few minutes later, dressed in a turtleneck sweater and a pair of jeans. I can't look at her face, I can't look at her tits, I can't look at her crotch, I don't know where to look at her now, so I just get embarrassed.

"Pleasure to meet you, I'm Adele," she says from a distance.

"Hi, I'm Al."

"Will you stop touching your popo?" Vittoria whispers to me.

"I wasn't touching it."

"You seem like a sex maniac . . . "

Adele comes over, extends her hand, and as I shake it I see that it's covered with scratches.

"What did you do to your hand?"

My eyes land on her face.

"Wow, that must have hurt!"

Thanks to my captivating smile, I manage to obtain forgiveness for my gaffe and get a smile out of Adele. After a few minutes spent chatting on the sofa, I start to get the hollow feeling in my stomach, the hot flushes to my face, and the unmistakable feeling that I've found the love of my life that appears every time a good-looking woman even looks at me. I care for you dearly. I love you. You're beautiful, even with that shiner. I have a crush on you. Considering that women use on average three times as much toilet paper as us men, I've decided to write the chosen declaration of my emotions, the last one, on the sixth square on the toilet paper roll. Unfortunately, it hadn't occurred to me that the first person to use the bathroom might be my sister, and I was forced to swear to her that I wouldn't try any more stunts of the sort.

We stayed inside all day long, partly because of the rain, but also partly because Adele found out that her boyfriend was looking everywhere for her, and she was afraid that sooner or later he might even come around here. When the two of them went to sleep, to reassure them I decided to stand guard in front of the window. I wanted to take advantage of the opportunity to jot down a few lines of the constitution, but outside a thundershower started. The house is full of noises. It sounds like a whole platoon of Adele's exes are trying to break in. The important thing is that Adele and Vittoria are able to sleep undisturbed, after all, I'm here to watch over them.

"Al, what are you doing here?" Vittoria asks me.

"What do you mean, what am I doing here . . . I'm protecting you."

"Go sleep in your own bed!"

The crazy boyfriend never showed up. That's the great thing about our house: you can't find it even if you're desperately searching for it. He must have done what anyone else would do, he must have gone to the last few apartment houses, checked the nameplates on the intercoms, then he might have gone a few hundred yards further down the road, seen the disastrous state of it, the countryside, and the intermittent light poles, and then turned back. It's impossible to get here without specific directions from us. This brings a brilliant idea to mind of how to contribute to our bottom line. I immediately tell Vittoria all about it.

"Yes, Al, that's exactly what we do need," she replies as she pours a cup of coffee for Adele, "but before we can rent out a room here, we're going to have to be able to build the partition walls. No one is going to want to have to sleep in a great big room divided by curtains."

"That will take months . . . "

"How much do people charge for rooms? What do you think? Like, ten thousand lire a night?" she asks me.

"No, much more, twice or three times that, at least!"

"What are you talking about, we're at the far end of nowhere . . . there's no public transportation, you can't even get a taxi to bring you here."

"Exactly, that's what you pay extra for. I'm not interested in having a permanent guest here in the principality, we need to focus on people who need to get away for a week or two, somewhere that no one can find them. Desperate individuals like Adele here."

There's a sharp report and then the table surges, overturning the mugs of cappuccino. A kick meant for my shins missed its target entirely. Adele laughs, while I gaze without a shred of compassion at that tremendous dumbass sister of mine.

"He's right . . . " says Adele, "the fact that this place is so peaceful is worth solid gold. I know people who'd be willing to pay more than thirty thousand lire even if there are no walls. Plus, if you decided to rent it by the hour, forget about it."

"You can rent rooms by the hour? What do people do with a room for a few hours?" I ask.

"Oh my God, Al, you're fantastic . . . never change," Adele says to me.

"There's no danger of that, tests and exams have confirmed it. I'll always be the same as I was when I was seven, a genius," I smile at Vittoria who first stares at me, openmouthed, and then gets up from the table with her head hanging low. I hurry to finish breakfast because we're already running late, there's a flag raising to tend to and an anthem to sing.

"The oleander has moved . . . " Vittoria says, standing motionless in front of the open door.

"Would you pass me the cookies?" I ask Adele.

"What is the oleander bush doing in front of the door?" she replies.

I follow her glance and in fact the oleander shouldn't be where it is, it should be a few yards to the right, next to the phone booth. I get up and, with Adele following me, I go over to Vittoria.

"What the devil! Everything has moved here, even the street and the light pole . . . " she says.

It seems absurd to me, but no matter how many times I try changing my vantage point, from the door, from the living room window, and from the bathroom window, the view appears to have changed perceptibly. Adele goes out onto the street and looks around. Then she waves for us to join her.

"Come away from there! It's the house that's moved!"

PART THREE

55.

The year 1986 has just begun but already everyone seems very determined. Gaddafi threatens to unleash "an interminable war" against the Americans, the Iranians are ready to launch yet another final attack against the Iraqis, Halley's comet shows no scruples about swinging dangerously close to Earth, President Cossiga is absolutely resolute, he wants to "put an end to all squandering of national resources which are the resources of every citizen." From his tone of voice, I'd have to guess that this might finally be the time they do something about it. The principality of Santamaria intends to rise to the same level and it continues to go its own way, even if we still haven't figured out which way that is. Adele, who studies geology, comes back every month to monitor the house's movements along with a friend of hers, a researcher at the university. After the initial survey done five years ago, the situation immediately appeared clear: the house has no foundation, it was built on a thick cement slab that was originally poised atop a tuff-stone ridge that must have suddenly broken off, perhaps because of the rain. Now the principality is on land that the geological maps of the area describe as former swampland, not suitable for construction. The movements aren't especially worrisome, it's only a few inches a day, a little more when it rains and the soil becomes unstable. It's impossible right now to say whether it will ever stop. The terrain is slightly sloping, there's a small basin a few yards further on and, if you ask me, worst case, that's where the house's journey will come to an end. It's hard to say because the principality seems to prefer moving toward the interior, but doesn't object to lateral movements, and even to retracing its steps. According to Adele and her friend, the only thing to do was to trace on a topographic map all the variations and check the structure's soundness from time to time, taking note of even the most insignificant cracks. That is what we did and for the moment not a single crack has been seen, therefore no immediate dangers are to be expected—partly because, among other things, the house is low and the cement slab on which it is built is very solid. From the sketch they showed us, it looks like the base of a Subbuteo tabletop soccer figure.

This idea that the principality is built on a cement raft that floats at the whims of the old swamp worries Vittoria greatly. I'm not especially concerned, it'll stop sooner or later, and after all, the distance we've traveled is a good thing, now when we open our window we no longer look out onto the street, but onto a lovely garden instead. The only technical problem that we've had to solve is how to maintain the hookup to the light pole, which from time to time would come loose. And so, the last time it happened, I called Raul and together we installed a nice long electric cable to accommodate future movements without breaking loose. There's always lots of things to do in an independent principality. Aside from the garden, now the Santamaria family also has a genuine bathroom, with a bathtub. It's a beautiful tub, easily seats two, the largest tub that could be installed in the space available, sacrificing all secondary accessories. In other words, just the thing for naval battles and the landings on Omaha Beach. Even though the decision to install the bathtub contributes to the physical and mental development of children, as well as to their happiness, and is therefore in compliance with the parameters of the Regulatory Criterion, Vittoria didn't seem capable of enjoying the surprise right away. When she got back from her umpteenth business trip, when presented with this magnificent bathtub, the first words to come out of her mouth were: "What happened to the bidet?" while the last were: "Don't be stingy with the bubble bath, I want at least a foot and a half of bubbles!" For years I planned to inaugurate it with a nice big cannonball dive. During the assembly I realize that the tub was big, but not big enough to contain the exuberance of a nineteen-year-old who is six feet tall and 165 pounds, and I remembered how Mamma always used to tell me to think twice before doing things. And in fact first I thought: "This can't possibly work," as I was getting a running start in the living room, and then, "What I'm doing is plain stupid," while I was flying through the air with my knees pulled up to my chest. I plummeted down into the center of the tub, kicking up a wave that knocked the mirror off the wall over the sink and then proceeded to dump me on the floor, legs high in the air.

The UN behaves exactly like the electric company, we never received a reply to our request for recognition. In any case the throne couldn't be left vacant, so two years ago we self-annointed ourselves as the reigning prince and princess *ad interim*. According to the provisions of our constitution, before taking office we were required to perform six months of volunteer service in a psychiatric institution, though we considered that requirement abundantly fulfilled because we've been taking care of that idiot Raimondo for years now, and six months in a hospital—I took care of that for both of us by secretly performing the invaluable service of guide at the Umberto I Polyclinic. After memorizing the location of all the various wards, the doctors' clinics, and the list of patients, I kept thousands of people from having to wander down hallways and through wards in search of some sign or map, while there were patients in hospital beds who urgently needed their care. For the past two years we've had our own coin, the Elvis. The coinage proved necessary in order to meet the costs attendant upon the strong migratory flow from outside the principality. An independent principality, isolated from the rest of the world, without old people getting in the way, with a constitution that is enlightened and, most important of all, actually observed, is an irresistible attraction to anyone in search of peace and quiet. At first we took in guests free of charge, then we decided to accept a voluntary donation, and in the end we became a bed-and-breakfast proper. We care nothing about inflation and the fluctuations of the Italian lira, because the Elvis has one-to-one exchange parity with the dollar. The use of bed, bathroom, bathtub, television set, and refrigerator is charged according to a price list that is updated on a daily basis. In the past few years, we have housed, among others, two former colleagues of Raul's, the principal of a vocational-technical school in Tor Bella Monaca who had been threatened by the relatives of a student who had been flunked, a draft dodger, a general practitioner working on the rolls of state socialized medicine who had been accused of having a significant number of dead people on his patient list, a female Somali refugee with her son, free of charge as specified by the constitution of the principality, and a Serie B soccer player under investigation for his involvement in an illicit betting ring, at triple the regular rate, as per Article 53, Clause D: "Solidarity taxation applied to citizens blessed by unseemly good fortune." To these we should add the friends of either gender who just wanted to spend a few days away from their families, husbands, or girlfriends. In short, the principality is growing, the average population has hovered around 4.2 people. For the past few weeks we have had as our guest a certain Dario, a friend of Raul's former colleagues. Dario is an ideal guest because he's never here, and when he does come, he just stays holed up in his room, attached to the microphone of his CB radio.

In spite of the fact that we're earning good money, we still don't have walls because our skimpy savings are periodically bled dry by the installments on the mortage and other unexpected outlays. The last one was yet another gift from the Italian republic: the collapse of the Banco Ambrosiano, where we had deposited all of our money. We were expecting interest on our savings, but instead we had to hire a lawyer. The only good thing about what happened is that now Vittoria is convinced of the need to liberate ourselves of this last constraint. Now we keep our money safe and sound, in the suppository box.

Every so often, I still overdose on sad information, but I haven't been back to see the calm lady doctor since Mamma and Papà went away. The last time I really felt bad was six months ago, though the TV and the press had nothing to do with it, the blame lies on whoever it is that issued a permit to build an apartment house in the countryside in front of the house. The construction site isn't that close, as the crow flies it's probably at least three quarters of a mile, but the view is irremediably ruined. It used to be that if we were in the garden or if we looked out the windows, all we could see were meadows and grazing sheep. It was a hard blow, all the work we'd done to beautify the principality, then from one day to the next the cement trucks of the Italian republic roll up and everything's ruined. I talked to Vittoria, we sketched together for a while, we took a nice hot bath with plenty of back massages, and I was good as new again, without having to lay out a cent.

In my human flesh diary I wrote: "Perestroika and Glasnost are original ideas by Al Santamaria, written in black and white on the draft constitution I sent to the UN. Sue Gorbachev for plagiarism," "Urgently need to have full sexual relations with a girl," "Outlaw the use in Italian of the words *look*, *VIP*, *in*, and *yuppie*," "Urgently need to have full sexual relations with a girl, check out availability of Vittoria's girlfriends," "Socialists close to fifteen percent, Christian Democrats recovering. Get

ID card that will allow me to leave the country," "Urgently need to have full sexual relations with a girl. Stop discarding the girls who believe that "Jailhouse Rock" is by Mötley Crüe."

56.

The bathtub has become our favorite place to read. While we enjoy the warmth of the bathwater, Vittoria reads the letter from Mamma and Papà, maybe the best one in the past two years, a dozen or so pages crowded with good news. For the past few years, they've even been moving from one country to another outside of Italy, they just arrived in Brussels because Papà has found a job as a singer. Apparently, in the Italian expat community, Elvis's songs are going great guns, as are Mamma's chocolate *ciambelloni*. For the moment, they've taken a room in a small hotel, then maybe they'll look for an apartment on the outskirts of town.

"'Be good, Al, listen to your sister and don't make her worry . . .'"

"Do they have to write the same thing every time? It seems as if I'm doing who knows what!" I say.

"Al, they're the worries that all parents have. Just listen to them . . . "

"Did they send the letter before leaving? Let me see the postmark."

Vittoria hands me the envelope.

"No, it's a Belgian postmark. They'd already moved," I say.

"What is it, Al?"

"They just keep getting further and further away . . . I don't want to spend another Christmas all alone."

"I know, it's hard."

"We ought to go see them, I don't even remember what they look like."

"Yes, maybe we should. Certainly, it's a pity that . . . "

"What is?"

"Well, what's done is done. We have the bathtub, all that's left to finish the house is the walls, and can you imagine what a nice surprise it would be to be able to tell Mamma and Papà that they can come home because the house is finished?"

It's the usual thing about surprises. I know, a surprise is only a surprise if you do everything right, if you don't say anything until the end, but Christmases at the Santamaria home were wonderful. Not just because of the presents, those come anyway, Mamma and Papà are very good about it, they always know what I want, even though I don't write it because I don't want to make them spend money. What I miss about Christmas is the atmosphere, the preparations for the big dinner, waiting for midnight and the arrival of Father Elvis Christmas.

"I know, I know. We've been saying it for years, but we're just too slow! Even if we spend a little money on the trip, what is that really going to change? After all, at this point, what's a month more or less," I protest.

"Well, it's our decision, Mamma and Papà never said we couldn't come and see them. We just decided to try to save every penny we could so the family could get back together as soon as possible, but if we change our minds . . . "

"I'm sick of this. No parent would ever go on a five-year honeymoon!"

"It's not a honeymoon anymore, they're working. And Tiziana's father has only come home for Christmas and summer holidays for the past fifteen years, so how bad is this? All we need to do is make one last effort . . . "

"I'm tired of it, all the same!"

"Then let's write it in the letter. But you go. I prefer to save the money. That way, if Papà's job goes well, then they can send us some money and we can finish the construction earlier."

"All right, I'll write it."

But of course I'm not going to write it. It's just a whim. Sometimes I wish that the aliens would bring back the whiny, incompetent little sister they abducted years ago, this mature, rational duplicate is so determined that she scares me sometimes. On my heart and on my brain I've written all the things that she told me on the subject: "Mamma and Papà were with us for eighteen years, there wouldn't be anything wrong if they decided to spend the next eighteen years on their own"; "Just think about how hard it has to be for them. They're far from home and from the two people for whom they sacrificed everything. We can't be the ones who give up"; "Their children's good comes before anything else as far as they're concerned. If they decided that this was best, then our only duty is to trust them." I've written down dozens, all of them true, all pitiless. If we went to see them, then they'd feel obliged to come home every once in a while because it's obvious that they miss us, you can read it in the letters, and that would be a disaster: everything would take so much longer. So I understand, I'll just go on writing that I miss them, like always, and that we're happy and soon we'll see them again. In the meantime, I enjoy the lukewarm water and the foot massage that Vittoria has started to give me. I'm not a child anymore, soon I'll have a job that will make us rich, Mamma and Papà will come home in a first-class berth, to their principality full of walls. What a wonderful massage, the steam on my face, the bath bubbles popping by my ear, the tickling on my ankles, the bath sponge sliding up and down on the sole of my foot . . .

"Al . . . "

"Huh?"

"Why is the water getting hotter?"

"How would I know . . . "

57.

Every time I think I'm going to get all sorts of things done, but then when Vittoria leaves for Milan I spend all my time in the house pacing back and forth and growing increasingly venomous at the sight of that reinforced concrete skeleton that's rising over the countryside. I don't feel like going to the university campus, I don't feel like playing, I don't even feel like eating. Grown-ups who are all intent on living alone just baffle me. What do they do all day? I'd go crazy. If at least Dario were here, but instead he came back last night and was already gone at sunrise. A genius like me should have other dreams. I dream of bricks and doors, while I should be thinking about graduating from university, of being courted by Harvard. I still have plenty of time to amaze the world, Pasteur spent twenty years on developing his vaccine, so I need to say calm, I'll find a way to finish the principality. But it's taken months to amass a loyal clientele, even though my business as an exam-and-paper vendor is now thriving at the university, just as it did at high school. The lessons are all pretty boring, I only go so I can take notes and resell them at a premium to others who have better things to do. On the other hand, it takes almost no effort to pass the exams. I don't work too hard to understand, I prefer just to memorize. At every session I expect a professor to ask me: "Would you be able to express the concept in your own words, or do you only know how to parrot what you read?" but instead they ask me: "Let's talk about the political inclinations of the sans-culottes," and I think to myself: book with pale yellow cover, title: *The Sans-Culottes: The Popular Movement and Revolutionary Government, 1793-1794*, chapter title "The Political Inclinations of the Parisian Sans-Culottes." Then they specify: "What can you tell us about their ideas concerning popular sovereignty?" and I remember that on the paragraph that discusses popular sovereignty, there's a tiny stain of chocolate, it's page ninety-five, the exact words are: "Popular sovereignty is 'an indefeasible right, an inalienable right, a right that cannot be delegated'; on November 3, 1792 (12 Brumaire, year 1), the *Cité* section concluded that 'every man who assumes to have sovereignty will be regarded as a tyrant, usurper of public liberty and worthy of death . . . '" Inside my backpack, along with my books and my sandwich, I bring with me ten or so tanks. There's a small lawn in front of the school of law with low, very dense hedges, ideal for my Battle of the Ardennes. Unfortunately, it's always crawling with students who seem to camp out there, so I've never dared to pull out my tanks. As it is, my popularity is hanging by a thread and I don't want things to end the way they did in high school: caught out the first year, the object of fun for the next four. As soon as I can, I join the little groups playing soccer or tossing Frisbees, but more than games they seem like sessions for the rehabilitation of the motor skills of the elderly. One time I dared to leap in the air to snag the disk, followed by a paratrooper's roll on the grass, and they all looked at me as if I were an alien.

I'm a shameless hit with the girls. My secret notes are slaying them. The older the students, the better it works. We're on the order of 70 percent useful results. I'm sweet, I'm a doll, if only all the boys were like me, so they tell me and then it's all hugs, kisses on the cheek, tousled hair. I ought to wear a Play-Doh T-shirt so I can take home casts of all the tits that press up against me throughout the day. But, actually, intercourse seems to be out of the question, I only get the girls who already have boyfriends or just went through a nasty breakup. Ever since Rock Hudson died, moreover, girls are more cautious, and I go everywhere with a condom in my wallet because I want to be ready for even the slimmest of chances. For the more difficult cases, I also have an authentic newspaper clipping that invites the populace to remain calm:

"Remember, AIDS is a disease that afflicts only homosexuals and drug addicts."

I take one exam after another, rapid-fire, and I get A-pluses even from the professors who are notorious sticklers and yet, in spite of my extremely high academic performance, I just don't seem to be able to find the shred of a job here at the university. I was hoping to get hired at the library, I tried to amaze the director by reeling off the titles and authors of the two hundred and six volumes contained in the "Modern and Contemporary History" section, but it wasn't enough, the vacant position was given to a professor's grandson. I'm not really all that surprised, because governments may change but the Italian republic always remains the usual place, the country of class opportunity. Every rich citizen has an equal opportunity to become even more so. That's the meaning of the Italian Dream.

While waiting for the people's revolution that in short order, perhaps even before the end of the soccer championship, will sweep away the established government, I put my genius to work at a pub for students. I like the job, spending my evenings surrounded by tables and mugs of beer makes me feel like a normal twenty-year-old.

"Here you go, three light medium beers, a red ale, a double malt beer, a Negroni, two glasses of gin fizz, and three glasses of Morellino red," I say.

"It was just two glasses of Morellino, I'd asked for a Dolcetto," a young woman replies with an annoyed expression.

Now I need to find a nice way of telling her that at least ten young women just like her come in here every night. They read the menu, they heave a sigh, they ask for advice, and with each piece of advice they reply with a: "No," with an: "I don't like that," and an: "I don't feel like that tonight." She kept me there like a fool for five solid minutes while she reread the menu for the fourth time, even though nothing about it had changed in the meantime, and in the end she said: "Okay, then, Morellino for me, too, no wait, make that a beer, I think that would be better . . . Or else, do you have Dolcetto? Maybe a Dolcetto, okay. Wha-a-at? Oh, let's just go with another Morellino!"

"You said: 'Oh, let's just go with another Morellino,'" I summarize.

"No, I said a glass of Dolcetto," she replies with the attitude of someone who's been accustomed to getting her way since she was three, and so has never had a good reason to grow up.

I think about my tip, I think about the poor bastard on her left who has to put up with her every blessed day, and I apologize for my mistake. I come back with a glass of Morellino, I tell her that it's Dolcetto, and she drinks it without noticing a thing.

I'm tired, I set aside my notes on the constitution, but before burrowing under the sheets I decide to mark on Adele's topographic map the principality's latest moves. I'd been meaning to do it for months and I don't want to put it off any longer. On the sheet of paper I sketch with dotted lines the direction of the movements, I add the observation date next to it, I connect it to the previous ones. First it was moving in a northeasterly direction, then northerly, then westerly, and now it's decidedly heading toward the east. Dang. Northeast . . . north . . . west . . . the situation is clear. Crystal clear!

"Are you asleep? Vittoria?"

"A-a-al . . . what is it . . . "

"I figured out where the principality is going."

"Good boy, now go back to sleep and you can tell me tomorrow . . . "

"Aren't you curious to know right now?"

"Sure, Al . . . just don't tap me on the shoulder."

"Do you see the chart of the movements? You see it?"

"Where?"

"Look at the direction . . . You see?"

"See what?"

"We were going northeast, then north, and now we're heading west! Venice, Munich, Brussels . . . "

"Oh lord, Al, I don't understand . . . "

"The promised home is trying to get back to Mamma and Papà!"

58.

To celebrate the fifth anniversary of the founding of the principality, Vittoria has decided to throw a great party. There will be thirty or so guests, all friends of hers. I circulated invitations to my few friends at the university, but the answers, all on the order of "If I can find the time, I'd be delighted to come," are all too familiar. The only one who accepted on the spot is Raimondo, who in fact made a point of coming well ahead of time to help out. Once Vittoria told me that Raimondo seems like one of those characters from an American comedy whom they present to you at the beginning of the movie as a small boy, dressed in a shirt, bow tie, argyle sweater, and glasses, and then, to tell you that time has passed but it's still the very same person, they show you an adult dressed exactly the same way. Aside from the bow tie, which he only wears for first communions and weddings, that's Raimondo, he always dresses the same way for fear that someone might lose track of his life.

"But what are you doing?" Vittoria asks us when she gets home from the grocery store with Tiziana.

"A soccer match . . . why?"

"You still haven't done anything!" Tiziana complains.

"Sorry, we'll help you right away," says Raimondo.

"As soon as we finish the match, we'll help you," I correct him.

Soccer matches, one-against-one with an unguarded goal, ought to consist of delightful touches, narrow dribbling, and finely calibrated shots, a sort of two-person dance in front of the goalposts. But it's a rare thing for Mother Nature to give good feet to those who have already been given a portentous brain; sometimes she won't even give them to people who left their brains stuck to the wall of a garage. One of Raimondo's Pruzzo-style kicks leaves the ball up a tree. One of my Zico-style heel kicks sends it sixty-five feet in the wrong direction, straight out into the street. Since I'm the one who had to climb the tree, this time responsibility for retrieval falls to my friend.

"What's that down there? A cargo truck?" Raimondo asks me from the street.

"No, it's just a semitrailer. I don't know, it's been there for a week."

"Maybe you should call the police . . . it might be stolen."

"It's outside the jurisdiction of the principality, if someone comes and gets it, fine. Otherwise, as far as I'm concerned, it can stay parked there forever."

We only return to the house after I've managed to tear victory from the jaws of defeat, exhausting my adversary with four overtimes and sessions of penalty kicks. Raimondo goes over to be enslaved by Tiziana, while I stall for time with Vittoria, hoping against hope not to get dragged into any activity.

"Is Adele coming?" I ask her absentmindedly.

"Al, forget about her. For tonight, she already had something to do."

"I was just asking . . . "

"Don't get obsessed. Look around, rather. Tiziana likes you," she whispers.

"How do you know?"

"I just know, it's obvious."

"What's obvious, how can you tell?"

"Trust me, there are certain things that a woman just knows. Try to strike up a conversation with her and you'll see."

I can already imagine what I'll say at the university: "These days I'm seeing an older woman, very experienced . . . "

"What are you thinking about, Al?"

"Nothing. All right, I'll try to strike up a conversation, then. I'm going, eh? You're not trying to make a fool out of me, are you?"

"With Tiziana? No, no, listen, go ahead and don't worry."

For the rest of the evening, I don't miss a single chance to make it clear to Tiziana, discreetly, that I'm interested in her. I place two notes in her hand, I hide a paper heart in her pocket, I lay a bouquet of flowers on her handbag. Each time, she smiles at me, but then she goes back to talking with her friends as if nothing had happened. After a while, I stop nurturing illusions, it's going to turn out just like all the other times, a kiss on the cheek and so long. When everyone gets up to go play the guitar in the yard, and I assume that I'm going to end the evening conceding defeat to Raimondo, Tiziana takes me by the hand and leads me to my room. I don't even have a chance to swallow the breath-freshening mint, which I put in my jeans pocket just in case, before I find myself locked in her arms. Her mouth tastes of wine and, in open contradiction of my reference texts on the subject:—*Flight from the Harem*, *A Nymph in the Woods*, and *Amorous Acrobatics* from Vittoria's collection of Harmony Romances,—her lips are cool, almost cold. She lifts my T-shirt, I understand that she wants to take it off so I do like with Mamma: I lift both arms in a V. From here on, though, we're in new territory. I'm about to beat the record. She starts to undo my pants, and to make it easier for her I sit down on the bed and raise my legs as high as I can. She laughs.

"What are you doing? . . . You must at least know how to take off your own shoes?"

She unbuttons her blouse, slips off her panties, lifts her skirt and, scampering across the bed, comes and lies on top of me. I try to concentrate on what I'm supposed to do next because I don't want to get it wrong, but she's faster than my thoughts. As soon as I think about touching her tits, she takes my hand and guides it under her bra. While I wonder whether it might not be a good idea to kiss her, at least out of gratitude, I find her tongue between my teeth.

When you get right down to it, things always turn out the same way. The time comes when the grown-ups tell you they're tired, that they just can't keep it up, that they're all sweaty, and that time always seems to come just when you were finally starting to enjoy yourself.

"Five more minutes!"

And they shake their head and tell you that it's been two hours that they've been at it and that they need a minute to catch their breath.

"Five more minutes and then I'll stop, I swear!"

And then they tell you that it's the third time you've said that, that it's a bad idea to overdo things, and that doing it six times in a row is the kind of thing you can't even tell people because after all no one would believe it.

While Tiziana puts her clothes back on, I try to make her panties disappear, but as soon as I reach out my hand to grab them, I feel my head start to go fizzy and my jaw go slack. She kisses me on the forehead, I'm tempted to hug her, but the impulse sent out from the brain evaporates before it can reach the limbs. From the garden comes a prolonged burst of applause and a chorus of whistles, and I hear someone yell: "Brava-a-a!" The cakes must have arrived, the celebrations for the inauguration of the principality are starting to heat up, and I decide to get a short nap, just a couple of minutes, then I'll go join them.

59.

Come on, answer, Vittoria, please, answer-e-e-r. I don't have the slightest desire to make this phone call, I guarantee it. I understand, I'm "waiting to be connected to the extension requested," got it, you don't have to tell me again! How I wish it was tomorrow. I'm-waiting-to-be-connected-to-the-extension-requested! What I wouldn't give to be curled up in my bed, between the sheets, waiting for everything to be taken care of without my having to lift a finger.

"Hello?"

"Ciao, Vittoria!"

"Ciao, Al."

"How are you? What are you doing today?"

"Al, I'm at the office . . . what is it?"

"*Oui, c'est ma sœur. Je l'ai trouvée.*"

"Al, what are you saying?"

"No, sorry, I wasn't talking to you . . . I was talking with a gentleman here . . . a policeman."

"But why are you speaking French to a policeman? Since when do you speak French?"

"I don't speak French, I just learned those two or three hundred phrases that are in the pocket dictionary . . . while I was on the train."

"On the train? Al, where on earth are you?" she shouts.

"Vittoria, nothing's happened, don't worry! I'm just here in Brussels . . . "

"In Brussels?" She shouts so loudly that the two policemen in front of me share a chuckle.

"Well, all right then . . . if you're going to get all mad then I won't tell you a thing!"

"Al, tell me immediately what you're doing with a policeman in Brussels!"

"If you don't calm down, I won't tell you anything!"

"Tell me right away, for fuck's sake!"

"Hee hee, you said 'fuck,' wait till Mamma hears about this . . ."

"Al, I beg you, I'm about to have a heart attack!"

"All right, all right, it's nothing. I just came to Brussels to surprise Mamma and Papà."

"Al!"

"With my own money, money I earned selling essays!"

"Then what happened?"

"I went to the hotel they'd mentioned in their last letter, Le Clocher, you remember, don't you? Well, to make a long story short, they weren't there, they must have left already."

"So what does the policeman have to do with all this?"

"Nothing, it's just that I was planning to stay in Mamma and Papà's room, so I didn't bring enough money . . . so I decided to sleep in the street for a while . . . and it turns out that it's not strictly legal around here. So now I guess I'm at the police station. Because, among other things, I don't really have a passport . . ."

"Al, I'm going to hang up now and call the embassy, I'll try to explain the situation . . . in the meantime, try to get a phone number where I can call you back."

"*Est-ce que je peux avoir votre numéro de téléphone, s'il vous plaît? Voulez-vous une tranche de* ciambellone *au chocolat?*"

I wouldn't have said a word about the principality, I wouldn't have spoiled the surprise for Mamma and Papà. At the very most I would have said: "You don't know what's waiting for you when you get back!" There's one thing I envy Vittoria for: she always knows exactly what will happen afterward. If you decide against letting someone see the classwork anyway, even though they're too poor to pay, afterwards you'll feel like a jerk; if you eat too much chocolate, afterwards you'll get indigestion; if you fall in love every five minutes, afterwards you'll feel as if you never even fell in love at all. I don't know how she does it, she has a very special talent all her own. No matter how hard I try, I just never seem to be able to take afterwards into consideration. If you go to see Mamma and Papà, afterwards you'll feel weighed down by a horrible sadness. It wasn't that hard, it should have been enough to think about it for a second. If at least I could have seen them, but instead they slipped through my fingers, and I was so frustrated I would gladly have set the passenger car on fire on the trip home. I spent the last hour on the train thinking about the fight I was going to have with Vittoria. But this time too the gaps in my ability to foretell the future were all too evident. Of course, she wasn't angry at all, she was scared to death, and when she threw her arms around me, she was just a complete mess. She trembled and sobbed. In my embarrassment I started smiling at the other travelers getting off the train, and so we were taken for a long-separated couple reuniting after a heartbreaking period apart. We slept together that night, curled up on her bed. She grabbed my foot, and it seemed like a massage, but it was really a leash.

When I wake up I decide to thank her with a full principality flag raising. It's 5:30 A.M., breakfast is ready on the table, flowers in a drinking glass, let's let loose with the anthem!

"*We are fa-mi-ly! I got my sister with me-e-e!*" I sing.

Vittoria gets up. Her face isn't really all that promising. She really reminds a lot of that morning in spring 1975, when she woke up covered with blisters and accused me of giving her chicken pox.

"*We are fa-mi-ly! Get up everybody and si-i-ing!*" I go on.

If I look at her more carefully, I see that murderous fury that I saw once before, on May 12, 1978, when I cut a pocket off her favorite skirt to make a tent for my Big Jim. Without the slightest sign of respect for the niceties of official ceremonial, she abruptly silences the tape recorder. Things are looking grim.

"All decisions of the reigning prince must be confirmed by the firstborn princess. Article 55 of the principality's constitution," she tells me.

My diversionary efforts didn't work. It was obvious that sooner or later we were going to have to deal with the subject, and this must be an unabridged version of the man-to-man talks I had with Papà.

"My decision respected the three fundamental parameters of the Regulatory Criterion," I reply, "and in fact seeing one's parents contributes to one's physical development, one's mental development, and . . . "

"No agency of the principality has the authority to make secret decisions concerning the good of the principality itself, otherwise we're starting to think like Andreotti and that'll be the end of that. Rough draft of Article 56!" Vittoria shouts.

"It's a fiduciary obligation of the reigning prince to take all due care of the assets of the principality in accordance with the juridical criterion of the good paterfamilias. Article 33!" I reply.

"What do the assets of the principality have to do with what you did?"

I stare at her with a horrified expression. I throw my arms wide in disappointment.

"The principality considers 'wealth' exclusively the accumulation and care of immaterial assets. Article 6! I'm surprised at you, if love for one's parents isn't an asset of the principality then I certainly don't know . . . "

"The utilization of the art of oratory to deceive the people and uphold patently absurd theses is to be considered a criminal act. Article 68!"

"I never liked that article! You insisted on it!"

"Certainly! I insisted on it because I know you!"

60.

At the pub I ran into Roberta. I hadn't seen her in at least three years, when her mother transferred her to another high school because of a joint she accidentally stumbled upon while intentionally rummaging through Roberta's purse. The woman's irrevocable decision, made for her daughter's own welfare, moved her to the same school, same class, adjoining desks, as the boy who she'd got the joint from in the first place, in exchange for who knows what.

Roberta came in with a girlfriend and, while I was wondering whether or not I ought to say hello to her, she walked straight toward me and gave me a hug. I didn't expect her to recognize me. Whereas she hasn't changed much, so I told her that she looked exactly the same, maybe a little fatter.

When her girlfriend leaves, Roberta waits for me to finish straightening out the tables and together we go out for a walk. We talk about our high school days, about our studies, our vacations, and what we're doing now.

"Do you remember back in kindergarten when you were still trying to find your way?" she asks me. "Since I have a grandfather and father who are both lawyers, I didn't have that problem . . . I enrolled in law school."

"Do you like it?"

"I don't know, that's like asking a train whether it likes going back and forth on the rails. I just try to get there on time and not to disappoint anyone."

"Do you live with your folks?"

"I've been living on my own for a few months now. But don't imagine anything romantic, I'm staying with a family friend, Papà pays the rent, and my landlady, who lives upstairs, keeps an eye on me day and night," she tells me.

"You ought to come live in the principality. There, you don't have anyone keeping an eye on you."

"What principality?"

"My house, me and my sister's house . . . we declared independence five years ago."

"I talk plenty of bullshit, but you . . . "

"No, really, we even have our own coat of arms. I designed it. Do you want to see?"

"Yes, show me."

"It's at my house."

"I should have guessed . . . "

She smiles at me, twisting her mouth on one side, creating a delightful dimple in her left cheek. I wonder if she'll let me stick my finger in it.

"And that look on your face? What are you thinking about?" she asks me.

"No, nothing . . . it's just that the principality is big. Me and my sister are the prince and princess, but we could find you a position as duchess, if you like."

We reach our destination in Tiziana's car, making time that would be very difficult to match if you obeyed the rules of the road. Vittoria isn't home and, as usual, she's forgotten to leave the front lights on. Luckily the moon is almost full and we reach the door, easily sidestepping potholes and projecting rocks. I show Roberta the coat of arms above the door, and she makes a funny face. She was convinced that it was all just a tall tale, but now something leaves her uneasy. She is immediately struck by the level of messiness that reigns inside the house. She says that it's clear we're living large, in complete freedom. Then she turns to look out the big living room window.

"You're very isolated . . . but you have a magnificent view," she says.

"Too bad about that monstrosity they're building."

"Where?"

"Over there."

But what I'm pointing at, right in front of us, is the hill.

"Right next to it," I correct myself.

Roberta leans out, but given the rotation undertaken by the principality, in order to see the construction site she'd actually have to go outside and even then make a certain effort. I remain at her side, admiring the hill. My legs shake a little. Hypothesis A: the principality moved in a perfectly normal fashion and I only just noticed that we now overlook the hill because I've been trying for weeks to avoid looking at the construction site. Hypothesis B: the principality actually has a soul, and in order to keep me from looking like a fool with Roberta, it swung around hurriedly the minute it saw us arrive.

In the meantime, she starts wandering around the house, and I take advantage of the opportunity to check and make sure there are no cracks in the walls.

"Where do your parents live?" she asks me.

"Here. In reality, we're the prince and princess heirs apparent, they're the real prince and princess, but since they're traveling for the moment it's all ours."

"And when are they coming back?"

"I don't know, maybe in a few months."

"Why, where have they gone?"

"On their honeymoon. At first they were only supposed to go to Venice, but then they liked it and started traveling quite a lot."

"How long have they been away?"

"Five years, one months, and twelve days."

"Wow, that is one long honeymoon!"

"Well, just consider that they postponed it for twenty years . . . "

"I love your folks. Those are the kind of parents everyone should have!"

I conclude the inspection in my bedroom, and the situation immediately becomes strange. I get the impression that she's studying me. I show her the box with all the games, she asks to see my ID card. After all, I knew that we weren't going to play anything, it was just an attempt, maybe when she saw the mini pinball machine she might have felt like a couple of rounds. We kiss, she never closes her eyes, I can't figure out whether she's keeping me under surveillance or just thinks I'm handsome. It must be the latter, so just as I did with Tiziana I raise my arms so she can take off my T-shirt. She doesn't understand. Maybe I ought to offer her something in exchange, like in the old days.

"Do you need notes on private law?"

"What?"

"Private law plus philosophy of law, last offer."

She coughs, she scratches her nose. She seems to be about to ask me something, but then not a word emerges from her parted lips. She takes me by the hand, she leads me outside. She stops for a moment to look at the hill, then she kisses me on the forehead and leaves. I felt much better years ago, when I just avoided girls, when I'd recoil and dodge anytime they tried to kiss me. Now I'm always in a state of tension, it's the whole body that needs it and the thought that once we get out of bed there aren't any other games I can play with them doesn't give me the slightest relief, that one game is more than enough. A new article is needed for the constitution of the principality: "The reigning prince has a right to one or more consorts." The issuance of an annual competition might prove to be a solution. I'm confused and, as always when that happens, I miss Mamma, the feel of her hand in my hair, her reassuring gaze. She knows that, it's why she made Vittoria come back.

"Who was that pretty girl I passed coming back?" she asks me.

"Roberta, we went to kindergarten together, she went to the same high school as us, too."

"I don't remember her."

Maybe I took the wrong approach, I shouldn't have taken her into my room. It would have been more romantic if we'd stayed out here on the lounge chairs to look at the hill. Luckily, there's Agnese's messenger, spending a few minutes with her will make me feel better.

"You see? Did you notice that now we're pointed toward the hill?" I ask her.

"Al! Please, stop!" She covers her eyes with one hand and goes inside. "Don't tell me these things, I'm doing my best not to think about them! Just let me know if any fissures open in the ground, okay?" she shouts at me.

Thanks all the same, Mamma.

61.

Anthem of the principality, flag fluttering, Casimiro standing to attention. Resigned sister who emerges from behind the curtain around her bedroom.

"Try and guess," I tell her.

"Al, please! I already told you not to talk to me about the principality's movements, because it makes me . . . "

"Oh, cut it out! It's better, much better than that!"

She needs to see it with her own eyes. I take her by the hand and drag her outside. We cross the field, arguing about the wisdom of going outside in our pajamas and the risk of running into someone in a place where you never see a soul in the middle of the day, much less at dawn, and then we walk up the street analyzing the pros and cons of how late I'm making her for work. We fetch up in front of the back door of the abandoned semitrailer, fighting like a couple of cats.

"Would you stop whining?" I shout at her. "Close your eyes a-a-and . . . look at the gift they gave us!"

"Toys?"

"Yes! They're boxes of LEGO bricks!"

"Nice, but they're not ours."

"There are thousands of them, if we snag just one box, who do you think'll ever notice?"

"Al, this isn't our property."

"But the trailer's been sitting here for months, it's abandoned!"

"Okay, take one box, shut the trailer back up, and forget about all this. Hey, I said one box!"

"This second box is for you. One apiece, and that's it . . . "

There, that's something I would have loved to invent: LEGO building blocks. They're simple, brilliant, suitable for all ages, educational. When I was one year old, I had fun stacking them up, and the structure would collapse immediately. I immediately discovered the benefits of the asymmetrical stringcourse, and when I was eighteen months old, I built my first earthquake-proof unit of modular housing, capable of withstanding the vibrations of our washing machine on spin cycle. I had a box of a hundred pieces, I used them up almost immediately. Now I have Vittoria's box, too, and a whole semitrailer full outside. I'm not supposed to touch it, I know, but if I slip a few empty boxes into the stacks, I'd love to see who would ever notice.

Here she comes now. Exhausted from a long day at work, from the walk home, nearly a mile, from the whole day away from home without me. But her exhaustion is going to dissolve in an instant.

"Al! You didn't even put a pot of water on the stove to boil!"

Just stop complaining and turn around. Come on, turn around turn around turn arou-ou-ou-ound!

"Oh, my God . . . "

"It's nice to have a man in the house, isn't it? He may not put the water on to boil, but still . . . "

Having completed the visual experience, behold, she steps closer in amazement for the tactile experience. She touches it gingerly with the tip of her forefinger, followed by further exploration with the palm of her hand. It's all true, Vittoria, believe it.

"What do you think?" I ask her.

"How on earth did you do it?"

"So you like it?"

"It's nice . . . but . . . will it hold up?"

"Eh-eh-eh . . . no, actually it won't. For the moment I've braced it up with furniture on either side. But I called Raul, he's going to come fix it in place tomorrow. He says that, if he's understood clearly 'exactly what the frick I've gone and dreamed up this time,' all we should need is some concrete, some industrial adhesive, and a dozen or so anchoring points."

We turned the sofa around and ate there, with our eyes locked on the first partition wall ever built out of plastic construction blocks. To work more quickly, I paid no attention to the assortment of colors, and the final effect resembles the staticky snow that you see on our television set when you unplug the antenna, only in full color. If you wanted to, you could try to introduce geometric motifs, say, polka dots, or pinstripes.

"I wonder what kind of sentence they'd give you for grand theft LEGO blocks . . . " Vittoria wonders aloud.

"At the very worst, misappropriation of abandoned property. It's not as if we hijacked the truck. And after all, semi-trailer freight is always fully insured, so don't start freaking out about toy factories going bankrupt or truck drivers losing their livelihoods."

"It's beautiful."

"You understand? Now we can tell Mamma and Papà to come home!"

Vittoria smiles at me. She sighs.

"No, Al, we'll tell them to come back when we finally have some real walls."

"Why, what's wrong with these?"

"What's wrong with these? Well, for starters, you can't hang pictures on them, much less put up shelving. And you know how Mamma adores shelves."

"They're beautiful walls, colorful, what do we need pictures and shelves for?"

"Al, the work you've done here is magnificent . . . in fact, now I'll help you to build another wall, that way we'll finally have all the rooms separated, and we can raise the rent on them."

The young lady's sharp as a tack. Hanging out with me isn't doing her any harm.

"Right. And with the rent money, we can build real walls, and then we can send for the old folks."

"Certainly! Let's go get some more boxes."

The principality preserves things, keeps them intact, here you can forget that you're the secretary to a powerful man or a genius bent on saving the world, and instead remember that at the origin of everything you may have eventually become, there always and in any case was a child. In no other home in the Italian republic and in the whole world are there two young people in their twenties playing with LEGO blocks in their underwear. I didn't have hair on my legs, she didn't have tits, but we were just sitting there, up on our knees, our butts perched on our heels, side by side. We were playing with Mamma's hair rollers, we'd build walls with the small ones, towers and bastions with the big ones, without realizing it we had begun that long spiraling path that brings the moments of life into repetition, never perfectly identical each time. This game gives me a profound and all-encompassing sensation of well-being. Brick upon brick, building the first yard or so of wall, I rebuild something even more important that I don't understand. I barely perceive it, in the frenzied confusion of acts, in the happy desperation of our fingers.

62.

After bracing up the last wall, Raul insisted on taking a picture of us with his Polaroid camera, he says that we absolutely have to send it to Mamma and Papà. We watch as the greenish emulsion turns light brown, the whites and blacks come to the surface, the facial features gradually swim into view like a distant memory of something that happened a minute ago. A faint stirring of uneasiness, the images that appear look like Agnese and Mario Elvis. Then there we are, Vittoria and Al, hugging in front of the wall, without a great deal of imagination, giving two thumbs up. We leave the picture on the table and follow Raul outside. He's beside himself with joy, he keeps jumping from one foot to the other.

"Well? What do you think of her?" he asks, slapping his hand on the roof of his little van.

"Nice, really nice, it hardly even seems used," says Vittoria.

Given his enthusiasm, we feel obliged to take a nice guided tour around the vehicle. On the sides the following words appear: "Call Raul. I Clean Out Apartments and Cellars."

"'Clean out'? Wouldn't 'declutter' have been better? Or 'empty'?" I ask.

"I don't know, that's just what popped into my mind . . . "

I'm happy that he's taken my advice. Because of the work he does, Raul knows all the junkmen and antiques dealers in the city. So I told him: Why don't you set up emptying cellars, with all the contacts that you have, you'll make twice as much money, from the people who hire you to clear out the cellar and from the junkmen and antiquarians. The idea worked, when the economy is going well, prosperity distorts reality, it attributes value only to what's new, which means that in every single cellar there's a treasure in old phonograph records, paintings, books, bicycles, and furniture. One lady paid him to haul away a motorcycle. It turned out to be a 1949 MV Agusta, and even though it was missing some parts, a collector bought it from him for almost a million lire.

"Oh, kids, I don't need to tell you that in a couple of months at the very most I'll pay you back every cent."

"Don't worry about it . . . " Vittoria tells him.

"Believe me, I know that you need it, I'll pay you back with full interest. Hey, who the frick is that?"

Raul points to a Citroën Dyane that comes to a halt in the field, lurching and bouncing like a water bed.

"That's our guest," I tell Raul.

Dario, a reserved sort of guy, in his early thirties, greets us as usual with a nod of the head. He puts the strap of his black shoulder bag over his neck and walks toward us, head bowed, ambiguous look in his eyes, hands in his pockets. Someone must once have made the mistake of telling him that he looks like the male lead in *9½ Weeks*.

"Ah, so that's him. I feel like I might have met him somewhere sometime . . . who knows," says Raul.

"Ciao, Dario," says Vittoria.

There's a glance between the two of them that kindles my hopes. Could it be that she's finally fed up with her crazy standard boyfriends and it's dawned on her that a remote, quiet type might just be the perfect fiancé for us all?

"Come on, I'll show you your new bedroom," I tell Dario.

"Have your folks come back?" he asks me.

"No, just new in the sense that there's something new about it."

Dario stops in front of the door to the house. He looks around.

"Wait, has the door always been right here? I remember that I used to drive from that direction and . . . "

"Dario, you say the same thing every time . . . it's just that you don't come very often, and almost always at night, so you lose your sense of orientation . . . one thing I can tell you for sure is that the house hasn't moved."

To keep him from mentally taking note of certain points of reference, I drag him inside and show him my masterpiece.

"Impossible. Don't tell me that . . . I mean, they must sell them in blocks and then you . . . " says Dario.

"No, we built the wall, tiny brick by tiny brick."

Dario goes into his room, looks around, touches the walls in disbelief. His tough-guy pose dissolves into a goofy smile.

"They're beautiful, I'm speechless."

"But now the price of the room is fifteen Elvises," I tell him.

"I expected as much . . . but how much does that add up to in Italian lire?"

"At today's rate of exchange: 23,710 lire."

"You're quoting one Elvis at almost sixteen hundred lire? You're just a ruthless speculator."

"The term is inaccurate, we're not in Italy here, this is the principality of Santamaria. 'The principality does not recognize the mechanisms of international finance and is free to assign to its currency the value that it deems appropriate,' Article 117 of the constitution. And in any case, you're in luck, until yesterday we were aligned with the British pound sterling."

"I'm tired right now . . . but later on you and me are going to have to have a little talk."

Now I understand why Mamma and Papà spent whole evenings at a time doing the accounts. Home economics has a mathematical logic that is hard to accept: (part-time work + freelance work + sale of notes and papers + room rentals) −

(mortgage + assorted expenses + unexpected outlays) = 0. It's been going on like this for far too many months, it's time to retrench. I also understand why most of the young men I know dream of working as a butcher, it's normal that they prefer to live with just one thought: "Ferrari or Porsche?" The Santamaria family is behind the times, the styles of consumption are changing, now people are buying exotic vacations, designer suits, second cars, while we're stuck at the ISTAT demographic profile of the average family of the Seventies, we're still worrying about a refrigerator and a washing machine. Sometimes I question the underlying assumptions of my plan: while we're struggling to keep our heads above water, the economy of the Italian republic is going great guns. In the outside world they're building hospitals that sit unused, sports arenas that never open to the public, superhighways to nowhere, viaducts that stop in midair. An impressive show of force, befitting a genuine superpower: So you spend billions to drop atomic bombs in deserts and on Polynesian atolls? We spend just as much to drop cement more or less at random. Maybe I should pave over the whole field and build a nice big parking lot, or maybe, just for the day, I ought to stop thinking entirely, because I'm starting to hear voices. Actually, I do hear them, insistent and crackling, and in fact they're coming from Dario's room.

"What are you doing?" I ask him.

"When are you guys going to make up your minds to install some doors, too?" he replies sarcastically.

"Sorry, it's just that I thought I heard voices coming from in here . . . "

With a smile he seems to apologize for his tone of voice. He waves me into the room.

"I was just listening to the police channel," he explains.

"And why would you do that?"

"It's fun, it's better than watching an episode of *CHiPs*."

"Can you listen to the firemen, too?"

"Certainly."

"Ni-i-ice."

"So listen . . . this whole thing about the principality, why is it so important to you to be a prince? Is it because you like to feel important? Give other people orders?" he asks me.

"No, not at all, it's just that I like to have clear boundaries."

"This is 1986! Everyone else is trying to knock down boundaries and you're trying to create new ones?"

"You see, Dario, strange things are happening out there . . . The Communist Party is going to hold its congress in the PalaTrussardi, you understand? We're allowing bishops, citizens of a foreign state, to urge Italian voters to support the Christian Democrats, telling them that to do otherwise is a sin and they'd make God upset? Boundaries are useful, believe me, otherwise you're forced to accept everything. With a clearly demarcated boundary, you can decide what to let enter your world and what to keep out. And after all, they started it."

"Started what?"

"You're strange, so you can't have a job, and you've been a housewife for too many years, so you can't have a job either, as for you, you have excellent grades, but since you're the son of a strange person and a housewife, you can't have a proper job, and your house is no good either because it's in an administrative black hole, and there's no one willing to come out and hook up the electric power or the gas . . . tell me that those aren't borders. So here you have us: This is the world's smallest principality, and it's governed by Mario Elvis and Agnese Santamaria, prince and princess of a genuinely secular micronation, truly independent, unfailingly peaceful. Here we welcome the weak, the poor, the disenfranchised, society's rejects . . . no disrespect intended for present company."

"Certainly, of course . . . Anyway, I'd rule out the poor, with the exchange rate you're talking about . . . "

"If you can prove that you're without means of support, you have a right to free accommodation for a month, plus all the winter nights that the thermometer drops below freezing. It's written in the constitution of the principality. Article 10, paragraph 3. Are you without means of support?"

"No, in fact, give me fifty Elvises, I want to take a shower and get something to eat."

"Fifty Elvises, certainly . . . and the first shower is free."

63.

The new letter from Mamma and Papà is a disappointment. The newspaper articles that I'd enclosed with our last response, as evidence of the waste of public money, did nothing to persuade them: once again they rejected my suggestion that we call them by retrieving tokens from the phone booth. Given my insistence, they wrote that from now on they'll call us, three times a week, at Tiziana's house or wherever else we want. They'll have to spend a hundred thousand lire or so every month, as much money as Mamma earns making *ciambelloni* all day, but we shouldn't worry, they've tightened their belts for a lifetime, and they're not going to refuse to do so now in order to satisfy a sacrosanct request.

"Let's have them call us at Tiziana's place, that's more convenient," says Vittoria.

I vanish beneath the surface of the water. I remain underwater for a few seconds, in search of tranquility.

"What's wrong, Al?"

Vittoria's voice is deformed, it seems to come from a megaphone tucked away inside my stomach.

"What are you thinking about?" she asks me.

How I wish I had the lung capacity of a sperm whale, just a quick glance at the world above every two hours and then down to the seabed, far from everything. I reemerge with a cap of bubble bath ill suited to my mood.

"I don't really want Mamma and Papà to have to tighten their belts . . . make more sacrifices . . . " I tell her.

"But what do you care if they're happy to do it!"

"They're not happy . . . It's obvious that they can't, otherwise they would have called us a long time ago."

"We'll make short phone calls, that way they won't spend much."

I tried that out for myself once, years ago, right after breaking into the token box. I called a hotel, chosen at random, in Paris, the tokens dropped down in a metallic shower, it ate up so many tokens I couldn't even hear the voice of the hotel switchboard operator. I told him that I wished to speak with Monsieur de Gaulle, Monsieur Charles de Gaulle, and in the time that it took him to look for that name in the registry and tell me that they didn't have any Monsieur de Gaulle staying with him, there were two more token avalanches. Mamma, I'm fine how are you? Are you two having fun? The university is going just fine, thanks, let me talk to Papà, ciao Papà, hold on, let me put Vittoria on. They'd spend five thousand lire just to tell us hello. Mamma used to walk a mile just to save four hundred lire on vegetables. She'd open perfume bottles and add distilled water so it would last longer. Papà got sore hips because he'd repair his own shoes, and one heel was always higher than the other.

"Papà would only eat chicken wings," I tell Vittoria.

"What?"

"When Uncle Armando was alive, he'd eat even fifteen meatballs at a time, then he suddenly seemed to think that chicken wings were plenty. He used to say to us: 'You guys go ahead and finish the chicken, I'm bursting at the seams.'"

"So?"

"I'm not feeling well, Vittoria . . . Let's stop talking about these phone calls."

"Al, you shouldn't be upset, these are perfectly normal things. All parents make sacrifices for their children. Just relax, if you want, we can talk it over tomorrow."

No, I never want to talk about it again. How could I help but notice that we were so poor? I've always thought that poor people were sad, that's why. Mamma and Papà have always been so unmistakably happy and I believed all the nonsense they told me. The reason we don't throw clothing away is that after spending all that time on your body, your clothing becomes fond of you, and we just could never be so cruel. We don't go to restaurants because Mamma's a better cook and it would only hurt the chefs' feelings. Small cars are the most technologically advanced vehicles available, just like with radios, television sets, and electronic calculators: the more things advance the more research succeeds in making them compact. I grew up with bedtime stories foisted off on me at every hour of the day, for twenty years I just luxuriated in one colossal slumber.

The time has come to look reality in the face: if an old and miserly duck dives into a mountain of gold coins, he'll just break his neck, if you're allergic to kryptonite then you'll die of anaphylactic shock, if at the age of fifty you're making a living as an Elvis impersonator, you're never going to become the commander of the Space Shuttle, the most you can hope for is copilot. Mamma and Papà were never really happy, in fact, they were sad, with all the work they had to do make us happy, sad and exhausted. It's time to come back to the real world, there's a principality that's waiting for its constitution to be completed.

64.

I never thought I'd see Roberta again. And instead she showed up on a flimsy pretext, she said that she just happened to be in the neighborhood. No one just happens to be in this neighborhood unless they intend to come to the principality. We ate dinner with her: she couldn't keep her eyes off the wall of LEGO bricks and swore up and down that when she has a home all her own, she'll call me and Vittoria as her masons. Then my sister said that it was time for her to get some sleep and shot me a wink. "Listen, she isn't the kind of girl who just slips off her T-shirt, she's not like Tiziana," I felt like telling her. In front of her favorite window, the one over-looking the hill, we talked about the principality, about future plans, and about how talented my father is, how when he sings "Amazing Grace" it's impossible to tell him from the real Elvis. In the fog of our kisses, we failed to notice that outside it had started pouring rain. So I took advantage of the opportunity, and I asked her to stay and sleep with me, I encouraged her by telling her that there was a game we absolutely had to try. We lay down on the bed, arms around each other, in an uncomfortable position that started pins and needles up and down my arm after a minute, but still I have no intention of moving. My hand, draped as if by chance over Roberta's breast, unfortunately transmits no information about what it's feeling.

"Now look out the window and memorize what you see," I tell her.

"All I see is rain, Al."

"Look carefully, concentrate on the details of the country-side."

"I can see a tree branch and in the distance, the lit-up sign of the gas station."

"What else?"

"Three . . . no, wait, four antennas on the roof of that apart-ment house over there."

"Now let's close our eyes for an hour and then you'll see . . . "

Roberta smiles, maybe she's thinking I'm going to spring

some trick on her. But she goes along with it, she shuts her eyes, leans her head against my chest, restoring feeling to my arm. To keep ourselves awake, we stroke each other's hair. I like to take the finest hair, the hair that grows around the temples, and let it slide slowly between thumb and forefinger. She prefers to roll the longest hair, on the forehead, around her finger. There's a scientific explanation for the fact that right now brilliant ideas are popping into my mind: Roberta's caresses are stimulating the blood flow to that prodigy of nature that is my brain. Responsible Neocolonization: a project for fair and ethical behavior guidelines for those superpowers that just can't seem to keep their paws off the wealth of Third World countries. Instead of destabilizing governments, installing dictators with piloted coups d'état, or relying upon armed interventions to put down civil wars specially fomented for the purpose, the superpowers would publicly challenge each other to duels over the construction of hospitals, schools, roads, and gelato shops. Whoever builds the most over the course of a year would have the right to exploit the country's natural resources for the following year. Every year, the riches at stake would be up for grabs again, until the authorities of the local government decide to say thanks very much, everyone, and we'll take over from here on in. Unemployment: unemployment would be considered a state-sponsored fraud, any person who has finished the mandatory course of studies has the right to be taken into the world of work and to be given a job befitting the studies completed or, as an alternative, they would have the right to the reimbursement of all their educational fees and tuition paid, from kindergarten on. Global Election: seeing that he claims to be the most powerful man on the planet, the president of the United States of America will have to be elected with planet-wide suffrage. Otherwise, let the Americans elect him themselves, but not put on such airs about it. First of all, though:

open-door policy at the UN. One day a week would be dedicated to listening to the voices of ordinary citizens, chosen on the basis of their IQs. Every idea suggested would be put to a vote and, if approved, transformed into law then and there.

"Why are you sighing? Is it time to open our eyes?" Roberta asks me.

"Shall we try?" I ask her. "On the count of three: one, two-o-o, three!"

Roberta looks out the window. She smiles. She looks more carefully. She stops smiling.

"Where's the branch? The tree branch is gone . . . and so is the lit-up sign!"

Now all you can see out the window are the crowns of a line of holm oaks and, further on, the roofs of apartment houses, bristling with antennas. I explain to her that the principality is built on a cement raft because, seeing that it is a free place, it is first and foremost free to go where it pleases. A thousand years from now, when the poles have melted and the water level has risen, the principality of Santamaria will be safe and sound on the hilltop, the sole surviving realm on this planet.

"Come on, let's try it again. Close your eyes," I tell her.

"But hold me tight, Al. This game is starting to scare me a little."

We opened and closed our eyes three more times before being overcome by sleep. The wild plum tree disappeared and reappeared, while in the background first the apartment buildings poked up over the horizon, then the hill.

When we wake up the wild plum tree is still there and, even more importantly, so is Roberta. I get up to make breakfast, and when the table is set and ready, I go out for the flag raising. I open the door, I lift the roller shutter, and then I become aware of the existence of a supreme being Who must love the principality very much.

"Vittoria, Roberta . . . look at this nice surprise!"

I walk around the house, sticking close to the cement running board. The principality has slid into the basin and now it's at the center of a nice big pond. Between the house and the shore there must be a good fifty feet of water. When I finish my tour, I return to find Vittoria and Roberta petrified at the front door.

"A little lake! With water lilies!" I cry, beside myself with joy.

"Al, those are garbage bags!" Vittoria replies.

"Could we try to refrain from being so cold and analytical and just try to consider that, once we've fished the garbage bags out of the water, we could install a nice array of water lilies?"

"Al, this is no game! I have to get to the university! And this water is stagnant, the mosquitoes will eat us alive!"

It's no good, they just can't seem to learn. No matter how hard I try, people can't seem to glimpse the beauty of the world. The principality has become a castle with its own moat, and the two of them are worried about mosquitoes and how they'll get to the university. While the two women grumble in the bathroom, I go and prepare the all-too-ordinary solution to this devastating catastrophe which is bringing grief and famine upon our family.

"Al, we've decided to call the fire department, maybe they could bring a drainage pump . . . " says Vittoria.

"The principality doesn't have a fire department."

"We could ask them to come in from outside of the realm . . . "

"The principality may not have a fire department, but it does boast a very well-run ferry service, with departures every five minutes, starting now!"

"Oh lord, Al, where did you come up with this? Do you think it'll take our weight?"

The old dinghy we bought in Torvaianica actually is much

smaller than I remembered. It's a child's rowboat, it can barely hold an adult, but this isn't the time for acting dubious, otherwise these scaredy cats are going to ruin everything.

"Certainly it'll take the weight. I'll carry you to shore, one at a time. For just two Elvises apiece."

"Al, you're a gouger!" says Vittoria.

"It's for the good of the principality, I don't want to hear any arguments."

I slip the plastic paddles into the oarlocks, and I take my seat before anyone else. When I was little, I used to be able to lie down on the bottom of the boat, now the only way I can fit in is by bending my legs.

"If we overturn, it's going to be a disaster . . . "

Having painted the grimmest imaginable scenario, Vittoria steps into the rowboat and entwines her legs with mine. I set the tape recorder on my thighs, press play, and, as Elvis sings "My Way," I start to row. On the second stroke, a section of oar, time-yellowed, breaks off. Vittoria doesn't even notice, she's too busy studying the progress of a microscopic hole in the bottom of the boat, through which minuscule drops of water are oozing. From her smile, though, I understand that she's starting to enjoy the crossing. When we're a few yards from the shore, I swing the boat around so that her side is the first to hit land.

Here in the principality we do things properly. Vittoria gets to her knees and with her usual style she leaps to shore, grinning from ear to ear.

"Al?"

"Yes?"

"You're the best brother in the world."

"Vittoria?"

"Yes?"

"You owe me two Elvises."

Me and Casimiro spent the whole morning cleaning up the little lake, we picked up two heaping boatloads of plastic bags, bottles, and rusty cans. While waiting for Vittoria to come home, there's nothing left to do but to get rid of some of the dirt. Keeping us company for the past few minutes are a man and a boy, dressed in black pants and white shirts. They're trying to find a way to bring a little religious comfort to our house. We pretended not to see them when they first got here, we ignored them while they were walking the circumference of the lake in search of a ford to get across. I think that at a certain point, the older man tried to persuade the younger man to take off his shoes and attempt the crossing. Before their arrival, we were thinking of excavating a drainage canal to let the water run off once it becomes stagnant, and instead now we're evaluating the feasibility of an inflow system, to keep the water level as high as possible.

"Excuse me? Are you acquainted with God?" the young man shouts to me, clearly uninterested in getting all muddy.

All it would take is a couple of inches of water and a drawbridge to keep salesmen peddling vacuum cleaners, magazine subscriptions, and supreme beings away from our door. I wonder how much piranhas cost.

"All your problems have a solution, did you know that?" the young man insists.

Casimiro, do you know what Raimondo would say if he were here?

"Do you have a pamphlet you could give me?" I shout.

All the old man has to do is glance in his direction. Without blinking an eye, the young man takes his shoes off and ventures a first step into the muddy bank. While the poor young man gasps and flails as he tries to reach the life preserver that his comrade is waving in his direction, I cross my arms over my chest and go inside, because it's starting to get cold. The principality of Santamaria will go down in history as the most protected and inaccessible state of all time. Without an invitation, not even the word of God could get in.

65.

There's no article in the principality's constitution that requires me to clean house. I already do plenty and I have no intention of sitting down to fold every single T-shirt in that multicellular organism that has now completely colonized my bedroom floor. Relegated to the minority by two women! They don't want to get mud on their shoes, they don't want the moat to become a permanent thing! Roberta came to lend a hand, but all she's done is vote against me and gossip with Vittoria. Forget about monthly cleanup, in half an hour all they've done is wash the coffeemaker.

"Al? What are you doing?"

So typical, just because I'm quiet and minding my own business, Vittoria starts getting worried. Still, the phrase stirs a cheerful feeling of nostalgia. That was the question Mamma always used to ask me.

"What are you burning?"

"Nothing," I reply.

At this point, if she were here, Mamma would emerge from the doorway anyway. This time, though, it's Roberta who looks out. Something tells me I shouldn't be so happy with this overlapping of roles.

"What are you making?" she asks.

"Nothing . . . it's just a gift for Mamma and Papà."

Roberta kneels before me and admires the album cover. She sees the labels with the dates, she pulls the strings, she's as amazed as a little girl. They're only flashes, like in all adults, but in her they're more frequent. That's why I like her.

"So that's you? And that's Vittoria?" she asks me.

"Yes, and that's the day she tried to kill me for the first time."

"She tried to kill you?"

"Someday I'll tell you the whole story."

"And now what are you doing?"

"I'm putting you in."

"That's me? Can I help?"

"No, tonight we're going out. Even though you don't deserve it, I'm taking you out to dinner."

Before going out, the women are obliged to go to the bathroom. These are difficult years for them, fluffy hairdos are in style. From the double-locked keyhole I hear the puffs of hair spray, the sighing and huffing, then running water, the buzz of the hair dryer, new puffs of hair spray, new sighing and huffing. I have a half hour, plenty of time to extract my favorite T-shirt from the pile, the one with Steel Jeeg, and my evening sweatshirt, the elegant black one. I also have time to brush a little dirt off my gym shoes, watch a cartoon, chomp down half a box of wafers. And finally Roberta emerges, looking exactly like she did when she went in.

"You're beautiful," I say, just to forestall tragedies.

"Well, where are you taking me?"

"To a place downtown."

Friday night is a good time to go out to eat in the Italian republic. All you have to do is ask around and make a few phone calls, and you can put together a little map of inaugurations and various buffets. At 7:30 there's an inauguration of a beauty parlor on Via della Scrofa; at 8:00, a gallery opening on Via del Babuino. And then if you're still hungry: until 11:00, samplings of typical Pugliese dishes in Piazza del Popolo. Things are jumping in the Bel Paese: Italy has become the world's fifth-largest economy, everyone thinks the future is bright. Even the beauty parlor, which has chosen the futuristic

name of "Hair Look 2000." Before we go in, Roberta is overcome by a sudden surge of shyness.

"But are we on the guest list?" she asks me.

"Watch and learn," I reply.

I go over to the proprietor, a woman who's busy showing
off an array of things. She has an orange complexion, the
result of a low-quality self-tanner. A pair of hoop earrings the
diameter of a 45 record. A hairstyle Madonna might have
worn in, say, "Express Yourself," though she clearly missed
the point.

"*Buonasera*, I'm Prince Santamaria," I begin.

My seriousness puts her at a loss. She hastens to grasp my
hand.

"Thanks so much for coming . . . " she says.

If there are still people in the Italian republic who are intimidated by a title of nobility, well, that's certainly not my fault.
She must have thought I'm an eccentric prince or a fallen aris-
tocrat, but still a VIP she can brag about to her guests. As long
as we have their eyes on us, we pretend to be interested in the
bold interior design: checkerboard floors, black walls dramat-
ically crisscrossed with large triangular mirrors and, in the cor-
ners, brand-new infrared heat lamps for longer lasting perms.
As soon as they look away, we head for the spumante and the
mini-pizzas.

At the gallery opening, things go much better. By the time
we get there, security has relaxed its vigilance and we are able
to enter without displaying the embossed invitation. Everyone
is taken by the exhibition of the work of a photographer who
immortalizes androgynous models in bodybuilder poses, their
hair slathered with product and standing straight up on their
heads, teetering on dizzyingly high stiletto heels. Undisturbed,
we fill two big plates at the buffet and we carve out a little pri-
vacy for ourselves on a sofa.

"I've never dined this way," Roberta tells me.

"Next time, if you prefer, I'd be glad to take you to a restaurant."

"No, this is more fun. My folks are obsessed with the Michelin Guide, and with them I only ever eat in the very best places."

"Do you like it?"

"I thought it was the greatest . . . yet another of the countless pieces of bullshit I've foisted off on myself."

"Do you lie to yourself frequently?"

"No, otherwise I'd stop believing myself."

I think I must have just grown up, in that exact instant. I feel as if I've understood for the first time what Vittoria meant when she told me that I shouldn't fall in love with girls just because of their looks, but that I ought to let myself by conquered by their thoughts, their words. I'm sorry that I didn't listen to her right away, but frankly the idea of taking advice from someone who fell for Solitary Puma . . .

"What does 'love' mean to you?" Roberta asks me.

Well, right now I'm a little baffled by the logical segue here. We were talking about restaurants. So where did this hard question come from? Now then, keep calm. "Love." In Italian: "*Amore*." Book: Devoto-Oli, *Vocabolario illustrato della lingua italiana*, ed. 1967. *Illustrated Dictionary of the Italian Language*; page: the one with the botanical illustration of the *Amorino* (*Reseda lutea*, in English, the yellow mignonette or wild mignonette); definition: "Between two people of the opposite sex, impassioned and exclusive devotion, instinctive and intuitive, striving to ensure reciprocal happiness, or well-being, or sensual pleasure." I ought to take this medieval, late-Christian Democratic definition, and improve upon it with words of my own. But I'm not used to doing that. I like "instinctive and intuitive," I like the idea that the "impassioned devotion" really is what they say it is, when it doesn't ask you to choose between "happiness, or well-being, or sensual pleasure."

"Don't you know?" she insists.

Wait a minute, just wait a minute! How am I supposed to explain to her that love is the instinctive and intuitive discovery of space? That at five or six years of age, you think you can devote yourself in an impassioned and exclusive manner only to your parents, and in fact at that age when people ask you who you want to marry, you proptly reply "Mamma," don't you? Then you grow up and become a man and you discover that your impassioned devotion is, in fact, exclusive but, miraculously, also extendable. Can I tell her that love is the discovery that you have lots of space inside you, and that it's a pity not to use it all?

"It's all right, never mind," she says to me with an unconvincing smile.

"It means that I have no doubts, that all questions have the same answer. Who do I want? You. What do I want to do? You. Where do I want to go? You. What do I want to eat? You."

I have to make a note of this gaze of hers. I need to write: "There's a very specific kind of gaze that means 'I am yours'. Description: intense, luminous, compliant. It resembles: a white flag fluttering from a trench, a castle drawbridge being lowered, a suicidal antelope offering its jugular vein to a lion." And then I ought to write about the value, at the same time anesthetic and exciting, of her face as it comes closer to mine, about the thoughts that go AWOL as her lips press against my cheek and then move slowly along with low-frequency smooches toward my mouth, about her breath as it feeds mine, about our tongues that speak to each other like the necks of giraffes in love. My favorite pranks, like sucking hard on her tongue, or blowing air unexpectedly into her cheeks, seem for the first time like sheer idiocy.

66.

"By virtue of the powers bestowed upon me, I pronounce you husband and wife," I say.

Raimondo plays "Love Me Tender" on Papà's Martin, the bride and groom exchange a kiss, the guests throw rice. With the idea of celebrating weddings in Las Vegas style the principality's average population has risen to 5.6 units. It may be garish and ostentatious, but an extra hundred Elvises now and then come in handy. And after all it's just a good excuse to party, to spend time together, to eat Mamma's chocolate *ciambellone*, which by now Vittoria makes beautifully. I push my way through the guests to reach Raul, who wanted to introduce me to his new girlfriend, but I'm waylaid by a friend of my sister's, a tall drink of water with milky white skin, lipstick intentionally smeared all over her mouth, and a black dress riddled with safety pins.

"Who is that good-looking guy?" she asks me.

She points at Raimondo, but it can't be true. Still, I struggle to accept it and I take her over to meet him, but only after checking to make sure he's the one she means, as if the individual in question weren't there.

"Who do you mean, him?"

"Do you think I'd meet someone who plays the guitar as well as him and not bother to talk to him?" she asks.

"No, it's just that I thought that your music . . . that is . . . he's more of a guy who . . . "

"Sex Pistols, Clash, Bad Brains," says Raimondo.

Because he absolutely detests punk music, but he seems to feel differently about the girl, as far as I can tell. They start talking about rehearsals, they exchange phone numbers, the pale one tells of a tour through the social centers of Puglia and Basilicata, he replies that he's weighing offers at the moment but the idea is certainly interesting. I'm not needed here. But witnessing a bullshit match without being able to compete is quite frustrating.

Roberta couldn't come, she had a prior commitment with her folks, and so I find myself besieged by Vittoria's friends who want to play. "Get the soccer ball!" "Bring out the fris-bee!" "Let's make water bombs with balloons!" If Mamma and Papà could only see me, with everyone chasing after me to play and me acting all standoffish, putting on a pose and then finally giving in with: "Okay, okay, I'll go get the balloons" . . . and then I rush inside because one of them might change his mind but instead, four against four, this is going to be an epic battle.

"Is all this ruckus going to be going on much longer?" Dario shouts from his room.

"The party has just begun . . . " I reply.

"Well then, you're going to have to take this whole day off my bill, because I paid to live in a quiet, out-of-the-way place, not in a commune of freaks!"

I decide to go in to try to calm him down. He must be on edge because he just got here last night and he must be tired, but what need is there to shout? I'll time the exact duration of the party with a chronometer and I'll take the exact number of minutes of lost peace and quiet off his bill.

"So what's that?" I ask him.

"Just forget you ever saw it."

"Firearms aren't allowed in the principality."

"I've read the constitution. There's nothing about weapons in it."

"Yes, it says that we're a peaceful principality. Besides, weapons do nothing to contribute to the physical development or the mental development or the happiness of the children, and so . . . "

"Listen, deep down we think about things the same way, we're both exiles for the same reason . . . You took refuge in this hovel and you think you're going to change the world by playing at being a prince, I want to change the world too, but I'm serious about it."

"You're going to put that pistol outside."

"Well, listen to him . . . and just how do you think you're going to make me?"

He comes toward and taps me on the chest with a stiff forefinger, pushing me a step back. I'm not afraid of people who are shorter than me and I instinctively wave my fist under his nose.

"Don't make me do it," I tell him.

"Just try if you have the nerve!" he shouts into my face. "Come on, just try! . . . Hey, hold on . . . what the hell are you doing! All right, cut it out, I'll put it in the car. As long as you stop!"

Vittoria arrives in the room. I stand in a corner with my face to the wall and scratch the paint.

"You made my brother start crying!"

"Me? We were having a man-to-man discussion and all of a sudden he . . . "

"Listen, Dario: first, stop having man-to-man discussions with my brother. Second, Al doesn't start crying for no good reason . . . something must have happened!"

"He has a pistol!" I say.

"Informer!"

"Is that true? Dario, let me see what you're hiding behind your back . . . right away!" Vittoria orders him.

Dario doesn't know what to do at this juncture. In the end, he sputters and shows Vittoria the hand he was hiding behind his back.

"A-a-ah! . . . Then it's true! Collect your things and get out of here! Now!" Vittoria shouts.

The effect of the surprise suddenly comes to an end.

"Kids, don't test me," he mutters through clenched teeth.

"I'll stay here as long as I feel like it. That's the way the world works, the man with the gun gives the orders!"

When the last little knot of guests leaves the principality, we gather on the street, over next to Raul's van.

"I just figured out who that guy is . . . you'd better forget about him, he's dangerous."

"Is he a friend of yours?" I ask him.

"Me a friend of that guy? What are you, kidding me?"

"No, certainly, but he *is* friends with Er Piattola, Er Gazzetta, and Tarzan . . . " says Vittoria, pointlessly reminding him of the exceedingly strange guests he's brought here.

"Look, you're getting me wrong, I never wanted to have anything to do with guys like him."

"So is he a terrorist?"

"Some terrorist, that one . . . He talks about politics to put on airs, but he makes a living by doing armed robberies and selling arms. He's a bad person, give him back all his money and tell him to get out of here."

"He threatened us, he said that if we send him away he'll report us for the illegal electric hookup . . . He's only going to leave when he's good and ready," says Vittoria.

Is this what we've come to? Just five years after the founding of the principality, we've already undergone the first armed occupation. So now what would a real prince do? Would he call the police? Would he hire a mercenary army? Would he scamper to safety with his women?

67.

Years and years of incursions into enemy territory have made secret agent Al and the Russian spy converted to capitalism Kasimir great experts in international espionage. Cunningly hidden in the lair of a notorious arms trafficker, they listen to his radio conversations.

"FDM-15 to Rombo. Over," says Dario.

"FDM-15, so we hear from you at last. Over."

"I had my hands full with that slut of a sister of yours. Over."

"I've got your mother here with me, and she wants me to say hi. Over."

The typical humor of the republic's gangsters leaves secret agent Al and Kasimir impassive.

"Can I ask what's become of you? Over."

"Still at the house of the retarded kid and the little whore. Over."

Calm down, Casimiro, calm down. "Actually, the retard would be you," we'll tell him when the time is right.

"Did you get hold of the pipes? Over."

"Right here under the bed. Three long ones and five short ones. Over."

So that's what's in this bag next to me. Agent Al and the spy Kasimir hold their breath.

"The nuts? Over."

"Two boxes for each pipe, as requested. Over."

"Two boxes? We asked for three. Over."

"Then there must be three . . . hold on and let me check. Over."

I'm under this bed because I'm a sleepwalker. I'm under this bed but I'm deaf since birth. I'm under this bed but I fell asleep and I never heard a thing, I swear!

I try to crawl away from the bag but I've become too big for this sort of escapade, with every movement I make, I run the risk that an elbow or a foot might stick out.

Dario's hand pats the floor frantically like the tongue of a giant iguana. Unless he finds it right away, I'm done for. This guy's going to kill me!

"FDM-15, hold on, you were right after all, we said two boxes. Over."

One of Dario's fingers grazes my forearm.

"Just when I'd found it . . . Then we're all good. Over."

"Where we gonna meet? Over."

"At the parking lot by the dance hall. Day after tomorrow, two in the morning. Over."

"But right under the dancers' noses again? Over."

"You really must be getting old. If I say it's safe, it's safe. The dancers won't be dancing that time of night, and after all, it's right near here, the less distance I need to cover with the pipes, the better. Over."

"Day after tomorrow, then. Over and out."

I, Al, prince of Santamaria, do solemnly swear that this will be the last nocturnal incursion of my life. I swear the same oath for Casimiro, as well.

68.

With what little information I possessed, it took me a full day to track down the location of the appointment. I was looking for a dance hall, but of course that was code for something else. The only building in the area that had a parking lot was the small Carabinieri station. An isolated place, dark, with plenty of escape routes, and, as I was able to determine, at the appointed time, there was a shift change, which means there were no officers on the streets. Having finished the investigative phase, I only had a few hours left to go into action. All alone, I never would have been able to do it, but with Raimondo as my accomplice and Casimiro standing lookout, there was even enough time to throw in a few additional gems. I'm lucky, I have trusted friends, always ready to hurry to my side when there's a chance of getting hurt.

But now I need to awaken Vittoria and Roberta, because the flash point of sulphur is 392 degrees Fahrenheit.

"Vittoria! Roberta!"

"A-a-al . . . what is it?"

"Wake up, both of you."

"No-o-o . . . where are you?"

"I'm waiting for you outside."

The temperature of a car's muffler reaches 1500 degrees F close to the engine. According to my calculations, the temperature drops about 125 degrees every eight inches, as you move toward the end of the exhaust pipe.

"Al, it's two in the morning. What are you doing up?"

"We need to drink a toast."

"A toast to what?" Vittoria asks in resignation.

"In the meantime, enjoy the evening, the stars, the crickets . . ."

By calculating the distance between the principality and the Carabinieri station, the car's average velocity, driving time, and air temperature, I ought to have been able to identify the exact point along the length of the exhaust assembly at which to place my creation so as to ensure that Dario's nocturnal operation turns out to be anything but silent.

"There's not even a single cricket," Vittoria complains.

"They're probably asleep . . ." Roberta points out argumentatively.

This is how you can recognize a leader's charisma. The crew grumbles but no one ventures to leave their post. They know that if their leader calls them, he must have a good reason.

The sulphur catches fire, the black powder explodes.

A first explosion makes them both jump. They look around, alert now.

Then a burst of gunshots in rapid succession makes them jump out of their seats.

"What's that? Gunfire?" Roberta asks in alarm.

"No, they're firecrackers," I say.

Through the trees we see the distant flashes of explosions. Another impressive burst. Three louder reports. Then silence.

"Maybe they're celebrating," says Vittoria. "Maybe some local neighborhood saint . . . "

"Sure, something like that. But hold on, it's not over," I say.

With a very narrow angle of trajectory, almost parallel to the ground, rockets take off. Some burst through the line of trees and shoot past us, vanishing into the countryside. The reports and shrill whistles blend with the sirens of the Carabinieri squad cars.

"And now? What the devil is happening?" Vittoria asks me.

Nothing, nothing at all is happening. Except that the principality is free once again.

Headline: "Car Blows Up Right in Front of Carabinieri Barracks. Prison Break Escapee Arrested." Article: "The car driven by Dario Barella, a convicted criminal already well known to the authorities for armed robbery, arms trafficking, and sex trafficking, was transporting explosives. Perhaps he was planning a terror attack, but the soldiers of the Carabinieri Corps went into action when they heard several loud reports from the street outside. The explosive devices, which blew up prematurely, led the Carabinieri to break up a military arms ring and, after a brief chase, to arrest Barella."

I'm tempted to cut out this article and frame it, but when Vittoria arrives, I choose instead to just fold up the newspaper and hide it under the sofa cushion. This time, I tell myself, "Good job, Al."

"What about Dario? His things are gone," she tells me.

"He left. Actually, I evicted him. I got him to pay up and I kicked him out."

"And just how did you do that?"

"Things men understand . . . I made it clear to him who he was dealing with."

"Why didn't you tell me? I'm sorry I missed the scene . . . "

I receive congratulations and hugs, I'll settle for just a small portion of what I really deserve. I had some doubts about the operation because I was afraid that, once captured, Dario might have revealed his hideout to the Carabinieri and caused us a world of trouble, but the marijuana I found hidden under his mattress set my mind at rest. The only thing still missing from his CV was a conviction for possession and dealing of narcotics. While Vittoria was asleep I tossed all his possessions into the dumpster, except for the grass and seven hundred thousand lire in cash which, along with our next salaries, will allow us to complete the principality and prepare for the triumphant return of Agnese and Mario Elvis.

69.

So 1989 is the year of farewells: the Soviets withdraw from Afghanistan, the Chinese students in Tiananmen Square say so long to their hopes for democracy, hundreds of Germans abandon the German Democratic Republic, scampering across the border between Hungary and Austria, Monsignor Marcinkus leaves the Vatican Bank, and the mayor of Rome resigns because he's under criminal investigation for irregularities in the contracts for school lunches. I took my last exam and said goodbye without too much exaltation to the too many useless books and their exorbitant price tags, the overcooked cafeteria pasta, the professors who teach courses without a hint of passion, the students who begin their oral exams by conveying the best regards of their illustrious father.

The principality enjoys enviable health, even though the Italian republic continues to undermine our financial solidity with tricks of every sort. The worst example was the fraud perpetrated by our state-funded physician who convinced Vittoria to get an operation to correct a defect in her nasal septum, which he said might cause respiratory problems and potentially grave cardiocirculatory deficiencies. After we'd scheduled the operation and even paid a sizable deposit, in part funded out of Dario's generous bequest, the police arrested him and the clinic's chief physician for fraud, falsification, and serious harm as a result of unnecessary operations. A year ago, we were once again on the verge of building walls, we already had an estimate in hand, and then a letter arrived from Mamma and Papà telling us that they were very happy to live outside of Italy, but they still really missed having a bidet. In order to reinstall it, we had to move the sink and redo all the piping. Room rental continues to play a major role in our GDP. A real piece of luck especially considering that, in the letter that came yesterday, Mamma and Papà wrote us that now they live in a house with beautiful furniture, and it's sad to think of our furniture, so old and beat up. Even if it's a burden, we want to make them happy, and so we'll delay the construction of the walls a little longer, so that we can understake the restoration work instead.

In my human flesh diary I wrote: "Women's weekly magazines might be a good business opportunity, consider the possibility of ginning up scandals in the principality," "Those who can't stop saying that if you weren't twenty years old in 1968 you can't understand what politics even is have finally won, there's no longer a single twenty-year-old who gives a damn," "Limit the number of drugs that are legal in the principality to those you can grow in the field behind the house," "Become independent as quickly as possible from the craftsmen and handymen of the Italian republic, especially plumbers, electricians, and carpenters," "New boyfriend for Vittoria: Piero the plumber?" "New boyfriend for Vittoria:

Sandrone the electrician?" "New boyfriend for Vittoria: Antonio the carpenter?"

The Italian republic rewards its brightest minds by preventing them from completing their studies in record time. I could easily have taken my degree at the age of twenty-one but the chancellor did everything within his power to delay the assignment of my thesis. Even if he won't admit it, the problem is that he thinks I'm too young. While waiting, seeing that my age is just fine when it comes to paying university tuition and fees, I've decided to find a real job. Something temporary, that won't distract me too much from my institutional responsibilities as prince, and which will allow me to earn enough to send the furniture to the cabinetmaker, build these blessed walls, and do whatever it takes to ensure that Agnese and Mario Elvis can be there to see me defend my thesis. Since the library continues to slam doors in my face, I've decided to fight back using similar weapons: I asked for a recommendation from one of our most recent guests, the son of a city councilor. I had helped him to rewrite his own thesis after it had become clear that every word of it was plagiarized.

Disguised as a hungry young capitalist, in a charcoal gray suit, white striped shirt, tie with a tight knot, and watch fastened over my left cuff, I stick my head into the office.

"Dottor Masci?" I ask politely.

"Yes."

Yes, my ass, this guy might have finished middle school at the most, and he acts as if he's a *dottore*, a university graduate.

"*Buongiorno*, I'm Almerico Santamaria."

"Santamaria, Santamaria . . . Ah, is this for the courier job?"

"Yes, Dottore."

"Come in, take a seat and I'll tell you about it."

I adjust my jacket, which is just a little long in the sleeves, and I step into the office. The fake doctor's jacket has the same defect as mine, so that when we shake hands the sleeves form a single tube connecting my suit to his. I take a seat facing his desk. On the leather desktop there's a hole where, over the course of the years, hundreds of nervous fingers have worked away. They didn't even leave me so much as a scrap of foam rubber padding to scratch at.

"There's no need for me to tell you how important letters and files are inside this ministry. Everything has to be delivered in a timely fashion, nothing must be lost."

"Certainly."

"The only thing that's certain in this life, my good man, is death . . . "

The man looks at me. He nods, raptly, impressed first and foremost by the profundity of his pearl of wisdom. I gratify him with a convinced affirmative nod of the head, and I pretend to muse over the pinchbeck pearl he's just palmed off on me.

"As you must have seen, this is quite a large ministry, hundreds of offices, thousands of people who don't do a blessed thing from dawn to dusk . . . It'll take you a while to memorize all the names. Maybe on the first day you could just learn the offices on this floor and then, day by day . . . "

"Berchicci L., De Santis L., Leproni F., De Rita M., Merolli M., Camera M., Rocca P., WC, Conference Room, Dott. Piermartini R., and Dott.ssa Giusti C., Registry Office, Dott. Scanabucci R. and Dott. Lancia E., Dott.ssa Gagliardi A., Dott.ssa Muzi S., and Dott. Masci S.," I say.

"When did you memorize them?"

"I read them while I was looking for your office."

"And all you need is to read something once and you memorize it?"

Now the smart thing would be to say no, to avoid the usual spot test and the cascade of "wow"s, "o-o-oh"s," and "never seen such a thing in my life!"s.

"Yes."

Masci stares at me, hard, for a moment, then he picks up his desk diary and starts with the test. He reads aloud his notes concerning his appointments for the week, dates, times, names, street addresses, and telephone numbers, two dense pages full of information, and, seeing me sitting there impassive, he decides on the second page to speed up as if the lack of pauses were somehow supposed to pose a greater challenge to me. When he gets to the end of his last note, he's out of breath.

He launches the challenge with a movement of the chin above which flickers an ironic little smile, the neon sign of stupidity which I'm always delighted to switch off. Twenty-two names, nine of them preceded by "Dottor" and three by "Dottoressa," four names of agencies, eight phone numbers, one of which must have been copied down wrong because it's a digit short, ten addresses with street numbers, six brief indications of the reason for the appointment. I repeat it all in the exact same order, without pauses, just as he did, from: "Monday the eleventh four P.M. dentist for new crown" to: "Friday the fifteenth ten A.M. call Dottor Martelli for his daughter's birthday."

"Never seen such a thing in my life! Someone like you shouldn't be a courier . . . You'd be perfect as my secretary!"

"That would be nice."

"The minute that senile old fool retires, I'll take care of you. A real job, with real responsibilities . . . "

"I'd like that."

" . . . full-time, with lots and lots of overtime!"

"Thank aaa sancarala, at's raalla an anarmaas plaasara."

We spend a good solid minute looking each other in the eye.

"What?"

"At's raalla an anarmaas plaasara."

"Does this happen to you often?"

"Daas what happan ta ma aftan?"

"Okay . . . well, in the meantime try to do your best as a courier . . . then we'll see."

70.

We were expecting a young man but instead our new paying guest is in his fifties. The minute we saw him we immediately began to worry about the state of the house, as if Mamma and Papà had just come home. Luckily he arrived at night. We thought that we would spend an agreeable evening chatting, but we immediately felt intimidated. Carlo, that's his name, wears a double-breasted suit and a tie, eyeglasses with thick lens, and long hair gleaming with gel. He showed up dragging a wheeled suitcase behind him. His bewildered gaze ought perhaps to have inspired pity in us, but instead it scared us like hell. When we accompany him to his room, we do our best never to turn our backs on him.

"You can hang your overcoat there, there's a hook in the wall of LEGO blocks," I tell him.

No answer.

"You are free to make use of the wardrobe and the dresser there at the foot of the wall of LEGO blocks."

Still nothing.

I get it, I'm not going to get any compliments from this man for my magnificent creation.

"Where's the telephone?" are his first words.

"Outside, in the phone booth."

We had another guest who used to put on the same expression. He was a government undersecretary. They're a media-modified species that favor the expression: "Now this is the life," employing it at least one million times, invariably the wrong way. The ones who go to a bank and, instead of speaking to a teller, insist on going straight to the director, who always seem to find a table at any restaurant, who are accustomed to hearing people say: "Dottore, for you I'll do the impossible," and who have a phone in every room, because if "he" calls, they must already be ready to answer.

"It's a safe number . . . no one's ever come by to do maintenance," I tell him, well aware that I'm giving him a useful piece of information.

For the first time, his facial features seem to relax. He takes off his shoes, lies down, and turns his back to us. Smiling courteously, we go into the kitchen to each get a knife.

"Who the hell did Adele send us?" I ask Vittoria.

"She's crazy! I told her that after Dario we only wanted reliable people!"

With a six-token phone call we learn that he's a very respectable individual, a highly placed executive at a bank that's in the midst of a major scandal, and that all he needs is a temporary change of scenery. In spite of all those reassurances, we still decide to sleep in the same room, with knives conveniently close at hand. While we try to decide whether it would be wise to go right to sleep or whether it might not be better to wait for the banker to drop off, we hear the sound of knocking on the wall.

"Excuse me? . . . It's me, excuse me . . . "

"Yes? How can I help you?" I reply.

The man sticks his head in the door, shyly.

"I need to make a phone call, but I don't have any phone tokens."

"You can have three in exchange for one Elvis."

He looks at me.

"We don't use lire here," I explain. "Now that you're here, you ought to exchange your money and purchase Elvises."

Now, instead of looking at me, he turns to my sister. Having obtained a certification of the authenticity of my words, he swivels back to stare at me.

"Would you be so kind as to exchange some for me?" he asks.

"The exchange office opens tomorrow morning at nine."

"Jesus Christ, Al, would you just give the man his phone tokens?" Vittoria hisses at my back.

You just don't seem to be able to enforce any rules around here. What's the good of founding an independent principality if in the end you just wind up doing everything Italian-style? Well, really, the office ought to be closed but for you, such an important person, I'd be glad to open it special. The cashier and the customer go into the living room, the cashier gets the strongbox out of the cabinet with the locked door, and the customer pulls a giant wad of hundred-thousand-lire bills out of his pocket. The cashier remains cool and composed, stifling a surge of understanding for the servile attitudes of the inhabitants of the Italian republic toward the rich and powerful. The customer says that he's sorry, he has nothing smaller, the cashier says that unfortunately, if he wants phone tokens, he's going to have to exchange the hundred thousand lire for Elvises. The customer says that that's not a problem. The cashier hands over the Elvises and the phone tokens and skillfully conceals his gratitude by whistling a little tune he's just invented then and there.

The banker goes to make a phone call and as soon as he turns his back on me, I run straight to Vittoria. I can't wait to wave the banknote in her face, forget about the suppository box, the principality is soon going to need a strongbox, then a full-fledged safe.

I hurtle into the room and smash into Vittoria lurking in the shadows. I feel a shiver, a strange cold burning, sharp and sudden. I still wave the banknote under her nose.

"We're rich," I tell her, and then faint in my joy.

I remain flat on the floor because now I feel pretty much the way I did that night after playing with Tiziana: my arms hang slack, I'd like to keep waving the banknote in the air but Vittoria is screaming, I raise my hand, but the hundred-thousand lire note is no longer in my fingers, it must have slipped out of my hand, I reach around for it and my arm knocks against a plastic handle projecting from my side. Forget about joy, the reason I fainted is because she stabbed four inches of fish filleting knife into my spleen.

"It's not in the spleen, it's just a flesh wound," says the banker.

"I'm calling an ambulance anyway," says Vittoria, her voice quavering.

"Why would you do that, we don't need an ambulance! It's just superficial, you can see the shape of the blade . . . we'll get it out right now . . . How the hell did you do this?"

"She's been trying for years . . . " I say, in search of sympathy.

I need to stop staring down at the handle sticking out of my side. I close my eyes and I abandon myself into the arms of the Creator. Let Him decide whether it's a good idea to let a genius die for such a trifle.

"Do you know how to do it?" my sister asks.

"At the bank, we've done dozens of these little operations . . . here . . . here . . . you see? He doesn't even need stitches."

"No?" Vittoria asks.

"He just needs a Band-Aid and he'll be fine."

"But what if he gets tetanus?" she asks.

"Dream on . . . " I reply. "You're going to have to kill me with your bare hands!"

71.

"This month again the balance sheet of the principality is

positive, we have 640,000 lire in the treasury and our projected expenses are 550,000 lire. Considering that at the end of the month, my salary will be added to yours, we can definitely start work on the walls," I tell Vittoria.

"Al, I think it's best to give precedence to the work of shoring up the house . . . "

"Vittoria, do you realize what that means? We're talking about 4 million lire at the very least. It means delaying Mamma and Papà's return for another year, maybe a year and a half. They weren't here for my eighteenth birthday, or for my twentieth birthday, and this means they won't be here for my graduation party either . . . It's out of the question."

"I know . . . you're right . . . "

"In fact, we've waited too long."

"It's just that I wouldn't want to spend all our money on the other projects and then risk having the principality collapse the next time it rains."

"But there's not even a crack in the structure, and after all it's not like we move all that much."

"By now we're a hundred yards away from the road . . . "

"Oh, I don't think so, must be fifty, tops!"

The truth is somewhere in the middle, tending toward Vittoria's side. In fact, completely on Vittoria's side if we consider that recently the principality had been following an L-shaped trajectory. A matter of a few more yards and we'll wind up completely behind the line of holm oaks.

"Now the door overlooks the countryside again," she tells me.

"So the principality has rotated slightly, so what?"

"Al, it's dangerous," Vittoria continues. "You decide, you're the prince, but just keep in mind that there's a risk we'll be throwing out all the work we've put into it."

I'm the prince. Why did she say that? Now I feel a surge of the magnanimity of Lorenzo de' Medici.

"And after all, Papà wrote that he'll be on tour for six months, so there's no big rush," she concludes.

"On tour? When did he write that? And didn't you say anything about it?"

"The letter arrived this morning."

"I thought we'd decided to always read them together!"

"Sorry, Al, I couldn't resist, but I swear I only read the first page."

"I'm going to fill the tub!" I say.

Enough is enough. I understand the worry, I understand the way that distance amplifies anxiety, but we can't go on like this. I've become a man by now.

"Now write: 'Dear Mamma and Papà'!" I tell Vittoria.

"I'm writing, I'm writing . . . "

"'I'm happy to know that you're well and before telling you a little about us, I'd like to clarify a few things: A) it's not true that I only eat french fries and chocolate cookies . . . '"

"Al . . . " the little gossip comments.

"Would you rather write them about the condom in your purse?"

"What's in my purse is none of your business. And anyway it belonged to Tiziana."

"The condom belonged to Tiziana and I don't only eat french fries and chocolate cookies. Write: 'By now I'm a grown-up and my diet regularly includes portions of fruit . . . '"

"Fruit gelato isn't the same thing as fruit."

"' . . . fish . . . '"

"Only fried."

"' . . . and legumes.'"

"When have we ever even bought any?"

"At Christmas, for bingo, quit busting my chops! 'B) I haven't burnt the fringe on the curtains and carpets in years now . . . '"

"Weeks, maybe."

"'C) I always obey Vittoria because she works so hard to keep the house clean . . . to cook . . . and iron . . . so it strikes me as the least I can do.' No quibbles on that point, am I right? 'D) I don't know how you found about the disgusting habit of selling thesis papers, but you can rest assured that I'd never get involved in any suspicious business. E) No, we didn't hear anything about a house that collapsed in Avellino, and anyway you have no reason to worry because the promised home is solid as a rock. You'll find the place intact, just as you left it.'"

"Anything else?"

"Yes, right before 'just as you left it,' put in: 'more or less.'"

72.

Our guest Carlo has begun to loosen up, at night we spend hours talking about economics and life in general. He's not a bad person, it's just that he was a child so many years ago that now, he hardly even remembers that he even had a childhood. While we're in the garden playing volleyball, he sticks his head out the door.

"Sorry . . . I just wanted to know what time the Olympics course begins."

He's embarrassed by the sight of Vittoria and Roberta in their underclothes so he turns his back to us as he speaks.

"Carlo, why don't you come play, too," Vittoria suggests.

"We could make it boys against girls!" I say.

"Just a couple of kicks, I haven't played in years," he replies.

For the volleyball game, we groom the field properly. We stretch out the clothesline and hang towels for the net. We gallantly let the women have the ball. Roberta serves, the ball lands a yard in front of Carlo.

"We just handed them a point . . . why didn't you go for it?"
I ask him.

"Go for it? How could I, I would have gotten all dirty . . . "

The day you play while taking care not to sweat, not to get
your pants dirty, not to tear up your shoes, well, that's the day
you've started getting old. There's a lot of work still to do on
this man. Vittoria and Roberta at this point no longer dare, if
you're going to play you have to play for real, otherwise you do
like the old folks and you sit down in an armchair and watch
yourself an episode of *Dallas*, that way you can be sure you
won't get dirty. Yesterday my sister skinned her knee while
we were playing dodgeball, and she looked at me and said:
"Look . . . now I'm going to get a scab. I haven't had one since
elementary school!" Carlo, on the other hand, has just remembered that he possesses secondary internal organs. He chased
after the ball and then yelled at me: "My spleen hurts! It's
ridiculous, it's been a good thirty-five years since I last felt this
pain."

The discovery of the spleen has put an end to our volleyball
game. We move onto the sofa where we boot up the
Commodore 64, we insert the Olympics cartridge, and we start
the twelfth lesson: "Losing with Style."

"How'm I doing?" Carlo asks me as he furiously manipu-
lates the joystick.

"No good, Carlo. You're being way too much of a loser . . .
you're not supposed to let him cream you, you're supposed to
let him win after a long head-to-head battle."

"I'm never supposed to win?"

"Just one game out of three. The important thing is never
to win the tiebreaker, just remember that."

"Never? Then he'll realize I'm letting him win and get
bored."

"A twelve-year-old? I can guarantee that won't happen."

A few evenings ago, while chatting about the model of

Luxembourg banks and offshore partnerships, Carlo told me that one day he'd like to talk to his son about these things. Why not, I said to him, and he replied that his son is growing up all wrong, all he's interested in are computer games, one time he even yelled at the boy to cut it out with that nonsense, but it didn't do any good. Nice move. If he's not interested in the things his son cares about, then he can hardly expect the reverse. I told him that his situation struck me as more worrisome—fifty years old, and there he is spending the day in front of a computer monitor obsessing over the fluctuations of the stock exchange, poisoning his mood because of a 0.2 percent drop in the textile sector. He got all offended.

"Look! I'm getting a blister on my hand . . . " he tells me.

"If you want to win the hundred-yard dash, you're just going to have to live with the blister. All Olympic champions have them, so stop whining!"

73.

Before going home, Roberta gave me an envelope closed with a rubber band. Inside were lots of sheets of paper and stacks of banknotes separated by rusty paper clips. I asked her what all that stuff was and she told me that it was all the money and exams and papers that she'd been given in exchange for a peek at her tits. Stacks of thousand-lire banknotes, some of them no longer legal tender, with the picture of Giuseppe Verdi. It was a lot of money, I told her that she was quite sought after, and she told me that all of that was my money, she'd spent all the rest. "What's that supposed to mean?" I asked her. "Try to guess," she told me. This must be one of those things you only understand when you're grown up, so now I ought to understand it. She kept the money because she was already in love with me. Strange, because even if she was in love with me, she would only date older boys. When she was a junior, she dated a guy who came to pick her up every day in a VW Golf Cabrio. When she was a freshman, rumors went around that she was dating a divorced forty-year-old. No, she probably just kept that stack of bills for the fun of showing it to her girlfriends and saying: "Look here, all the money that fool Al spends on me." I don't understand and I never will. Can resignation be a sufficiently powerful weapon to conquer a woman? If only that were my one doubt. There's an underlying error at the foundation of the planetary economic model that I just don't seem able to understand. Of course unemployment is high: you either slave away or you stay home, there's no compromise. Dedicating your life to your job ought to be a choice, not a requirement for keeping your family from starving. Vittoria, with her part-time job, really lucked out.

"But how do people do it?" I blurt out.

"You have to be really motivated, and we just aren't, right?"

"I don't know, Casimiro. Do you realize that we have to go every single day, every single blessed day?"

"It's just like school."

"No, it's worse. At school you got out at one, here you're nailed to your desk until five thirty. I absolutely need to address the matter in the constitution. 'The principality is founded on part-time labor.'"

"What a complainer. Everyone else does it, we can do it too."

"In fact, it's a clear case of collective madness! What with work, getting ready for work, commuting to work, you waste nearly twelve hours a day, then you spend eight hours sleeping, and you're left with just four hours to enjoy yourself. I don't want to live four hours a day!"

"If we'd chosen ourselves a more interesting job, then you wouldn't think those twelve hours a day were wasted."

"If we'd chosen ourselves a more interesting job, then the hours we're talking about would have become fourteen, without mentioning the possiblity that you'd be tempted to work on Saturday and Sunday too! Shall we call in sick?"

"We were just hired, that's out of the question!"

"We'll just pop by the amusement park . . . "

"I'm not listening to you."

"One ride on the Tagada, a doughnut, and then we'll go to work!"

74.

First she was ashamed and now she's rolling on the ground laughing. Whoever understands her is better than me. The whole time the movie was playing, she kept telling me: "Sssh!" "Don't make the gunshot sound!" "Don't repeat the things they say aloud!" And now she's sprawled on the sofa with tears in her eyes.

"Vittoria, you should have been there!" says Roberta, between one gasp and the next.

"What did he do?"

"Well, at a certain point, he shouted at Batman to hit Joker in the no o ose!"

"Al . . . "

"I didn't shout it . . . I just said it."

"He even stood up! I swear, I felt like I was at the parish movie night . . . "

I walk over to the window, because the two of them, once they start backing each other up? There's nothing you can do but ignore them. Outside, in the darkness, a van leaves the road and plunges across the meadow.

"Did you call Raul?" I ask Vittoria.

"No, why?"

The van stops behind the phone booth, Raul jumps out and runs toward the door. He runs along hunched over, maybe to protect himself from the strong wind that's gusting. I open the door a crack and he slips through, where even a sheet of paper wouldn't have fit.

"Come on, you gotta come away with me, Dario broke out of prison!"

"Dario? Dario the tenant? What was he doing in prison?" Vittoria asks.

Raul looks at me.

"She didn't know a fuckin' thing, did she?"

"Al! Raul! What's this all about?"

"Listen, the two of you, you can explain it all later, we've got to get going because that guy's on his way here now, to make you guys pay!"

"Pay for what?" Roberta shouts.

I briefly explain that Dario was a dangerous criminal, and that I sent him to prison, me—the hero of the story. I don't expect an equestrian statue but at least a bit of recognition, yes, that I'd like.

"Oh, then, that night . . . it wasn't actually the neighborhood festival!" Vittoria deduces. "You're crazy! We need to call the police, right away!"

"No, Vittoria, the best thing is for us to disappear for a couple of days. Dario is a wanted man, he can't stay around here to hunt us down," I tell her.

"And then what do we do? Just live with the nightmare that he might come back any day, any minute?"

"Vitto', whatever you do, we need to leave now," says Raul.

Maybe just for a day or two, or maybe in an hour we'll change our minds and call the police, in any case having to abandon the principality in haste and fury is a hard blow. At the door, Raul stops us.

"Get back inside, someone's pulling up."

"Come on, let's play the curfew game!" I say, pushing Vittoria and Roberta inside.

"We're supposed to do what?"

"Let's turn off all the lights."

"Is it him?" Vittoria asks.

"I don't know, the street is far away and you can't see a thing with all these trees in the middle."

The car zips past quickly on the road. A short while later it reappears, in reverse, slowly, and then disappears from my field of view.

"What's he doing?" asks Raul.

"Al, I'm afraid," Roberta tells me.

Her terrified gaze makes me change my mind. Taking advantage of the darkness, I try to get to the phone booth, but the car appears again, this time creeping along at walking speed. It comes to a halt far from the cone of light under the streetlamp. The car door opens and out comes the shaft of a flashlight beam, followed by a dark figure, slightly hunched over, with a loose-limbed gait. Now I recognize him: it's Dario, sure enough. The end of my uncertainty also puts an end to any aspirations to take heroic initiative. In fact, I can't even seem to take the initiative of an ordinary man. I don't move a muscle, otherwise it would be clear just how badly that muscle is trembling. I observe the criminal as he scopes out his surroundings, walks down the street, flashes the beam of light over the field, here and there, increasingly impatiently, as if he were lashing it. He seems bewildered. The fact that we are concealed by the darkness and are completely outside the range of his flashlight beam is cold comfort. I envy Raul for the fact that he's still able to think. He goes over to open the bathroom window in case we need to make a sudden escape. I try a defective imitation of him, I wave Roberta and Vittoria away from the window with a panicky wave of my arm, then I try to say something too, but in my anxiety, my tongue sticks to the roof of my mouth, an anomalous surge of blood chokes my throat. I don't feel safe, the darkness weighs upon me, I want Mamma and Papà. Dario takes a few steps onto the field, the wind-tossed tree branches conceal him fitfully from view, each time he reappears, he's closer. We just barely manage to stifle a scream when the strong wind slams the window that was just opened. The noise attracts his attention, he tries to identify the source of it, he aims the flashlight in our direction without illuminating us. When he starts to run across the field I take a step backward, involuntarily prompting Vittoria and Roberta to run, so that they immediately scamper away to Raul, leaving me all alone. I don't go any further than that one backward step, I'm afraid that if I move even a little that could help him to find us. I want Mamma and Papà more than I ever have in my life. A slight leakage of bodily fluids warms my thigh. I hear the whispered cries of my companions in misfortune, their urgent invitation to come join them arrives already old, like a memory of something I ought to have done once, only now it's too late. Outside the murderer runs back and forth, shouting things that the wind transforms into the barking of a dog. His change in direction is so sudden that it doesn't offer me even the slightest relief. Why is he running toward the hill now? Is this a tactic? Is he trying to attack us from behind? He seems to have gone mad, he stops, he takes a few more steps in our direction and then he starts running again, but in the opposite direction now, back toward his car. Someone grabs me by the arm, and a small new leakage of fluid slides down my leg.

"Would you stop trying to be a hero?" Vittoria snaps at me angrily.

The hero with the soaking pants thanks the downpours of January 5th, March 18th, August 22nd, and September 14th of 1987, and blesses the summer of 1988 which was one of the rainiest on record in the postwar period. While Dario was in prison, the principality traveled extensively, he keeps looking for it next to the road, he's furious, every so often he turns his flashlight toward the interior, but far from the target. He even begins to suspect that it might be hidden behind the trees.

75.

I think I may have overdone it with the celebrations for the liberation of the principality. I swear that I won't eat french fries for a year. I'll never eat them again as long as I live. My stomach feels like a garbage bag. I'd like to take it, tie a knot in the top, and toss it in the dumpster. I'd like to throw out my tongue too, it's greasy, having it in my mouth makes me nauseous. Before going to work I need something cool, a healthy breakfast, but there's nothing in the fridge that can help me get rid of this nasty taste, only empty bags and cans. Maybe this would do it? It's certainly cool.

"Cheers!" I say to Raimondo's photo as I latch onto the whipped cream spray can.

I wish we could have celebrated the event with him, but I'll have to settle for this picture that he sent me a few days ago from a heavy metal festival in Pordenone. After breaking up with the punk chick, now he's seeing the bassist for a hard rock band, a pretty girl, her head shaved clean and tattooed from head to foot. He hasn't changed a bit, he's dressed the same; the only concession to his new musical creed is that he wears a few oversized skull rings. I take another gulp of whipped cream, thinking of the day he returns to Rome and the phrase: "Mamma, I'd like you to meet my girlfriend."

"Al, what's wrong? Are you not well?" Vittoria asks me.

No, genius, I'm fine. The fact that a geyser of acid is corroding my throat and bits of french fries are plugging up my nostrils certainly shouldn't make you think I'm not well.

"Into the bucket, Al. Into the bucket!"

So where's the bucket? My eyes are swampy from the effort, I fumble for it blindly while Vittoria shoves me, and from my stomach I feel another surge of undigested food come welling up.

"Here, Al. In here!"

The only thing she cares about is that the projectile hits the intended target! I can't even breathe, between one surge and the next I barely have time to ingest an uneasy mouthful of air before my stomach spits it back out, mixed with gastric juices and spew.

"Here, put your head right here, good boy."

"I'm done . . . I think I'm done . . . " I tell her.

"Do you feel better now?"

"Why do you stink like that?"

"Al, you've inundated the the kitchen with vomit, I'm not the one who stinks!"

"I feel disgusting."

"Now you tell me what kind of crap you ate and I swear that that junk will never be seen in this house again!"

"Why, nothing, really . . . just fruit, vegetables . . . "

I had every justification to call in sick, and this is my reward for my devotion to my work. If they were to tell me: instead of being here right now, you can choose to sit through the entire congress of the Italian Liberal Party, I'd take them up on it.

"Santamaria, you really have disappointed me . . . would you tell me where you go every morning?"

Even if they asked to go make a fool of myself on TV on *The Dating Game*, I swear I'd accept.

"What's wrong, cat got your tongue? Santamaria, just for starters, tell me where you were yesterday. Why didn't you come in?"

"I was sick, Dottor Masci. I had a cold."

"Two days for a cold? The health inspector came to your house, did you know that?"

I'm done for. So long job, so long walls. He must have seen me playing volleyball with Roberta. Or worse, while I was using one of Vittoria's bras as a catapult to launch water bombs. Masci picks up a file and reads it.

"Domicile not found . . . Can I ask where you live, Santamaria?"

"Via del Fossone 125, it's written on all my documents." I show him my ID card. He compares it with the address on his file.

"Well, let's just say that, thanks to this not particularly tenacious inspector, you got away with it, but now you tell me why you're never here before ten in the morning."

"No, no, Dottor Masci, it's just that my grandma hasn't been well, and one time the bus broke down . . . "

"Santamaria, don't dream up excuses, I wasn't born yesterday, you know!"

"These aren't excuses, and anyway nobody's in the office before ten!"

"A-a-ah, so the truth comes out, at last! Santamaria, if you punch in after eight thirty just one more time, and I mean even 8:31 A.M., you're fired, is that clear?"

Good heavens, now that everything is finally going along swimmingly, the Italian republic threatens to cut off my financing. No more outings to the amusement park, the walls of my home are at stake, this is no joke!

"One last thing. I've noticed the way you deliver the mail. I'd like to request that you do no more than push the cart in the accepted fashion and lay the mail on the desks, instead of throwing it from the hallway."

"But why? I've sped up delivery by forty percent and I'm able to ensure two more rounds of deliveries every day, the office workers are all contented . . . plus I'm having fun!"

"From now on, you'll deliver the mail the way I told you, even if it's not as much fun!"

That's exactly what's wrong with the public administration and the government offices of the Italian republic: there's no room for innovation, no one has fun while they work, the office workers all have a stirring of emotion on payday, and then starting the next day the grim blanket of sadness descends again. I'd just say to hell with it, I'd like to keep shooting along at top speed on my mail cart, but today the old man really has nothing better to do than traipse along after me. Now we're coming to one of the best rooms, the office of the accountant Ganapini, who's bought a baseball glove so he can catch the mail I throw him.

"Well, Santamaria? What is this feeble behavior?" he asks me.

"Dottor Masci's orders."

"Just tell that old jerk to go fu . . . "

"What, has Santamaria arrived?" shouts Leopoldi. "I'll bet breakfast at the café that you can't drive a proper racing curve without fishtailing!"

And from his desk he tosses a glass of water onto the floor. Masci nods, pays his regards to the employees as he passes by their offices, mentally taking note of all the acts of insubordination. I need to hasten to earn what I'll need for the principality because by this point the truth is unmistakable, it may be possible to save the world, but not the ministries of Italy.

"You need to sign here," I tell Roberta.

"On the dotted line, right?"

Even though the UN won't deign to answer us, I've decided to send a registered letter to the International Olympic Committee to enroll the principality of Santamaria in the next Olympics. They're going to be in Barcelona and it's an opportunity I don't want to miss, for the moment we can't afford to travel to America or Asia. Since we haven't been recognized by the international community, I decide to make the request more authoritative by adding a petition. One hundred percent of the inhabitants of the principality are in favor of both independence and participation in the next Olympic Games.

"Do you ever think about the future?" Roberta asks me.

"Certainly, how could I be prince if I didn't have a clear vision of the future?"

"Al, I'm talking about the two of us."

"I understood . . . well, we'll get married, we'll go on our honeymoon, and then we'll have children."

"And after that?"

"And after that we'll live happily, is there some problem?"

"We'll live happily where?"

"What do you mean, where? Here, in the principality."

"With your sister . . . "

"And my folks, certainly."

No, wait a second, here there's something that doesn't add up. After all, when people grow up, they leave home, they go and live in another house. I don't know, I just can't seem to imagine this part of my life. When I'm all grown up, certainly, I'll leave home, but I'm only twenty-two now, I haven't even taken my degree, so there's no hurry.

"That is, when I'm grown up, I'll have a house all to myself," I correct myself.

Roberta looks at me, she encourages me to go on.

"I feel strange. Why are you asking me all these questions?"

"It's nothing Al, don't worry."

Maybe this is how all geniuses feel. Capable of grasping the greatest mysteries of the universe and then fragile when confronted with simple questions about their own future. There's nothing wrong, I'm very focused on the principality, that's why I can't seem to imagine myself anywhere else, without Vittoria, without Mamma and Papà. No, that's not it, I *still* feel strange,

I try to go on, past my plans to complete construction, and I run up against a black wall. Where is the future?—and I don't mean mankind's, I mean my own. I'll do all the things that other adults do, why can't I seem to focus on them? I'm starting to feel dizzy, what I'm living isn't a life, it's a dream, and it's not even *my* dream, it's Mamma and Papà's dream of having a home all their own. And yet nothing outside of here seems to have any meaning. I'm feeling restless, I waver uncertainly as I try to peer beyond, toward the day when I take care not to get grass stains on my pants when I play.

"A postcard arrived from Carlo!" Vittoria shouts, and I take advantage of the opportunity to get out of that room.

"Al, are you all right? You're staggering . . . " she says to me.

"I must just have stood up too fast," I reply. "Where is the postcard from?"

"London."

"What does it say?"

"'Commodore Olympics World Challenge. Sixth place! Signed: Carlo and Gianni.'"

76.

Mamma's calculator must be about fifteen years old. In its day, it was a very advanced model, with scientific functions, one of the first ones with a red LED display. One particular feature of this calculator, though, is that has never once given good news to the two generations of Santamarias who have lovingly encouraged, begged, and even supplicated it. Now that I'm adding up the end-of-month accounts, with my salary for the first time, the bastard has broken just when things were getting good, as I was pressing the "=" button. I happily recalculate the numbers in my mind.

"Here, this is to pay the mortgage, this is to build the walls, this is to pay for first-class tickets for Mamma and Papà . . . and in our coffers we still have three hundred twenty-six thousand lire!" I shout at the damned thing.

"Al, we'd decided to shore up the principality first . . . " Vittoria tells me.

"No, Vittoria, we decided that once we put the walls up, we send money to Mamma and Papà so they can buy their tickets. I doubt that the principality is likely to collapse after years of shifting from place to place without so much as a hairline crack."

"We'd also said we were going to buy them a new bed, with all the people that have slept on it . . . "

"But how would they even know! Unless, as you usually do, you added something to the letters without telling me about it, they don't have even the slightest idea that anyone's been staying in the promised home!"

Vittoria and Roberta exchange a glance. It's one of those exchanges of glances that annoy me because it means that for days or months now they've been scheming and making decisions without checking with me and now, with this imperceptible bob of the head, they've finally agreed that they're going to condescend to bring me in on it, whatever it is.

"First of all, there's a piece of good news, Al . . . " Vittoria tells me.

"Did you make lasagna?"

"No."

"The *ciambellone*!"

"No, Al, this has nothing to do with food . . . "

"Then why do you keep touching your stomach?"

I make a note of this moment. I immediately write it all down in my human flesh diary because I don't want to forget anything. Even though these two women are embracing me and getting all sticky and sentimental, I take note that my first thought is that my sister has had sex. The fact was obvious but in spite of everything, that's the first thing that occurred to me. Only afterward did I realize that soon I'll have a nephew with whom I'll be able to play endlessly with toy soldiers, no, make that, I'll have a *niece* with whom I'll be able to play endlessly with toy soldiers and who will listen avidly to the story of the founding of the principality, the adventures of Prince Al. I also think of Ciccio, the various Clays, and the grilled cat, and shivers run up my spine. As soon as Mamma and Papà come back, we're going to have to review the project of the principality, we're going to need an extra room, because in Vittoria's room she'll be sleeping with . . .

"Wait, who's the father?" I ask.

"It doesn't matter."

"What do you mean, it doesn't matter? Who is it?"

"I don't know, Al."

"Did it happen while you were asleep?"

Now what's that look on their faces? Are they smiling? So I guessed it, didn't I?

"Al, maybe she doesn't know because it could have been more than one guy," Roberta tells me.

"I knew that! I was just asking . . . to make sure . . . "

It doesn't take a lot of thinking to figure out how a sister can become a bit of a slut. Studying, working, a principality to run, the parents far away, too much freedom, her brother's magnanimous attitude, a legislative lacuna in the principality's constitution.

"At least we can rule out the idea that it's Dario, I'd like to hope."

"Certainly Al, don't even joke about it . . . " she reassures me.

"Or Lorenzo, I hope."

"You're right, Al."

"Or Cris, Albert, Gianluca, Francesco, Guido, Sasà, and all the other geniuses I've met!"

"This is my daughter, your niece, and that's all that counts."

Please God, I can't take care of everything myself, just don't let it be Solitary Puma.

77.

"NSU Prinz 4L! Five standard seats, price 750,000 lire plus 20,000 lire for the front disc brakes!" That's what I said, I can still remember. And that's when Papà threw in: "And what did the Santamaria family say about the front disc brakes?" And in chorus we replied: "Plthththth!"

It all ended on account of the 20,000 lire. "The Santamaria family lacks nothing!" My ass, the Santamaria family has always lacked everything and now we can no longer pretend that's not the case. I'll walk without stopping, I'll cover enormous distances, I'll reach places no other human being before me has ever reached on foot, and people will remember me as the Walking Prince who died of hunger and exposure after an epic journey around the world.

"Right, C-c-casimiro?"

I threw my life away, I failed at everything, I wanted to save my family but I couldn't do that, I wanted to save the world but I couldn't save so much as a thousand-square-foot principality. I'll weep till the day I die, I'll go down in history as the Dehydrated Prince, the greatest genius of the twentieth century who died of grief, because he was betrayed by fate and his sister Vittoria.

"You tell her, C-c-casimiro, that she's a traitor!"

Now I go back out onto the road, because I can't walk on the meadow, I can feel my feet sinking in. It's no good though, they sink in here, too. It's not the ground that's giving way, it's me. Mamma and Papà were the equilibrium and the solidity under the bottoms of my feet. I'll go down in history as the

Wobbly-Footed Prince who died because he sank into himself. That liar Vittoria follows me, she hangs back at a safe distance, the coward. I'll sprawl to the ground before her eyes, she'll see what her lies have done to me and she'll go mad from the grief.

"Right, C-c-casimiro?"

Now I'll worry her, Casimiro, I'm going to start walking right down the middle of the road. It's a straightaway, the cars ought to have no trouble avoiding me. And if they don't manage, then one of those absurd things will happen, like I'll wind up sitting on a cloud, I'll be reincarnated as a pink flamingo, or I'll find myself surrounded by seventy-two sticky virgins.

"Al, not in the middle of the street!" Vittoria shouts at me.

Yes, in the middle of the street.

"I'll walk in the street, too, that way they'll hit me first!"

Mamma and Papà have wound up just like Grandma Concetta, Uncle Armando, and Ciccio. Vittoria takes me by the arm, for a second I hope that it's just a joke after all, but this isn't the face she puts on when she's kidding around, it's no good, I keep on looking at her but she doesn't have the right face! This is the joke that she's played on me, for the past eight years.

"You made a fool of me . . . you all made a fool of me!"

"That's not true, I didn't tell anyone else. Tiziana knows it because I was at her house when the police called. Roberta and a few others figured it out for themselves, but there was no plot! I was just afraid . . . "

"All those l-l-letters . . . th-th-there were even postmarks on the envelopes!"

"Al, I was beside myself, I didn't want you to feel the way I was feeling. Every day I couldn't wait to write something that would make you happy."

"But the postmarks?"

"The company I work for has offices in Munich, Vienna, Paris, Berlin, and Brussels . . . I'd send the letters every time I traveled, sometimes I'd ask colleagues to do me a favor . . . I knew that sooner or later you'd check the postmarks."

"All those trips just to make a bigger fool of me!"

"No, Al. That's my job, I travel with my boss."

"A college graduate who still w-w-works as a secretary . . . "

"What college graduate are you talking about, Al! I had to quit school immediately and find a job!"

"So yet another lie . . . you never took your degree!"

"We needed the money to pay the mortgage!"

"Then Mamma and Papà never sent us money . . . It was all from you . . . "

I turn and run, I no longer want to listen to her. The hope chest where Mamma kept her dowry is full of those letters. I weighed them, they're thirteen pounds, twelve ounces, and one hundred forty grains of lies. Can you believe it, Casimiro? It's absurd, we fell for it for years. It's an inexplicable thing. And we let that incompetent fool sister of mine pull the wool over our eyes!

"Al, I was too young myself . . . I couldn't bring myself to inflict this pain on you, I was afraid you'd have one of your fits! I was just waiting for the right time, but it never came," she shouts.

"Are you t-t-trying to tell me that you waited eight years to tell me: the good news is that you're going to become an uncle, the bad news is that you're an orphan?"

Then there's another question, Casimiro: Where are Agnese and Mario Elvis? Where are they buried? If they're really dead, then there has to be a grave somewhere.

"So wh-wh-where is it that th-th-they're buried?"

"Nowhere . . . they found the car but not their bodies."

"Then wh-wh-what are we talking about? Why are we standing here wasting time, why don't we go look for them right away?"

"No, Al. It's been eight years, I kept my hopes up at the

beginning, but we have to make peace with the idea that they're dead, they fell into the sea and the current swept them far away."

"Far away where? Let's g-g-go find them! Maybe they're in the Suez Canal and they don't know how to tell the Egyptians that they want to come home!"

"Al, they're dead!"

They died because the Santamaria family has always lacked everything, even the money to pay the tolls on the highway. Who knows what provincial back road they took, one of those roads that are all curves the whole way, and they died all alone, while we were sleeping. We should have been in the Prinz ourselves, I could have done something. I'd have taken a nice deep breath on the way down and then, once we were in the water, I'd have gotten one of the doors open and then I could have rescued everyone.

"Isn't it t-t-true that I could have saved them, Casimiro?"

Instead, we left them all alone, they must have flown off the road saying: "Mario," "Agnese," no, actually, screaming: "Mario-o-o!" "Agnese-e-e!" Oh God, no, banish that picture from my head, Mamma and Papà screaming. Now I start beating myself until that thought flees. I'll go down in history as the Brain-Damaged Prince, who died by carving his head open and eradicating the bad thoughts from his brain one by one. I can hardly breathe. Mamma and Papà are my sternum and all the muscles that expand my thoracic cavity. Now I'll climb up that hill, perhaps from there I'll be able to glimpse the sea and get an idea of the currents.

"Al, stop, please, my feet hurt."

"C-c-casimiro, tell her to stop following us!"

"Stop torturing yourself, there was nothing we could do."

"You could have done something! At age nine, a person ought to know how important a car's b-b-brakes are! You should have told Papà to spend the extra twenty thousand lire!"

"The brakes? Al, he dozed off . . . "

"They died in their sleep?"

"Yes. Do you remember what Mamma and Papà always said about death?"

"C-c-certainly, they wanted to die in their sleep, or else while doing something nice."

"And it went just the way they wanted, Al. They died in their sleep, while doing something nice . . . both at the same time!"

Is there anything worse than your parents' death? Sure there is: a retarded sister who tries to console you. What good are such low hills? You can't see a thing from up here. But I'm not stopping, walking is the only thing that will do me any good, even if my feet continue to wobble and my knees seem to do whatever they want. Nothing makes sense anymore, I'm finished as a man, finished prematurely at the age of twenty-two. I could have saved the world, but since the Santamaria family lacked everything, instead I had to think about heaters, walls, and bathtubs. I'll just die here, in these woods, I'll collapse to the ground, dead in despair.

"Al, wait for me!"

"C-c-casimiro, why don't you tell her to go away? Casimiro? . . . Would you answer me?"

What's become of him? Why is he hiding?

"You knew it, didn't you, C-c-casimiro? You knew it all along!"

Betrayed by everyone. That's how Almerico Santamaria is going to wind up, alone like a dog, betrayed and abandoned by his nearest and dearest. There's a hole in the ground up there, it's not very deep but it's large enough to hold me in my last few hours, I'll end up eaten by ants and worms, disassembled and carried off piece by piece, stockpiled in dens and hives in fragments so small that no one will ever be able to put them back together and weep over my corpse. I lie down in the hole, with my ankles I gouge out the last few inches I need to remain completely stretched out. Now I cover my legs, my belly, my chest with dirt and leaves. This is the time to say farewell, I cover my face, my hands disappear beneath the soft, damp pile. I wait for the end to come.

"A-a-al?"

No one will ever find my corpse, but when people come into these woods, on nights with a full moon, they will hear my spectral voice.

"A-a-al?"

I'm going. I'm going into the realm of the Santamarias.

"Al, I see you . . . "

No one has ever found Al Santamaria when he decides to hide.

"I told you, I can see you."

"It's not true," I tell Vittoria.

"You're under the leaves."

"How did you spot me?"

"I can see your nose."

"Now I'll cover it up and I'll die of suffocation. You just go away and don't tell anyone where I am."

"Then I'll die here with you. My life means nothing without you."

I can tell that she's laid down next to me. And now that doesn't bother me a bit. Soon it will be pitch dark, and I don't feel like dying all alone and in the dark.

"Maybe you're right . . . dying is the best thing to do. I'm sort of sorry about the principality . . . " she tells me.

"Think of your daughter, the principality is utter nonsense."

"No, Al. The principality is the most courageous and meaningful achievement of the twentieth century. That doesn't mean that we shouldn't both die . . . it's just that, oh, I don't want you to say bad things about the principality."

"A filthy mess of a house without walls!"

"That's exactly the magnificent thing about the principality, so tiny and so powerful . . . without royal halls, without banquet halls, reception halls, and ballrooms, without precious stuccoes, Renaissance paintings, or golden candelabra! There's not another place in the world where you can feel like a princess without needing anything in particular!"

"Well, I deserve no credit, I didn't really do a thing."

"You saved my life, Al, if it hadn't been for you, I'd be dead now, or I'd have gone crazy. Instead, day after day, you made me realize that my life still lay ahead of me, that I would have other beautiful days, and that, thanks to you, I would have them all the time."

"No, Vittoria, I didn't do a thing."

"Al, all credit for the principality belongs to you."

"You built it with your own money."

"That's not true, I always set the money from my paycheck aside . . . I was afraid that the principality might collapse or sink into the marsh and I didn't want us to have to live in the street."

"How did I fail to notice?"

"I lied a little bit about what I was earning, I padded the expenses, falsified the ledger books . . . "

"You are Italian to the marrow . . . "

"What counts is that it's all your doing. You found the promised home, you transformed it into a principality that endured and prospered despite a thousand challenges. There's no other place on earth where such happiness reigns, and it was you who made it what it is today. Who else has ever succeeded in doing such a wonderful thing? Geniuses your age go on TV to show off what prodigies they are by multiplying three-digit numbers!"

"This is true. Still, the fact remains that nothing will ever be the way it was before, so I'd rather end it all."

"Of course you will, I wasn't saying it to keep you from dying. It's just that I was thinking the same thing myself, that nothing will ever be the way it used to be, and that's partly true, but what still exists is just as wonderful . . . We have our baths in the tub, our candlelit evenings, the commemoration of Elvis, the flag raising at dawn, lots of people who love us, and who knows how many other projects to improve the principality."

"You can run the principality, that's the right thing. I've failed at every turn. I wanted to save the world and I wasn't even able to save Mamma and Papà."

"No one could have saved Mamma and Papà. If only. But you did something impossible: we're still a family, you ensured the survival of the Santamarias! Your plan to save the world is actually working . . . "

"What do you know about it, I never told you a thing."

"Do you remember at dinner when you told Mamma and Papà that you'd figured out how to save the world but that you'd never reveal it because it was a surprise? Well, that night I waited for you to fall asleep and then I read what you'd written on your hand . . . 'It isn't possible to make the whole human race happy all at once. The battle for the salvation of the world has to be fought house by house.'"

Well, we certainly lost our battle. Or, really, I lost it. I hate that fact, I did everything I could to win, including cheating, but whoever figured out the rules of this game must have been good at his job, because there's no way of cheating that will bring back Mamma and Papà, there's no trick that can turn the principality into a success. Only by making the principality a happy place could we have gone on to contaminate other people, other families, with an exponential contagion that would have led the planet to evolve on the model of the principality of Santamaria in the course of no more than two generations. But instead, who did we contaminate? Adele and Roberta, for sure. Raul and Raimondo, yes. Also Carlo and through him, his son Gianni. Then certain other guests—Dario not included— all left with smiles on their faces, and Vittoria's friends, no doubt, at least when they're here, are happy. Also the clerks at the ministry, not all but many of them, whistle while they work, and sixty-four of them signed up for the next weekly competition of "Stamp and File Away the Application." But Agnese and Mario Elvis are certainly not happy, and so it's all pointless.

"Leave me here. Think of your daughter and don't tell anyone where I am," I tell Vittoria. "Understood? Understood? Vittoria? Where are you?"

"I'm going back to the principality . . . " she shouts from a distance, " . . . to carry on the legacy left unfinished by my brother!"

I can just picture how she'll carry on the legacy.

"Wait for me, I'm the chosen one!"

78.

The year 2012 will be remembered as the year of reunification. After zipping all over the field, gravitating around the holm oaks, after tucking itself away at the foot of the hill and pirouetting freely, the principality autonomously annexed itself to the Italian republic, city of Rome, nineteenth district, with a last stirring of rebellion, between the street numbers 91 and 93 on Via del Fossone. It took thirty years to travel two hundred fifty yards as the crow flies and to win recognition. Annexation to the Italian republic wasn't a particularly traumatic event, we interpreted it as the crowning achievement of Agnese and Mario Elvis's dream of a normal life, including utility hookup. The experience as an independent principality has formally come to an end, even though we actually enjoy keeping our political institutions, and feel more comfortable with the constitutional charter we drew up ourselves.

We haven't rented the room since the early Nineties, when a flood of businessmen and politicians started seeking asylum, and thanks to the solidarity fees we charged, we earned so much money that even now we can afford to offer hospitality free of charge to those who really need it. Vittoria lives far away, in a promised home all her own, and recently I've been seeing more of her because her daughter, Agnese, has problems with her math tests and is only willing to be tutored by me. She's a twenty-year-old with a good head on her shoulders, she devotes every free minute she has to studying, at least the time left over after sports and going out with her friends. Sometimes a fair amount of time will go by without me seeing my sister. In these cases, generally within the space of twenty days at the most, one of the two of us will receive a letter full of invented occurrences, as an homage to the good old days. It's the signal that now the most important thing of all is to meet in the bathtub, with at least a foot and a half of foam, lit candles, and letter in hand. I'm very lucky, because I have so many most-important-things-of-all, all of which take absolute precedence, all of them must-do items. Work, too, is one of these. I continue to work for the ministry of finance, with a part-time contract as an outside consultant to the office of economic and financial planning. Even though the offices have been completely computerized, I still start my workday delivering the mail with the cart that they gave me when Dottor Masci retired. He got a gold watch, I got a customized four-wheel-drive vehicle, painted fire-engine red, with high-performance tires. A little exercise before sitting down for a four-hour stretch does me good. I have three degrees, I could aspire to higher positions, but I work to be happy, not to become rich. Our money is enough for us, because *we* are enough for us, we don't much care about what restaurants serve as a backdrop, what vehicles contain us, what monuments frame us in our photographs. The principality is no longer independent, but we've become even more independent ourselves. For the past few years, I've even started working as a volunteer fireman because: "The principality encourages the expression of one's own talent in the interests of the collective." Article 22. I'm in charge of sprinkler systems, specializing in arson. But nothing is as important to me as Roberta. She took her law degree and for a few years worked as a lawyer in her father's office, among wealthy clients and cases befitting a prince of the court. One day she said to me: "I'm not happy," and so I told her: "Stop doing whatever it is that's making you unhappy, immediately." Luckily, that didn't mean me. Two months later she opened a small law office near our home. Her last client was our daughter, and she too is more important than anything else in the world. Her name is Maria, I would have preferred Maria Elvis but Roberta correctly pointed out that the appellation of Elvis is one that has to be earned on the field of battle, and for the moment, she only sings cartoon theme songs. Maria has recently proclaimed her bedroom to be an independent principality. When I slipped Article 5 of the constitution under her door, which reads: "The principality of Santamaria is one and indivisible," she replied that she would speak to me only in the presence of a lawyer. Maria is seven years old, I have a perfect understanding with her. Someone told me once that I'm an ideal father, because no one understands children the way I do and that it's unbelievable that I feel like playing with her the minute I get home from work. What else would I want to do? I think of nothing else all morning long. Sometimes we argue, but never because she doesn't listen to me. When it happens, I try to follow her line of sight, to understand what it is that's calling her, toward what discovery her mind is running. I'm pretty good at it, I can still sense the old calls, the eye of the reclining doll that remains half open, a solitary ant everyone else assumes is in search of food but which is actually just out for a stroll, this noise in the street that sounds just like Mario Elvis's Prinz.

"Papà? Did you hear what I said to you?"

"Certainly, you said 'Papà,'" I reply to Maria.

"And before that?"

"Uhmmmm . . . you said . . . "

"Urghhh, I asked you: "Who is this man . . . Papà?""

With a special *ad personam* amendment, Maria has ensured the goodnight fairy tale without giving up the independence of her bedroom. She pulled the string for 1989. This is one of her favorites—the game is to tell the story again, each time as though it were the first. Roberta, too, pretends not to know a thing and curls up under the album cover, waiting for the story.

"This man is Dario, a ferocious criminal that Prince Al, Princess Vittoria, and Duchess Roberta arranged to have arrested through a cunning stratagem. In 1989, thanks to a daring escape and the reductions in corrections personnel, Dario regained his freedom. The first thing he decided to do was come back to the principality to make them pay dearly for his arrest. It was a dark and stormy night, the lightning flashed through the clouds, illuminating the criminal's black car, the pistol he clutched in his fist, his bloodcurdling smirk! It looked like the prince, the princess, and the duchess were done for. The criminal was driving rapidly down the road that he'd driven in the dreams he'd dreamt every single day and every single night in his cell . . . his vengeance would be tremendous. He drove past the last few apartment houses, the stretch of countryside, and . . . the principality was no longer there!"

"And then what happened?" Maria asks.

"Dario was beside himself with rage, he searched the length of the street not once but twice, he got out of the car and ventured out into the fields, using a flashlight to find his way, and he found . . . nothing! The principality had vanished into thin air."

"And then?" asks Roberta.

"Furious at having been unable to take his savage revenge, he started shouting at the top of his lungs: 'Where are you, you bastards?' and shooting his pistol into the air! Bang bang bang! 'Bastards!' Bang bang!"

"And then?" asks Maria.

"And then, their interest attracted by the shouting and the shooting, the Carabinieri arrived. The ferocious Dario was arrested once again, on charges of escaping from prison, grand theft auto, resisting arrest and assaulting a law enforcement officer, possession of firearms, disturbing the peace . . . and everyone in the principality lived happily ever after."

"He didn't manage to find the principality . . ." says Maria, "just like those gentlemen who said you were tax evaders, or the journalists who were looking for that missing singer . . ."

"I'll tell you the story about the financial police and the female English rock star the next time. Now it's time to go to sleep."

"No, the last one, tell me the last one! That one about the principality in the pond and Mamma getting into the dinghy!"

I'm no longer the little boy who wanted to save the world. Many years ago, Vittoria told me that no one can save it alone, because it's a wonderful thing to save the world and everyone should do it together. Right then and there I thought: "Then where's the surprise?" I was still just a kid, I thought I could give six billion people a nice surprise. It took me a while to get used to the idea, but Vittoria's point of view is important to me, I always believe her, as a joke I tell her that she deserves the utmost consideration because she's the only person who's been able to outflank the greatest genius of the contemporary era.

We don't know how to lose, me and Vittoria, that's our secret, we force life into overtime, and into overtime on the overtime if necessary. We rewrite the rules in the middle of the game. The world I thought needed saving was our world, a challenge well beyond human abilities that still today demands all I can do. Roberta is starting to feel old, last time I got a smile out of her was by offering her money in exchange for a peek at her tits, but it's not going to work much longer; Maria has normal ankles and times change, her secret admirer might not get off with a paper heart and a note. And so when she was born I gathered my best ideas and sent them to the UN, in 194 copies, one for each delegate, telling them to put them to the service of mankind and could they please take care of it because I was just too busy. Two delegates wrote back, the delegate from Zimbabwe and the one from Samoa, with effusive thanks and compliments, especially for the idea of ethical neocolonialism, from Zimbabwe, and for the Regulatory Criterion, from Samoa. Mario Elvis was always right, the revolution will start from the bottom, from the world's south.

No one will write my biography, History will ignore me, but I'm a big boy now, even if I don't turn my back on my origins as a little child, I've learned the importance of what comes afterward. In fact, I've decided to repair the projector because, later, it will help to refresh my memory, to build important tiles in the mosaic of Maria's memory. I also purchased a Super 8 movie camera so I can go on celebrating Santamaria's Day with a steady supply of new footage to view, and so, when we go to the beach or for a picnic to the park, we'll be able to compare them with the old movies and see that everything that's changed around us lacks the power to change us. But in the meantime, now, immediately, in the present I enjoy the inheritance of Agnese and Mario Elvis carved onto Maria's face, the inheritance of the principality that emanates from Vittoria's serenity, Roberta's, and my own. We are family. We are all that I have.

The laws of physics still can't explain the power of my brain cells, capable of establishing contact with yours even through a closed door . . . relax, Maria-a-a, go on sleeping, this is your father speaking to you-ou-ou . . . you are going to be the heir to the former principality of Santamaria and all its immaterial possessio-o-o-ons . . . respect its laws and those of the republic written by the founding fathers, which you should never confuse with those scrawled by politicians found guilty of fraudulent bankruptcy, extortion, bribery, misappropriation of public funds, stock manipulation, corruption, association with the Mafia, and false accounti-i-i-ing . . . respe-e-ect the-e-em . . . and then tomorrow open this blessed doo-oo-oor . . . ah, one more thing: trust me on this, don't be in a hurry to grow u-u-u-up. On the count of three you'll receive this information and you'll be happy-y-y-y.

One . . .

two . . .

ABOUT THE AUTHOR

Fabio Bartolomei lives in Rome. He is a writer, a screenwriter, and a teacher of creative writing. His debut novel was *Alfa Romeo 1300 and Other Miracles* (Europa, 2012) and with *We Are Family*, his second novel, he won the *Elle* Magazine Readers' Grand Prize.